REBIRTH—OR DEATH

In the house of screams, of pounding blood, of the heat of death, Ray screamed. His hands moved very fast on the wheels of the wheelchair. He flew from the room and hit the second floor railing. And then—

Ray suddenly felt his legs, solid beneath him as of years ago. He was running, felt the warm grit of the sand between his toes as he leapt into the surf, laughing with happiness, the water covering his head. He kicked down deep, and deeper, and touched the sandy white bottom.

But he couldn't push himself back up. . . .

DON'T MISS THESE BANTAM BOOKS
BY AL SARRANTONIO

House Haunted
October
Moonbane

HOUSE HAUNTED

AL SARRANTONIO

TM

BANTAM BOOKS
NEW YORK TORONTO LONDON SYDNEY AUCKLAND

HOUSE HAUNTED

A Bantam Spectra Book / May 1991

Chapter 7, in a substantially different form, first appeared as "Pigs" in Shadows 10, *edited by Charles L. Grant.*

ISBN 0-553-29146-7

Published simultaneously in the United States and Canada

Bantam Books are published by Bantam Books, a division of Bantam Doubleday Dell Publishing Group, Inc. Its trademark, consisting of the words "Bantam Books" and the portrayal of a rooster, is Registered in U.S. Patent and Trademark Office and in other countries. Marca Registrada. Bantam Books, 666 Fifth Avenue, New York, New York 10103.

PRINTED IN THE UNITED STATES OF AMERICA

RAD 0 9 8 7 6 5 4 3 2 1

For
PETER SCHNEIDER,
MELISSA SINGER,
GINJER BUCHANAN
and
JANNA SILVERSTEIN,
Who
Believe in
Ghosts

Why do you weep?
The bells are not ringing,
The town is asleep.
The night at your window
Is nestled in deep.
The stars in the heavens
Are gently singing—
Why do you weep?

—*French lullaby*

ONE: THE FOUR POINTS

1. WEST

In the early morning he looked out through his window to where the green of the lawn sloped down the hills to show a thin band of the Pacific, the ocean's blue-orange glint a metallic complement to the living color of grass.

Sometimes during the day he sat at the window and read, or moved his head to the right or left, or imagined that his legs worked. Sometimes he imagined that he could climb through the open window and run down the slope of living lawn over the hills to the hot sand of the beach, and feel its soft grit slide between his live toes, and then leap feet first into the water, and feel the cool-hot slap of salted wetness on the pads of his feet, and feel the wet up his legs, displacing the air on his body, rushing to cover his eyes and head until there was nothing but ocean surrounding him. And he imagined himself opening his eyes beneath the water, his cheeks puffed out like a breathing fish, to see the white sandy bottom, making it rise in languid dust-devils. And he imagined pressing his hand flat on the bottom, feeling the swell of the tide, the lap of waves against his legs as he pushed himself upward, the tight uncomfortable feeling just beginning in his chest. And he imagined rising majestically to the surface, letting the deoxygenated air out of his lungs with a satisfied blow and pulling dry, sweet, new air into himself.

Sometimes he imagined that.

Sometimes he sat with dull eyes in front of the television, or pushed the buttons on the arm of the wheelchair that rolled him into the white kitchen to the lowered sink and stove, where he put water into the pot and boiled it, waiting for the insistent whining push of steam, listening to the roiling, churning, tortured water yanked out of tranquillity and thrust into hot air. When the water was boiling, he turned the heat down and poured it into the filter brewer, watching water metamorphose into coffee as it dripped into the deep carafe sitting on the electric plate that kept it warm. He drank a lot of coffee. Sometimes he listened to the woman from Mexico who came to clean the house. He listened to her stories about her country, her family, her solid Catholic faith. He watched her eyes, the deep certainty in them, looking for and finding the long pain she had endured. One son in a Mexican jail, caught smuggling; another son an illegal, somewhere in Nevada; a husband who had renounced his faith and divorced her to live with a girl of twenty. He made her sit and have coffee with him, studying the deep lines of her face as she talked. There was a daughter who wrote her regularly, who had married a Colombian businessman; she prayed he was not involved with drugs, because he had money and never spoke of how he made it. She said she kissed her daughter's letters. She kissed the stamps on the envelopes. He would listen to her until she would rise abruptly, thinking she was foolish to pour her heart out to him, uncomfortable at the gringo's staring silences, and say she had work to do.

Sometimes, he knew, she looked at him as if he were mad.

He never left the house. In the front room, the television was always on. In the bedroom, the radio always played, tuned to a news channel: sometimes, when he concentrated, the radio gave him the illusion that there was a human voice with him, overriding the memories, the demons in his head.

When he was with the Mexican woman, sometimes her voice, her careful English, overrode the memories.

When the housekeeper went home in the early afternoon,

he went to the front room and looked out the window again, at the clear green line of the far water or the green of the sloping hills or at the flowers that bordered the path down the hills to the water. When the men came once a week to cut the grass on the front lawn, he watched their slow work, watched the uneven wild green lawn become a smooth pleasant carpet. He tried to smell the odor of new mowing from his window.

He kept the grounds neat. A man came in to fix the porch in the back when it needed painting or when boards needed replacing, and he had the foundation of the house shored up when it began to sag. The house looked as it always had. At night, the wide windows stayed open, and he looked out at the stars or the clouds, watched the moon's slow progress and changing shape. Often he slept in the wheelchair, and awoke to find his shoulders aching from the angle of his rest or his hand asleep on the telephone beside him.

Sometimes, he thought about the bag of white powder in the locked desk drawer under the telephone. He thought ironically of the Mexican woman's fears for her daughter's husband.

Perhaps the Mexican woman thought him mad because there were telephone extensions throughout the house, in every room. Even when he looked through the window, or talked with the housekeeper, listening to her stories, or gave in, before sleep, exhausted, to the screaming memories in his head, his hand was always on a telephone. Sometimes it rang, but he knew the difference, that it was only someone calling to ask him to subscribe to *Time*, or to ask him to take out insurance for his credit cards. He never answered the phone when it rang like that. When it rang the other way, then he would answer. Bridget had told him the call would come, and when it did, he would go to her wherever she was and destroy her.

Sometimes he sat staring out the window at the back of the house, toward the woods, and the memories in his head talked. And sometimes he listened, because it was good to remember why he waited day after day, with patient, long hate, in a house haunted by memories.

Memory . . .

• • •

They called it the Haunted Hut, because, the bigger kids said, the spirit of the hobo who'd hung himself there still inhabited it. The hobo had lived in it for years, after the Korean War. He never bothered anybody. Rusty Kranepool, who was in the third grade but came over to play toy soldiers with Ray because his father had taken all his away, saying, "No kid of mine is going to play with war toys" (forgetting, of course, that he'd done almost nothing else himself when he was Rusty's age, and he'd turned out a CPA and not a blood-guzzling war lover), had told him that his older brother Dan had once sneaked up on the lean-to with his friends to spy on the hermit. At first it was quiet, but then they'd heard something going on inside the shack. There were scraping sounds and a low voice. There was silence again, until the front door suddenly burst open and the hobo came out, waving a hickory cane in front of him, screaming, "Get away from me! Get away!" At first Danny and his friends thought the man was yelling at them, but the hobo turned away from them, waving the cane over his head and running into the woods. They waited a little while. When he didn't come back, they decided to creep up to the shack. They had just stepped out of their hiding place when the hobo returned, moving the cane weakly in front of him and sobbing, muttering to himself. When he saw Dan and his friends, he began to scream again, but in a different way, "No! Go away!" He charged at them with his cane raised, cursing, and they ran off into the woods. A month later he was found hung inside his shack. He had looped a belt over a big hook screwed into the center beam of the ceiling. There was a kicked-over chair at his feet. The only strange thing about it, something that one of the sheriff's new deputies wanted to look into until the sheriff told him not to bother, that folks didn't care, was that apparently the man had tried to burn down the shack before he hung himself in it. In one corner they had found a can of kerosene, half empty. He had doused a rolled-up rug and lit it. The rug and part of the floor was burned black, but it looked as though the fire had gone out on its own. The new deputy thought that maybe someone had tried to burn the place down to hide the fact that they'd hung the hermit, but the sheriff had told him to go down to Route 22 and catch speeders instead of thinking so much.

"You want to go see it?" Rusty said. They were in the clearing in the woods out behind Ray's house, moving regiments of Ray's toy soldiers from the sitting rock that looked as though it had dropped from the sky to the spot next to the sandpit.

"No," Ray answered, not looking up.

"You scared?" Rusty said, with the insinuating sneer any ten year old uses when playing with an eight year old.

Ray stopped posing his GI Joe in the sand and looked at his friend sideways. He shrugged.

"Not allowed?" Rusty smiled, immediately knowing he had scored a direct hit.

"I could if I wanted to."

"Why don't you want to? I've been there plenty of times."

Ray shrugged. "I just don't want to."

"That's bull," Rusty pursued. "Your mom said you can't go out there, and that's all there is to it."

"She's not my—" he started to say, but then he said nothing, trying to turn his attention, and Rusty's, back to the soldiers embedded in the sand battlefield.

Rusty wasn't going to give up. "Come on," he said, standing.

Ray looked down at the clutched soldier in his hand. "No."

"Look,"' Rusty said earnestly, kneeling on one knee in front of Ray. "I'll be with you, and your mom won't even know. We'll come right back. I just want to see what it looks like."

"I thought you said you've been there."

"I haven't seen it in a while," Rusty answered defensively. He stood up, started to walk in the direction of the thick woods. "Coming?"

Ray looked at Rusty's face, the daring on it burning into him, telling him, *Go ahead, defy her, she's not your mother anyway. She wants to be but she's not; she's only a woman named Anne who married your father and tried to take your mother's memory away from you. She's too nice, nobody's that nice. All she wants is to suck your mother out of you like a vampire and put herself inside. She's not your mother.*

Go ahead.

And then he was up on his feet and following Rusty. Only Rusty had stopped at the edge of the thick woods. He stood still, his face red, staring past Ray, and Ray turned around and there was Anne, holding Tony in her arms, looking at the two of them, standing quietly on the path leading back to the house.

"Your mother called, Rusty," she said. "She wants you home."

They went back to the house, and Rusty went home, and Ray had a snack, and then he asked if he could go back to the sandpit and Anne said yes. She was doing the dishes; Tony, in the playpen next to the kitchen table, waving his hands in the air, making little sounds.

Anne was poised over the sink as he got up to leave. She was humming in a low voice to an old song by the Temptations playing on the radio she kept on the counter next to the sink.

"Wait a minute," she said, stopping her humming as he walked behind her to get to the back door.

"Sorry." He went back to the table and picked up his plate and glass and brought them to her. She put them in the sink and turned back to him,

"Was Rusty going to take you to that shack in the woods?" she asked.

"No," he answered, too quickly.

"Are you sure?" she said. She was talking as if she were his mother, and part of him wanted to cry and tell the truth. But she wasn't his mother.

"We just played with soldiers."

"All right." She frowned. "But I don't want you back there. It's dangerous and it's not part of our property. You hear me?"

"Yes."

Her eyes stayed on him, trying to be his mother, but then she turned back to her dishes and began to sing with the beginning of another song on the radio.

"Remember what I said, Ray," she reminded him in her quiet voice.

He went out past the tree with the tree house in it, past the toolshed where, when his mother was still alive, they had once found a dead cat after coming back from vacation. He went into the stand of trees, threading his way expertly to the clearing with the sitting rock and sandpit. The afternoon was quiet. There were high trees around him, with the leaves on them that sounded as though they were whispering to one another when the wind blew. There was no wind, and no whispering. Ray looked into the sandpit, at the scattered toy soldiers. There were plastic dinosaurs buried there, and a lucky silver dollar he had hidden in a box and buried below the sand. He'd figured anyone looking for it would stop digging when they hit the bottom of the sandpit, so he'd gone down five inches farther into wet cold dirt.

He played with the soldiers awhile, having them line up on a lip of the rock and then charge down into the sand, throwing cloudfuls of sand up to simulate a sandstorm on Mars, making sand mountains to be ploughed by the superior artillery of GI Joe.

His eyes wandered to the thick trees leading to the Haunted Hut, to the mostly overgrown, thin path that marked the way.

Go ahead.

He stood, dropping the two soldiers he held into the pile of sand at his feet; a weak plume of sand dust rose, the end of the battle. He stood facing the path and the trees with his hands in his front pockets.

She's not my mother.

He started for the trees.

The way was easy when he got onto the path and away from the clearing. The trees weren't as thick as they looked; there was a lot of dead wood, big trunks split by lightning, trees growing too close together losing the fight for available sun. The path became wide enough for a small truck—and, indeed, he saw two faint ruts overgrown with weeds and grass where tire treads had once rolled, when the hobo's hut had been the one-room, Walden-like summer home of a reclusive writer in the twenties.

The trees thickened, then suddenly cleared out.

Go—

He stopped cold, suddenly standing before the Haunted Hut.

Something besides guilt (*She's not my mother!*) told him to turn back. A creeping spider of hair rose up his back at the sight of the place in the summer afternoon. A breeze had come up; the trees had started to whisper.

Afraid.

He stood still, hands in pockets, staring at the wood frame covered by a mass of weeds. It looked like a tiny, neglected house—like the witch's house in *Hansel and Gretel* ten neglected years after the witch had been baked in her oven. There was a white, chipped wooden bench in front. There were shutters on the windows, one of them hanging crookedly by its top hinge. They had once been painted a deep green, but now were flaking paint, revealing an earlier brown coat underneath.

Get out, his guilt and that other thing, the whispering fear, told him.

She's not my mother.

There was a gaping hole where the front door had been. The corner to the left of the door was charred through, showing rough, singed timber and wallboard through the encroaching weeds.

Ray took his hands from his pockets and moved tentatively to the front entrance.

It was dark inside. There were four windows, glazed with dust; two were blocked from daylight by tall grass. He edged in closer, stepping so that he was neither in nor out of the house.

Go.

Stay.

He stepped in.

It was very dark. A wave of fear passed over him, taking the air from his lungs. His eye caught movement.

Someone was behind him, moving across the entrance.

He turned, but the doorway was empty.

Panic filled him. He looked back in the Haunted Hut; in one corner, he imagined flames rolling off the kerosene-soaked rug, licking the walls, flat sheets of orange fire rising and joining, racing around the top of the shack to form a whirling tornado of heat. Then he saw the flames snuffed by an invisible hand. He saw the hobo beating at the air with his cane, then saw him suddenly swinging from the rotting overhead beam, legs kicking helplessly, seeking a chair that had been yanked aside.

Go. Run away.

She's not my mo—

"Hello, Ray."

He turned to see his mother standing in the doorway of the Haunted Hut. No—it wasn't his mother. But it was as if his mother's unknown double had been poured out of the invisible air before him. He felt a gasping sob of recognition and longing rise up his throat.

"You—"

"My name is Bridget," she said. She smiled his mother's smile.

"You have hair like my mother's," he said.

"I know."

She held her hand out to him, and he took it. It was like his mother's hand. She led him to the white bench, guided him to sit in it. She sat beside him. There was an odor about her that he recalled. It was the way his mother smelled on nights she went to parties with his father. She kept a little vial of the perfume she used on the round tray on her dresser. One night after she had gone to a political dinner with his father, Ray went into her bedroom and took the vial down. He wanted to smell the odor again. The cap was a little glass one. When he pulled it, it came out too easily and he spilled the perfume all over the front of his pajamas. He looked for other pajamas, but they were all in the wash.

He stayed away from the babysitter and waited for his mother to come home. When she got back, he was almost asleep in a chair in his room. When she came in, he ran to her, crying, and told her what he'd done. He thought he had destroyed her smell; that she would never smell like that again. She laughed and held him and rubbed his back in a circle. She told him that she would get more of the perfume and would smell like that for him always. She told him that it smelled better on him than it did on her.

She changed him into a T-shirt and put him to bed. And as he fell asleep he heard through the long crack of hallway light that came in through the bedroom door, his mother telling his father outside in the living room how wonderful he was.

Bridget smelled like that, and she had red hair like his mother's. She put her soft hand on his and looked at him with her green eyes.

"I know how lonely you've been, Ray. You won't be lonely anymore. I've been lonely, too."

"Anne isn't my mother."

"Neither am I," Bridget said, smiling down at him the way his mother used to. "But I want to be just like her."

He looked at her, and he believed her. Anne was tall and dark blonde; she laughed loud and covered her mouth with her hand when she laughed; when she put her arm around him, she patted his back instead of rubbing it. Anne was nothing like his mother.

"You know, Ray," Bridget said, in the kind of voice his mother used when she told him a story, "I've been waiting for someone like you for a long time." She looked very happy.

He looked at her, and his life had changed. "How long have you been here?"

"Pretty long."

"Did you know the man who lived here?" Ray asked. "The hobo?"

She smiled deeply and laughed. For a moment she pulled him close. "Yes, Ray, I knew him. He was a foolish man, not a nice man at all."

"Did he really hang himself?"

She said, "Someday, I'll show you what happened to him." Impulsively, she pulled him close to her again, giving him that wonderful party-perfume smell. "Oh, Ray, we're going to be such good friends!"

And then he was crying. He buried his face in her, clutching her as if she were his mother returned, a thing he was terrified to lose again. She was his mother. And he cried and cried, sobbing out his fear and loneliness, and he couldn't stop. "I don't love Anne!" he cried. He couldn't stop himself. She looked so much like his mother, with her red hair and her smell, and her pale soft white hands, he couldn't stop. "My dad married her after my mom died, and he didn't even wait a year, and he brought her home from Washington to live in my house and use my mother's things. She sat in the chair where my mother used to read me stories, and she watched my mom's TV, the same shows in the afternoon, and she used the same closets and put all her stuff in my mom's furniture and threw out all the stuff she found, put it all in boxes and left it out on the curb like garbage. *Like garbage!*" He looked at her, at her soft face, her red hair. He was still sobbing. He wanted to tell her all of it.

"I took it all back in," he went on, "and put it in the back of my closet. She found it all one day, and she made me throw it all out." He couldn't stop telling her everything. "I screamed at her, and she told my father, and he tried to talk to me in a low voice. I hit him. His eyes got hard, and he took all the stuff out in the backyard that night and burned it, like it was leaves or garbage, and he locked me in my room. I threw the chair from my desk through the window and tried to climb out and stop them." He sobbed, and there were rivers of water flowing out of him, two years of pent-up bile and rage flowing hotly out of him. He clutched her the way a drowning man clutches the wet wood of a broken mast.

"But I couldn't stop him! I screamed and begged, but he burned it all. He said he understood, that he knew, but he didn't! He's hardly ever here anyway. He's always in Washington. And then *she* came into the room and tried to touch me! She tried to hold me!" He burrowed deep into Bridget. "So I hit her, *Oh, God, oh, God!*"

"There," Bridget whispered. "Shhh." She held him, and she drew all the bile and the fear and loneliness out of him.

"And then," Ray sobbed, "they had Tony, and they brought him home, and it was like I wasn't even there. She gave everything to Tony, and she treated me like I was visiting the house." He was whispering now, small broken sobs into her breasts. "*Oh . . .*"

The tears came from him again, a long anguish expunged, a burst dam draining bad water, and she held him and let him.

And then when he was finished, he sat up, shaking, and she still held him, putting her arm around him, rubbing his back in little circles, enfolding him, protecting him, letting him calm down.

"I'm sorry," he said.

Her arm around him squeezed, let go. "Don't be."

For a long while she said nothing. He leaned his head against her, hearing the birds in the woods, looking at the soft shade of tree light, the peek of afternoon sun through the leaves and branches, the gentle sway and buzz and hum and click of a summer afternoon.

"Do you like this?" she asked, finally. "Are you glad for this day?"

"Yes," he said, holding her.

"I'm going to be with you, and you never have to worry again." She looked down at him, smiled. "I'm going to take good care of you, Ray."

Again she held him, and only the tiniest flicker of fear passed through him from the whispering trees.

2. THE ASSISTANT

Harold was worried that Gary would not show for their chess game. Whenever he worried, which was seldom since his retirement from the garment business and since his wife had passed away ("God bless her! *But* . . ."), the acid in his stomach burned and he grew uncomfortable.

He ran his fingers over the outside of the pocket of his topcoat to make sure his antacid tablets were there, feeling the slightly shaped bump that told him they were.

He had come to rely on the games with Gary. Most days he spent in Washington Square Park, watching the regulars play chess with the amateurs they called potzers. Potzers all looked the same, hunched desperately over one of the concrete chess tables lining the park side of MacDougal and West Fourth, while the regulars on the other side of the board waited for them to concede and give up their money. When he was younger, Harold used to play, and sometimes beat, the regulars, but now he was content to watch, sitting comfortably on a bench, legs crossed, leaning slightly forward to observe the nearest game, eyelids half closed, the eyes behind alive, calculating strengths and weaknesses, estimating how long it would be before the potzer threw up his hands and asked for another game.

But on Thursday afternoons he moved away from the other players, setting up his folding board over the concrete one farthest from the others, putting each hand-carved piece in place, and waiting patiently until exactly three o'clock, when Gary invariably arrived to play.

He fingered the antacid tablets through his coat pocket again, beginning to feel that this would be the first Thursday in two months that he would have to go back to watching the potzers play. Worry was already turning to the disappointment that soured his stomach.

A pigeon strutted too close, its dull black-bead eyes regarding him stupidly, looking for popcorn or bread. In seventy years of life in New York, he had never fed a pigeon; his mother had screamed that they were dirty, his wife had screamed that they carried disease, and these thoughts had never left him. He bent down slightly to shoo it away, thinking to use the momentum to bring himself to a standing position from which he would repack his board and return to the other regulars, when he saw Gary walking toward him, gently swinging his gym bag.

A smile nearly crossed Harold's face, but he held it in check. From the first, his games with Gary had been real tests, serious business. In effect, they were two opponents meeting on a battlefield. Their conversations had been little more than pleasantries; it was as if they lived their isolated, separate lives, only to meet purified over the chessboard. At least that was the way Harold had come to justify in his mind the fact that in all their previous meetings, he had not gotten one bit of gossip or information out of Gary about his life, his hobbies, his girlfriends (or boyfriends; this *was* New York City in the 1980s, after all), or anything else. The young man was always pleasant enough, but he seemed interested only in playing one extremely good game of chess and then going away, returning a week later at exactly three o'clock.

It was three-thirty now, and Harold thought this, at least, worthy of comment.

"You're late?" Harold said, making it an inquiry.

Gary said nothing, only smiled slightly, giving a shrug. He

wore his customary turtleneck shirt under a patched leather jacket. He looked as though he had gotten a haircut lately; his thinning blond hair was shaved short in the back, brushed back away from his face. His round, wire-rimmed glasses always made his eyes look dimmer than they were: when he took them off to clean them, his eyes nearly jumped out of his face, they were such a clear, clean blue. Powerful eyes to go with a weak body: he was long and skinny, with long, thin-fingered hands and a pale complexion. Only the eyes were strong and, when he smiled, which was not often, his mouth.

"Chilly for September," Harold offered as they both looked over the board, the polished black and white squares of hardwood expertly set and bordered in polished briar, the root usually reserved for making pipes. As far as Harold knew, it was the only set like it in the world. At least that's what he liked to think. The pieces, brown and white, were carved from briar and meerschaum, small but extremely hard and strong, witty representations of pipe smokers.

Gary made no answer to Harold's comment about the weather, but nodded slightly when Harold said, "You do like this set, don't you?"

Harold had found the set one day in a shop that sold almost exclusively junk. It was half hidden under a pile of old *Playboy* magazines. The cashier, a Pakistani, hadn't even been able to find a price on it and had given it to him for an extremely low amount—a financial conquest that Harold had kept in his heart ever since. It had been the bargain of his life, one of the prizes of his collection.

Harold hid the two queens, holding his enclosing hands out for Gary to choose. As always, the young man picked the one holding the white queen.

"I'd like to know how you do that," Harold said.

Gary gave his enigmatic smile, holding the white queen up for inspection before placing it neatly in its square. "Shall we play?"

They played, and the gray sky, the pigeons, all of New York and the world, went away from Harold as he concentrated on the game. Gary was as uncanny with his play as he was with his choice of queen, constantly making unorthodox moves that had Harold playing out a hearty, if vain, defense. The young man seemed invincible, and after an hour that passed as a few minutes, Harold once again found himself hopelessly trapped. He capitulated, foregoing the last few, useless moves.

"You know," he said to Gary, dusting each chess piece with his fingers before carefully placing it in its felt inset inside the folding board, "I used to get angry when I lost chess matches. But not anymore. I'll tell you why. I tried one off those computer chess games, thinking that if I lost I wouldn't get mad because it was only a machine. The board had little red lights on it, and when you beat the computer, they flashed on and off in salute. They stayed on when the machine won." He looked up at the sky for a moment, feeling what he thought was a drop of rain. "I found myself gloating when the lights flashed on and off, and getting very angry when they stayed on. After a while I put the machine away and started playing people again. I found that I couldn't be angry at them when I lost anymore. After you get mad at a machine for beating you, it seemed kind of silly to get mad at a human being, someone with a real name and face who gloats if he wants to, but doesn't have to. Those little red lights on the machine went on whether the machine wanted them to or not. The machine had no choice." He waved his hand, holding the last pawn. "If I ever want to get angry over chess again, I can always take out my machine."

To his surprise, Gary was listening to him. Usually, when he talked one of his harangues at the end of a game, the young man sat politely, obviously wanting to go and only waiting for the opportunity. But today he was looking at Harold with concentration and actually *listening*.

"I tried one of those chess computers myself, once," Gary said. His mouth formed one of his tiny, mysterious, thoughtful smiles.

"Did you like it?" Harold asked.

"No." The young man reverted to his customary withdrawn silence, then turned to Harold once more, his smile widening. "The computer was plugged into the wall, and I was about to make checkmate when there was a power outage. The game was erased from the computer's memory. I became quite annoyed."

He kept smiling, and Harold broke into a grin and began to laugh. "Oh, ho! I bet you did!"

He put the last of the pieces into the folding board and closed it. Normally, this would be the end of their weekly meetings. Today, the young man lingered.

"Harold," the young man said abruptly, shyness tainting his voice, "do you remember, the first time we met, telling me about your collection?"

Harold blinked in surprise. He had told the young man, all right, about his chess pieces and boards, and at length; but he could have sworn at the time that he was talking to a wall for all the response he had gotten. He looked at Gary expectantly. "I remember."

"Does your offer to show them to me still stand?"

"Of course!" Harold replied, his face brightening. He had been dying to show the young man. He clutched the box of his traveling set under his arm. "Would you like to come now?"

"I'd love to."

Harold rose and motioned the young man to follow. Gary fell into step beside him.

As they passed a concrete table by the edge of the park, Harold took Gary lightly by the arm. "I once played Stanley Kubrick, the famous director, at that table. He played there all the time when he was a young man. Nobody knew what he would become. Around here, he was just another regular. Not a potzer at all. He made enough money to feed himself. And he was *good*."

They left Washington Square Park and turned uptown. By the time they reached Harold's apartment building, he realized that he had been indulging in a monologue for nearly a half hour, that Gary had not uttered a word.

"You sure you want to see my sets?" he asked.

"Yes."

The elevator jammed a floor below Harold's apartment. He hit the button with his elbow to get it started again. "Every machine in New York stinks, Gary," he said. "Not just the chess machines. They should do away with all of the machines, let people do the work. And they should let people play all the chess."

Gary nodded absently, the blue eyes behind his spectacles holding a quiet, thoughtful look.

As he moved his key toward the lock on his door, it occurred to Harold that he really didn't know this young man all that well. After all, he had only played chess with him. Maybe he was making a mistake. What if this young man was a thief and had only ingratiated himself with him to steal his collection? Wasn't it possible? He had stopped reading the *New York Post* a long time ago, had tried not to be paranoid, but it was not easy. What he had found was that the more paranoid you were, the more lonely you were, too. It was good to be careful, but there was only so far you could go without becoming all but dead. He stole a tiny glance at Gary. Could this boy really have befriended him, played chess with him every Thursday afternoon for the past two months, only to steal from him? It was possible, wasn't it? Yes, it was. He could call the whole thing off, even now, couldn't he? Yes, all he had to do was say that he was terribly sorry, that he had completely forgotten an appointment and must hurry off to meet it. Anything would do. The dentist.

But the point was, did he want to do that? Did he want to surrender a chance to share his beloved treasures by being a paranoid old man?

Behind his belt, he felt the beginnings of acid in his stomach. He might as well start buying the *Post* again. Even better—if he didn't show this boy his collection, he might as well start playing chess with the computer again.

His key slipped into the lock, and he heard the comfortable click as he turned it and opened the door.

"Gary," he said, taking the young man by the arm as they entered the doorway, "I hope you enjoy what you see."

The apartment was clean, thank God. The woman had come on Wednesday, dusting, straightening up. The only untidiness was the dish and teacup in the sink from this morning's breakfast.

He took Gary's jacket, laying it over the arm of a chair by the doorway. Gary put his gym bag down next to the chair. Harold then led him through the living room, down a short hallway. Two doors at the end were ajar; one on the right showing a bedroom done in blue and white, illuminated by light from two windows facing the street; the other led into darkness.

Harold turned to Gary, unsuccessfully trying to cover the pride in his voice. "My museum," he said, touching a light switch on the wall and pushing the door open.

Gary followed the old man in.

The room was suffused with sharp fluorescent light that fell on stands and racks of glass cabinets. They were the kind used in department and jewelry stores, some of them floor to ceiling. The shelves were clear glass, showing off the chess sets and individual pieces from all angles. There were collections of carved ivory, one from northern China with figures sitting on grotesque animals. There were ironwood and stone pieces, some of historical interest: one assemblage, in red and deep gray bisque, represented the Battle of Hastings. There was a set of painted porcelain figures from *Alice in Wonderland* in the style of Tenniel, another from *Through the Looking Glass*, the figures of pure clear crystal. At one shelf, higher than the others, Gary stopped. Harold hurried to stand beside him, whispering in rapture, "Eighteenth-century Spanish. I felt very guilty about acquiring this." He smiled, not at all guiltily. "But I got over it. I was told, and later had it authenticated, that each of these pieces was carved from human bone." The pieces stood, a rank of skeletons for pawns, towering spectral figures for the remaining pieces. Each queen's face was covered by a shroud held by a skeletal hand; the kings wore pointed crowns fashioned from the caved-in domes of their own skulls.

Gary smiled and moved on to a set of Napoleonic painted figurines; Napoleon faced by Wellington as opposing kings. There was another comprised entirely of Harlequins. Harold brought the young man to one case, opening it to remove a rook and put it in his hand.

"Cast iron," he said, taking it and placing it back with its fellows. "Identical to a set given to Morphy at a testimonial dinner. Only, his were cast in gold and silver."

They finished their tour, and Harold led his guest from the room, closing the door behind him and switching off the lights. On the way back to the living room he stopped to show Gary his collection of chess books, set in a single tall mahogany bookcase. Lining the edge of the bookcase shelves were pawns of various styles. "Philiodor, the great French player, said that pawns are the soul of chess," Harold explained.

He looked at his guest with concern, realizing that once more he had been doing most of the talking. Gary had become remote; though he had shown interest, his eyes had begun to wander.

"Did you like it?" Harold asked.

Gary's eyes and lax smile came back to him. "Yes. Very much."

There followed an awkward silence. They stood by the front hallway, next to the wing chair with the young man's jacket draped over it, which Gary made no move to retrieve. Harold felt suddenly unsure of himself. It had been so long since he had brought anyone to his home. Should there be something he should say or do now?

"Would you by any chance have a glass of soda?" Gary asked, suddenly.

"Yes, of course!" Harold replied. "Please." He motioned back into the living room. "We can talk."

"May I come with you to the kitchen?" Gary asked.

"Yes, if you'd like. We can sit there, at the kitchen table."

They went into the kitchen. Again Harold was glad that the woman had been in to clean the day before; normally there would be more than the few dishes in the sink, complemented by a scattering of the previous week's newspapers on the butcher-block table.

He hurried to the refrigerator and withdrew two cans of 7-Up. He held them out for approval, and when Gary nodded pleasantly, he placed them on the counter, reaching up above to one of the cabinets to get two glasses. He brought everything over to the table and motioned for Gary to sit.

"Do you by any chance have a can opener?" the young man asked.

Harold pointed to the self-opening tab on the can. "You don't need one."

"I have to be careful of cuts."

You're a hemophiliac? he nearly blurted out, managing to change it to an, "Oh." He added, "I'll open it for you."

"I prefer to do things myself," Gary answered, sounding almost hurt.

"Of course," Harold quickly replied. He slid open a drawer next to the dishwasher and, after some rummaging, located a can opener.

"Thank you," Gary said, taking the can opener, his other hand closing hard around Harold's outstretched arm.

"Oh—" Harold gasped, at both the pain of Gary's grip on his arm and the widening realization that he did not know this young man after all.

Gary smiled, showing his teeth, and pushed Harold backward, still gripping his arm tightly. Harold came to rest hard against the kitchen counter. Incongruously, he felt the beginnings of a sour stomach and thought of his antacid tablets. He felt the outline of the counter against his back and the rectangular gap that traced the now-closed drawer from which he had taken the can opener to hand to this young man, who now, for the first time since Harold had known him, showed his teeth in his smile—small, yellowed incisors that made his face look paler, his hair more blond, his eyes as bright as if he had removed his glasses.

"Gary—" he begged, but the young man did not listen to him. He pushed Harold back, bending him over the counter and holding him under the chin while he tore down from the throat in ragged scraping lines with the can opener.

The old man shrieked out Gary's name and then gurgled, and then he didn't make any more noise.

After a long time, when the taut muscles of Gary's working arm began to ache, he finally stepped back and let the thing that had been Harold drop to the floor.

Gary cleaned the can opener with his handkerchief, then dropped it next to the body and walked deliberately to the kitchen table. He picked up one of the 7-Ups and opened it, using the pop-top. He poured it carefully into one of the glasses and drank it.

When he finished, he cleaned the glass and can and set them down on the table and went to the front hall. He picked his gym bag up, placed it on the chair, and opened it. Inside was a clean white turtleneck, a clean pair of chinos, socks, and sneakers. He changed into the clean clothes, rolling up the blood-soaked ones he had been wearing and stuffing them into the bag. His jacket was draped over the arm of the chair, and he smoothed the cracked leather with his hands. He put it on, over his white turtleneck. He picked up Harold's folding briar chess set, which was on the seat of the wing chair, opened it, cleaned each piece with his handkerchief. He tossed the set back down on the chair.

He crossed the living room and walked down the short hallway, switching on the fluorescent lights in the room on the left. He went in, walked to the tall glass case enclosing the chess set made of human bone. Using the handkerchief, he opened the case, knocked over the king on the board, and reclosed the case.

He returned to the living room, picked up his gym bag, and left the apartment, closing the door behind him.

A half hour later, in his front room, Gary waited for the phone to ring. He hadn't removed his jacket. He brought the phone to the window, studying the deceptive beauty of Gramercy Park, the meticulously tended trees, the fat healthy squirrels.

When the phone finally rang and he picked up the receiver, there was the customary silence filled only by space and the faint tickle of static.

"Is there anything you want me to do?" Gary asked.

The voice that was strong but sounded as if it came from far away said, "Not at the moment." There was static, then: "Are you enjoying yourself?"

"Yes."

"Good. In a short time there will be much to do."

"I'll be ready."

"I know you will, Gary." A kittenish, purring quality came into the voice. "Do you feel strong?"

Gary's hand holding the receiver clutched it tightly; he felt as though he could crush it if he wanted—could crush *anything* if he wanted.

"Yes, I feel strong."

"I know." Before the voice faded into the neutral vast silence of the phone wires, it asked, "Doesn't it feel good to be invincible?"

3. EAST

A woman with chin hair came to get him each afternoon. He guessed the time to be about one o'clock. She was not a fat woman, as you would expect a woman with hair on her chin to be, but slim, almost shapely, with doe-dark eyes and soft, thin black hair brushed away from her eyes the way a man with such hair might do. Her nose was slim and straight, her mouth large, the lips moist, nearly always lipsticked. She had ample breasts, evident beneath her uniform smock, which was a shade softer in material and color than those the other attendants wore. In many ways, she was a desirable woman. But the presence of hair on her chin—long, black curls of it that grew down under the ledge of her chin to rest their points against her upper neck—negated all of her feminine qualities. Jan could not understand this one monstrous anomaly that made all of her femininity, her lipstick, her dark eyes shaded with eye shadow, ironic. She reminded him of the nuns who had taught him at school. Some of them had seemed almost feminine; behind their habits you could detect the outlines and allure of a woman. But invariably there would be one trait that would set them apart from normal women, one flaw, physical or psychological, that branded them as different.

"Come, Jan," she said. He had tried once to look into her eyes, but there had been such depths there, such unminable territory, a life so completely alien to him that he had looked away in embarrassment.

"Come," she repeated, in her soft voice.

She led him down the hallway, through a series of corridors. They turned right, left, left, right. He tried to keep track of the turnings, the lengths of corridors. The walls smelled of damp. There were deep rivuleted cracks, evidence of cement long neglected. Jan would know from the damp alone that he was underground; it was always chilly, and even when the lights were turned out, he could not tell if it was night or day.

He knew that they were buried deep. One day during the first week he had seen an elevator open, in one of the corridors he had not been taken to since, and out of the corner of his eye, he had seen the huge lift entrance, as wide as a barn door. When the doors had suddenly opened, offering him a view of the vastness of the compartment, he had felt, down in his gut, the huge weight of that elevator and the slowness and extreme length of its descent. Now, whenever he thought of that elevator, he thought of the surface, of night, day, sunlight, leaves dripping wet on trees, rain itself, the world without pain.

"Stop, Jan," the woman with chin hair said. Her voice was as soft as if she had asked him the time in a tavern, trying to get a date with him. They stood before two doors. Each had a mirrored round window in it. His attendant, who had not told him her name when he had asked, before he had learned to be fascinated with her depths, and to fear them, gave him her mysterious smile. It was the smile of the Mona Lisa. *Which do you want?* it said. *Which door should we choose?* and *Will you choose the right door? Have they changed them this day? Did we walk down this corridor to these two doors the last time?*

"Choose," she said suddenly, laughing, startling Jan, sending a chill through him.

Before he could choose, she said, "Right door."

She reached for the handle, but it was opened from within.

Someone had been looking at them through the porthole, the one-way glass.

The room was bright, white tiles and silver chrome. He had been going to say, "Left." That would have brought him isolation, an empty dark room, mere loneliness. This meant the other thing.

She did not touch him; he stumbled into the room as if in a dream.

"Pain," she said softly, smiling sadly, her doe eyes dark.

He fainted, and remembered no more.

Later, in his room, he heard other screams. He did not remember his own screams. He did not even remember if he had screamed. Perhaps he had laughed, or tried to fight the attendant with the chin hair, or even the other attendant, the man with muscled arms and a head covered with small tight blond curls. He did not even remember the needle going into him. Perhaps they had made the muscles stand out on his arms, or his mouth twitch as if it had been jolted with electricity, or his privates engorge with blood or to the point where he blacked out. Maybe they had asked him questions the answers to which he did not know or, finally, one that he did know the answer to. Perhaps they had finally found that place in him they wanted and had drained it dry, leaving no memory in him of their excision, and now they would let him go, or kill him.

But there were other screams now. There were no faces to go with the screams, because he had never seen any of the other prisoners. There was a shrill, begging, high scream, the scream of a very young man. There was another young man, whose scream was level and low, like a barking angry dog fighting its pain. And there was a third, the scream of an old woman, a husky, deep, begging voice.

The very young man was screaming now, high wails punctuated by gasps, through which Jan could faintly hear an electric sound, the sound of sparking voltage.

In a little while, the young man would stop screaming, and then, after a short hiatus, one of the others would begin.

He turned to the wall by his bed. By his reckoning, and by

the schedule of screams he heard, the lights would soon go out, signaling the beginning of his underground night.

Jan closed his eyes and tried to make night come sooner.

He thought of Bridget. He had never had her, though he knew that someday he would. She had told him that, the day she had shown herself naked to him. There were times when he thought she was imagined, a vivid creation of his mind. But she had come to him enough times now, times when he was not drugged or so deep in despair that hallucinations—of his mother, his friends—would rise unbidden, that he was convinced of her reality. He had really been convinced the first time, even before he had been brought here. And she had told him then that he would someday have her.

He had never had a woman. He had often bragged that he had, before he had ended up in this place, when he and his friends, all of them below the age of twenty, had told the same lies about being with women. One of their group, Karol, had a girlfriend, but they all knew she had never let him have anything, only because they all knew her and knew the strict religiousness of her family, and mostly because Karol claimed she had let him have everything. The more a boy claimed to have received from a girl, the less he had. It was a rule they all knew, but wouldn't admit to. They all called Karol's girlfriend The Nun behind Karol's back.

There had been one girl whom Jan had known well, and it had almost happened, but the girl's father had come into the barn for some hay and she had quickly buttoned her blouse. They had been drinking beer at a fair all afternoon, and things had progressed to this logical point, but after her father left, she seemed to have sobered and refused to have Jan near her. A week later she was with another boy, not one of Jan's friends, and apparently she had kept her blouse unbuttoned for him, because three months later there was a wedding, when she began to show.

But Bridget would be his; she had promised him. And she had returned so many times to renew her promise that he believed her. For his sanity, he had to.

He opened his eyes and stared at the concrete wall. If he touched it, his finger would come away with a bead of wetness on it. The lights had not gone out yet. The screaming of the young boy had stopped.

He rolled over on the cot and sat up, his feet lying heavily on the floor. He felt numb, a dead man made of damp concrete.

He wanted Bridget now. He wanted not only to imagine but to see her, to touch her. He put his hand gently to his groin and found himself hard. He tried to conjure her up, as she had appeared to him that first time, on the day they took him. He tried to see her now.

She was as young as Jan. Her eyes were the color of blue spring sky over the river. He had seen such a blue sky one day when he was fishing with his father, when he was twelve, and the Vistula River was so cold and clear that it reflected the purity of the sky and seemed to make it twice as blue and clean. They were large eyes, in a round face, not the face of a peasant but not one of royalty, either. She had fair skin, with freckles lightly set around her nose. The freckles were so faint he could only see them when he was close enough to kiss her. He wanted to kiss her now. Her mouth was full and large, her teeth almost perfect, small, white and even.

Her hair was red, not the dull red of some Warsaw girls, not the flaming wild color of some of the Irish girls he had seen on magazine covers, but a rich, dark red, the color of harvest plums. It was cut neither short nor long, cropped straight around her neckline. It looked as though it might once have been very long, over her shoulders. It was hair that should be allowed to proliferate, to grow the way wet rich plants grow. In his mind, he had put his hand through it, and though it was straight and thick there was a softness to it, a fineness, that was one of the most sensual things he had ever felt. He thought of it as the full feeling of water at the exact, cool temperature to tingle and refresh the skin of the hand on a hot, dry day.

Her hair and her eyes together made her extraordinary. She was short, with pale hands, and, like her nose, the backs of her hands were sprinkled with freckles. The skin was clean as milk, nearly as white. Her body was thin, with the delicate bulges of small breasts that stood straight out from her body, capped by large dark areolas and wide red nipples. He thought of the delicate line of her thigh where it merged into leg . . .

Her smile showed hidden depths, like that of the female attendant with chin hair. But where the attendant's gaze was direct, Bridget's came from under her eyes, as she bowed her head forward, shading her ocean-blue eyes, almost, and smiling from under the exquisite face, the freckles on her nose, the lips of her wide mouth parting slightly, showing the whiteness of her tiny, perfect teeth. He had imagined the way her tongue would feel against his mouth, his face, within his own mouth. He had imagined kissing her, knowing that her tongue would be sharp and thin, that it would greatly excite him.

His hand had moved down behind the long, badly cut, rough-stitched prisoner's overalls he wore; he took himself in his hand. He wanted Bridget, *now*.

And suddenly she stood before his cot, her face bent slightly down to him, the ring of her plum-red hair framing her face like a Rembrandt portrait, the luminous vision of her filling him.

"Jan, my poor one." She smiled.

She was as real as his own flesh, standing naked as she had that first day. For a moment, he felt a need greater than that in his loins. She represented all that was left of sanity to him. She was the earth itself, not its dying bowels, but its living surface, the warming sun enfolding it as he longed to enfold her in his arms.

"*I want you,*" he almost sobbed.

"You will have me soon."

He tried to get up. She put her creamy white hand on his shoulder and he did not move.

"Have me," she whispered, her smile deepening, taking his hand and pressing it back to the hardness at his groin, "like that." He put his hand back behind the trousers and began to milk his hardness, his eyes locked on hers.

"Yes. Yes," she whispered. "Jan, do you remember the day they took you?"

For a horrible moment he was sure that his greatest fear was realized, that she, too, was part of what they did to him in the room of pain. He felt the jab of a needle in his arm, the taut pull of a strap around his middle, around his arms and legs, the sharp blurt of electricity through his head, the swim of lax white faces over him, asking him, asking . . .

"Oh, God . . ."

"No, Jan, they don't own me. You own me. Don't you remember?"

She let his hand, a finger, touch her as he came.

"Never forget, Jan," she said.

She moved away from him. Her form mingled with the wet, cold walls. "Soon," she whispered. He felt the wetness in his hand, and, for a moment, he possessed her. She left him slowly, her head slightly tilted, her shaded blue eyes, with her smile, vanishing . . .

He fell back on the cot, turning to the weeping wall, his lust and need draining away into the cement, the damp floor, sucked into the mole-tunnels of the underground world that had captured him. He heard screaming, his own, and a long time later, he awoke from dreamless sleep to see that his hands were bloody and that the wall before him, the weeping cement wall of his cell next to his wooden bed, was stained in blood, showing the perfect outline of a hand, the imprimatur of a weeping man, the red copy of perfect fingerprints.

He brought his reddened hands to his face and cried.

"Soon . . ."

4. SOUTH

Standing on tiptoe on the highest limestone shelf of his mother's roof, Ricky could just see the water.

That made him proud. It was said that there was almost no place in Bermuda where the water was not in sight's distance. He had always thought that their house, the lowest in the line of houses on the road, blocked in back by a line of trees bordering the golf club, hampered in front by hedges and the sweeping curve of the winding roadway, was one of the few exceptions. But now, in his fifteenth year, after a spring of sudden growth that had stretched him to two inches under six feet, Ricky caught sight of a thin crystal-green ribbon of water.

He had climbed up to the roof to make sure the water trough was clear. The roof's white limestone tiers were pure white, clean as a baby's bottom, and after clearing the remains of a dead bird from the water gutter that ran to the tank at the side of the house, he stepped up to the very top of the roof and stood tall against the sky. He imagined for a moment that this little, square, pink stucco house, in the middle of this road whose silence was broken only by the waspy buzz of a lost tourist's motorbike or the mail car, was in another place. The sun, high above, between the puff ball clouds, was a spotlight. He was standing on the flat bright wood of a Broadway stage, bowing for an audience that had come to see him dance and sing, he, Ricky Smith, the equal of Ben Vereen, Tommy Tune, Gregory Hines, a Broadway star as great as any.

And then his eyes had caught a pencil-thin flash of pure green light, and there, at the top of his height, with his arms above his head, his feet on tiptoe: there was the water.

He was filled with happiness and pride, because he was within sight of water as the tourist brochures bragged, and his mother's little pink house was not so little and insignificant after all.

He stood admiring his discovery, savoring his Broadway dream, until a bulging line of gray-bottomed clouds from the east moved in, blotting the sun, his spotlight. It had rained only once in the past two weeks, a brief night shower dropped from a low scudding storm front that was gone almost before it was noticed. Since then there had been high wisps of cloud only momentarily obscuring an otherwise perfect string of blue, high days. Perfect June weather. The *Royal Gazette* had taken note of it every day, mentioning repeatedly, for the sake of the tourists, that this was why everyone came to the Islands of Bermuda—and, of course, why they would certainly come back again.

But today looked as though it might be different. The gray clouds had elbowed their way in and looked ready to stay. The air smelled thicker, less fresh and open. The tourists wouldn't be happy.

Neither would Mr. Harvey.

Ricky made his way down the steps off the road, lowering himself to the ground and calling out, "Roof's fine—off, Mum!" through the half-open doorway. From somewhere inside he heard her say, "Bye," as he pulled his motorbike from the wall. He boarded it and kicked off.

Any day, rain or shine, was too good for work. He'd much rather be with Spook and Reesa and Charlie, down at the ferry dock, jumping with a shout into the clear water, scattering the angelfish. You could see straight to the bottom, which wasn't always a good thing, since some of the tourists chucked their Heineken bottles from the boats, messing up the seafloor. Ricky had once caught Spook chucking a ginger beer can off the quay and had pushed him in after it, telling him he might as well be a tourist himself. Spook had laughed it off, but later on, when Ricky was talking to Reesa alone, sitting at the far end of the pier, bouncing his naked feet off one of the huge rubber bumpers that held the ferry off the concrete of the dock, Spook had snuck up behind and lifted him up under the arms and into the water, the soda can following.

"Off with you—and pick it up yourself!" he shouted, only he had been laughing so good-naturedly that Ricky had only come up from the warm water, laughing himself, with the can.

But today there would be no swimming. He sped by the turnoff for the dock, consoling himself with the fact that even if Reesa and the others were down there, their swimming wouldn't last when the storm came.

Ricky braked, then gave the bike a little gas, pulling out carefully on the Somerset Road, eyes alert for reckless Americans on motorbikes or the occasional bus driver with his mind on his wife or his rum, and took the long, slow curve into the village, past the cluster of shops and the Bank of Bermuda. In another moment he had passed the police station, giving a quick lookout for Constable Wicks, who wasn't in his accustomed spot, leaning against the doorway, looking at the weather, lost in cop's thoughts.

Not seeing Wicks, who didn't like speeders, Ricky gunned the bike, skimming right and then left to the Cambridge and then Daniel's Head Road before turning abruptly into the short lane cut into the curb that led up to the house.

He parked the bike on the side drive, jumping off, moving with a springing step to the back door. The front was locked tight from the inside, the historic house open only on Tuesdays and Thursdays to visitors. The shuttered windows, too, were locked, because Mr. Harvey liked the place closed tight when it wasn't open to the public. Which made it quite stuffy and uncomfortable inside. But Mr. Harvey cared more about protocol than about stuffiness.

He expected the old gent to meet him at the back door. But instead there was a note. It read, "GONE THE DAY TO ST. GEORGE'S, DO THE BACK ROOMS," and was signed, James Harvey, in the old man's florid script. Mr. Harvey fancied himself original stock and acted accordingly, constantly commenting on his former duties with the Tucker family, as well as other former governors. Ricky knew the truth, because the old man's wife had told him one day with a wink behind his back, that he had come from Ireland in 1965 and she with him. But Ricky had never said anything, letting the old man have his dreams, just as he himself did. Just like everyone in the world did.

Ricky knew his own dreams well enough. His mother laughed, and Spook did too, and sometimes even Reesa, though none of them, especially Reesa, ever laughed mean at him, only gently, shaking their heads and giving him looks that said, *dream, Ricky, dream*. But he would make his dreams come true. He would go to the High School for the Performing Arts, just like the one in that TV show *Fame* he sometimes saw off Mr. Bigg's satellite dish, and he would learn to dance, and be at the head of his class, and go to Broadway and be more famous than Ben Vereen. He loved the way Ben Vereen danced, but Ricky knew he would be even better.

He would dream, just like Mr. Harvey did, and someday he would make his dreams real. But for now he would do the back rooms like Mr. Harvey wanted.

He lifted the note off the door. He was fishing out the key when he saw a shadow pass lightly between the half-closed shutters on the window next to the door.

He shivered, something he might not have done had the sun been out. But then the shadow, if it had been one, was gone.

There were stories about Chambers House, of course. There were stories about nearly every house in Somerset Parish that was over fifty years old. Springfield, another old Bermuda family home a mere half mile away, which had been restored as the Somerset Library, certainly had its share. And there were others. But Chambers House was the oldest, and because people craved superstition so much, there were more stories about it than most. It was one of the earliest built on Bermuda, which made it a tourist attraction. There were more rooms than in most houses on the islands, which again made it a topic of conversation. There were stories of piracy, of murdered slaves and buried treasure, which made it all the more romantic, a great lure to Americans especially, whose movies filled them with a lust for adventure.

Ricky had never believed any of it. Spook did, which was why they all called him Spook. He believed in demons and ghosts. He read Hawthorne and Edgar Allan Poe and H. P. Lovecraft. Ricky and the rest of his friends told him his head was filled with nonsense.

Old Mr. Harvey pooh-poohed the stories, except when drunk on his weakness, rum, which was the reason his wife wished they had never come to Bermuda. She said that at least in Ireland he drank rye, which she favored, and could share with him, but rum made her sick. Old Harvey didn't drink often, but when he did, he became a different man, all his stuffy manner evaporating as his face flushed and his brogue surfaced. "I was clearing out the cellar once," he told Ricky one day, when the house was closed and they were supposed to be cleaning the cellar themselves. But it was August, and the heat so blinding hot, that they went out on the back porch and watched the flowers and the trees, and smelled the water, and waited for whatever wind might blow at them from the east, "when I swear something touched me on the shoulder." Harvey's eyes got wide and he ran his hand back through his thinning hair. "Oh, Ricky, I jumped like a frog, I did." He leaned over in his wicker chair, giving Ricky a hard, unmistakable tap on the shoulder. "It was just like that. And the hell of it was, when I turned around, I saw something fly away from me like a ghost in the storybooks, white gauzy linen and all, in the shape of a dress. When I blinked it was gone." He ran his hand through his hair again, then picked up his rum glass. "Ten minutes later I was in the fresh air out here and looking at the blue of the sky and trying to believe I'd seen it at all." He drank and put the glass down. "And I've heard things, seen things fall where no one pushed them, found things moved when I opened up the house the next day, after closing it myself."

The next day Mr. Harvey was sober as a calf. When Ricky asked him about the stories, he just waved his hands and said, "Bah."

As Ricky stood staring at the shutters the shadow passed across them again.

He rushed to the window, pressing his face to the angled wooden slats. He saw nothing. He could view the entire room from where he stood. It was the cooking cellar, next to the kitchen, and there was little in it to begin with—two chairs, a table used for cutting vegetables, a deep, waist-high fireplace with a thick iron grate over it.

"Hey now," he called nervously, "anyone there?"

He felt foolish—as if Spook had gotten him scared with one of his stories. Spook had a scary story about everything from the full to the new moon and back again.

As Ricky stood, staring into the room through the shutters, the shadow passed once more, an invisible yet substantial thing.

A fist of fear formed in Ricky's stomach. There was nothing in that room, and yet there was. He wondered what Mr. Harvey would say if he went home and begged off sick. He already knew the answer. He would lose his job. If he could catch Mr. Harvey in his rum, there might be a chance of getting away with it, if he told him what had happened with the shadows, but there was little chance of that since Mrs. Harvey had gotten him to give the rum up, saying the very smell of it made her ill. And without the rum in him, Ricky had no chance with the old gent. Especially since he wasn't here today and was relying on Ricky to get the house ready for tomorrow's visitors.

So the choice was between losing his job or staying and doing his duty.

The shadow hadn't reappeared. Ricky turned around and saw a close-hanging tree branch that *could* have thrown its shadow, even with the near absence of sun, across the window.

He waved his fear aside and unlocked the back door and went in.

The green-painted door banged shut solidly behind him. It didn't bounce and bang again the way it normally did. Ricky looked back at it. It looked as though it were glued. He resisted the urge to go and check it, and then remembered that with the humidity in the air from the coming rain, the wood would swell, making the door stick.

"Foolishness," he said out loud, to himself.

Stepping into the kitchen, he peeked into the cooking cellar.

It was empty. But as he turned his head away, he saw something move.

"No way," he said, inspecting the still-empty room.

He shook his head and walked out.

The house was dark. The big overhanging window shutters in front and on the side windows were fastened down. He lifted a few of them, letting light and air into the house. It didn't help much; the air was muggy, the day so cloudy that the rooms stayed gloomy. As he straightened and dusted one of the back bedrooms he sang, his voice pleasantly high. He liked Bob Marley, and performed, "I Shot The Sheriff," beating out the rhythm on his chest or a passing piece of furniture.

As he finished the song, his hands slapping the last reggae beat on a chest of drawers, there was a crash in another room.

He stopped cold, fighting off a rush of fear.

Finally, he went to investigate, his hands continuing to slap the beat of Marley's song nervously against his side. The sound had come from one of the middle rooms. When he looked in, he saw a vase he knew had been centered on a small rectangular table in pieces on the floor, the table unmoved.

He heard another crash, at the front of the house.

Slowly, breathing through his dread, he edged down the hall and stared into the main dining room.

The heavy glass door in the center of the china hutch was open on its hinges. On the oriental rug lay the smashed shards of one of the dinner plates that nested inside.

Ricky snapped his head up at a sound. Above him, the tin-plated chandelier began to swing on its chain, slowly and then with widening arcs. One of the candles flew from its beaten-tin holder to break beside him.

"Lord Jesus," Ricky whispered, crossing himself.

Another dinner plate tipped out of the hutch, crashing

beside the first. One of the side doors of the cabinet opened leisurely, and a heavy gravy boat and ladle tipped out and fell to the floor.

From the rear of the house he heard his own voice singing "I Shot the Sheriff," and then there was a heavy crash.

The singing voice moved closer. When it reached the room where Ricky stood, shivering, the singing stopped.

In the adjoining living room, a painting fell from the wall over the couch, the corner of its frame cracking.

He backed cautiously out into the hallway. Silence fell and stayed. His body tense, waiting for the next assault, he took another step backward.

He felt a tap on his shoulder.

Gasping, he slapped his hand at the spot, whirling about in time to see the retreating leg of a figure vanish into one of the back bedrooms.

From the same room, his own voice began to sing Bob Marley's "Redemption Song."

There was a shuttered window in the dining room, and he walked to it. He was sure it was one of the windows he had opened when he came in. It was closed now. There was a hook and eye holding the large green shutter down; to open it, he had to slip the hook and then push the shutter out.

His voice in the other room continued to sing, louder.

He fumbled with the hook, not getting it to come out the first time. It had gotten very dark in the house. He thought he heard a roll of thunder, the first tentative splatters of big raindrops. He wanted to be in the midst of that storm, speeding home on his bike, hot wet rain falling on him. The rain would wake him up from this nightmare, and then the warming sun, later, would make him forget.

If Spook had told him a story like this, he would have laughed. Spook had told him lots of stories, on nights when they sat on lawn chairs in front of Spook's house, Spook sipping rum from his father's bottle, pulling it out every once in a while from the bush behind the chairs, leaning back his big wide frame and laughing, keeping one ear open for his parents. Spook made Ricky scold or laugh with his stories about ghosts in trees, or the ghosts of dead buccaneers that were supposed to inhabit one corner of Hamilton Harbor, asking a penny of any passing soul on a certain late summer night, slitting their throats if the penny wasn't offered.

This was worse than any of Spook's stories, and it was no comfort to know that if Spook had told him this he would have laughed long and hard.

From the bedroom down the hallway, the singing became very loud. It was as if an amplifier had been turned up. Then, abruptly, in mid—lyric, the singing stopped.

The hook on the shutter slipped from its eye in Ricky's fingers. The window shutter moved out a half foot before stopping.

Something touched Ricky's shoulder and stayed there this time.

"Ricky," a voice whispered, "don't you want to listen?"

Ricky screamed, pushing futilely at the shutter, banging it with his fists, before giving up and suddenly turning around to face his attacker.

The dining room was empty.

But someone's finger was still pressing into his shoulder.

"Ricky," someone whispered in his ear.

He cried out and turned, ramming both fists ineffectively at the shutter. Outside, rain fell just out of reach. Thunder growled.

"Jesus, Jesus," he pleaded, pushing with all his might as the shutter began to close.

He could not hold it back. It shut, and the hook slipped back into its eye.

The finger on his shoulder became a heavy, bruising grip.

"Come, Ricky."

The hand on his shoulder pushed him to the back of the house. He stood before the whitewashed door that led to the cellar. The wooden latch flipped up and over, and the door creaked open. Ricky was propelled toward the stairway, forced down one step at a time.

The light at the bottom snapped on, its pull chain swinging wildly. The light was brighter than Ricky remembered it.

The cellar was chilly, musty smelling. Along one wall, library shelves stored house records; rows of visitor registers and account books jutted out into the room. Behind them was an area bordered by stacked boxes and furniture in storage or in need of repair.

The hand on Ricky's shoulder pushed him toward the storage area.

The overhead bulb blinked on, flooding the area like a spotlight.

Ricky screamed, covering his face with his hands.

In the neat square area lay the mutilated bodies of everyone he loved. Charlie and Reesa were facedown in one corner, hands tied behind their backs. The skull of each had been crushed like a robin's egg. Reesa's face was closest, her head on its side, her eyes staring into nothingness. Spook sat with his back against an unused chest of drawers, his eyes wide open, his severed head not quite aligned with his blood-washed neck on which it rested. Mr. and Mrs. Harvey sat on chairs directly under the light; they had been bound together back to back, their blue-strangled faces staring sightlessly around the world at one another, tongues licking out for air that wasn't theirs. Worst of all was his mother. She was on top of a dining table, laid out neatly like a waked corpse, with three screwdrivers set into her body in a line down her chest; her hand was frozen around the sunken handle of one, vainly trying to remove it. Her mouth was an open cry, eyes pleading unseeing with the ceiling.

"No, God, no!"

Ricky fell to his knees, burying his head in his arms. The hand on his shoulder bowed him to the floor, and he lay there, weeping.

Suddenly, the grip on his shoulder was gone.

Ricky looked up, and the storage area was empty, save for an open box of discarded magazines supporting the leaning handle of a sweep broom.

Ricky slowly got to his feet. He was shivering, unable to drive what he had seen from his mind.

From near the stairs, the voice that had whispered came to him. It didn't whisper now. There was nothing subtle about it.

"Go to New York, Ricky," the voice said. It was a woman's voice. "If you don't, I'll bring you down here again, and what you see will be real. Do you believe me?"

"Yes." He shivered as if he were naked in the snow.

"Maybe you'll even dance on Broadway. Would you like that, Ricky?"

Ricky did not answer. Tears pressed at the corners of his eyes. His mouth worked a silent prayer.

From upstairs, he heard his voice singing "Redemption Song." He heard the muffled taps of his feet, dancing a routine he had created in the style of Ben Vereen.

"Leave, Ricky." The voice sounded amused. Upstairs, the singing and dancing ceased.

All was quiet.

Ricky took the stairs two at a time. Through the back door it seemed the day was bright again, but when he pulled it open, he saw that the sky was black overcast. There was a deft cut of lightning, followed by the deep booming sound of thunder, its mate. The drops of rain were large and insistent, cold against the skin.

He ran to his bike, ramming it into life, and fled. As he passed the front of Chambers House he saw that the green shutter in the dining room window was thrown wide open.

He sobbed, his crying mixing with cloud-tears of rain.

He bounced down the driveway and into the road, nearly skidding into a pink Hamilton-bound bus as he made his too-quick turn. The rain and thunder made a sound, but it was not loud enough to block out what he heard behind him: his own voice singing, and a laughing voice that said, "Boo."

5. THE ASSISTANT

For the first time, Gary hit traffic on the way down. He was mildly annoyed, because the Taconic State Parkway was usually one of the least traveled and most pleasant roads in New York. But today, at the start of a chilly, overcast end-of-summer weekend, which no one but the diehards would be spending at their upstate retreats—and they'd be going the other way, anyway—he'd hit a slow-moving crawl and now, suddenly, a complete backup.

He put up with it, jamming a Miles Davis tape into the deck of the old Datsun. Twenty minutes later his patience was rewarded and annoyance abated when he passed the remains of an accident by the turnoff for the Saw Mill River Parkway. It looked like some idiot in a Volkswagen had tried to make the turnoff from the left lane. He'd been punished by having the right side of his bug torn off by a white Cadillac. The Caddy must have been moving; it looked relatively unharmed, but the Volkswagen had been totalled. From the appearance of the windshield on the passenger side and the red-speckled glass swept onto the shoulder of the highway, they'd needed an ambulance, if not a meatwagon.

Gary glanced idly into the interior of the bug as he rubbernecked by, but whatever had been left in there had already been hauled away.

From then on, as he got onto the Saw Mill Parkway, the traffic was light.

It had been a good trip, as these trips went. He'd been able to get Bridget's business out of the way, still leaving plenty of time to get home and take care of his own.

He smiled, gripping the wheel hard. *Business. Like old Harold and his chess.*

The Invincible Man.

He gripped the wheel harder. His entire body had become tense, his smile set. Why not test it now? Maybe he would tear the wheel right off its shaft, send the old Datsun into a concrete overpass. Maybe he'd wait until he got off the Major Deegan Expressway, send the car over the Third Avenue Bridge. If the impact didn't get him, the water would, since he couldn't swim.

But what if she was lying?

He nearly broke the wheel in confused anger, his eyes filling with blind rage. He was passing a huge diesel rig; he could run the Datsun sideways, jamming it under the bed; the dragging crush of the wheels would—

She wouldn't lie to me.

He loosened his grip on the steering wheel. His smile loosened, too. There was no reason to total the car. Why would she have told him all these things if she didn't mean them? A trade, she'd called it. He did a few things for her, was a kind of assistant; she gave him . . . *invincibility*. A fair trade. And he knew she could do things that weren't . . . normal. She'd proved that to him.

What if she's using you?

He was gripping the wheel again. Deliberately, with an act of will, he calmed himself. He was getting upset over nothing. It had been a good trip, a good day; it would be a good night . . .

What if—

In the confines of the Datsun, he shouted, "*Stop it!*" He banged his fist down hard on the dashboard, feeling the cheap padding give with the blow until metal somewhere underneath met and resisted his hand.

Stop . . .

He felt better. He stretched his hand out on the seat next to him, letting the pain spread from his fist to his arm, concentrating on it, tasting it.

In a few minutes, he was himself again.

He turned his attention back to the road. He was already on the FDR Drive. Even with the delay on the Taconic, he had made good time. His spirits rose. He reversed the neglected Miles Davis tape.

In five minutes he had reached his exit, passed a couple of stoplights, made two quick turns, and was into his underground garage. The car bounced and squeaked at the bottom of the short ramp, and he thought, *Have to get new shocks.*

He was in a good mood by the time he locked the garage door behind him, made a quick trip to the corner deli to buy the three papers ("Hello, Bob"; "Hello, Gary," a meaningless conversation that hadn't changed in twelve years), and entered the elevator. Mrs. Fogelman was in it. She'd lived in the building since Gary was four years old and had known his mother. "Hello, Gary," she began, trying to rush into conversation, looking for gossip. He waved his hand at her noncommittally and pushed the up button.

The elevator was slow; the gate creaked and momentarily stuck when he pulled it open. As the car finally arrived he looked at his watch. Six o'clock. Plenty of time.

He locked his door behind him, took off his jacket and laid it carefully over the back of the couch. He put the three newspapers on the corner of the coffee table. He reached beneath the couch and slid out a flat square scrapbook, the old-fashioned kind with black pages for snapshots mounted with gummed corners.

The first three pages were covered with newspaper clippings. He opened to the fourth page, revealing a black-and-white photograph of his mother and himself and a man he didn't recognize. The man had an arm around his shoulder. Gary was standing in front of a low brick wall. He was about six years old. Above where he stood, on top of the wall, was a huge plaster Humpty Dumpty with its arms and legs flailing, trying to regain its balance, a look of extreme alarm on its face. A sign, partly hidden by his mother's smiling face, read: "Couldn't put . . . again."

Gary removed the picture, tossed it aside. He pulled up the four gummed corners and discarded them.

He turned the page. Another snapshot showed a similar scene, with him and his mother, but a different man. He didn't recall this one, either. The man had a broad-brimmed hat tilted back on his head. Gary was about seven, now. He was mounted on a saddled horse, his mother's hand holding the reins. The man's arm was around her waist, pulling her close.

Gary lifted the picture out and slid the gummed corners off. He went on until he reached a page that held a huge picture, eight by ten, set in sideways to fit. It was of his second-grade class at the Lexington School. It was the only class picture his mother had ever bought. He sat in the row farthest from the camera, in the end seat. He could barely be seen, his crew-cut blond head partially hidden behind a girl with a red thick kinky mop that stood out from her head. Only half his face was visible, showing a lopsided smile. He looked as though he were half asleep. The teacher had even said that to him once or twice, that he acted as though he were half-asleep. His mother had said that, too.

"Bitch," he said, yanking the picture from the page and removing the corners with his fingernails.

He gathered all the photographs together with the school shot and put them under the couch, brushing the gummed corners after them.

He pulled the three newspapers on the coffee table up close, going through them page by page.

It had taken them a week, but they had finally found Harold. The *Daily News* had a story about him on page four. There was a photograph, blurred, of the sheet-covered body on the kitchen floor, and another of his chess museum. In the kitchen shot, a cop in plain clothes stood next to the body; two uniformed cops were pulling the sheet up around Harold's head.

The caption said the plain-clothes detective's name was Falconi.

Falconi was in the story, too, claiming he had no real leads but that he was certain they'd solve the crime. "We'll get the S.O.B.," he was quoted as saying.

Feeling vaguely disappointed at the *Daily News* coverage, Gary clipped the article and used a glue stick to paste it into the photo album.

He searched through the *Times*, which had the same story with fewer, fancier, words. There was a clearer picture of Falconi—he was short and looked stout but his tie was straight.

The *Post* had the headline he had hoped for. "GAMES KILLER," it read. He pasted the story, a lurid copy of the other versions, underneath the headline, carelessly ripping one section at the bottom. He didn't get angry at himself. It was the headline, in two-inch tall type, he wanted to stand out.

He glanced at the school clock in the hallway and *did* get mad at himself. It was seven-fifteen. He had nearly let himself run late.

He added his clothes to the pile in the hallway and showered. Then he shaved, pausing to wipe the steam from the mirror carefully before each stroke.

He dressed slowly, in blue oxford-cloth shirt, gray crewneck sweater, tan chinos. His cordovan loafers were shined, his hair brushed neatly to the side. He cleaned his glasses and set them carefully on his face.

He took his gym bag from the closet, packed an extra pair of chinos, belt, navy blue turtleneck. By the time he was finished it was nearly seven forty-five. He went back to the mirror in the bathroom to make sure he looked the way he wanted, then left the apartment.

Out on the street he thought about Meg. She once told him that he dressed the way she remembered boys dressing in high school. She liked that. She said that when she was in high school everything was nice. That was before hair got long and everybody turned into slobs. She told him that he reminded her of high school, of the junior prom. She'd lived in the suburbs, then. She'd gone to the prom with a boy named Mike; he'd come on time and he'd given her nice flowers and he was polite and they had a nice time. The senior prom she didn't like to talk about; but once when Gary got there she'd been drinking a lot of her gin, and after a while she'd told him. She called him Mike, the name of the boy she went to her junior prom with. She said that this other boy, the one she went to the senior prom with, was named Bill. She had gotten her father to let Bill take his car for the night. She thought she was in love with him. They had a good time at the prom, though Bill drank a lot at the place they went afterward. And then, on the way home, he parked the car by the curb where there wasn't a streetlight nearby. His breath smelled like beer and bourbon. He leaned over and kissed her, and then put his hands on her where she didn't want him to. They'd had little, teasing fights about it before, and he'd always given in. But tonight he didn't. He touched her and then he pressed his hands on her, and before she knew it, he had slipped his hand into the top of her dress behind her bra and smoothly down over her breast, touching her nipple.

Meg was very drunk with gin while she told Gary this. She called him Mike again. She sobbed, and then she told Gary that she tried to get Bill to stop, but he wouldn't. He pulled her dress away from her back, the dress she had agonized a week over, hoping it was just right, hoping he would like it. He pulled the dress forward, slipping it down over her arms, pinning them. He slipped his hand out of her bra and down her front into her panties ("Oh, God. Oh, Mike"), and he touched the hair down there. Then she screamed and ripped her dress, and screamed again. He moved back away from her, alarmed, and said, "Shhh, Meg, Shhh." She screamed at him to drive her home, *now,* and finally he did. He moved the car slowly from streetlamp to streetlamp, so drunk he wasn't sure where he was. She was terrified he was going to hit another car parked at the curb, wrecking her father's car on what should have been the most beautiful night of her life. ("Oh, Mike.") She was crying and trembling, trying to fasten her dress back up the back, screaming at Bill when he turned to help her, telling him to stay away, just *drive*. When they got to her house, Bill parked the car in the driveway, leaving it at an angle, partway on the grass. She told him to get out and ripped the keys from his hand, running into the house past her mother dozing in a chair in the living room, waiting for her.

"Gary, oh, Mike," she cried, putting her head on his shoulder briefly before sitting up and pouring more gin into her glass. She drank the gin and blew her nose, and told him that she slammed the bathroom door and cried for forty-five minutes before she let her mother in. Her father vowed to go out, at three in the morning, and find Bill and beat him to a pulp. And even though she wanted her father to do that, she wouldn't let him.

Idly, Gary wondered how drunk she would be tonight.

At eight o'clock he rang the bell to her apartment. He could hear her coming to the door, and he stood in front of the peephole so she could see him. She opened the door. She wore a red plaid skirt and dark green sweater, with a gold pin over one breast. Her black hair was parted in the middle, hanging over her shoulders. She wore her high-school ring on one hand.

"Hello, Gary," she said, her breath bearing the sweet-sharp odor of gin.

Behind her, on the coffee table, he saw the cribbage deck and board, the pegs neatly in place to start. Next to it was a half-empty clear bottle and her glass. There was also a folded copy of the *Post*, the red banner above the tall block headline making it instantly recognizable.

"You know," she smiled, letting him in, taking his gym bag and leaving it by the door, "after reading tonight's paper, if we hadn't been playing so long I wouldn't let you in." Her smile widened: a gin smile. "Especially your name being Gary *Gaimes* and all."

6. NORTH

Laura Hutchins awoke to the sound of rattling cutlery. Her first thought was, *My god, someone's in the apartment*. Then, when her mind cleared: *My God, the first night*.

She grabbed for the notebook and pencil on the night table next to the bed. She missed on the first attempt, unused to the location of the furniture, but found the book, her fingers closing around the pencil, on the second try. As quietly as possible, she pulled the chain on the small lamp on the bedside table, flipping open the notebook to an empty page.

In the kitchen, the rattling noises continued.

She glanced at the clock radio and began to write. *Twelve forty A.M., October . . .* She couldn't remember the date. She counted up from Peter's birthday, which had been on the 21st. Four days. She wrote, *October 25*. Then she crossed out 25, remembering that it was past midnight.

October 26. First night in my aunt's apartment, and already an audible manifestation. She began to write faster. *Dr. Brennan was wrong. Sound of knives and forks scraping together, being thrown about. Someone looking for something.*

She stopped, almost jumping. *Dropped utensil. Loud. Maybe thrown down. Angry?*

The pencil froze over the notebook, and suddenly she was completely awake, realizing that this was her first night in a new apartment in a strange city, and she didn't even know if the lock had been changed before she moved in.

Suddenly she thought, almost writing it down, *maybe that's not an audible manifestation after all. Maybe there's someone in the apartment.*

The rattling sounds had ceased. She sat listening for footsteps, the bang of a leg or foot against an unfamiliar object, a human cough or breathing. She heard two utensils scrape lightly together, followed by continued silence.

She counted to twenty, then turned off the lamp on the nightstand. She rose, wincing slightly at the ever-present pain in her leg. Stifling an "Ouch," she hobbled to the open door of the bedroom, her notebook and pencil brandished as ineffective weapons.

Down the hall, an eerie glow emanated from the kitchen. Beyond it, through the living room, the tenth floor picture windows showed an ironically tranquil view of Ottawa at night: a scattering of overhead stars blessing the silver glint of the Rideau Canal, straddled by the Parliament buildings and the majestic turrets of the Chateau Laurier.

The coldness that had crept down her spine at the sight of the otherworldly glare in the kitchen evaporated when she remembered that there was a digital timer with fluorescent green numerals set into the range hood over the stove.

She stood still in the doorway, waiting for something to happen. Minutes passed. Then suddenly the weak green glow from the kitchen was vaguely shadowed and there was the sound of something sliding over the floor. She saw the blade end of a steak knife slide out into the hallway and stop.

Visible manifestation, she scribbled in her notebook, in the dark, hoping the words would be recognizable later.

A step at a time, with pauses for held breath, brought her, after what seemed an hour, to the doorway of the kitchen. She glanced in. The dim green light revealed an empty room with the kitchen utensils she had put away earlier that day scattered on the counter and floor. Some were bunched into patterns.

There was a curious triangle of interlocking forks that abruptly fell apart.

She jumped involuntarily, but then remembered the notebook and began to write.

Open utensil drawer, she noted, studying the room. *Positive it was closed. Forks and spoons—*

The pencil froze in her fingers. In the center of the counter, above the utensil drawer, was what appeared to be a deliberately cleared spot. She felt along the wall past the telephone and flicked on the overhead light, giving a little gasp to see a single knife, the sharpest paring instrument she owned, standing straight up in the countertop. The blade was sunk deeply into the wood. Something had been done to the countertop around it—

The telephone rang. Startled, she dropped her notebook and pencil. By the third ring she was calm enough to pick up the receiver.

"Laura?" Peter's voice said.

She stifled the urge to yell at him.

"Laura, are you there?"

"I'm here."

A few beats went by. She had the feeling, from the tone of his voice, that he was fighting to swallow his pride. And that he had been drinking.

"I want to apologize. I—"

"It's not the right time, Peter," she said.

"If we have another fight like the last one, it might be the last."

"I thought it was."

He paused before answering. "We both said a lot of things we didn't want to." Another pause. "At least I did."

Despite her resolve, her voice softened. "So did I."

He took a deep breath. Relief? "Thank you," he said, adding quickly, "for not hanging up on me."

She laughed a little, knowing the way he was, what it must have taken for him to call her like this. "You sound tired, Peter."

"I haven't been sleeping very well."

"You should go to bed."

"I sleep better with you there."

She yielded to affection. "I didn't have to give you the number here."

"I know. If you hadn't, I think I would have known I'd fucked things up for good. I know it's late, but I sat by the phone since seven o'clock, trying to work up the balls to call you."

You said you were sorry we fought, but you still haven't said I've done the right thing. She was suddenly angry, but she held it at bay, realizing that the very fact that he had called her was a victory against his stubbornness and need to be right. "You didn't wake me."

She moved the receiver to her other ear, shifting her weight to a more comfortable position. Her foot kicked a spoon, and suddenly she remembered why she was up at this hour.

"Jesus," she said.

Peter's voice became wary. "What is it, Laura?"

She battled with herself whether to tell him or not. She knew it would probably only restart their fight. But if she didn't talk to him about it, make him see that if he wanted to be part of her he had to understand what all this meant to her, then she might as well hang up now and forget about any future victories over his obstinacy.

"The apartment is active," she told him. "The same kinds of things Dr. Brennan said had happened elsewhere."

She heard his sharp intake of breath. "But he told you not to go up there."

"He was wrong. It woke me up. Utensils were scattered all over the kitchen."

She felt him trying to control himself; when he spoke, his voice was low and reasonable.

"You could have left the drawer out too far when you put all those things away, and they fell out."

"The drawer was shut before I went to bed."

"Maybe—"

"I heard it, Peter. With my own ears."

"Laura—"

"*Goddamnit, Peter, I heard it!*" She nearly hung up on him, stopping her hand before it drove the receiver into its cradle. When she spoke again, her voice came from between clenched teeth.

"I'm here and it happened. My own ears *heard* it. The drawer was closed before I went to bed. Something opened it and pulled all that stuff out. That's it. That's all there is."

There was dead silence on the other end. She thought that Peter had hung up on her. Then, when his voice came, it was filled with pain.

"Oh, God, Laura, don't you know what this is doing to you?"

She heard him from a growing distance. She knew what he was going to say; he had said it before and only the tone of his words had changed. But she listened to him anyway, from that faraway place.

"Laura, how long can you keep doing this?" And then suddenly he was crying. "I love you! Can't you see they're gone? *I'm* here for you now." His sobs consumed him. "They're *dead,* Laura!"

She looked at the countertop, at the paring knife jammed into the center of it. She head Peter, but his voice had suddenly become very distant. She wondered if something was wrong with the phone lines. Peter's voice grew thinner and higher, like a mouse's. She held the phone receiver away from her ear, but it wasn't a phone receiver anymore. It was a boomerang, a smooth polished curve of hardwood. She was about to throw it. It seemed the right thing to do. She threw the boomerang and it made a long, graceful half circle into the bright sunlight. She was standing in a field that had just been mowed. It smelled like cut dry grass. There was a single apple tree off to her left, growing fat with apples that she would soon pick. She knew her father had had this field mowed just for her, because she wanted to play in it. It was her favorite place.

There was only one cloud—a fat, lazy white one, hovering high above the apple tree. Behind her, partly visible over the lip of a sloping hill, stood their house, with open windows in the kitchen. There was a blueberry pie on the sill.

She laughed, and her father laughed, still dressed in his long pants from the office and his suspenders, his white shirt open at the collar, his tie thrown down at his feet, his white thinning hair framing his full face, his mouth laughing under his white mustache. He reached up for the ball he thought she was throwing to him, the one she had tossed behind her as she pulled the hidden boomerang from under her sweatshirt. He watched the boomerang spinning a curving circle up and over him, curling back in a neat helicoptering sweep to land at his daughter's feet. And he stood there with his hands still up for the feinted catch, laughing at her joke, jumping up to make the grab that would never be.

"Oh, Laura," he shouted to her, "you make me laugh so."

Her mother appeared on the hill behind her, shouting, "Supper, you two!"

"Coming, M!" she shouted, beginning to run. She called her parents M and P, short for Mom and Pop because of their age, a term of affection they cherished. "Coming, M!"

Her mother's smile turned to pained concern. "Oh, Laura, don't run! You know you're not supposed to run!"

Laura stopped, gasping at the shooting pain in her right foot, and slowly hobbled back to the boomerang. Tears of pain filled her eyes. She wanted to throw the boomerang again, wipe the anxious looks from M's and P's faces, stop them from running to her, make them laugh, make them forget that she had run, had disobeyed them, disappointed them, wanted to make the pain in her foot go away, the blue day with the mown grass and single beautiful high white cloud come back, the happiness come back . . .

She bent over and picked up the boomerang. There was a mouse's voice coming from it. She put it to her ear and the voice grew loud into Peter's voice. Her eyes stared at the knife standing straight up in the countertop. She heard Peter, but she didn't listen to him. There were lines etched in the wood around the paring knife. She moved closer to the counter. She heard Peter very loud in her ear. "For God's sake, Laura!" he screamed.

Laura's hand dropped the phone. The receiver hit the floor, springing up and then tapping the floor again before settling into a slow, bobbing swing. Peter's voice was far away, a mouse's voice again.

She stood over the countertop, staring at the deep gashes

that had been carved in shadowed relief by the paring knife. She put her hand on the knife, feeling as she yanked it out like the boy who drew the sword from the stone. The knife resisted, then pulled free.

She stood back, the knife limp in her hand. Thawed hope welled up into tears in her eyes. Reaching out a single, trembling finger, she lightly traced the words of the message etched deep into the countertop:

SOON
LOVE, M&P

7. EAST

Today, Jan didn't faint when the door opened onto the room of pain. The woman with hair on her chin helped to strap him to the table, tenderly, almost, and put the needle into him, searching for an unused vain, trying to spare him some of the hurt. There was no unused place on his arm, and she ended up utilizing a raw, swollen spot anyway. "There, there," she said, her dark eyes below her dark hair looking truly sad. She patted his arm below the vein bulge, which only added to the sharp, tearing agony spreading through his body and mind.

"Tell me about the day they took you," she whispered. She was a mother soothing a troubled, sleepless child. He began to hear his own screams then and went to the place the drugs took him, where he told them everything they asked of him . . .

The day they took him was like any other day. The sky over the Vistula was fat with billowy gray clouds, "thick puffs from God's pipe," as Tadeusz had once said of such clouds. He stood on the bank of the river with Tadeusz and with Karol, leaning on the thin rope bridge, the three of them sharing one cigarette. Jozef did not smoke, and did not approve of it, so they took the opportunity to smoke while they waited for him. It was late September, cool but muggy. Tadeusz had his cap pushed back on his head, which always forecast the weather, because Tadeusz would pull it down tight over his ears in cold or wet weather. He did not like the cold and complained bitterly when it rained, calling it a punishment from God for some great sinner in the city. "In Warsaw," he once told Jan, as they sat hunched over the smallest table by the smallest window in their tavern, so close together their pints of beer were pressed into their coats. The noise in the café was nearly unbearable. They looked out at the rain pelting the tiny window, at the thick wash it sent across the four panes intermittently, because it was either look at that or into each other's close faces, or into the coats of the standing patrons surrounding them—damp wool that would suffocate their conversation. "In Warsaw, when a great man, some member of the Party, commits a great sin, there is rejoicing in heaven. They laugh loud and long, because another Communist has proved himself weak and human, not equal in purity and character with God himself. You know," Tadeusz continued, poking Jan's nose lightly with his thick finger, an annoying habit, "that this is the great fault of Communism. In seeking to abolish God, it merely replaces him with man. That is why it's doomed to failure. And God knows this. So, when a party official commits a great sin, one of greed or lust, God and his angels laugh until they can no longer contain themselves, and God allows his angels to relieve themselves on the city of Warsaw. It is a just and mighty retribution—as well as a great relief for the angels. Unfortunately," he said shivering at the rain outside, "it's a pain in the ass for those of us who live in Warsaw."

"What about God?" Jan asked him, gently warding off Tadeusz's finger, heading toward his nose to make another point. "Doesn't God ever piss?"

"Of course he does," Tadeusz answered, offended. "But he is God, and his bladder is vast. It's as large as the Milky Way Galaxy. And if you're going to ask me if he'll ever use it, the answer is yes. He's saving it, though, for a very special occasion.'' Tadeusz leaned close, pushing Jan's head around so that only his ear would hear his next words. Jan smelled the sourness of Tadeusz's breath, the odor of sausage and beer and stale tobacco before he felt the rough stubble of Tadeusz's mustache at his ear. ''God is waiting until the biggest man of all, the Big Man himself, the one in Moscow, commits the biggest of all sins.'' He turned Jan's face around, moving his own back. He smiled. ''And then—BOOM! The big rain, right on you-know-where, and then you-know-where won't exist anymore.''

''And then?'' Jan asked, smiling in a friendly way.

Tadeusz held his hands out in his confined spot, palms upward, indicating what surrounded them. ''And then this is ours again.''

They looked out through the small window silently, before Tadeusz added, slyly, ''There's only one catch. I have it on very good authority that you-know-who in Moscow has already fucked a chicken, and,'' he sighed, ''nothing happened.''

They turned to their own thoughts, watching the sliding wet sheets of rain on their tiny window, in their tiny space surrounded by heat and the smell of damp shorn sheep, until Tadeusz added, ''And why do you ask about God, Jan? I thought you knew all about him. It's you who was going to be a priest.''

At the bridge, leaning lightly on the rope railing, smoking and waiting for Jozef, who now approached them sullenly, the words of disapproval of their smoking probably already forming on his never-smiling mouth, Jan thought of the priesthood and wanted to laugh.

''And what do you find so funny?'' Karol said, nudging him to look at Jozef. ''Now *there's* something worthy of laughter. Our friend Jozef was born with a frown on his face.'' Karol, who almost never frowned, laughed heartily.

''He doesn't even smile when he gets off a good fart,'' Tadeusz said, throwing the remains of the cigarette that had been passed to him into the river and turning to meet Jozef, who had now reached them.

''Save your breath,'' Tadeusz said, slapping Jozef on the shoulder. ''We've heard all your lectures on smoking. And we're late for work as it is.''

The look on Jozef's face made him stop his joking.

"What's wrong?" Karol asked, a cloud of seriousness descending.

"They're looking for Jan," Jozef said.

"What do you mean?" Tadeusz nearly shouted, and then he barked a laugh. He lay the back of his hand on Jozef's brow. "Are you ill? have you been drinking? Who is looking for Jan?"

"The police."

"A mistake," Karol spat.

"No," Jozef replied. His dour face was pinched tight. He turned to Jan. "I saw them come out of your mother's house as I passed. They must have just missed you. I waited until they were gone, and then I went in. Your mother was at the kitchen table, weeping. I asked her if they had hurt her. She said no—but there was a pot of oatmeal broken on the floor, by the stove."

"Bastards," Jan said.

"She might have dropped it herself, when they came in," Jozef continued. "She was very upset, Jan. She said they wanted to speak with you, but she could tell by the way they came in, knocking once and then nearly throwing open the door, that they were there not to talk but to take you away."

"*Why?*" Karol shouted, indignantly. "What could they possibly want Jan for?"

Jozef shrugged. They saw now how frightened he was, his big-knuckled hands working one over the other, his thick coat pulled tight around him, the collar up as if protecting him from a chill wind.

Jan said quietly, as much to himself as to the others, who now faced him as if waiting for an explanation, "I've done nothing."

"Of course you've done nothing," Tadeusz said, scratching the black stubble on his chin. "But we have to hide you. We can't let them take you. When the storm passes over, it will be like nothing ever happened."

"There is no place to hide," Jozef said, his eyes on the ground.

Karol, in anger, grabbed Jozef by the front of his lapels. "Of course there is."

"I've done nothing," Jan repeated, as if in shock.

Tadeusz said, "We must get him to my house, off the street, then move him to a place that can't be connected to him." He took Jan by the arm. "Quickly."

Jan looked at him. Comprehension of what was happening to him on this fine day, with its cool, late-summer breeze and fine gray clouds—on this day when he had smoked a cigarette with his best friends, and leaned on a rope railing overlooking the roiling water of the Vistula—dawned on him. Something out of his control was closing in on him, a machine in the form of a hunting hound had been set in motion, with his name imprinted on it, and unwavering instructions to bring him to tree. The police would not go away. They had been told to talk him, and they would.

"I'll give myself up to them," Jan said.

Karol's face came before his own, flushed and angry. "Come with us," he said. *"They're not going to take you."*

Tadeusz's grip on Jan's arm tightened. Karol took his other arm. For a brief moment Jan felt as though he were going to faint. But then the world, the gray sky, the billowing gray clouds, the smell of the moving river, came back to him.

They moved briskly away from the bridge, Jozef darting glances behind them, and ascended stone steps to the street above. "Walk casually," Tadeusz ordered. They began to converse, trying to keep the tension out of their voices.

The street was filled with late factory workers hurrying to their jobs. Some wore winter coats, since the last few days had been colder than today, but they were opened at the collar, enjoying the last hint of warmth before the damp winter settled in. Most carried black lunch boxes.

They walked along with the workers. The pace quickened as the clock in the church steeple near the end of the street began to toll the hour, promising reprimands for those not at work by the time it had ceased. Jan and his friends hurried along until Tadeusz said, "This way is quicker," and brought them through a narrow alleyway lined with discarded boxes to the next street. "Stay back," he ordered when they reached the far end. He went ahead, slipping out onto the street before motioning for them to follow. They crossed the road and mounted a flight of wooden steps to the second floor.

Tadeusz fumbled a huge iron key out of his pocket and turned it in the lock. Below them, on the street, someone rounded a corner, a man in a trench coat and brown hat. "Shit, he's right out of the movies," Karol said as they pushed Jan into the flat. The man in the trench coat was followed by two uniformed policemen, who kept a discreet distance.

They watched through the window as the man in the trench coat stopped and waited for the two uniformed men to catch up with him; there followed a discussion over a piece of paper that the man in the trench coat produced, which escalated in volume, with the uniformed cops arguing and the man in the trench coat waiting for them to stop.

"Are they the ones you saw come out of Jan's house?" Tadeusz asked Jozef.

"I think so." He squinted hard through the window, then pulled his head back. "Yes."

"Jesus," Tadeusz said, "they must have gone right to the factory and found we weren't there. They're looking for this place."

The man in the trench coat suddenly threw his hand up and his companions ceased arguing immediately; the three of them then proceeded down the street away from them.

"They'll be wanting a telephone, and then they'll find the correct address," Tadeusz said. "We can't wait here. There's no time to waste." He reached into his pocket, pulling out a clip of bills and handing it to Jan. The others did likewise, Karol cursing when he could produce nothing more than one small bill and a handful of coins.

"You must get to a bus," Tadeusz said to Jan. He held him by the shoulders, looking hard into his eyes to make sure that Jan understood what he said. "You must get out of the city. Go to a hotel in a town called Kolno. It's about a hundred kilometers northeast of here. I had relatives there, once. There are only two hotels in the village. Pick the less conspicuous one. I can't remember the name. It had a pot of flowers by the sign out front. On Sunday, two days from now, I'll meet you there. We'll get money together. I'll go to the priest and he'll help. They all will." He squeezed Jan's shoulders tight, bringing him close. Then the three of them, Jozef muttering good-bye, Karol punching Jan on his arm with his fist, looking angry and impotent, were gone, leaving Jan alone in the room.

They'll all help, Tadeusz had said to him. But even as his friend was saying it, even as their eyes met while he was uttering the words, they both knew that, in the end, the police would find and take him.

Jan stood in the middle of the empty, cold flat. He looked down at the money in his hand. Suddenly, for no real reason except that he refused to give up, a sort of life came into him. *Maybe they won't take me.* Maybe there was escape. Even if there wasn't, he would not let his friends down by not trying. He owed them something. He thought of his mother, in her tiny kitchen, cleaning the remains of his breakfast, which he had cavalierly refused because he was anxious to get out of the stuffy little house, to smoke cigarettes with his friends. (*No, mother, I can't eat it, I'm not hungry*), the almost arrogant way he had refused her cooking. He thought of all the little things she did for him, her mending his boots, the way she had replaced the lining of his coat after he had had it ripped during a brawl in the pub the previous March. She hadn't even scolded him about his fighting—though, later, he had seen her in her bedroom, the faded, colored quilt still tucked under her pillow, the mattress of the bed high and uneven from the old filling it possessed, kneeling with her elbows on the quilt, hands clasped around her rosary, head bowed. When he went to his own room, he would find a holy picture tucked under his pillow, just as he had every night since he was a boy, since his father was killed during a worker's strike. Jan thought of his mother, and his eyes filled with tears. She would never see him again. She had been in her kitchen, probably scraping the remains of his uneaten breakfast back into the pot, to save for later, perhaps to serve with the potatoes at dinner, and the policeman had come into her house, and had asked her rough questions, and then had left her, not laying a hand on her, perhaps, but just as well striking into her body, into her heart. He cried not because he would never see her again, but because she would never see him. He was the one thing in her life she truly cared for—Jan, her only son, the image of her husband preserved in youth, the boy who would, perhaps, be a priest.

He had told her that once, when he was young, with his tongue connected to a boy's confused heart, mostly because she had wanted to hear it so badly. Yes, he had said, he would become a priest. Later, when he had realized that he was now a man and not a boy, he had almost stopped speaking to her because he realized that he could never be what she wanted of him. He resented her for wanting him to be something he could not be. She had never said anything to him about it, had never mentioned the priesthood again, but still, every night, under his pillow the holy pictures, the image of Christ, the Sacred Heart burning in His open breast . . .

I'm sorry I couldn't fulfill your dreams, Mother, he thought. *I'm sorry I didn't tell you mine.*

More than anything, he must get away for his mother. If she knew he was safe, she would be all right.

Jan's eyes were dry by the time he opened the door. The street below was empty. But it would not stay so. At any moment, the man in the trench coat and his two thugs might reappear, heading with certainty toward the very spot where he stood. That would be the end of it. He would have betrayed his mother. He would have betrayed his friends—and their money, which they had thrust into his hands and which the police would quickly confiscate, would be gone.

He turned his collar up and descended the stairs. As calmly as possible, he crossed the street, heading for the alleyway Tadeusz had taken them through. From the next street he could reach the bus depot by mingling with the shoppers in the marketplace.

"You there, just a minute."

He was turning into the alley when someone called to him. He thought of turning with his fists out. He could use the boxing move Karol had taught him, which they had used to such good purpose during the bar brawl last winter. But there were three of them. There was no way he could overpower them. The one in the trench coat would be a few steps behind him, his two companions to either side, guns drawn, already aiming at a point between his shoulder blades. There was nothing the cops loved better than a prisoner resisting arrest. It was sometimes a quick road to promotion to add the shooting of a wanted man attempting to escape to one's record.

"I—" he began, turning around. Confusion was replaced by elation. It was one of Tadeusz's friends, a man named Jerzy who had sometimes observed their chess matches. He was a pensioner who lived alone, and though he never spoke while he watched, Tadeusz claimed that he recorded every move in his head, learning the game voraciously. "One day," Tadeusz said after one of their matches, when the old man had limped down the stairs to his own apartment, giving Tadeusz the chance to bring out his good tea, which he hoarded, "he will beat us all. His eyes are a hawk's eyes."

"I say, Jan," the old pensioner said. The glow of concentrated purpose that Tadeusz had spoken of was in the man's eyes. "Do you think I might have a game of chess with you sometime soon?" He trembled; he must have practiced the speech before approaching Jan. His great shyness, and the great need bursting now from within him, made Jan reach out and put his hand on the man's arm.

"I—"

Behind the old man, Jan saw the man in the trench coat with his two henchmen approaching Tadeusz's flat.

He gripped the old man's arm tenderly.

"I'm sorry, Jerzy, not anytime soon."

He turned away, nearly as much in avoidance of the disappointment on the old man's face as in haste.

As he had hoped, the marketplace stalls were busy. He was able to blend with the crowd of haggling women, schoolboys playing hooky and the young marrieds out together to buy vegetables and, perhaps, a little meat for dinner. He mixed with the hagglers, arguing himself over the price of a bag of chestnuts, which he leisurely ate as he strolled.

When he reached the last stall, Jan thought it must be at least noon. But, to his great surprise, the clock over the bus depot showed it to be only twenty minutes past nine. His initial feeling that the bus station would surely be watched by the police was replaced by a conviction that it was not. They had been looking for him for only a little more than an hour. At this point, there would only be the three men he had seen after him. When he was not located, there might be more, and a general alert would be posted, but now it was three against one.

His theory was proven correct when a covert inspection of

the station revealed no sign of police activity. Jan's spirits were further lifted when he discovered that a bus heading out of the city in the direction he wanted was preparing to leave. He had no difficulty hiding his features from the ticket seller, who was more intent on his magazine than on studying the faces of bus passengers. He took the same precaution handing his ticket to the driver, using the opportunity to glance out over the driver's shoulder to see if his three pursuers might have shown up. They had not, and a few moments later, as Jan reached an empty seat halfway toward the back of the bus and away from the driver's direct gaze in the rearview mirror, the bus lurched forward.

Twenty minutes later, they were out of the city and passing into the rural region north and east of Warsaw.

Though Jan never actually closed his eyes, a great feeling of lassitude overcame him. He felt as if he had been detached from himself, floating above the unfolding drama of his life, watching his own plight on a television camera. With some interest, he wondered what would happen next. In the drama, the man had eluded his pursuers, but now what would the script call for? In every television crime show he had ever seen, it was easy to plot the destiny of the felon. If he was a good character, he would elude his hunters and ultimately triumph. If he was a villain, he would be caught and brought to justice. But what was Jan? Was he hero or villain? If the police wanted him, did that not make him an automatic villain? On the television productions, whenever the state wanted a man, he was obviously a criminal, to be judged and sentenced. But what had been Jan's crime? Why did the state want him? It didn't matter.

About halfway to Kolno, the bus stopped to let passengers off. Jan waited for them to continue, but instead the driver left the bus. Jan nervously waited for his return. After fifteen minutes he was sure that word had somehow spread and that policemen would appear momentarily and drag him from the bus. But as he was rising to leave, the bus driver suddenly reappeared, reclaiming his seat and pulling the door shut behind him.

Jan was filled with anxiety, undecided as to whether he should stay or rush to the front of the bus, throw the door open, and flee, until he overheard one of the passengers in the seat in front of him laugh and say to her companion, nodding toward the driver, "There he is with his loose bowels again, it never fails." And the other one replied, knowingly, "Sausage for breakfast as a habit will do that. I tried to tell him that our last trip, but he wouldn't listen."

"Men never do," the other woman answered, and they both laughed and nodded their heads.

Jan settled back into his seat.

The trees thinned, showing dry farmland, but then trees reappeared again. And then, suddenly, they had reached Kolno. The two women in front of Jan got out ahead of him, stopping a moment to scold the bus driver on his breakfast habits. The bus driver waved them on impatiently, and Jan hurried out behind them, keeping his face averted from the driver and from the two women, who were nosy enough to remember a face. The bus doors closed with an airy hiss and the bus groaned off. Jan noticed that it leaned slightly to one side in the back, another state vehicle in need of repair it wouldn't receive.

The bus had left him at the edge of the small town square. So as not to draw attention to himself he went to the statue at the other end and sat down on one of two benches there. An old woman occupied the other bench. She was blind, one of her hands rubbing softly at the blue-veined wrist on her other arm. Her black cane rested against one hip. Her eyes calmly stared into blackness.

"Excuse me," Jan said.

"I'll tell you anything you want," the woman said, "if you buy a pear from me." She lifted the corner of her cloak, revealing a small wicker basket of pears nestled beside her. "It will cost you five hundred groszy."

"Certainly," Jan answered, drawing out one of the coins Karol had given him and pressing it into her hand. "Can you give me change for this?"

"I don't have change to give," she answered.

Jan was about to say that she could keep the whole coin, but realized her game. "I'm sorry," he said, reaching to remove the coin from her palm, "I can't buy your fruit, then."

"I'll give you change," she said, smiling mischievously.

She pulled a purse from beneath her cloak. She drew out coins, shorting him one to see if he would notice. When he protested, she handed him all she owed him.

"I'm looking for the hotel with a pot of flowers out front," he said to her.

"Oh, I can't help you," she said. Her mischievous smile returned.

"You promised to help me. I can tell you you won't get another groszy from me, old woman."

"I was playing with you." The old woman laughed. It was a hoarse, unpleasant sound. "It's just outside of town. It's haunted, you know. Demons. Are you sure you want to stay there? There's another, much finer hotel on the other side of town, and for another hundred groszy—"

"That's where I want to stay," Jan said impatiently.

The old woman shrugged. "There's a horse path behind us, and you take that for about a half kilo. It's on the left side. A man named Edward runs it." She laughed again. "A skinflint like me. Don't let him cheat you. There isn't a room in the place worth more than ten. The best rooms are in the rear, where there's plenty of sun in the morning."

Jan stood up. The woman's sightless eyes followed him. "Are you going to stay long? Perhaps there are other things I could tell you, people you should watch for."

"Thank you for your help," Jan said, not trying to hide the annoyance in his voice. He moved on.

It was a longer walk than the woman had said. After what must have been a kilometer the road narrowed, leaving space for barely a cart, certainly not two horses abreast. The day had grown almost oppressively hot, an anomaly for this late in September. There were thick hedges beside the road, the branching trees getting their brown coats of turning leaves overhead. It was like walking through a close burrow. Jan began to feel claustrophobic. He carried his coat over his arm. He rolled his shirt sleeves up and loosened his tie. It felt like July; the humidity in the air was palpable. He wanted to sit and rest, but the hedge was cut so close to the road there was nowhere to do it. His entire former life seemed like a dream, something he had left behind only a few hours before but which was a lifetime away from him. He tried to conjure up his mother's face, or Tadeusz's, but could not precisely remember what they looked like. If someone had told him a day ago that in twenty-four hours he would be stumbling through a darkling, hot tunnel, hiding from the police, running from a crime that was unknown to him, he would have laughed or executed the fighting move with his fists that Karol had taught him—the quick one-two.

Or maybe he was dreaming. Perhaps he would awaken at any moment, pushed gently on the shoulder by his dear mother, and would look up into her face, and tell her that he had had a dream of guilt, that he loved her more than anything, that he was sorry he had not told her of his feelings for her in such a long time. He would tell her that he was sorry that he had grown arrogant and distant; perhaps he would embrace her. Hopefully, the breakfast he had left on the table this morning was yet to be faced, waiting for him out of this dreamland on the kitchen table at this moment; and his mother stood over him right now, ready to end this guilt dream, about to give him that gentle nudge, this mother who had awakened him so many times, gotten him off to school, changed the sheets on his bed, seeing the stains he had sometimes left there with his wet dreams—his mother who was closer to him than anyone . . .

Oh, Mother—

He did not wake, because it was not a dream. But suddenly he came up short, nearly walking into a black wrought-iron post curving out above the road to hold a brass basket of white and red roses. Riveted to the pole was a tarnished sign that said, KOLNO INN.

Flanking the sign was a lane, and he turned into it.

The path was lined with rosebushes, trellised up nearly to Jan's height. He could see where some had been clipped for the basket out front, strong green stems covered with thick red thorns, which ended suddenly in sharp, slanting lines. But there were more than enough, in various states of bloom. The largest, in full flower, was wider than his closed fist. But these vague observations, which battled with all of the other fears and anxieties that had been in his mind since this morning, were pushed aside at the sight of the hotel.

It seemed to appear before him out of thin air. One step he

was on the rose-enshrouded path, and the next step he was in the courtyard. His first thoughts were of a peasant cottage on a monstrous scale. There were three stories. The front was flat, lines of ornamentally shuttered windows set on a dark chocolate-brown façade of diagonally laid planks of wood. The roof was edged in scrollwork, and at the four corners, there were turrets, each with a small, square window.

The front door of the inn was low and wide. Dark flat stones led up to it.

Fearing only what lay behind him more than what lay ahead, Jan walked to the door and used the heavy brass knocker.

The sound echoed once and then was swallowed from within. No one came to let him in. He pulled at the wrought-iron handle, curved against the door in the shape of a long, open-mouthed gargoyle. His fingers drew back; he thought fleetingly of the old woman's words about "demons." But she had only been seeking money. He put his hand on the monstrous door handle and tried the door.

It opened, and he entered.

At the end of a short hallway, through an entranceway was a small lobby. It looked as though it might once have been a taproom. The ceiling was oppressively low. The front desk might once have served as the bar. Above it, abutting the ceiling, was a thick square beam that ran the length of the desk. On it were intricate carvings of animal grotesques. Jan shivered. There were bloated pigs with the faces of wild men, mouths grinning, sitting on their haunches, bellies sliced open to reveal hanging strings of sausages and bacon slabs immersed in twisting clouds of smoke. There were goats with the heads of women, sprouting great tufts of hair, open mouths full of sharp teeth. Some were biting themselves; one had its head thrust into the gaping stomach of an adjacent sow. Above these fantastic animals, at the line of the ceiling, had been carved scenes of violent weather: fat thunderclouds with thick jets of rain pelting down, hailstones square as bales of hay, blizzards of snow stacked up in leaning drifts against the unheedful animals below. Jan studied the bizarre scenes, moving along the desk slowly from depiction to depiction. The thick black beam drew him, mesmerized.

"What do you want?"

The rough sound of a human voice startled him. A short man was now facing him from behind the front desk. A door behind him, which had been closed, was now open wide. The man had a shock of white hair like those of the fantastic goat-women above him. But there was no goat body below his neck, only a hard torso sporting a green felt vest. In one sharp-fingered hand he held a piece of bread that had been torn from a loaf and a slice of sausage, which he now pressed together before bringing them to his mouth. Half of this meal disappeared into his mouth, and he chewed, waiting for Jan to speak, regarding him with his unfriendly eyes.

"Are you Edward?"

The other continued to chew, his hand holding the remaining sausage and bread, pressing them together. He started to bring his hand up to his mouth but stopped and said, "You have a reservation?"

"No. Your hotel was recommended to me by a friend."

"Recommended, eh?" For a moment the man's stare lessened, but then he put the rest of his meal into his mouth and wiped his hands across the front of his vest. "It will cost you extra if you don't have a reservation."

"How much?"

"Twenty for the room. And ten more for not phoning ahead."

"That's too much," Jan bluffed, remembering the old blind woman's warning about the proprietor being a skinflint. "When my friend stayed he said it was ten for the room."

"Twenty." Edward shook his head. "Costs go up."

"I could stay at the other hotel."

"Go on, then," Edward said, but he added, "all right. Ten it is for the room. In advance. And ten more for not reserving."

Remembering the blind woman's other words, Jan said, "I want a room in the rear of the hotel."

Edward looked momentarily surprised; his surprise quickly turned to impatience. "Fine," he said. "Just pay in advance."

Jan paid him and was taken to a small room in one of the back corners of the third floor. It was hot. It looked out onto an oppressively close stand of oak trees. What little light reached the room filtered through the sway of branches. Looking out through the small window, he saw the entire back of the hotel was suffocated by encroaching trees. *Damn old woman*. So much for her advice about morning sun.

When Edward had left him, Jan lay on the bed. He found it lumpy, tilted annoyingly to one side. It smelled of old feathers and mildew. He laced his hands behind his head, finding with his fingers a rip in the pillow. He stared at the ceiling, trying to think of nothing, to make this day, what had happened to his life, vanish. But it would not. He saw it all again, as if played on a television screen: the haunted look on Jozef's face as he approached them on the bridge with his news; the smug visage of the man in the trench coat, sure of his job and his prey; and his mother's face, looming over him, telling him to get up for work, then weeping alone in her room after the police had gone, her rosary clutched in her praying hands, kneeling over the quilt, crying and praying to God crucified over her bed on his crucifix—

He pushed himself up on his elbows at a sound of movement, and there at the end of his bed was a girl he had never seen before, holding her hand out to him. She was short, her pale face suffused with freckles, her hair straight and red. She did not look Polish. But when she spoke, she spoke Polish to him.

"Don't worry, Jan. My name is Bridget."

He reached his hand out to her, and she took it in her own. Her touch was gentle, but in the fingers he felt a fierce hardness. He sensed that, if she wanted, she could grip him so tight it would feel as though his hand were in a vise. And yet she held it now as gently as a lover.

"Come with me," she said, in her beautiful, soft, enigmatic voice, letting his hand go.

He rose from the bed. She walked into the far corner of the room. He thought she had disappeared. But then he saw that the shadows in the corner lengthened and the walls did not meet. There was a door there.

Jan entered the shadows, leaving all but faint tendrils of light behind. He felt the walls with his hands. Abruptly, there were stairs. He climbed. Above him, the stairway ended, and he faintly saw the girl.

"Come, Jan," she called tenderly to him.

He reached the doorway. Inside was an attic, dimly lit by red light falling through a small, round, stained-glass window. At first he did not see the girl, but then he located her at the far end of the room. The girl was standing over a bed, a mattress laid on the floor, covered in silken sheets. She smiled at him. Wordlessly, not taking her eyes from him, she removed the shoulder straps of her gown. The gown fell to her feet, revealing her naked to him. She was a mixture of girl and woman. Her face, the perfect white lines of her body, were childlike, yet the rise of her breasts, the V of deep red hair below her belly, the loving smile and the magnetic sexuality of her look and stance aroused him deeply. She held her hand out. He went to her, and as he took her hand she lay back on the bed, pulling him down above her. She lay very still, looking into his eyes. Her hair was almost the color of cherries. She let his hand go so that he could touch her. There was a perfect mole on her right shoulder. He wanted to kiss her. She looked into his eyes. "Soon, Jan," she whispered, a moan. "Soon you will have me."

She vanished beneath him.

Someone struck Jan roughly, on the back. He was on the lumpy bed in a stuffy back room of the Kolno Inn. He was pulled away from the bed and turned around, then pushed back, feeling the lumps of the old mattress under him.

The man who had pushed him now held him with his hand on Jan's chest and sat down next to him on the bed. It was the man in the trench coat. Behind him, to either side of the window, stood the two uniformed policemen. They looked tired; one of them yawned into his hand.

The man in the trench coat took his hand off Jan's chest and flipped open a small notebook.

"You are Jan Pesak?" he asked, matter-of-factly.

Jan said nothing.

The man in the trench coat looked down at him; when he spoke he sounded almost bored. "I can make one phone call from downstairs," he said quietly, "and it would be very hard for your mother indeed."

He looked at Jan dispassionately.

"I am Jan Pasek," Jan said.

The man in the trench coat wrote something in the notebook and then closed it, putting it into his pocket. He studied Jan's face for a moment. He, too, looked as though he wanted to yawn.

"You caused me great inconvenience," he said, and then he swung his fist in a high arc over the bed and hit Jan squarely on the nose.

Jan felt an explosion of pain followed by numbness. Another blow struck his face. Dully, he looked up to see that the two uniformed cops had moved to the bed. The man in the trench coat stepped back. The uniformed men began to beat him methodically, raining blows on his ribs and stomach. He tried to roll into a fetal position. They struck his head and legs. One of them pulled him to the floor between them, and they began to kick him.

Through the curtain of torment that was lowering him to unconsciousness, Jan heard the man in the trench coat tell them to stop. He heard the word "dinner." Turning his head, he saw through one nearly closed eye the man in the trench coat leave with one of the uniformed men. The other sat on the bed, trying to light a cigarette with an uncooperative lighter.

Jan attempted to sit up. The uniformed cop put his lighter aside on the bed. "Feel like fighting?" He laughed, dipping his boot toe into a sore spot in Jan's side, rolling him over onto his back.

Jan felt another deep push of pain in his side and then blacked out.

When he awoke they were carrying him through the lobby of the hotel. Edward, the proprietor, had another sandwich of sausage and bread in his hand. He turned his face away from Jan as he was dragged through the front doorway, his shoes scraping over the flagstones outside. Jan caught a glimpse of the roses through nearly closed lids. He could smell the flowers; their sweetness was mingled with the odor of his own blood.

He was carried a long way. They had not been able to get their big car down the road to the hotel and so had had to walk. They dumped him once on the way, to rest. Jan heard one of the cops grunting, the other making fun of him for being out of shape.

"You would be, too, if you relied on using your head instead of your fists," his partner replied. The other mocked him in return until the man in the trench coat told them to stop bickering.

They dragged him to the town square, near the statue, where a dark sedan was parked at an angle. The blind woman was still in her accustomed spot. She cocked her head up and smiled at Jan as he was taken past her.

"You found your way to the hotel?" she said, giggling throatily, but Jan didn't know whether she spoke to him or the policemen.

He was thrown into the backseat of the car. One of the uniformed cops got in heavily beside him. The other got behind the wheel, the man in the trench coat beside him in the front seat.

The car wouldn't start. The driver cursed, the uniformed man next to Jan, mocking his friend's ability as a chauffeur. Sharply, the man in the trench coat told them to shut up. The engine turned over, the driver shouting in triumph as they pulled away.

Jan lay on the backseat, watching the slate gray of the sky go past through the rear window. The face of the uniformed cop hovered over him. "Enjoy it now." The cop smiled. He nodded at the sky with his head. "You won't be seeing that where you're going."

After a while Jan slept, the needs of his beaten body aided by the soothing motion of the automobile. At first, his sleep was dreamless. But later, as they approached their destination, the underground place in whose elevator only the bureaucrats and the dead ever rose, he dreamed not of his mother but of Bridget, the red-haired girl, holding her naked body out to him and telling him, gently in his ear, "Soon."

8. WEST

It was hardest to stay away from the cocaine when his legs hurt.

Some days it was his neck that hurt, or his lower back. Some days, when the clouds were low and gray and wet over the Pacific, he hurt all over, a dull aching as if he were a giant throbbing tooth.

He had switched to coke when the doctors took the morphine away from him in the hospital; some of them had even remarked what a wonderfully easy withdrawal he had had from the morphine, which, they insisted, he had become dependent on.

Withdrawal, my ass, he had thought at the time. *All I did was change accounts*. One of the doctors, the shrewd young one who had come out of the Peace Corps and was stupid enough to be in medicine for reasons other than ego or money, guessed what had happened, but Ray had become very clever himself and began to hide the cocaine, taking it only when the doctor, Madelaine, wasn't around. She had taken to showing up unexpectedly, and once had walked into the living room while a long line of coke lay waiting on the coffee table for the straw Ray was looking for. But he had been able to distract her away from it, eventually having to dust it off the table onto the rug while she turned to look at a Mondrian print he pointed out to her on the far wall. Later in the day he had spent two hours cursing and crying, pulling his useless legs out of the wheelchair till he collapsed on the floor, sucking at the dirty fibers with the straw he had finally located, getting as much grit and nylon up his nose as diluted coke. The two hours had hardly been worth it, and finally he had fallen asleep, exhausted and worn with frustrated rage. Madelaine had found him the next morning when she came in with the housekeeper, and the only satisfaction he had gotten out of the entire affair was her inability to find any more coke in her search of the house.

But that had been early in the rehabilitation, when the doctors still hovered around him, when he knew he needed something to drown out the awful memories in his head, the awful sound of Bridget's laughter . . .

After a while he had come to an accommodation with the drug. They lived in peaceful coexistence, and he was proud of the fact that he had fought it to the point where he had convinced himself that it was a medicine only, to be taken only when the pain got bad . . .

The pain was bad today. He rolled himself from the window, leaving the clouds making moving shadows over the rolling lawn (*his dream to run down that lawn to the beach beyond, to the ocean, his legs moving him, throwing him into the blue Pacific . . .*), and went to his desk and pulled out the file drawer. He pushed the green hanging folders back and lifted the thin plywood panel on the false bottom beneath. The white powder was already measured (*doctors measure, medicine is measured*), and he dusted it out expertly in a line on the top of the desk, lowered the straw he had removed from the hollow in the drawer, sucked the (*medicine*) up into his head . . .

The telephone—all the telephones in the house—rang.

He screamed suddenly, throwing his head back, the powder driven up deep into his sinuses like a pounding headache. The ring sounded again. He sat frozen in his wheelchair, staring at the black instrument that lay not two feet away from him on the corner of the desk over the file drawer.

That was not the ring of the man selling *Time* magazine, or the call of an aluminum-siding salesman.

He knew if he took the phone apart, unscrewed the bottom panel and found the ringing mechanism, that it would not be ringing at this moment.

The telephone rang again.

Bridget.

His hand reached out for it; somewhere in the back of his mind and body his arm ached feebly. The cocaine was making the ache lessen, but the arthritic throb suddenly strengthened. He cried out. It felt as if his arm had burst into flame, the fingers burning stick twigs that would incandesce into white fire and ash, filter off his hand—

"Oh, Jesus!" he called out, as the fire shot up his arm, through his chest to his legs. It felt as if someone were hammering on his legs with pure strikes of heat. Flames wrapped up through his neck into his head; he felt his hair on fire.

Suddenly, the heat went away.

The phone, all the phones, stopped ringing.

He sat gasping in the wheelchair, overcome with chills. He hunched painfully over, holding himself. The heat was being drawn out of his body as if it were being sucked through a straw, leaving a vacuum of cold.

"Jesus." He shivered.

He looked at the phone.

His hand trembling like an old man's, cold hunching him over arthritically, he reached out to pick up the receiver.

As his finger touched it, a shot of pure heat went through his hand to his shoulder.

"Shit!"

He drew back in pain; then, slowly, he reached out to the phone again.

He lay his hand on it gently, hovering until sure there was no more heat.

His fingers like claws, he picked the phone up and brought it to his ear.

Hissing. He heard the hissing of long distance, distant voices swimming. They didn't sound like they were having human conversations. A thin, faraway crackle of laughter was pierced by an equally distant, high, humming scream.

The hissing intensified. He could *feel* her waiting out there for him.

"I know you're there," he said.

The hissing modulated to what sounded like laughter.

"I—" he began.

"Hello, Raymond," she said.

Her voice was so crystal clear, so much like he had remembered it, calm, the way he had heard it in his waking and sleeping dreams for so long. He had known that this would be the way she would sound. He had played this moment out in his mind a thousand times. He had rehearsed each word he would say, the tone of his voice, the inflection of his calm outrage. But now that the moment was at hand, his powers of reason and reflection deserted him. Her voice was like a lancet piercing him; he was immobile with the very fear he had successfully battled, turned to bitterness and plans for battle, for so long. With her two calm words, "Hello, Raymond," in her perfect, clear voice—clear as if she were standing beside him, whispering into his other ear—she had undone him.

He began to cry. He clutched the receiver so tightly to his ear that the thick plastic of its casing cracked in protest. He was frozen in fear and in loss: he thought he had battled her all this time, come to know her so intimately that her worst horrors could no longer trouble him, and with two simple introductory words she had easily mastered him.

"Would you like to destroy me, Ray?" she asked.

He wanted to use his voice, wanted to get out his words through the crying and the rigor of his limbs and thoughts.

"Yes."

"Would you like to destroy me now?"

"Yes."

"Do you remember why you want to destroy me? Do you remember all the bad things I've done?"

Ray's lips trembled around the word. "Yes, Oh, God, yes."

She laughed, gently. She was almost as gentle as his mother now. "Do you really hate me that much, Ray?"

"Yes! Jesus, yes! I want you to DIE!"

"You might get your wish yet, Ray. But you have to remember why you want me to die. Remember, Ray."

He wept. "Noooo . . ."

Memory . . .

His father's charter was late. Which wasn't surprising, since snow had been falling since morning and there was a good deal more predicted before nightfall. But the American Airlines clerk he'd spoken to before leaving for Stapleton International had assured him that the flight had left on time and that the airport would stay open for at least the next six hours.

"They have everything under control, sir," the clerk had told him.

Sure, he'd thought, hanging up the phone, *just like I do.*

It was no secret that he didn't want to see his father. He never did. They had never gotten along well since the death of his mother, and since . . . well, since that other thing had happened, they had gotten along even less. Ray had thought for a while, with the glib analysis that young men often give to complex problems, that it was because they were just too much alike. But he knew now that glib analysis was just that, good for television but little else, and that the enmity that existed between himself and his father was a many-layered thing. Though they had the same blood, it ran in different directions. It always had. It was something Ray was ready to accept, and act on, with the kind of benign neglect he'd enacted the past couple of years.

But that didn't seem to be good enough for his father. For a time Ray thought that his father had learned his shallowness in Washington, but on deeper reflection he knew that the shallowness, the insistence on the surface details, the smiles, the friendly banter, the flatulent exchange of pleasantries, and, above all, the accordance of due, had always been there. As a boy, Ray remembered his father insisting on a regimen, an attention to details, that seemed on cursory examination a hewing to tradition, but on closer inspection revealed itself as an almost pathological need to control. At Sunday dinner there were "traditions": his father would carve the roast just so, would serve just so, would enact by rote the same dialogue of approval to Ray's mother—"Great roast, Abby." "Wonderful potatoes." "Fine greens."—and this, even if the roast was burned, the potatoes lumpy, the greens drowned in butter or undrained cooking water. There was such a need of control in his father—for after these epithets of approval would follow the required and inevitable assent from Ray himself, the withholding of which would result in the hardest of stares followed by a black mood that might last through the afternoon or entirely through the week.

And his father had never changed. The Senate had only emphasized and enriched these qualities. And, with Ray's inevitable rebellion from their stricture, a rupture in their relationship had followed and widened.

Only, it had always been there, as Ray had finally come to realize.

As Bridget had told him—

He pushed Bridget from his mind. It was a measure of his father's domination over him, over his thoughts, his anger, that Ray had managed to forget Bridget for most of the car ride.

The old man had eight years on you, Bridget.

The snow was falling in huge flakes, but it seemed to have let up a little. The Volvo was doing the job so far, the Michelin radials churning him toward the airport a few exits away. As if to reinforce his thoughts, he heard the hissing whine of a jet engine as the huge belly of a landing 747 passed low overhead, its lights making the snowstorm into a Christmas scene.

At least if this were Christmas, not the end of February, he could understand his father coming to see him.

"Ray, old boy," his father would say, "good to see you. Great tree you've got there."

The expectant stare.

"Yeah, Dad, great tree—"

He threw his father from his mind and Bridget immediately filled the void. For a chilling moment he felt her sitting beside him in the front seat. The heat of the Volvo rose measurably. He saw her as he did in his dreams, reaching out to put her soft hand on his shoulder like a mother, whispering in his ear, telling him that she'd done everything for him—

He gasped and looked to his right. He had swerved too far over, and a station wagon was honking at him, the driver beating the horn angrily, yelling at him wordlessly through the closed window and the snow and the night.

For the briefest moment, as he swerved back into the center lane, he thought he saw Bridget's fading outline in the passenger seat.

He concentrated on the road, getting his breath back. He looked briefly sideways; there was no one in the seat. It held his scarf only. The station wagon, not trusting his driving, had roared ahead, throwing up a plume of snow behind it.

He looked up and saw the lit exit sign for the airport.

He pulled into the wake of the station wagon and edged off the highway. Ahead, the airport loomed, quiet. The blinking green and red and white lights of the landed jumbo jet, taxiing quietly away from him, was the only activity.

"Shit, here comes the wait," he muttered.

He parked the Volvo in the visitor's parking lot, grabbing his scarf as a last thought before closing and locking the door. Again something seemed to move on the passenger seat, but his stare produced only patterns of snow shadow from the sodium-vapor lamps overhead.

He wrapped the scarf around his neck and ran for the American Airlines terminal.

The American representative had, of course, been wrong. They were stacked up fifteen deep over the airport, and there was a possibility that Stapleton would close in the next half hour. His father's American Eagle flight was somewhere overhead, doing a slow circle, near the end of the pack.

"There's a possibility they'll get it down within the hour," the rep said.

This time Ray said out loud, "Right."

He found a gray padded seat near the observation window at the arrival gate and sat down. Snow melted on his topcoat—big flakes with patterns. They were beautiful, but for their transience. As he would begin to admire the symmetrical geometry of a flake's construction, it vanished before his eyes, transforming from art to a droplet of water on his Scotchguarded coat.

"Sir?"

It was Bridget's voice, and he started—but looked up to see the face of an American Airlines attendant. It had only sounded like her voice—

"I'm sorry," he said. "I was dozing off . . ."

"Are you Raymond Garver?" she asked, her smile returning.

"Yes."

"Your father has landed, sir. He was given priority, but they had to use a runway at the far end of the airport. He'll be in at Gate Fifty-two."

"Thank you."

She nodded, her smile following him as he rose and walked off. He had been staring at her, remembering that voice. She had obviously taken his stare for something else.

Gate 52 was not only at the far end of the airport, he had to leave the terminal and cross a parking lot in front of the Hertz Rent-A-Car terminal to get to it. It was a small private-plane terminal, little more than a hangar with a waiting room like a cab stand. His father was waiting for him.

"Where the *hell* have you been?" he said immediately.

"The American Airlines people—" he began, unable to halt the familiar apologetic tone.

"Screw American Airlines! I told them an hour ago to get you. We'll see what happens when those deregulation talks come up in May. If they think I don't forget things like this, the bastards are dumber than I thought. Where's your car?"

He told him, and his father's face turned beet red. "Goddamnit, you think I *enjoy* this shit? I spend three-quarters of my time in Washington dealing with assholes, and I have to come to fucking *Denver* in the middle of a fucking snowstorm to find *more* assholes?"

Ray began to walk away.

"Where the hell are you going?" his father called after him. Unaccountably, some of his anger had abandoned his voice.

Ray turned, snowflakes dandruffing his coat, his scarf, his hair. "I'm not going to take this shit anymore," he said calmly.

Once more his father's face reddened; he fought to bring it under control and had managed to almost smile before the black look took him over.

"I don't ever want to hear you talk like that to me again," he said, evenly.

"Then don't listen. And don't call me." Ray turned and began to walk off again.

A landing Delta 727 screamed overhead at that moment, or he would have heard his father's footsteps crunching the snow, hurrying to catch up to him. "Wait a minute, son," his father said, taking his arm, causing an almost physical repulsion.

Ray stared at him.

His father smiled—a smile as smooth and polished and layered as his psyche. "Let's just forget it, all right? Can we start over?"

Ray regarded him wordlessly; a snowflake blew into his open eye, blurring his sight, but when it blinked clean, his father was still showing his best-friend smile.

"Airlines are always screwing up," his father reasoned, "let's blame it on them."

In his life, he's never apologized to me, or anyone, Ray thought suddenly.

"Come with me," his father said, taking his arm and steering him back toward the tiny terminal building.

One phone call and ten minutes later, they were dropped off by an American Airlines staff limousine in front of Ray's car. His father smiled mischievously as they climbed into the Volvo. "Maybe I'll let the bastards off the hook yet in those hearings," he said, then added conspiratorially, "and maybe I won't." Then he laughed and said, "Let's go, son."

After missing the airport exit once, during which his father stifled a red rage and merely muttered, "Just find it," they were back on the highway. The snow had intensified. The Volvo's wipers, which hadn't been changed in three years, were streaking clumps of snow across the windshield in Ray's line of sight. The night had turned white and black. Near silence was punctuated by the swish of wipers and the occasional hissing slush of a passing car to either side.

Ray reached for the radio to end the silence, then drew his hand back.

"The hell with it. Why are you here, Dad?"

His father feigned preoccupation, turning from the windshield to squint at Ray. "What's that?" His thinning gray hair was plastered back away from his forehead by melted snow.

"I was going to wait until we got to my place and had a couple of drinks to ask; but I can't be bothered. What the hell are you doing here?"

"Son," his father began, putting on his best meeting-the-constituency face. The face collapsed into a grin, also false and calculated. "I need something from you."

"What do you need?"

Once again Ray had swerved too far to the right, and amid his father's curses, he had to interrupt their conversation to get away from a honking, light-flashing tow truck that roared past, throwing slush at them from huge chained tires.

When they had settled on the road again, his father said, "Son, I've always given you everything you needed—"

"Cut the shit."

Senator Garver's face hardened. For the briefest time the mask dropped and showed the face of the man underneath. It was the face of every caveman with a weapon and no fear of his enemies; any spiteful little boy with no concept of reason or layers of sophistication, no boundaries of lawful behavior to restrict his impulsive and chaotic wish to destroy a balky toy or anything else that wouldn't bow to his will. It was the face of pure selfishness. The glimpse lasted only a moment—the senator quickly remasked it with layers of sophistication, knowledge of law and punishment, and the hope that his wishes would be satisfied by subtler and acceptable means. "I've never asked much of you, Ray," he said, his face still hard, but set in an altered hardness, to inspire guilt.

"You haven't given all that much, either."

His father took a deep breath. "I don't want to get into any more of this now. I need you for something, and I expect you to do as you're told."

Ray laughed. "As I'm *told*?"

His father held his hand up. "I'll rephrase that. I expect you to do what has to be done."

Before Ray could reply, the senator added, "I'm running for president."

The words hung in the air for a few moments, unreal, stopping somewhere between Ray's ears and brain. His initial instinctual reaction was to laugh again. But laughter did not come. His father's face precluded that: it was not a comical face, but a frighteningly powerful one—and though the power had at its root the absolute obsession by and passion for an attainment, it triggered in Ray the remembrance of the more primal power and fascination that his father had had over him from his earliest memories.

"You're serious?" he managed to get out.

"This wasn't my idea, Ray," his father continued. "I was approached by Rafelson and Murphy and a number of others who did the scout work. They're positive it can happen. All the groundwork is already in place." He shifted his weight, looking wistfully out the windshield for a moment—a gesture calculated for effect. "I'm not so sure myself, of course. But I'd be lying if I said I didn't want it." He turned to look at Ray. "I do want it. But there is a problem, which I haven't told them about yet, and which I have to make absolutely sure won't bother me if I make the run."

Everything became clear to Ray. A bone-numbing chill of remembrance went through him. Once again, the temperature in the Volvo increased. He felt the tiny prickling of fear that Bridget was with him. He could almost feel her breath on his neck, the outstretched, hovering caress of her fingers near his neck, and she leaned forward in the back seat—

"You *do* know what I'm talking about?" his father said, studying his face.

Ray nodded. "Yes."

His father leaned back, breathing deeply again. "Can't you get this goddamn foreign car to move any faster? Where is this place of yours anyway?"

"We'll be there in a half hour," Ray said, his mind still lost in memory.

"I know it hurts to go over this," his father said solicitously.

"It hurts me, too. But we've got to review it and gloss it up."

"Gloss it up?"

Something settled on the back of Ray's neck and he cringed, waiting for Bridget's voice. But it was a droplet of melted snow, which fell into his collar and dissipated.

His father's face hardened again. "Yes, Ray, *gloss it up*. That's exactly what I mean. It could sink me right out of the dock, and you know it. Now, I didn't say hide it, which would be impossible, or even lie about it, which would be stupid because those goddamn media bastards would sniff it out anyway—you know they already know the basic facts from my second Senate run. This time, though, they'll go over it with a fine-tooth comb. They'll pull it every way, turn it upside down—" His voice was rising, and he paused to calm down. "Anyway," he resumed, his tone businesslike again, "we've got to make it as good as we can without changing one little fact. We've got to . . . gloss it up."

Without warning, tears sprung into Ray's eyes.

"Now, you know," his father continued, "there are certain things we can't hide. We can't hide your stint in the . . . counseling center. We can't hide the fact that you tried to kill yourself. But we *can* put the right spin on these things, Ray. You were young; you'd just watched a horrible thing happen. We *all* saw it happen. But . . ." His father shook his head ruefully. "Ray," he said, "there are some things we can't spin away. They just have to . . . disappear." He waved his hand. "Like all this hideaway stuff, this recluse in the mountains business. Grief, the media can understand. Pain, they can understand. But nuttiness . . ." His father turned to him. "Ray, I want you to come back to the house in California. A reconciliation type thing. Happy son, happy father. Understand?"

He almost wished his father had torn him apart like a balky toy. This was much worse . . .

"I won't help you," Ray heard himself saying.

"Now, Ray—"

The tears came and would not leave. Ray tried to blink them back, to have hard thoughts, to make them go away. But hot knives of memory were scooping the water out of his eyes, pushing the tears down his face as he drove, eyes on the road.

"I won't help you," Ray repeated.

"Son—"

Ray turned his face to his father, ignoring the tears that came on their own. *"Why the hell don't you just have me assassinated, if I'm such an embarrassment? Why don't you just fucking kill me?"*

But for the toiling push of the windshield wipers against snow, and the crunch of crushed snow beneath the tires, there was silence in the car. His father sat immobile, his face unreadable in silhouette. Ray turned his attention back to the highway; once again the car had wandered, and this time he pulled behind the offended sedan and stayed in the right lane. The guardrail off the service lane had reflectors; he could gauge his position by those. He drove for five minutes, and then his hand strayed toward the radio to turn it on, to have sound.

His father's hand was on his wrist, and for a foolish moment he thought there was tenderness in the touch.

"Do what I want, Ray."

He shook his hand out of his father's grasp. "Fuck you."

"We'll go to your little cabin in the woods and talk all about it—" his father began sarcastically.

"I said, fuck you."

"Turn the car around."

Ray pulled over into the service lane abruptly and braked the car. His father sat motionless.

"Is that what you want—"

"Turn the car around," his father repeated. "And when I'm through with you, Ray, you'll wish you *were* dead."

The engine idled. Ray turned to stare at the rigid, tight-lipped, unspeaking statue in the passenger seat, and then he put the car into drive and pulled back onto the highway. He began to search for an exit ramp.

As he saw a sign for an approaching exit, he felt a touch on the back of his neck. This time it was not a bead of water. He felt her fingers, thumb and forefinger, circle the back of his neck and squeeze, almost tenderly. He felt her breath close-by, felt her heat as she leaned over toward him.

"Ray," she whispered into his ear.

He began to shiver. His tears had dried to salt on his face, and there was only fear now.

"Ray," she whispered, tenderly kissing the back of his ear, "I'm going to help you."

The exit ramp appeared, curling into darkness off the highway, thicker with snow than the traveled macadam. He felt Bridget lean over him to his left, between him and the door, and saw her grip the wheel in her hands.

Ray cried out, and his father stared at him. His eyes widened. Later, Ray was sure his father had seen her. She laughed and turned the wheel sharply. The car took the exit ramp in a curving skid.

Ray pushed his foot to the brake. Bridget laughed—it was not the brake but the accelerator pedal, which had switched places with it, that his foot hit. The car sped up and skidded sideways. The headlamps, piercing falling snow, picked up covered roadway and the lip of the exit roadway. Something indistinct was parked ahead, off to the side.

Ray jammed his foot from accelerator to brake, but there were two accelerator pedals. He alternated between them, screaming for one of them to be the brakes. He took his foot from the pedals, but it was too late; they had locked. The car continued to whine against the icy roadway, sliding sideways toward the thing parked on the side of the exit ramp. Through the snow and lights it resolved into a bed truck bearing a yellow, snow-covered bulldozer. The bulldozer had been thrown sideways, facing them, its shovel dropped over the side of the bed.

They glided toward it.

Senator Garver said, "Oh, my dear God," as the white-black sky became filled with the curving hard metal solidity of the huge shovel. Ray ducked as he saw the straight bottom edge suddenly outlined starkly in the slipping beams of the headlights. They slammed straight into it. His father screamed and Ray turned to see him beheaded, and felt the crushing weight of the collapsing car against his mortal legs—

"Go back to your cocaine, Ray," Bridget said. With the phone receiver clutched in his hand, he felt her grip on the back of his neck, pushing him toward the rest of the cut line of coke on the desk. She pushed his nose into it, and he felt the tickle of white powder against his nostrils. He dropped the phone on the desk and began to cry, turning his head sideways on the desk and closing his eyes. Her hand let him go with a departing caress, and he heard her voice, half distinct through the receiver.

"Here's what to do," she said. "Here's where to go to destroy me . . ."

He listened, and in a while she had stopped talking and there was nothing but hissing on the line, and faint, unrecognizable laughter and screams, and soon Ray had turned his face to the table and found his tiny straw, and was pulling the medicine up into his nose to his brain and making himself strong for the journey.

9. NORTH

Somewhere in Montreal, Peter Wayne got lost. First, the jerkoff at the border-crossing booth gave him the wrong directions, probably for fun (Peter had sensed his leg was being pulled—"You go about eighty miles west, hey?" the idiot had said, saying it in such a way, by going back to the paperback book he was reading, that Peter knew he wasn't going to get anything else out of him), and then when he finally got into Montreal and needed directions to Ottawa, the fog had rolled in so thick that he could barely see all the new construction going on around him (*What is it with these Canadians—they made of money?*), and the proprietors of the two 7-Elevens he'd stopped in had pretended they didn't know a word of English (*Bilingual bastard country.*). And by now he was lost good, and asked the last person he felt like asking anywhere, anytime, about anything, especially with an open cooler of beer on the floor behind the driver's seat, with empties scattered around it, a cop. But, lo and behold, the cop had smiled and said, "Sure, what you want to do is . . ." and had given him exact and precise directions to Ottawa, and then Laura's *building,* that had gotten him to the capital city in less than ninety minutes.

The upshot of which was it was two-thirty in the morning when he finally pulled into a parking spot in front of Laura's apartment complex, instead of ten o'clock as he'd planned. By this time he didn't give a damn if she wasn't expecting him; he just wanted to sit down and drink two or three more of the beers in the cooler behind his seat and then start yelling at her.

Pulling his jacket and the cooler from the back seat, and cursing when he banged his head standing up, he slammed the car door and trudged to the front lobby of the building.

He had to admit Ottawa didn't look too bad—at least at night. There was no fog here, as in Montreal, and the canal looked beautiful, a perfect river of dark, clean-looking water reflecting the pretty lights of the city from its cool surface. Everything in Canada looked clean and brand-new. It was as if America had opened for business twenty minutes ago.

He shrugged. *Maybe it looks shitty in the daytime.*

Somehow, he doubted it.

The lobby had a new panel of lighted buzzers. He cursed when he couldn't find Laura's name. He knew she had moved in only five days before—exactly five days, since the last time he'd spoken to her had been Thursday, when she had hung up the phone on him and started mumbling garbage about that jerk Brennan and all that poltergeist stuff being real. Peter's drinking jag had started the next day, which he had been unlucky enough to have off (or lucky, if you considered drowning your sorrows in Coors good medical treatment), and by the time Monday morning had come around, he'd been in no shape to go to work. He'd had a little time coming to him anyway, and when he'd called in sick, he'd sounded sufficiently lousy that there would be no questions. "What the hell good are you to me on the floor if you're going to puke on the customers?" Charles had said, and when Peter said he'd take the whole week off because he'd felt run-down anyway lately, Charles had just said, "What the hell, it's slow now anyway."

"Goddamnit, Laura, where are you?" Peter said to himself, studying the panel. There were names in all but two panels, and he put the cooler down on the lobby floor and pushed the first. There was no answer. He counted to thirty and then pushed it again, longer. Still no answer.

He turned his attention to the other buzzer, and again there was no reaction. Once more he counted to thirty, then leaned on it for a count of twenty. Nothing.

He cursed and began to study the panels with names in them, looking for a clue, when the light on the second blank panel lit and a voice said sleepily from the speaker, "Hello?"

"Laura?"

"Yes?"

"It's me, Peter."

"Peter . . ." The grogginess didn't leave her voice. He waited for it to, but when she spoke again, her words were still heavy. "What do you want?"

"Laura, let me come up."

"Go home, Peter . . ."

Before he could think, his hand had slapped at the speaker. "Goddamnit, let me in!"

He thought she had turned the intercom off. There was a long silence, and then she said, no more brightly, "Okay."

He grabbed the cooler and yanked at the door as the buzzer unlocking it went off briefly. If he hadn't lurched at it, he would have missed it. He was halfway into the open elevator when he realized that he didn't remember what number her room was. 1212 or 1221? He held the elevator door open with his hand, trying to visualize the number next to the empty name panel. He couldn't do it.

"*Shit.*"

He stalked back to the lobby door, opened it, and wedged the cooler into the opening so it wouldn't close. The number was 1214.

He went back to the elevator and took it to the twelfth floor, reflecting that an optimist would have pointed out that he'd at least gotten the floor right.

Fuck optimism.

The elevator door opened, and he walked resolutely to 1214. There was no answer. A brief fear that he had read the wrong number on the panel downstairs assailed him. No, he was sure at least of that. He felt cold, and shivered; there was an open window down the hallway and he closed it.

"Come *on,* Laura," he said impatiently, knocking on the door again.

He leaned close, listening, but there was no sound from within.

The doorknob turned and the door opened.

"Laura?"

It was pitch black inside. He waited for her to appear in the doorway. He could hear the muted hum of the refrigerator in the kitchen, but nothing else.

"Laura?" he called into the apartment.

"Peter?" he heard from somewhere in the back.

"What the fuck—" he cursed, stepping in, feeling for a light switch on the wall. There was one, and it was up. *Fucking Canadians probably do it ass backward.* He flipped the switch down. There was the tiny click of the mercury element inside, but no light went on.

He switched it up and down a couple of times. Nothing happened.

"Laura?" he called again, not hiding his annoyance.

"Hmmmmm . . ."

She sounded half asleep. Or drugged.

He stepped into the darkened apartment. Immediately, he tripped over something. As he regained his balance it abruptly occurred to him that there might be an intruder in the apartment.

"Are you all right, Laura?" he said, worried now.

"Yes . . ."

Peter felt someone behind him, put his hand out suddenly—and there was someone there. A hand touching his, then pulling away.

"Who the hell—"

He backed away from the door. There were other objects in his path. He tripped and fell. There was a noise behind him at the doorway. He got up and walked to it and looked down the hall. It was empty.

Whoever it had been was gone.

He returned to the apartment and found himself in the entrance to a room. There was a green glow, and his heart jumped—then he saw it was a digital readout over a stove. He was in the kitchen.

He yelled, "Laura?"

"Yes, Peter," she said.

He checked the bathroom, but there was no one there.

Next to the bathroom was a door that proved to lead to a linen closet. Another door stood open at the end of the hall, filled with darkness. There was another light at the end of the hallway. He flicked it on. The shadows retreated into the room at the end of the hall. He saw the outlines of disarray: pulled-down bed sheets, clothes on the floor, drawers on a dresser against the wall pulled out, a bra hanging forlornly from one of the pullout knobs.

"Christ," Peter said. The implication of what had happened dawned on him. He remembered the felt touch in the front room, hoping the intruder had indeed left. A tendril of fear told him his hope might not be right.

"Laura?" he shouted, loudly, hoping that any neighbors might be awakened. "Lau—"

"Here, Peter."

Her drugged voice, close-by, in the bedroom.

"Where are you?" His voice was tinged with hysteria now.

"I'm here."

He entered the room and groped for the light switch. There wasn't any. There was an overturned lamp near the dresser; he picked it up and twisted the switch. Nothing happened. He felt along the cord till the plug came into his hand. He patted the wall for an outlet but couldn't locate one.

He yanked the dresser away from the wall in frustration. The tepid light from the hallway wouldn't reach. Cursing, he moved the flat of his hand around for the protrusion of an outlet. It was there, at the far end. He butted the dresser away viciously to get at it.

He pulled the lamp into his self-made cave, turned it on.

Light hurt his eyes. He blinked and stood up, putting the lamp onto the dresser.

"Jesus."

The room was a bigger mess than he had imagined. Everything had been tossed around or rearranged. Kitchen utensils were scattered about on the floor, glasses and plates in low piles near the bed. The sheets had been pulled from the bed, exposing the mattress, which had seemingly been raked with a sharp instrument. Tufts of padding were pulled from ragged holes. A chair lay broken by the clothes closet.

"Laura, where in God's name are you!"

"Here," she said weakly, from the closet.

He pushed his way across the room and yanked on the closet door.

A smell hit him as he saw her, and the odor, as much as the sight of her, repulsed and shocked him. But then his eyes became the dominating sensors.

"Oh, *God*!"

She lay in the back corner of the closet, huddled like a child, naked. Her hair was matted thick with blood and what looked like human waste, her body covered with bruises. She was smeared with a coating of excrement that in some places caked her flesh completely.

"Oh, Jesus, Laura."

"Hello, Peter."

Her eyes were open and too clear. She smiled up at him, moving her hands, which had been holding her knees, up over her thighs to her breasts. She rubbed at them, exciting the nipples before reaching down with one hand to pick up one of the turds that lay nearby and bringing it up to her mouth and putting it in.

She chewed slowly, lowering her hands to cup her breasts and held them out to him.

Peter began to tremble. Shock gave way to outrage. He reached down to lift her out of the closet, but she suddenly stretched her body out lengthwise on the floor and pulled her legs apart, bending her knees. She felt around on the floor and found another turd, thrusting it into the encrusted cavity between her legs, trying to work it into her vagina. She moaned, putting her weight on her toes and shoulder blades and lifting her pelvis off the floor.

"Peter, that feels so good, *please* do it again."

She searched for another turd with one hand, still writhing, her other hand working between her legs.

Peter bent down and grabbed her hand. He turned his face away to avoid the odor. He began to gag.

"No! What are you doing?" She fought him, trying to make him let go. His stomach heaved, but he held on. She clawed at him and he cried out, but he retained his grip, hoisting her up and then securing her under the arms, walking her back out of the closet.

"No! No!"

"Goddamnit, Laura!"

"Leave me alone!"

He pulled her toward the bed. Suddenly she said, "For you, Peter," in a silky voice and he felt wetness on his leg. She had spread her legs and was urinating on him. He cursed, continuing to drag her body, and she said, "And this for you, Peter," in the same sex-drugged voice, and she pressed her buttocks against him. He heard and felt the sourness of excretion as a runnel of shit left her and ran onto his leg.

"Oh, God, oh, Jesus," he said, fighting the urge to vomit. But suddenly it was too strong, and he loosened his grip on her, setting her down on the floor. He turned his head away and threw up. All the beer he had drunk during the ride up churned up into his throat and out, all the rotten sour food he had eaten the past twelve hours came up and out of him in a thunder of revulsion. He heaved endlessly, doubled over, until there was nothing left in his stomach. He heaved dryly, eyes closed, hands on his middle, then gagged, spitting bile, trying to blind himself to the sour taste in his mouth.

"That's *good,* Peter," Laura said. She had turned over at his feet and was lapping like a dog at his vomitus. "Good!" she cried, pulling herself forward into the puddle, covering her body, rolling over to look up at him with a horrible inhuman face. She smoothed vomit over her breasts, her belly, into the thatch of hair between her legs. "Yes!" she shouted excitedly, opening her mouth, vomiting, gagging out bits of dried waste and sour food.

"No more!" Peter shouted. He bent down and hit her. The blow caught her on the cheek. Her eyes brightened and she said, "Yes!" before he hit her again, flush in the face.

She fell back unconscious.

He stood shaking, wanting to vomit again, bending over but unable to bring anything up. He moaned and stepped over Laura's unconscious form. He stumbled out of the room, hands on the walls for support, to the bathroom.

He turned on the hot and cold water, making a hard jet run into the sink. He took off his jacket and rolled up his shirt sleeves. He cupped his hands under the water and washed his face. He looked for soap. There was none, so he brought great handfuls of water up and scrubbed into his pores and his neck and into his hair, then washed around his wrists and lower arms. There was one towel thrown over the bathtub; it looked unwashed but he didn't care, and he dried himself with it, ignoring the moldy smell of it.

He turned on the water in the bathtub hard, as hot as he could get it, and then he went back into the bedroom.

She lay where he had hit her, head turned to one side. He reached down to check her pulse. It was strong. He bent down in a weight-lifter's crouch and lifted her, grunting, and brought her into the bathroom.

The mirror was steamed. He checked to make sure the water was not too hot before laying her in the tub.

He soaked the towel in hot water and began to rub at the filth that covered her body. He had to stop frequently, turning his head away to gag, but he kept at it, starting with her feet and moving gently upward. He let the putrid water drain and refilled the tub. He resumed his washing until the water became filthy again and then repeated the process.

When he was finished, he filled the tub once more with a few inches of warm water and rolled the towel and pillowed her head with it. He stood and looked down at her. A shiver ran through him. He had seen her naked only four or five times, when they had made love up at his parents' cabin over holiday weekends. He had seen her plenty of times in bathing suits. But she had never been this skinny. He had seen her a little less than a week ago, and he knew she hadn't looked like this then. Her bruised ribs showed unhealthily below her breasts. Her cheeks were hollow, her arms overly thin. He could almost curl his thumb and forefinger around her ankle. Her body was covered with scores of black-and-blue marks, scratches, half-healed cuts and gouges. In places there were neat lines of round little holes; it looked as though the tines of a fork had been pressed into her. She looked like an inmate from a prisoner of war camp.

"Jesus, Laura, what happened to you?" he asked. He wanted to cry. He noted with a wince the bruise that was forming over her lip on the right side where he had hit her.

He left her soaking in the tub and returned to her bedroom. The thought occurred to him that he should call the police.

But he hesitated. What would the Canadian police say, finding him here at three in the morning, half drunk, telling wild stories about someone trapping her in her own apartment for a week and turning her into someone who only wanted to eat and have sex with her own shit . . .

He took a leg of the broken chair and checked through the rest of the apartment. As he had thought, whoever it was had left. He stared hard at the open front door for a moment, but then he closed and locked it, put the chain across it, and went back to the bedroom.

He straightened the bed as best he could, finding some clean linens in a closet in the hall. The pillows were covered with filth, so he fashioned one from a clean pillowcase stuffed with what clean clothes he could find. He gathered the plates and glasses to bring to the kitchen, noting with disgust that the yellow liquid in one glass appeared to be urine.

The kitchen was a mess, also: drawers pulled out, the refrigerator wedged open. A foul stench issued from inside. He kicked the chair holding the door open aside and let it close. The kitchen sink was stained, and next to it he saw a paring knife jammed deep into the wooden countertop. Something was carved deep into the wood, the etched grooves stained in what looked like blood:

SOON
LOVE, M&P

He felt a chill. He left the dishes he had brought in the sink and went back to the bathroom.

She hadn't stirred. He had found a single clean towel in the linen closet, and he lifted her from the tub and carried her to the bedroom and laid her on the end of the bed. He patted her dry, wincing at the sour smell that still impregnated her hair as he toweled it dry. Then he put her in a relatively unsoiled nightgown and laid her on the makeshift pillow. He drew the sheets up over her and left the room.

The next two hours he spent cleaning the apartment. He started with the kitchen, sponging rancid milk from the floor, scraping broken tomato sauce jar fragments, along with bits of dried onion and stale bread into a pile, which he then gathered into the unused garbage pail in the broom closet. He piled all the utensils and glasses and dishes into the sink and let them soak in hot water.

The living room showed less evidence of neglect; the furniture had been moved around, and there were stains on the rug from an overturned bottle of red wine. One leaf of the dining room table had been cracked off, as if someone had sat on it, and one of the chairs was missing its back.

He was cleaning the tub in the bathroom when he heard Laura stir. He walked slowly to her bedroom door and looked in. She was sitting up on her elbows, looking around her as if lost. When she saw him, her eyes widened.

"Peter?" she said in a very small, unsure voice.

He entered and sat on the bed next to her. The glaze was gone from her eyes. She looked like someone suffering the effects of a hangover. He studied her face, waiting for her to speak.

"How—?"

"You don't remember anything that happened tonight, Laura?"

She shook her head tentatively.

"None of it?"

"No . . ."

"Did someone break into your apartment? Has someone been keeping you here against your will?"

Her memory was striving to inform her. "No," she said, finally.

"What have you been doing the last five days, Laura? And there *was* someone in this apartment tonight." He was trying very hard to keep an accusatory tone from his voice.

"Peter, I don't—" But then a spark of memory ignited and her face was transformed.

"Oh, Peter, yes." She tried to rise from the bed. He held her down by the arms, bending over her.

"Let me go," she said.

"Tell me what's been going on," he said, angrily.

"It's M and P." A light had filled her eyes.

"Do you know how I found you tonight?" Peter said, deliberately. "Did you know you've been living in your own feces for days, possibly since I talked to you? That you haven't eaten anything since God knows when? I found you in that clothes closet"—he pointed, a suppressed rage evident in his shaking fingers—"covered with your own *shit*. Do you know any of this?"

He let go of her arms and stared at her, trembling.

"Peter, you've got to listen to me," she said. She wanted to rush on, but she composed herself. She touched him tenderly on his arm and held her fingers there. "Peter, you have to believe me. I don't remember anything of what's happened. All I know is that M and P are *there*. They can be reached. There was a message—"

"You mean those scratch marks in the kitchen?" he said scornfully.

"There's more," she continued. She put her hand back on his arm. "*Please* listen, Peter. I've been told I can see them."

"Who—" A sudden suspicion invaded his thoughts. "Has Brennan been up here?"

She shook her head. "No. I called him, but he was away." Her voice became vague. "His machine took a message . . ."

"Then who *told* you?"

She took a deep breath. "Someone. I'm not really sure. But there was contact with something, that same night you called me. I thought it was my aunt, but it wasn't. Something that promised me I would be able to reach them. A house in New York—"

"*Jesus Christ!* What's *wrong* with you? Don't you see what's been going on here? Are you that *blind*? Something's *wrong* with you, Laura—don't you *see* that?"

The light in her eyes was constant, unfluctuating. "Peter, I'm telling you, this force contacted me, and—"

For the third time that night, he hit her. Not as hard this time, but his guilt was worse because he knew it was as much out of frustration as necessity.

She sat straight in bed, stunned, putting her hand to her cheek. She stared at him, and then abruptly the light softened in her eyes and she began to cry.

"Oh, Peter," she wept. She looked at the room, the open door of the closet and what lay on its floor, the stains, the broken furniture, the torn clothes. She registered the distinct, faint uncleanliness of her own body, her own hair.

He put his arms around her, and she cried for a long time.

When she had stopped crying, he held her tight and then laid her back against the pillow and held her hands. Her eyes were swollen red with tears.

"I'm going to take you home," he said quietly. "Something strange happened here. But even if it's all in your mind, we're going to fight it. I'm going to make you well again."

She nodded, on the edge of renewed tears.

"I know how you feel about your parents," he said gently. "But what they did to you was wrong. They were selfish, Laura. They loved you so much they wanted to make sure you never left them, so they told you things that weren't true. You *know* there's nothing wrong with your foot. They told you that to tie you to them." He leaned very close to her. "But they're *dead,* Laura. They're *gone.* And I'm here to take care of you and make you well."

"Peter," she said, in a whisper, beginning to cry softly again.

He looked deeply into her eyes. "You'll let me take you home?"

"Yes."

He kissed her forehead. "Good."

The front door slammed.

"What the—"

He distinctly heard the chain being slid in its socket, then the front door was opened again and then slammed, very loud.

Laura looked at him fearfully. "Peter—"

He was already up, finding the broken chair leg he had wielded on his earlier search of the apartment.

"Peter, please—"

He walked out into the hallway and looked at the front door.

It was closed and bolted.

He walked slowly to it, noting from a distance that the chain was in its slide and locked, just as he had left it.

The lights blinked out. He felt a light touch across the knuckles of his hand holding the chair leg.

He swung at the unseen presence.

He heard a faint brush of laughter in his ear, felt fingers slide like a spiderweb across his wrist.

The front door flew wide open. He saw the chain tapping

against the door edge. A rectangle of outside light spilled into the apartment.

There was a touch on his wrist and cheek, simultaneously.

He heard laughter in one ear, then the other.

In the near dark, he was pushed, hard, toward the open doorway.

He turned. No one was pushing him. Laura stood in her bedroom doorway. Her nightgown had been removed. She was smiling, the hard bright shine of madness back in her eyes, her hands cupped between her spread legs as she urinated on them.

"Good-bye, Peter," she said.

He was pushed by the unseen presence, knocked backward to the front doorway.

"Laura!" he shouted, swinging the chair leg. It was caught in midair and pulled from his hand. It hung suspended for a moment, then dropped to the floor.

Peter was pushed out of the apartment and down the hall.

Shouting, he turned to see the window he had closed on the way in. It was wide open.

Laura stood in her open doorway, watching him.

"Laura! No!"

Screaming for help, he was pushed past three other apartment doors. Only silence answered.

Cold night air pushed against his back as he moved toward the open window.

"Laura, oh, God!"

The backs of his knees rammed against the window ledge. His feet left the floor as he was forced back and out.

He fell into the night, screaming, the far-off ripple of the beautiful canal his last glimpse of the world before the ground below threw out its hard arms to embrace him.

Laura closed, locked, and chained the door. Favoring her right foot, she walked back down the hallway to the bedroom. As she passed the kitchen, drawers slid open, utensils jumping out of them onto the floor. The refrigerator opened. A half-filled container of sour milk tumbled out, spilling the rest of its contents in a cheesy puddle across the floor. Someone laughed in the living room. The furniture was pulled and pushed by unseen hands; a dining room chair lost its back with a splintering crack, and the other leaf of the dining room table buckled and split. In the bathroom, the medicine cabinet hinged violently open, belching lipstick tubes and glass cold-cream jars out into the sink. They broke, mixing a sickening cosmetic cocktail. The tub backed up, pushing drained dirt and vomit into the sink.

Laura returned to the bedroom closet. She drew her knees up, smearing feces around them, resting her chin on them.

Suddenly she looked up, with the quick eye-snap of a bird. She smiled.

"Yes," she said. "Thank you." She rose, left the closet, and began to gather clothes. She took those with the least amount of ruin to them, tossing the rest aside. She put a pair of panties, a bra, a turtleneck shirt, and a pair of jeans, along with a pair of white crew socks and her Reeboks, off to one side.

There was a blue cloth suitcase under the bed, stained with vomit and feces. She slid it out, opened it, and packed, neatly and carefully.

When she was finished packing and had closed the suitcase, wiping at the most obvious stains with a discarded blouse, she dressed herself. She straightened her clothes, went to the bathroom and brushed her hair back with her fingers. There was a smudge of human waste over one eye and she toweled it off.

She brought the suitcase to the front door, found her jacket on the floor next to the sofa and put it on. She found her bag with her wallet in it and slung it over her shoulder. She found Peter's car keys in his jacket pocket.

She opened the door, looked into the living room.

"Yes?" she asked, breathlessly, excited. "You promise?"

An answer came. Her face radiated happiness. She picked the suitcase up, went out into the hallway, and locked the door, sliding the key underneath, back into the apartment.

On her way to the elevator—on her way to New York State—she paused to close the open window because the soft night breeze that came in momentarily chilled her.

10. FALCONI

There was a big chart on the wall behind Detective Richard Falconi's desk, which he swiveled in his chair to look at ten or twelve times a day. He swiveled to look at it now. It had been handmade on the back of a Bruce Springsteen poster he'd found in the garbage pail in his fourteen-year-old daughter's room ("I never want to see his face again after he left his wife," she'd said in explanatory indignation), and on it was everything Falconi, and anyone else for that matter, knew about the murderer the *Post* had called the Games Killer. There were a lot of categories—Physical Description, Modus Operandi, Area of Attack, Psychological Profile, even one titled Games, which listed all the victims by the kind of game they had been playing when they were killed—and though there was a lot of information, including subcategories such as the one under Monopoly that elucidated the progress of the game at the time the Games Killer had lured Marilyn Fagen, age forty-five, widow, mother of two boarding schoolers, resident of the Upper East Side, thought, through unsubstantiated reports, to have occasionally cruised the bars on Second Avenue and to have been open to any sort of sexual activity that might follow a successful prowling expedition away from the game board to the bedroom where he had calmly bound her hand and foot, gagged her, and then beheaded her. Noted for anyone interested, and Falconi was very interested for one reason, the game was about to be won on the next roll by the player using the pewter race car as a playing piece. It had been dusted and there were no prints on it; a partial of Marilyn Fagen's right forefinger had been taken from the other piece, a spinning wheel. How had Marilyn Fagen, hot in the pants as she must have been, waited so long to try to get what she wanted out of him? Was he very handsome, or otherwise alluring, and worth the wait, which he probably had insisted on? Perhaps she could not wait for that final roll, but the killer had been satisfied that it was imminent. He had won the game.

He had won the game. He *always* won the game—that was the one solid lead they had after all this time. Otherwise he was nearly invisible; a man who appeared quietly, established a relationship almost invisibly, killed, and went into the ether. Under Physical Characteristics were a couple of possibilities: a homeless man who lived on the benches in Washington Square Park "thought" he'd seen Harold Moss playing chess a couple of times with a young man in a black shirt—he couldn't remember a face; a deli owner "sort of recalled a man in his thirties or forties" with Marilyn Fagen when she came to buy a loaf of Italian bread the night she was murdered.

He likes to win. This, Falconi knew, was all he had, and he had written it at the bottom of the chart, underlined twice. HE LIKES TO WIN. Which told him—what?

Which told him nothing, because everyone he knew liked to win, everyone he'd grown up with in Astoria liked to win at marbles, at stickball, at anything.

He has to win. Yes—which told him something, because there was a need in him so strong, so all-persuasive, to dominate his opponent, to *destroy* him, to the point of murdering that opponent after he had been vanquished in mock battle. "This individual takes no prisoners," Minkowski had told him; and Minkowski was the one he trusted more than all the others. Minkowski played pinochle—and Falconi could attest to the fact that he liked to win at that. "This particular person's behavior is in many ways like that of the black widow spider; though in the black widow's case it is sex and not the playing of games that is the operative area."

At this point Minkowski had smiled his Cheshire grin, cluing Falconi that he should divert Minkowski from the lecture he was about to deliver on the relationship between the sex act and the playing of games of any kind, as studied by Friedman and Wallach, 1965, and Borgen and Robbins, 1973; a diversion that Falconi had accomplished by saying, "Just stick to the point, Mark."

"Also," Minkowski had gone on, "it is the female black widow that does the killing, and in this case, the male is the one who kills. But as you know, the female black widow kills her partner after the sex act has been completed. It is not enough that she dominate him, as she does physically, being four times his size; she must perform the ultimate domination of him, murdering him afterward."

Falconi, feeling a little foolish, as he always did when asking a question of Minkowski or any of the other psych people, feeling like a schoolboy, said, "So why does he kill them if he's already beaten them?"

Minkowski, seriously lecturing now, answered without humor, "It's a power thing. I would imagine that we're dealing with someone from a classic broken home, most probably with an overbearing mother, one who may have compromised his love for her with other men. He has a rage in him that can only be assuaged by beating, in proxy, his mother. In effect, each of those he kills is his mother; he's beating his mother, dominating her the way she dominated him." The sly grin returned. "All speculative, of course."

Falconi threw up his hands in exasperation. "Great."

Minkowski slapped Falconi's knee and got up. "Don't look so glum," he said, stretching. "Even if I'm wrong, you'll be catching him soon."

Falconi's interest immediately piqued. "What do you mean?"

"He's getting bolder, more confident of his invincibility, cockier. That bloody turtleneck shirt he left at the cribbage woman's apartment, what's her name—"

"Meg Greely."

"Right, Greely. That shirt was left deliberately. He probably nicked his finger while he was cutting her up. It's a sign that he's ready to up the odds in your favor. The fact that his blood type is O positive is irrelevant. He knew he'd be giving you relatively little to track him down with there. He's teasing you; wants to see how good you are. I wouldn't be surprised if he gives you a call soon, or one of the papers."

"You're sure about this?"

Minkowski winked. "All speculative, of course."

"Mark—"

Minkowski laughed. "Look, Rich, don't be so tentative around me. I know my business, but I'm not God. And neither are Borgen or Robbins. I can tell you for a fact that Robbins published a paper a few years ago that's complete bullshit. He pulled in theorists that were discredited forty years ago to try to bolster his thesis, and he got away with it. I'm sure he believed what he was doing; probably still does. But the paper is still bullshit."

He leaned down toward Falconi. "Don't be so intimidated by it, Rich," he smiled. "Most of it is bullshit. The mind's a mystery, like Plato's Cave, only most of the time we can't even catch the goddamn shadows."

"Now I really feel great."

"Oh, most of what I've told you is good enough to use." He walked toward the door, pausing to stretch again. On the way out he said, "Purely speculative, of course."

Falconi threw a wadded piece of paper at him, but it fell short of the doorway.

Shit. There was some things that weren't purely speculative. Like the fact that his head was being fitted for the scapegoat platter if they didn't get a break soon.

His eyes wandered to the double-hinged picture frame resting on the corner of his desk.

Still, some things are worse than being a scapegoat.

The picture on the right was of Grace and Amelia—his wife smiling, his daughter with a glum, little girl's look on her face. Falconi remembered it had been their last day at Disney World, and Amelia hadn't wanted to go home. It had been taken three years ago, the last time she had looked like a little girl. Before Bruce Springsteen.

The picture on the left was of a blank, anonymous-looking woman in her midthirties. Her hair was cropped sloppily close to her head. She had on a nondescript spring jacket and stood on a slush-covered March city street, staring into the camera as if uncaring if it was there or not.

Minkowski had asked him why he kept that picture, had even hinted there was something unhealthy about it. But Falconi knew why it was on his desk. There were some things worse than being a scapegoat—

Fuck that. Let's just get this creep.

He stared hard at the chart; annoyingly, he could just see the outline of Bruce Springsteen's tight fanny and upraised arm through the back of the poster. Springsteen's ghostly hand, holding a wired microphone, was pointing to the category marked Games. Falconi was mildly satisfied to see that the Psychological Profile category was right over Springsteen's fanny; he would have to tell Minkowski that one. Under the Games heading was listed, in Falconi's tight scribble, Monopoly, Cribbage, Chess, Trivial Pursuit, Bridge; under that was the word *Next* followed by a question mark and then: Pictionary, Pinochle (the word *Ha* was scribbled next to it in red ink, in Minkowski's hand), Life (again the word *Ha*, this time the irony crossed out, again, in red ink), Clue (Falconi's own *Ha*), Parcheesi, Video Games (a double question mark after this; so far, the killer had had nothing to do with electronics), Poker, and a dozen others.

Falconi stared at the list, felt nothing. *So much for Bruce Springsteen.* He rubbed at his eyes and yawned; the sourness in his stomach was gone, which meant it was time for another cup of coffee. He reached behind him to his desk, felt his finger down into his coffee cup, and found it still half full. Cold. Good, he could have another cup and not feel like he had lied to Grace. "Two cups of coffee a day, tops," he'd promised her. He had it down to seven.

Once again he stared at the poster; Springsteen's phantom hand holding the mike sprouted something curling beneath it. He leaned closer. Part of the mike—the cord. It started at the end of the word *Games* and snaked down and over to the category Physical Characteristics. It went through the heading and stopped somewhere in the middle of the list. *Coffee,* he thought. Instead he leaned closer, playing out his own game, emptying his mind, peering close to see the end of that cord. Down through Height, Weight, Clothes (*Black Shirt* scrawled next to this; question marks with *Jeans?* and *Windbreaker? Coat?* next to it), Eyes, Name—the microphone cord ended there.

Name. Falconi stared at the word, let his eyes drift back up through the curls of cord, settle back on the word *Games*.

Games? It was a stupid idea, but all of his ideas were stupid to him in the beginning. He began to think about it. Could the killer's name have something to do with games? Minkowski had said it was odd that there had been no communication by this time between the Games Killer and the media or the police; they had of course made sure Falconi was prominent in the news stories, was the focus of the investigation, just to make sure the killer had a name, a nemesis, to concentrate on. It had worked before. Minkowski had said it *might* be because he was getting everything he wanted already.

Games? Gaymes? Hastily, Falconi pulled his pen from his shirt pocket and clicked the ballpoint out. He wrote, hand cramped against the wall, under a dash next to the word *Games,* making a subheading: Games, Gaymes, Gaimes, Gaemes, then, after a pause, Gaames, putting a few dash marks down a line after it to leave spaces for other possibilities.

He leaned back in his chair, contemplated the new entry, absently clicking the pen closed and slipping it into his pocket. He felt a tiny thrill run through him, the kind he had had many times before and which sometimes—just sometimes—led to a break.

His eye caught the opaque trace of the microphone cable and he traced it leisurely up from one link to the other.

Why not.

He swiveled around, away from the poster, turning to his phone. As he put his hand on it he felt the familiar doubt, the relic of hesitation, the fear of looking foolish that always assaulted him when he needed to ask anyone else's opinions on his hunches. He ignored it, knowing that second thoughts were part of his nature and that they should be ignored. They were nonproductive and vain. If he needed further incentive, he need only think of his head resting on that platter on the front page of the *Post,* surrounded by cut vegetables, an apple stuck in his unemployed mouth.

If he didn't keep working, his daughter wouldn't be able to buy a poster of the next teen idol.

His hesitation had been instantaneous; even as he had these thoughts he was dialing Minkowski's number and waiting for the pickup on the other end.

11. SOUTH

When Ricky was not happy, it was never a secret.

He couldn't help it. He was normally so open, so outgoing, that when anything really bothered him the change in his nature was instantly apparent.

For two weeks he had tried to keep to himself what had happened at Chambers House. Arriving home that afternoon, soaked and shivering, his mother had thought he was sick and had made him take a hot shower, get into dry clothes and get into bed. But by the time he was under the covers she had known that he was not sick and that something was bothering him.

"What is it? What's wrong?" she had said, scolding him gently, which was all it had ever taken to get him to open up.

But this time he had only shivered and said, "Nothing, Mum. Just a shiver from the rain," and turned his face to the wall.

Shiver from the rain it wasn't, and she'd known that immediately; and over the next few days, when he'd stayed in bed through glorious sunshine, claiming illness that wasn't there, she'd known that something had happened to him. She had even asked Mr. Harvey—whose patience at Ricky's absence from work, as well as his forgiveness for the items that had been broken at the landmark, was beginning to disappear—if anything had happened to him at Chambers House that day, but Mr. Harvey had only answered that he hadn't been there himself, and Ricky had better come back soon, because there were special groups coming through soon, and the work had to get done by Ricky or someone else. Mr. Harvey's regret at saying "Someone else," was evident, but so was his resolve.

Finally, on the eve of the third day of his bed-taking, after a day of seventy-five degree temperatures and beautiful breezes, and high layered clouds like sheets of heavenly gauze breaking the deep blue, after yet again turning his friends Spook and Reesa and Charlie away, without even seeing them, she went into his room in the light of dropping evening and pulled the hard-back desk chair close to his bed and made him look at her.

"This has got to stop, Ricky," she said, fighting to keep her voice firm. He had rustled away from her when she came in, and lay staring at the white plaster of his wall.

After a silence she said, "You hear me?"

"Yes, Mum," he replied.

"Roll over, boy. Look at me."

He did as he was told, finding her large face filled with concern and love. She lay the back of her hand gently on his cheek and withdrew it. "This isn't my Ricky. You're looking at me from some dark place." She brushed his cheek again, feeling the tremor in his flesh. "Tell me."

He almost told her. Instead, he decided what he must do. Down inside, in a dark place he was not accustomed to being, he fought the little demon that wanted to tell her everything, make her wash the pain off him, making it her own, as if he were her little boy again. But he was not a little boy and could not do that.

In the dark place, he controlled the tremor in his skin, turned his face into part of a smile.

"It's a girl, Mum," he lied, but even in his lie a relief

flooded through him because he was able even to pretend to unburden himself to her.

"Oh?" She lifted her face up, and the only dim surprise she registered told Ricky that he had hit something along the lines of what she had expected. "And who would this girl be?"

"I . . . can't tell you that." He was filled with panic, not knowing where to go next.

"I see." She was silent, turning her face away from him, hands in her lap, thinking. Ricky knew for certain now that he had said the right thing.

She turned her face back to him, patting her hand on his knee below the sheet and leaving it there. "I had a feeling we might be having this talk someday," she said. "Thinking about this day coming made me wish—and that was the only time I ever wished such a thing—that you had been born a girl. For I don't really know how to go about it." She looked away uncomfortably, then back at him with a level gaze. "Did you get her pregnant?"

"What?" Ricky almost laughed. "Why, no, Mum, of course not!"

He saw her task immediately made easier. "Then what is this trouble? Do you feel love for her and she doesn't love you?"

Ricky reached quickly, thinking of Reesa. "She loves me, Mum. But she already has a boyfriend."

"I *see*." His mother now seemed to be relishing her role, playing out daytime soap opera plots in her mind. He imagined she knew whom he was talking about. "And would this boyfriend be one of your *best* friends?"

So caught in his own lie that he half-believed it now, Ricky blushed.

"Ah," his mother said. She squeezed his leg and stood up leisurely, reaching around to rub at her back. Ricky saw that there was a smile, a sad, perhaps memory-drenched, smile on her face.

"Ricky," she said tenderly, looking down at him with all the love a mother could contain (down in the dark place he trembled, seeing her, briefly, flat on a table with three screwdrivers in her chest and the look of "Why?" on her frozen features), "Ricky boy, there's nothing anyone can do for you. You're filled with love like a puppy, and you have to let things work their way out. It's something we all do." She gave a relieved sigh. "You had me so worried! Ricky," she said, putting her hand to his face, "this will pass. Believe me it will. What I say may sound foolish to you now, and may *be* foolish, but we all must be our own fools in our own way. One thing I know," she said, slapping his cheek playfully, "is that you cannot stay in bed forever. You have to drink up sunshine. And rain, too. You have to live in the world. Now get up out of your bed and let your problems live in the world, not in your poor head."

She smacked him again, and he found himself almost laughing—and then actually laughing, sliding on the bed away from her playful smacks, finally yelling, "All right! All right, Mum!" He hopped out of bed. "I'm up! See me? I'm up!"

"Good boy!" she said, taking his face in her hands and kissing his forehead. "Now go outside where you belong." She shook her head and sighed as she walked from the room. "Oh, for heaven," she added as she walked from the room, "it's times like these I wish your papa were still alive . . ."

Twenty minutes later, Ricky was heading to Spook's house on his motorbike. It was the only thing he could do. A false burden had been lifted from him by his mother; perhaps Spook could help to lift the real one.

Spook was not home; nor was Spook's father. The lawn chair sat empty on the front lawn. Of course, Spook's father would be at work. It was Saturday, and his shifts had begun to run through both Saturday and Sunday, leaving him two days midweek to sit on his lawn and get quietly drunk and think about his rotten wife, Spook's mother, who was a fine woman but never good enough.

There was only one place that Spook would be. Feeling a twinge of guilt at the story he had just told his mother, and feeling a tiny guilty poke because he really *had* begun to notice Reesa as more than one of the chums, and maybe if Charlie didn't want her for anything more than a friend there might be a chance for him with her yet, he gunned the motorbike onto James Road and off the long sidestreet down to the ferry dock.

They were all there. A ferry had just left, tooting its horn merrily, tourists waving lazily at the three of them, and at Charlie especially, who was wet and had obviously just completed one of his trick dives into the water. Sometimes he jumped in and held to the bottom of the boat with his flat palms, letting it take him out until he had to breathe and pushed himself away and up, popping through the surface like a dolphin, then swimming slowly, clownishly, back to the dock.

"Did I miss much?" Ricky said, trying to put on a convincing smile.

"Ho! Who's this fellow!" Charlie crowed, still huffing from his swim, dripping water to the concrete. Reesa smiled and Spook held his hand over his heart and stumbled back in mock surprise.

"Risen from the dead!" Spook said.

Coldness went into Ricky, but he held his smile.

"Say, what's been wrong with you?" Charlie said. "Been sick or something?"

Ricky nodded simply. "Much better now. How's it going?"

"Same as ever," Spook said. He came up close to Ricky, peered into his face. He did it in jest, but something he saw there made him start. "Sure you're all better, Ricky?"

Ricky flashed a smile and hit Spook on the back. "Bad cold, Spook. Just about gone."

Charlie was toweling himself off; behind him, over the water, the ferry boat had dwindled to a paddling churn of water and steel and wood. The late afternoon sky was lowering; the sun had become orange, and there was the slightest of chills in the air.

Charlie shivered, finished with rubbing his hair, and folded the towel under his arm. "Coming, Reesa?" he said, approaching his bike.

"Sure," she said. She came to Ricky and looked at him; his guilt rose again briefly as she smiled. "Missed you, Ricky."

He nodded as she turned to retrieve her own bike from

against its wall and mounted it to ride off after Charlie. "See you!" she called back.

"Sure!" Ricky shouted with false brightness.

When he looked back at Spook, he saw that he hadn't fooled his best friend for a moment.

"Let's talk about it," Spook said.

In the approaching dusk they sat on Spook's front lawn. The rum bottle had found its way out from the bushes. "The old man's on till midnight," Spook explained. "Mum won't be home till nine."

They passed the rum and sat in silence. The clouds were high soft wedges, bottoms tinged with sunset. The breeze brought sea smell to them.

Spook drank, then said, "So tell me, Ricky boy."

Ricky stared at the passed rum bottle for a few moments, then drank from it quickly. "There's a ghost in Chambers House."

There was true silence, and then Spook exploded in laughter. "What!"

"No joking, Spook. There's a ghost and I saw it. It talked to me."

Spook fumbled for something in the near-dark. He abruptly turned to Ricky and hissed, widening his eyes, opening his mouth, showing off the glowing plastic vampire teeth he had put on.

"I said no joking, Spook," Ricky said quietly.

Spook continued to stare at him; he reached into his mouth and took the plastic teeth off and put them away.

"It was a *real* ghost, Spook—"

"There *aren't* any real monsters, Ricky—didn't you know that?"

"I'm not talking about your stories, Spook, I'm talking about something real."

Spook took the bottle from Ricky's hand and drank. "That's just the point, Ricky boy. They're *all* stories. You think H. P. Lovecraft believed all that crazy stuff he wrote? It's just *stories*. For *fun*."

Ricky looked at his friend, and then he told him everything, including Mr. Harvey's stories, right through the horrible vision Ricky had been shown in the cellar. Somewhere in the middle of the telling, Spook began to drink seriously from the rum bottle. At the end, he stared at Ricky and laughed.

"Man, you ought to write that down, make some money on it."

Anger, born of frustration and alcohol, crested up through Ricky. *"I told—"*

"Settle down, boy. Settle down." Spook put one of his large hands out and checked Ricky's forehead for fever. "Ricky, you're as sane as the night. You have to show me this ghost."

"No." Ricky stood up, knocking the lawn chair over.

Spook looked up at him calmly, cradling the nearly empty rum bottle in his hands. "I said take me there, Ricky, or there's no way I can believe you."

"It said it would hurt you! It said it would hurt all of you if I didn't do what it said!"

"And what was that?"

"Nothing, yet. But I *know* it doesn't want anyone else near."

"How do you know that, Ricky?" Spook said reasonably. A bright, captivated gleam had come into his eyes.

"Well . . ."

"Exactly!" Spook rose from his chair, handing Ricky the rum to finish. "Wait here, Ricky boy, and then we'll do what we have to do."

Not wanting to think, Ricky finished the rum in his hand. But thoughts flooded him. He had been desperate to share his frightening secret with someone; now that he had, fear had grown to encompass guilt. A dim part of him said that he was right to trust in Spook's knowledge; the brighter, keener edge of his mind said that he had merely acted a coward and dragged his friend into his problem.

He saw the night, the darkened clouds moving across the winking stars, the close-cropped sweep of Bermuda leading to the ocean spread before him over Spook's front lawn. And suddenly a fear so deep and true and cold possessed him that he was out of his chair, nearly weeping, and trying to kick start his bike when Spook reappeared.

"Ricky, what you doing!"

A stifled sob escaped him; he kicked and kicked at the starter, but it wouldn't catch.

"This is how you do it," Spook said from behind him. Spook mounted the bike, forced Ricky's foot away from the pedal, and instantly snapped it down into life with his own sneaker.

They tore down the driveway into the road. Spook laughed. "Don't you worry about any old ghosts." He held a zippered bag up in front of Ricky's face. "Everything we need to fight ghosts is in here."

Spook laughed again, and Ricky, finally, gave himself up to the relief of having his friend with him.

The shutters at Chambers House were closed tight. That in itself made Ricky feel the beginnings of security, because that was the way it was supposed to be. They rode the bike through the gate and up to the front porch, dismounted, and Ricky leaned it against the steps.

Spook was already bounding up to the front door, flashlight pulled from the kit bag and snapped on, its beam bouncing up the stair.

"No, the back door," Ricky said.

Spook bounded ahead, then waited impatiently while Ricky fished his key from his pocket. He took Spook's hand with the flashlight and swung the beam toward the kitchen window next to the back door. It, too, was shuttered tight.

"All right," Ricky said, breathing deeply, and pushed the key into the lock, snapping the metallic mechanism open.

The door swung back into darkness.

They hesitated on the threshold. Spook handed Ricky the flashlight and told him to shine it on his kit bag. He opened it and rummaged around inside, getting Ricky to pull the light right over the lip of the bag. "Son of a . . ." Spook said, but then he said, "Ah," and pulled two large crucifixes out of the bag, handing one to Ricky.

"You think this is a *vampire*, Spook?" Ricky asked. His faith in his friend began to evaporate.

"Nothing evil can stand up to the cross," Spook said. "I've made a study of it. In the books, a ghost is nothing by itself. To act, it has to have power behind it. If it's an evil power, the crucifix will guard against it."

Spook stared at his friend levelly. "*Believe* me, Ricky boy."

Eager to prove his point, Spook snapped closed the kit bag, took the flashlight from Ricky, and pushed ahead into the house.

He moved past the opening to the kitchen, ignoring it. Ricky, following, looked in to see, for the briefest time, in the moving shadows of the flashlight, another shadow move against it.

"Oh, Jesus, Spook," he said, clutching his friend's arm, pointing into the kitchen. "Something's in there."

"Let's see." Spook moved into the kitchen entrance, nearly filling it with his bulk. He played the flashlight over the floor, the ledge, the fireplace grate, the ceiling, the furniture.

"Don't see anything, Ricky boy," he said. He rotated the beam out of the room toward the back door they had entered, stopping it dead.

"Oh, Jesus, yourself," he said.

The door was closed.

Spook leaned forward to try the knob. The flashlight went out. He turned his attention from the door in the dark and pushed the flashlight switch back and forth. It clicked, but there was no light. "Shit, boy," he said. Only the tiniest cracks of light leaked through the tight wooden shutters into the house. Spook reached out in the darkness and pulled on the door.

It wouldn't move.

"I say shit again," Spook said.

He held his crucifix out like an offering. "Ricky?"

There was no answer.

"Ricky boy?" he called out loudly, hearing the faintest of echoes as his voice sank into the deep corners of the house.

He reached farther into darkness, expecting to find Ricky cowering against the wall. No one was there. Wedging the kit bag under his arm, he held the flashlight in his right hand and desperately snapped the switch back and forth. "Friggin' ghosts," he said. He wedged the crucifix under his arm with the kit bag and began to shake the flashlight.

Faintly, he heard his friend call him.

"Ricky, that you?"

Again he heard his own night-echo, followed by the faintest of answers.

"Yes . . ." Ricky's voice said.

"Where are you, Ricky boy?" Spook shouted.

There came no immediate answer—and then he heard Ricky singing.

A light went on somewhere down the hall. At first Spook was blinded, but his eyes adjusted quickly. The light was segregated within the frame of an open doorway.

"Ricky, what you doing?"

Ricky was singing loudly Bob Marley's "Redemption Song." His voice seemed to come from the lighted doorway.

Spook put the flashlight in his back pocket and replaced it in his hand with the crucifix. Cautiously, he moved toward the open door.

He stopped and looked into it. Steps led down.

The cellar.

Ricky's voice was definitely coming from the cellar. Now he was singing a song Spook didn't know, something Bob Marley might have written with different words:

"*Spook, oh Spook . . .*
Come down the cell-ah . . .
Spook, say Spook . . .
(I say now) Come down the cell-ah . . ."

"Ricky?" Spook shouted down into the cellar, and suddenly Ricky's singing stopped. He heard his friend laugh.

"Ricky, you been playing tricks on me?" he shouted, the first trace of hysteria coloring his voice.

Ricky's laugh suddenly ended, and he said, "Oh, Spook, I'm so sorry. I didn't mean to frighten you bad. Just a joke."

"The whole thing?"

"Yes, Spook." Ricky sounded sorry. "A joke to scare you a little. You and your foolish scary beliefs."

"The flashlight, Ricky—"

Ricky laughed so good-naturedly. "I fixed it when you gave it to me to hold. A little twist on the top to loosen it."

Spook fished the flashlight out of his back pocket, and sure enough, the top was loose. When he twisted it back on, the light flared up in his face.

"Come on down here, Spook!" he heard Charlie say, and then he heard Reesa's laughter, too.

"Didn't mean to scare you bad," Ricky said. "Just a little surprise. We have a party all set up! Mr. Harvey is gone all week and I thought—"

"You *thought*!" Spook howled. His feigned rage turned to laughter. He gathered his things and stamped down the stairs. "You rascals, I'll—"

The door above him slammed shut. He saw below the ceiling line that the cellar was empty of everything but a swinging, sour low-watt bulb and some dusty shelves and a long wooden table.

"Come down, Spook," a voice said, a female voice, and then the swinging bulb went out and his flashlight went out, and as he fumbled vainly with his crucifix, he was pulled down the stairs and began to scream.

Ricky was having a most wonderful dream. He was in New York City, in a grand long black limousine, with an open top. The lights of the city shone down upon him like stars. People hung from the windows of the tall buildings and dropped confetti and their best wishes on him. They loved him. He loved them.

The limousine stopped under the largest marquee Ricky had ever seen. It loomed out over Broadway itself, nearly covering the street. Written in huge black letters against the lit white background was his name, RICKY SMITH, and under it, APPEARING TONIGHT! In front of the theater was a huge crowd of people waiting to see, to touch, him. Police made a path for him. He threw his cape back and left the limousine and walked through the people, stopping to wave, or nod, or kiss a dainty female hand. The line waiting to see him stretched down Broadway as far as he could see, to meet with the stoplights, the horizon.

He went through crystal glass doors, under crystal chandeliers that showed his smiling self in a thousand perfect miniatures. Someone took his top hat and his cape.

There was a blink in time, and he was on a darkened stage. He waited for the lights to go on above him, and he held his cane very tight. He heard the audience rustle, waiting for him to dance. But the lights didn't go on. He began to be afraid. The audience began to make noise. Someone screamed, and he clutched his cane—

Ricky awoke in the kitchen of Chambers House, curled on the floor, in darkness. He held something in his hand. His cane? He felt along its surface in the dark. It was a crucifix. He heard screaming.

The screams intensified to a short series of pain-filled brays, then ceased.

"Spook?" Ricky called out, trembling.

"Here, Ricky boy," he heard.

Then he saw the beam of the flashlight cut across the opening to the kitchen.

"Where are you, Spook?"

"Come see, Ricky," Spook said excitedly.

Ricky stood and felt his way to the kitchen opening. The flashlight still bobbed out in the hall. He looked around the corner at it and was blinded.

"What are you doing, Spook?"

His friend laughed, a hearty pleased laugh. "I got your ghost, Ricky boy."

"Don't be kidding me!" Ricky shouted, rounding the corner, getting the flashlight in his eyes again. "Lower that thing, Spook!"

The flashlight beam was lowered toward the floor. Ricky saw the outline of his friend standing by the open cellar door. Fainter yellow light backlit him into shadow.

"In the cellar?" Ricky said, his fear returning. "She showed me things in the cellar—"

"The cellar was the place she didn't want you to *go*,

Ricky. The place where she hid her power.'' Spook laughed again, delighted with himself. ''It's where I *got* her!''

Ricky paced forward. The flashlight beam followed his feet until he stood next to his friend. The flashlight turned toward the cellar. Ricky felt his friend's heavy hand on his shoulder.

''Ricky, let me show you!''

The firm grip of Spook's hand pushed Ricky on, down into the cellar. The light at the bottom was on. When he reached the bottom, he saw nothing but smooth dusty floor and the bookcases that formed the storage area.

''Where . . . ?'' he said, trying to turn his head to face his friend, but Spook's hand merely squeezed Ricky's neck, and his happy voice said, ''In the back.''

Ricky's stomach tightened as he crossed toward the storage area. The memories of what he had been shown—the horrible mutilated bodies of his friends and family—came fresh into his mind. ''Spook—''

''Go on, Ricky.''

''I don't want to.''

''Go *on,* Ricky boy!'' Spook's voice said. But now it was coming from behind the bookcases. It sounded as if Spook had thrown his voice. Ricky turned to ask Spook, but the hand on his neck became very cold and thin and held him very tight. Where Spook's hand had been, he felt small strong fingers with nails longer than a man's.

''God, no,'' Ricky said. The iron grip of the hand pushed him forward as if he were attached to a machine. It steered him around the open end of the bookcases to the storage area.

''*No!*'' Ricky wailed. He saw blood against the far wall. The iron hand propelled him on. Below the blood was a *thing,* a crushed melon of a thing, that had been Spook's head. It lay upon his sitting, rag-doll-looking body as if it might collapse into itself at any moment.

The cold hand pushed him down toward the blood on the wall. Toward the head.

''Oh, God, oh, Lord . . .''

His face hovered six inches from Spook's destroyed head. He heard the settling of bodily fluids down in his body, the drip of crushed matter.

''Please! No!'' he begged.

Spook's head twitched; then, slowly, it rose up into itself, a pulpy misshapen mass. The eyes opened and the mouth opened and smiled and then laughed.

"Ricky boy! Too late for old Spook! Should have listened to her, Ricky!"

Parts of the head collapsed, leaving a smashed ridge of bloody moving mouth. The eyes melted out of the head and dripped over onto Spook's body.

"Should have listened!"

Ricky thrashed against the vise grip that held him as he was pushed down closer to the gurgling, flapping mouth.

"Should . . . have . . . listened . . ."

What was left of the head gave a sound like an egg being opened. Then it spilled over away from the red-fleshed neck cavity.

"Let me go!" Ricky screamed.

The grip pressed him down close over the open neck.

"Oh . . . God . . . Ricky. . . ." he heard, down inside, retreating into the distance.

There was silence.

The voice that went with the iron hand, the female's voice, said, "Here's what you're going to do." The hand squeezed Ricky's neck so hard he felt he would black out. "If you don't do *exactly* what I say, right now, the rest of them will be down here looking like your friend in one hour. I'll start with Reesa. Do you understand?"

The hand held him so tight he could barely cry out, "Yes!"

"Listen . . ."

Thirty five minutes later, his motorbike abandoned against a nearby tree, Ricky stood before the huge, gleaming, spotlighted length of the cruiseship S.S. *Eiderhorn*. Its height, its row upon row of tiny round portholes, its triple, massive smokestacks, completely dwarfed the pier. In the night, in the brilliance of its illumination, its stark colors of black and white and red, it was a beautiful, dreamlike thing. Ricky had seen it a thousand times; it docked in Hamilton Harbor every Tuesday, bringing tourists from New York City, mostly old people with a hunger for sweater and rum shopping, and every Saturday, like this Saturday, it pulled its anchor, turned, and headed back the way it came.

As Ricky watched, trembling, waiting for the hand on his shoulder to guide him, a steam horn blasted proudly into the night, signaling last call.

"Aboard!" someone shouted.

Across the street, a clutch of last-minute shoppers hurried toward the ship. One beautiful black woman, holding her hat on and managing to wave at the *Eiderhorn* with her other hand, which clutched four huge shopping bags, was followed to the gangplank by ten or twelve others.

"Now," the cold female voice said to Ricky. The cold hand propelled him forward until his path suddenly intersected that of the running woman with the packages.

"May I help you, ma'am?" the cold voice said beside Ricky. Only now it wasn't cold, but warm, filled with charm, much like Ricky's own voice. Ricky's head was pressed down, and not waiting for an answer, his hand was shoved toward the woman's shopping bags.

"Why—yes!" the startled woman replied. Ricky took three of the bags and bounded ahead of her up the gangplank. As Ricky reached the porter above, the cold hand turned his head down toward the woman and the voice, so much like his own, said, loud enough so that the porter but not the woman, would hear: "Meet you in the room, Auntie!"

The hand on his neck propelled Ricky forward. After twenty yards the voice, cold again, said, "Put down the bags," which he did. It pushed him on.

He was guided to a stairwell, and they descended. The bright deck gave way to softly illumined passageways. The ship was being readied for departure, and busy employees passed. No one questioned him. They continued downward; the lights became less soft, more infrequent.

Finally, they reached the bowels of the ship.

The hand forced Ricky to sit. He felt something buzzing at his back; felt the metal deck beneath him vibrating with a different tone. Far off, he heard the sound of hissing steam. He was in near darkness.

The grip on his neck loosened. Ricky felt out along the

walls. His hand found a bucket with a mop in it, a shelf close over his head. In front of him was metal deck, a metal sliding door that was open a crack.

The door slid closed.

The grip, near-strangulation, returned to his neck.

"Stay here until the ship arrives in New York. If you don't, I'll take you back to Chambers House. Understand?"

Choking, wanting to weep, Ricky nodded.

"Good," the female voice said. It softened, the grip on his neck turning to caress. In the darkness, the hand touched his face.

"Don't cry, Ricky boy," the voice said, suddenly sweet. "Your dream is going to come true."

12. BRENNAN

Ted Brennan turned on his meter at three o'clock in the afternoon and found that the batteries were dead. "Shit," he said, carefully removing one of the dangerous lead cells, which sparked meekly as it came away from its contacts. He had spares; he remembered bringing them with him, but he couldn't find them. After rummaging through his camera bag, his briefcase, the gadget bag that he kept the meter in (the most logical place for replacement batteries—therefore, the least likely place for them to be: and, of course, they weren't there), he gave up and was feeling into the pocket of his raincoat, which was draped over a chair in the living room, for cigarettes, when his fingers came across the plastic bag containing the extras.

"Bully for serendipity," he said to himself, sarcastically. He ripped open the battery package and pulled the cells out.

He spent the next five minutes smoking, trying every possible combination of alignment before he got the batteries to work.

He was about to light another cigarette when he suddenly remembered his father's simple statement: "You smoke, you die.'' Those four words had worked better at making him at least *think* about stopping than all the antismoking campaigns and all the born-again nonsmokers he knew: the same assholes who had chain-dragged two or three packs of Camels a day in medical school, on top of whatever weed was around, and laughed when anyone—especially any *doctor,* tried to tell them what they were doing to themselves. They weren't doing shit, seemed to be the response; they were twenty-fucking-four years old and the only thing that was going to kill them was if the president pushed the wrong button on his bedside table while fumbling around for his teeth, and blew all the medical students and all the people in all the world, straight to atoms. Which was pretty much out of their hands.

But Ted Brennan was thirty-eight now, along with all those born-again jerks who had formerly been friends (they were born again about *everything*, it seemed—kids, conservatism, even religion), and some of the messages of middle age were getting through to him.

''You smoke, you die.''

The image of his father, the famous surgeon, lying wasted to whiteness on his hospital bed at the age of fifty-seven, his lungs riddled with healthy cancer cells eating him alive, pointing to Ted's own cigarette pack but pointing just as well to all the two-packs-a-day he himself had smoked over forty years of his addiction, rose into Ted's mind. The weary gesture that went with the statement, which held so much more than a deathbed warning about smoking, got through to Ted.

''Ted, I'm sorry,'' his father had said.

''Please tell me.''

His father had tried to rise on the bed, couldn't find the strength. He'd fallen back, exhausted, pale as the sheets that engulfed him. ''I can't.''

''I have a right to know.''

His father had nodded, wearily. ''Yes. But my promise . . .''

You smoke, you die . . .

Brennan crushed the second cigarette out, which he had unconsciously lit while deciding not to smoke it.

Back to work.

With a grunt, he rose and went back to the bedroom.

All the windows were open; had been, the landlord, Beauvaque, told him, since the girl had left two days before. Beauvaque had done nothing but whine from the time Ted had tracked him down in his top-floor apartment—the best in the building, facing out over the Rideau Canal. The landlord's apartment had smelled of heavy perfume. A lot of cats were moving around in it. Beauvaque wore a flowing paisley robe, and his eyes, outlined in eye shadow, showed nothing as Ted explained why he wanted to see the apartment. Then, holding his slim white hand out, giving Brennan what was supposed to be a soulful look, which had come across as sad and calculated, Beauvaque had dropped the key into Ted's palm.

"The police wouldn't like it if they knew I gave you this, sugar," the landlord had said. "You *do* appreciate this?"

"I certainly do." Ted had answered, leaving the landlord as quickly as possible. He had expected a return visit from the man by now, but so far he had been left alone.

The batteries in place, Brennan turned on the meter.

"Jesus," he said to himself. The meter reading was higher than he had ever seen it.

A flare of hope went through him. Maybe—

Take it easy, Ted.

He had been through this kind of thing enough times before. Often what started out as a routine poltergeist event showed some quirk that promised more—but, inevitably, the house of cards built on hope would tumble down, and he would be left with anything from a hoax to another paranormal event with no proof and no chance that it was part of what he sought. The standard always remained, in the end, just that—standard.

Still, he knew that soon, maybe this time—

Take it easy.

Standard, if anything, was the way this had looked up until now. Laura Hutchin's own notebook, which Beauvaque had hidden from the police and given to Ted, had maintained that there had been poltergeist activity the first night: drawers pulled open, silverware scattered, a message, seemingly from her parents, carved into the wooden counter in the kitchen. Even what had followed was standard enough, pointing to something worse than a hoax: a disturbed person acting out a psychosis in a paranormal framework.

The single time he had met Laura Hutchins, two weeks before, she had impressed him as neurotic. She had haltingly, and with some embarrassment, asked him if it was possible to contact her dead parents. She said there was an apartment her aunt and cousin had lived in in Canada, and supposedly it was haunted; she had rented it and perhaps she could contact her parents there. She had read an article about him in a magazine.

Brennan had given her the usual two-minute lecture about how he couldn't help her, maybe she wanted a medium; though in his opinion mediums were fun, but completely full of shit; he had politely listened to her stupid questions, then sent her on her way explaining that he was interested only in one certain type of paranormal event connected with one specific type of haunting, and that if she came across such a thing, she should certainly contact him, but otherwise please leave him alone. Along with her phone number, and the number of the apartment in Ottawa she insisted on giving him, he had described her in his logbook, as he did everybody who came to see him; a quick thumbnail sketch: *Laura Hutchins, 5'4", brown hair, brown eyes, nice breasts, serious demeanor, embarrassed but neurotically determined about contacting dead parents, nothing concrete to give me. Gave lecture, explained that popular articles like one she read about me were unauthorized bullshit. Obsessed enough to keep trying.*

That was all he knew of Laura Hutchins until he got back from a promising trip to Phoenix (a hoax, it turned out) to find a particularly frantic phone call from her on the tape machine. She had at least been smart enough to identify herself, leading him back to the thumbnail. The taped message was nearly hysterical: "Dr. Brennan, I've . . . just gotten off the phone with my boyfriend, oh, God, I hope the tape goes long enough, he's very mad at me, but I think I've found what you're looking for. I'm in the apartment in Ottawa I told you about, where my aunt and cousin died. I've only been here tonight and I've gotten a message; there were knives and forks scattered and—oh, damn, the tape is o—"

The tape ended there, but she was a smart girl and called him right back. She sounded more worked up now, barely identifying herself and going right back into it: "I . . . the knives and forks were out of the open drawer, and the drawer was pulled out [stopped to regain breath, sobbed a little, losing control; a count of ten and then she regained control]. Okay, I was on the phone with my boyfriend, Peter, and I had a waking dream, a hallucination *as I was holding the phone*. I saw my M and P—that's my mom and dad—I was *with them*, back home, when I was younger, and I was with my father, and M called both of us for supper—"

The second tape recording ended, followed immediately by a third. "Damn!" she screamed, then, "Oh, God, and then I put the phone down and I saw the kitchen counter next to the phone and it said 'Soon Love, M and P' on it; M and P are my mom and—[More hysteria, real crying, and he thought he heard her tell someone "No!" but he couldn't be sure; she had pulled the phone away from her mouth for a moment. She continued talking, rapidly.] They're my mom and dad, and Peter hung up the phone. I know he's going to come up here eventually; we had a fight—oh, God, I'm scared! The lights are going—["No!" he heard distinctly this time as she pulled the phone away again] The lights are on and off! I heard something in the other room." [Brennan had replayed this tape fifteen times, gone so far as to have it analyzed, but there was no other sound in the background.] "I just want to see them again! I want to tell them—oh, God, what's happening in here! Lights outside the window, too! Like lightning—"

He had run through the rest of his messages quickly, looking for any more: one call from his ex-wife ("Money! Money!"—His answer: "Fuck you! Fuck you!"), a computer voice from his bank trying to get him to take out a home equity loan. Then at the end of the tape, two days after the first calls (his wife had called again, reminding him that forty-eight hours had passed and that the rest of eternity would pass before he got to fuck her again), a final message from Laura Hutchins.

"God, Dr. Brennan, please listen to me! Come here, please! There . . . [part missing, a hiss spot] . . . things I see! I . . . [hiss/miss] . . . I can hear her talking to me! Her voice!

She says she'll take me to M and P. Her voice is *cutting into my head like a knife!* She . . . [more hissing till the tape runs off]."

That was all. A sound analyzation had shown nothing out of the ordinary: in the kitchen the faintest of hums, from the refrigerator. G.E. Model, probably. An intermittent tapping sound, semirhythmic, the girl tapping her fingernails nervously on some surface—the kitchen countertop, the wall. Nothing else.

So the question became whether to follow up or not. The Phoenix trip had depressed him. There was probably nothing to this, either. She sounded like a kook, and he would just be wasting his time.

Still, there had been one sentence on the tape that intrigued him: "She says she'll take me to M and P." And that insistent little pressure in the back of his mind, pushing him on . . .

He decided to follow up. But when he'd called Laura Hutchins on the phone, he'd gotten a disconnect message, and when he arrived in Ottawa, he discovered she was missing.

Brennan had asked the landlord point-blank about anything strange ever taking place in the apartment. Beauvaque had been evasive. "The apartment's been unavailable for quite a while," he said vaguely. "If I hadn't know that Hutchins girl's aunt and cousin, I wouldn't have let her have it."

"Laura Hutchins told me the apartment was haunted—"

"I wouldn't know about that," Beauvaque had snapped.

Was Laura Hutchins crazy? Possibly. Brennan had talked to her roommate and found that Laura had been depressed since her parents died, the year before. The roommate had hinted that Laura had been *too* close to her parents, that they had smothered her—an explanation for her obsessive-compulsive behavior. The roommate also said that Laura and Peter had fought over her parents, and that the fights had gotten worse.

He had come to Ottawa expecting to find the thumbnail sketch all too right, the voice on the telephone messages faked or delusional. He had expected to find overwhelming evidence of a psychotic episode.

He had fully expected to find another in a long line of dead ends.

Up until he had turned on the meter, he had still expected that. But now he had . . . hope?

Maybe this was the one he was meant to find—

Take it easy, Ted.

He did a slow circle around the bedroom. When he passed the closet, the needle jumped even higher. He pointed the meter at the closet, and the meter reading held, more than three quarters of the way up the scale.

"Jesus."

There was a cold, empty, unpleasant feeling in the pit of his stomach. It was as though his insides had been scooped out and filled with ice water.

A mixture of elation and fear.

He paced slowly toward the bedroom closet. He checked the meter reading; it was rising. The icy feeling became stronger.

He stepped into the closet.

The meter reading went off the scale.

Instantly, Brennan's head was filled with a blinding flash of light. It was as if someone had set off a flare behind his eyes. He stumbled back out of the closet. His legs found the bed, and he fell onto it.

He blinked furiously, a spot like the burn from a flashbulb filling the middle of his vision. When he closed his eyes, the spot flared green behind his eyelids; when he opened his eyes, he could see clearly around the edges for a moment, and then a blackness settled into the middle of his sight and spread outward.

He coldly realized that the effect was not going away.

Something moved in the room.

He pushed himself up on his elbows and blinked furiously at the closet. Green flash, sight at the edge (a figure dashing out of the closet at him?) and then blackness.

"Jesus."

There was commotion around the closet—scratching, something tapping on wood.

"Get away! Keep away from me!"

Something jumped onto the bed.

Brennan flinched. He felt the brush of fur against his side. He strained his eyes to see.

"Get away!" He swatted at the thing as it moved against him.

His hand struck something solid, covered in fur. It hissed, falling from the bed.

"Get—!"

"What *is* all this now?" a voice said. Brennan strained his eyes at the bedroom door. Fighting the edges of his vision, he saw a shape.

"What's going *on* here," the shape said. "Did he *hurt* you, Muffin?"

"Who is it?" Brennan shouted.

"Dr. Brennan, are you all *right*?"

With relief, Brennan recognized the voice: the landlord, Beauvaque. "I . . ." He waved his hands before him. "I can't see."

"My *Lord,*" Beauvaque said. Brennan tried to blink sight into his eyes (green flash, total blackness now; the green flash fading to black). He felt the weight of Beauvaque sitting on the bed; felt Muffin, the cat that was with him, move against his side, purring . . .

Fighting panic, Brennan said, "My retinas may have been burned out."

"Let's have a look," Beauvaque said.

Brennan acquiesced. Soft hands pressed lightly around his eyes, holding them gently open. He could feel the other man staring closely into his own eyes.

"I can't *see* anything wrong with them."

Beauvaque took his fingers from Brennan's face. Brennan stiffened as the other man squeezed his shoulder.

"Listen to me, Dr. Brennan. I used to be a nurse, in a real hospital. I'll take care of you."

Brennan sensed embarrassment.

"No touchy-feely, if that's what you're worried about, sugar. I'm not *like* that." Beauvaque snorted. "Come on, let's get you up."

With Beauvaque supporting him, Brennan got to his feet. He began to walk. He felt like he had been reborn in a world without light.

"We're coming to the door, Dr. Brennan."

He felt himself walk through the bedroom door.

Brennan felt himself leave the apartment, felt the rub of Muffin against his leg.

"My equipment," he protested, turning to look blindly back into the apartment.

"I'll get it later," Beauvaque said.

They stopped, and Brennan heard the landlord rattling keys, closing and locking the apartment door. "Right now let's worry about your eyes."

Brennan leaned on the other man for a moment as they stepped onto the elevator and quickly pulled back. He felt very tired and upset.

"Dr. Brennan, you're shivering!" Beauvaque said.

Suddenly, Brennan didn't mind the other man's closeness. He leaned into Beauvaque, and Beauvaque put his arm around Brennan's shoulder and held him.

"Poor boy," Beauvaque said, opening the door to his apartment.

In Beauvaque's bedroom, in the midst of the odor of cat and strong perfume under an army of quilts and blankets, Ted Brennan fell asleep sightless, shivering, with terrible fear and hope in his head.

13. EAST

The woman with hair on her chin came for him at seven o'clock. She usually came for him at eight. He was still curled asleep on his hard bed, face toward the damp wall, arm thrown over his face. He was dreaming about a turtle, a marvelous slow turtle, a dark clean shade of brown, with green mottles within its shell sections. It was as beautiful as painted ceramic, and its leathery legs, fresh from the water, were as clean as the rest of it. There was a spot of bright orange behind its wizened head; its eyes were like two tiny dark smooth pebbles. It blinked a dinosaur blink and moved from beach to a clean cut of green grass.

The turtle pulled into itself, becoming only a perfect piece of pottery. Jan started and blinked open his eyes. He saw white light against the walls instead of accustomed darkness.

He lifted his arm away from his face and turned his head over, yawning awake, to find the face of the woman with hair on her chin inches from his own.

She smiled at his surprise. He waited for her to lift her head away, but instead she lowered it, twisting her mouth sideways and opening it like a little animal and putting her mouth over his.

He jerked his head back, meeting the solid dampness of the wall behind him. She lifted her mouth slightly from his and said, "Don't."

He lay back and let her continue to kiss him. Her kiss was like dry paper. He thought of the remains of fallen leaves after their burning. Her eyes were open, looking into his. They were beautiful eyes, round, limpid, a shade between amber and chocolate. He found himself responding until she adjusted her mouth against his and he felt the curl of her chin hairs against his cheek. He suddenly wanted to vomit. But again she sensed his feelings. Once more she lifted her face from his and said, "Don't."

This time she smiled, sly, secret, her Mona Lisa smile, and stood up. He saw her almost as shadow in front of the overhead light. She stood up straight and lifted her cream work smock up over her head like a dress. She stood taut for a moment, relishing her own tenseness. He could sense her using the cold of the room, bathing herself in it. She wore nothing beneath. Jan was momentarily thankful that at least she was a woman, of which he had never been positive. During the brief time when her dress had been hiked up over her head, when he could only see her body, he became instantly aroused. Something told him that this was something he had better use, and by the time she had tossed her smock away he had lidded his eyes, not looking directly at her face. He knew that if he saw or thought of those chin hairs again he *would* vomit. He knew what kinds of horrors might follow such an episode.

She kept her taut ballet stance for an instant (her underarms were shaved—why in God's name didn't she excise the hair from her chin!), then quietly, almost sweetly, she said, "Remove your clothes."

Averting his eyes from her face, he removed his pants and pulled his prison top over his head and tossed it to the floor.

"Good." In a lithe balletlike movement she straddled and mounted him on the bed.

It was over in a moment. Holding him within her, she arched once and stayed there, straining every muscle in her body. Jan could hear her grunt with effort. Then there was a quick movement within her, and she had pulled from him what he had, nearly before he knew it. It was as if she had been a vacuum cleaner. Then she was off him, stretching, touching her toes, climbing quickly and efficiently back into her dress.

Without looking at him, she left the room.

She returned at eight o'clock. There was no change in her ordinary demeanor. It might have been her ghostly twin he had coupled with. They made their rounds of the corridors, as always ending eventually at the two doors.

"I'll choose for you today, Jan." She smiled, her secret smile. "Right."

The door opened, showing him the large attendant with the tight curls, the antiseptically white room.

"Pain," she said.

They strapped him onto the gurney, and there was pain.

When she took him back to his room, when he was crying, she whispered into his ear, delicately holding it between her thumb and forefinger, "Later."

And he saw what she meant, because she lifted the hem of her gown, showing him the long dried track of his seed on the inside of her thigh.

When she left him alone, he did vomit. There was only a bedpan in his room to contain it, and he barely pulled it out in time, noting with disgust that it had not been emptied while he was out. He heaved everything out of his stomach. It felt as though he was expunging everything he had ever eaten. He thought of the last meal his mother had made him, the cracked pot of oatmeal the police had left on the floor, and his retchings became uncontrollable. He felt he might pull up his own guts and spit them out, his own soul, along with everything else in the bedpan.

He began to gasp; he could not gain his breath. His retchings continued. But he was not breathing, only throwing little gasps of undigested food out of his mouth. He clutched his stomach and rolled onto the floor. He could not breathe. Ragged, convulsive heavings were coming out of him. He thought he might die. And then suddenly that was fine with him, because what was there but death, now that this *creature,* this vampire, had decided to victimize him. He had never had a woman, and now he had *this*. He had seen the full, mirrored look of satisfaction she had worn while sucking his seed from him. He had not given it. There had not been even a glimmer of mutuality. She had taken it, and would continue to take it—

Even through his gasping agony, he could hear the screams of the other inmates. There was one less scream tonight—the shrill, high keen of the very young man was gone. That explained it: she had killed him with her cold self-passion, or the pain had killed him, or he had succeeded in killing himself, and now Jan was hers. If he died, so be it; the pain, or the chin-haired vampire would get him eventually anyway. Let death come to him now.

He heard himself fighting for breath from a very long way off. A dark curtain, a velvet buffer, began to descend on him, and he heard another sound, a peaceful sighing, a giving way of self, that also came from him. He began to see himself sleeping, putting his hands under his head like a babe and sleeping . . .

Someone called, "Jan?"

"No!" he shouted through his dropping sleep, fearing it was the vampire's voice.

"Jan! It's me! Bridget!"

Her voice was so pure, so beautiful, more beautiful even than his acquiring sleep, that he rose on his hands, pushed himself up on his unfolding hands, and listened to her.

"Jan!" There was urgency in her voice as well as beauty.

"Yes?" he answered, not knowing if she could hear him.

"Jan! You can't go away!"

He loved Bridget, but he was nearing the other place and rest and sleep would be so good . . .

"Jan! YOU MUST NOT DIE!"

"I must . . ." he said.

"No! I'll get you out! I'll get you out of that terrible place!"

He felt her reaching for him, pulling him back.

Her voice mixed with the sound of his own coughing breath.

"Yes, Jan! Yes!"

His lungs filled full with air. He choked it out and began to breathe.

He opened his eyes, gagged, threw himself away from the mass of putrefaction in the bedpan.

He heard her say his name distinctly, softly.

She sat angelic on his bed. She wore the dress she had worn at the inn in Kolno. He trembled, remembering her touch. Her red hair shone like a halo; the freckles on her skin stood out in beautiful transluscence, tiny petals floating on milk. She looked pensive, disappointed.

"Jan, what did you almost do?" she said. She shuddered, her tiny body a single tremble.

"I . . . I'm sorry."

"Didn't you believe me?" When she looked up at him, her eyes were filled with tears.

"That . . . *vampire* took me! I wanted you to be the first, the only . . ."

He looked at her again; silent tracks of tears marked her face, and then, in an instant, she seemed to collapse into herself, becoming as small as a girl, weeping into her hands.

"Oh, Jan, Jan, I want you so badly, the thought that you would go away from me . . ."

Jan reached out, desperate to touch her. But his fingers moved right through her.

"I'm sorry," he said. He sat on the bed beside her and put his hands in his lap. "I'm so sorry." Suddenly he put his fists to the side of his head and squeezed. "God, I'm so confused!"

"Jan, I love you so much. If only you'll listen to me." She had stopped crying. Her eyes were large, puffy with tears. Her hair looked like spun red silk; framing her face, on the sides, where her tears had wet it, it glistened. Her hands had drying tears on them. Her face shone with a radiance Jan had only seen upon the moon at certain times, in its fullness, when it seemed, not dry dirt and blasted craters, but the shimmering face of Eve.

"Jan," she said, in a small voice, but she was looking directly at him, the blue eyes of the angel lighting into him like lamps. He shuddered when she put her own hand over his and he *felt* the soft, tear-wet flesh of it. "Do you love me?"

Tears leapt into his eyes. "You're the only thing that matters. The only thing in my life. I want to be with you always."

She held his hand over her breast, moving it down slightly so that he felt the swell and the rising hardness of her nipple. She smiled shyly and raised her other hand, putting a finger to her lips. "Then listen to me. I'm going to bring you to me. You're going to leave this place and come to me and be with me forever."

When the woman with hair on her chin came for him again in the afternoon, Jan was waiting for her at the door. He smiled at her meekly, and she returned his smile, briefly, chillingly, knowingly. She closed the door and turned to Jan.

"The bed," she said simply.

Instead, Jan put his hands around her neck.

She stiffened. She looked into Jan's eyes with contempt and reached to activate the call button on her belt.

Jan pushed her against the wall, holding her neck tight with one hand while ripping the call beeper from her grasping hands. He dropped it, returned both hands to her neck and redoubled the pressure.

"Die," he spat.

She hissed a loud silent scream, and her face turned bright red and then purple. Her eyes opened wide. The mottling of her face only made her look as ugly as she was—not the hidden deformity of the nun, but true ugliness. Jan's throttling hands lifted her off the ground. Her hanging was complete, free of gravity. A stain spread on her smock at her crotch as her face froze in place.

When Jan let go of her, the body collapsed to the floor and a hissing, her last breath, vented into the atmosphere.

Jan opened the door and stepped out into the hallway. He closed the door behind him.

"Quickly," Bridget's voice said close-by his ear. "As I told you."

He turned right and walked purposefully to the end of the

hallway. It was the beginning of a trip he had taken many times before. There followed a long, tense walk through the maze. Jan's heart seized as he recognized the turnoff for the hall with the two doors ("Pain!"). He heard the husky, deep, begging cries of the old woman, very close. He hurried on.

Soon he was in unfamiliar territory. There came to him the faint smell of cabbage, of other vegetables—carrots, potatoes, *meat*. These were smells he had not sampled in more than a month, and he stopped dead as if hypnotized, tasting them with his nostrils. "My God . . ." he said, beginning to tremble, a precursor to weeping.

"Jan! Go on!" Bridget urged.

He stumbled ahead, as if his roots had been pulled from the spot. The smells strengthened, and now there were voices—not cries of madness but laughter, true conversation. He passed a low wall, heard the clanking of silverware, the hiss of cooking steam. Two women's voices, arguing politics; one of them saying, "Walesa is a *great* man, a saint!" and the other grunting, giving in to the point, begrudgingly, "Well . . . maybe not a *saint*, though . . ."

Jan continued. There were office doors cut into the concrete walls now, painted a cheery blue, with smoked-glass windows set into them. He heard typing, the ring of a telephone.

"Turn left, Jan."

He thought of the woman with hair on her chin making him turn right, turn left. He nearly laughed in his nervousness.

"This one, Jan."

He had walked by an entrance. He felt Bridget close-by. He backtracked to stand before a large wooden door with no window, no sign on it, a smooth polished aluminum doorknob.

"Turn the doorknob and go in."

He rubbed his hands together, hesitating. Then down the hall he heard two voices, two men walking side by side, talking.

"*Go,*" Bridget said.

He turned the knob.

He entered a spacious office. There was an empty secretary's desk; behind her small partition, the room opened to luxurious dimensions. There was green, thick-piled carpeting on the floor. Plants in large pots bookended the filing cabinets. A deep red leather chair with a coat draped over it squatted in one corner. A long, polished wooden table abutted the far wall. Lit from above, it showed off models of several large sailing vessels. Against another wall, behind the partition, was a huge desk with chairs in front of it, and a tall leather swivel chair of the same wine-red color as the other.

"Walk," Bridget whispered.

Jan stepped around the partition and all the way into the room. A stout man with his uniform tie loosened sat behind the desk. In front of him on the desk was a bottle of vodka and two glasses, which he was filling. The bottle was half empty. He handed the second glass to a man who now sat down in the wine-colored swivel chair. The man in uniform behind the desk stopped pouring his own vodka and looked up at Jan; when the man on the other side of the desk turned to look at him also, Jan was startled to see how much he resembled himself.

"Who are you?" the stout man behind the desk said, in a curt, hoarse voice.

"Go to the coat and reach inside the right pocket," Bridget said. Jan strode across the room, lifted the coat from the leather chair and drew a pistol from its pocket. A fat silencer was screwed onto the barrel.

"Use it," Bridget's voice said, urgently.

"What—" the stout official was saying, rising from his chair as Jan turned and shot him in the chest and throat. He sat down heavily, blood pouring copiously from his mouth and down over his uniform. He tried to gag the flow, to speak or scream. Jan shot him again, and his face erupted in blood. He fell forward to the desk.

Jan turned the gun to the other man, who stood and stepped back, away from the desk. He looked at Jan calmly and moved lithely into the center of the room. He was dressed impeccably, Italian tailoring, his thin red tie knotted to perfection.

"I'm sure this shooting is none of my business," he said to Jan, beginning in Russian and then repeating and changing to Polish. "You're Polish Intelligence, I take it? I'm sure our friend Stefan here had his enemies." He smiled, and now Jan saw how nervous he really was. "What I'm saying is," he said, his cool demeanor beginning to crumble, his eyes darting left and right, back to Jan, searching for any kind of opening, "I hope we can work something out."

"Shoot him, Jan," Bridget said.

Jan aimed. The man looked at Jan imploringly, and Jan hesitated. "Damn it, man, call Roskolov in Moscow! He's KGB like me! He knew about the smuggling—it was all so *innocent*! A few cases a month! One of them went to Roskolov for his Kremlin buddies. Hell, two can go to *you* if you want!"

"Shoot him," Bridget repeated.

Jan fired a single shot into the man's forehead. "You . . . can . . ." the man choked out, before he collapsed and was silent.

"Quickly, Jan—take his clothes."

Jan went to the man, trying not to look at his contorted face as he removed his clothing. Everything was nearly a perfect fit, even his shoes, which were of fine leather and looked English.

"Under the desk, take the briefcase," Bridget said. "Button the jacket and put on the topcoat."

Jan did as he was told, putting the gun into the coat's right-hand pocket. There was even a scarf, bright red, which he wrapped around his neck.

"Go."

Jan put his hand to the doorknob, and after drawing a breath, he turned it and opened the door.

He stepped confidently out into the hall.

Bridget guided him back the way they had come, until he turned abruptly into an offshoot of the main passage. He passed more offices. There were more sounds of typing and paper shuffling. He kept his head down, looking thoughtful, his briefcase swinging easily at his side. Two more turns. Suddenly he was in a large hallway.

He was hit with a sense of déjà vu. He had seen this place once before—and then he knew it. His eyes registered the huge steel doors in front of the elevator.

"Step up to the elevator," Bridget said, "and wait for it to open."

Jan did as he was told, holding his briefcase in both hands

before him until the doors slid back. "In," Bridget said. "Tell the operator to take you all the way up."

Jan did so, noting the gray uniformed man in the corner who eyed him with boredom. He waved his finger at the man, indicating that they should go up.

"Ground level?"

Jan glared at him, and suddenly the operator went rigid and pale.

"I'm *sorry,*" the man stuttered. "I didn't recognize you for a moment, sir. It's . . . it's been a long day."

Jan broke off his glare to regard the doors in front of him. The elevator man fumbled to bring the elevator into service.

There was a bump and then a jerk upward. The elevator rose.

It seemed a half hour went by. Jan had the feeling the elevator was moving slowly, but there was also the impression of rising through a great amount of earth. Jan could feel the pressure lessen in his ears. He nearly became light-headed.

The elevator jerked to a stop. The operator fumbled with the door mechanism, giving short glances at Jan, who remained impassive.

The doors opened.

Jan squinted and put a hand up before his eyes at the brightness that hit him. He hadn't realized just how dark the underground world had been, how few lightbulbs there had been, strung far apart and of dim wattage.

The smells of the earth assaulted him. He must have swooned, for the elevator operator was at his side, blubbering, giving aid. Jan stood straight and pulled away from the man, who immediately scrambled back into his doorway and closed the doors.

Jan could faintly hear the slow machine returning to the bowels of the earth.

It was late afternoon. Jan smelled wet leaves, cut grass, maple trees. He smelled pine sap. His nose was assaulted with the odors of mown hay, far off, and apples and pears. It was as if his nose had never been used before. He smelled motor oil, and rain, though the ground was dry. There were thickly stacked white-gray clouds overhead, moving toward twilight, and the sun was orange and tinged the edges of the clouds orange. He *smelled* winter coming, far off, beginning to gain strength and stretch its limbs and think about its season.

He stood on a spot of tarmac; behind him, the elevator doors were set back in a barnlike building that looked for all the world like a farmer's storage area. He had a feeling he was in the extreme north of the country. Empty, harvested fields stretched off to a strong-looking chain-link fence about a quarter mile away. To Jan's left was parked a Soviet limousine, angled away from neatly painted parking spots that held three Polish automobiles.

The car door opened on the limo, and a man got out. He stood up next to his open door and regarded Jan.

"Lower your head and get in the car," Bridget told him.

Jan stiffened.

"He won't know the difference. And he's Polish, so you can tell him whatever you want."

Jan straightened his coat and walked over to the car.

The driver bowed and opened the back door. Jan got in. The door slammed shut behind him.

He nearly gasped at the accommodations. A long leather backseat was flanked on one end by a bar, on the other with a writing desk complete with telephone (red! Jan noticed). There was a television and radio set into the partition between driver and passenger.

Bridget told Jan to tap on the partition window. The driver slid back a small window.

"Yes?" the driver inquired.

Following Bridget's instructions, Jan said, "Take me to the airport immediately. Does your phone work up front?"

"Yes, sir."

"Very well. Estimate our time of arrival and tell them to have my plane ready to go by the time we get there. Tell them we are going to New York. Call my office in Moscow and tell them the same. There is very important business at the embassy in New York that I have to attend to. Tell them I'll be back in two days. I'm going to take a nap now. Don't disturb me until we get to the plane."

"Yes, sir."

The partition slid closed.

As the limousine pulled away, Jan saw another car pull up before the elevator doors. Two men got out of the back. Then the driver emerged from the front. Jan recognized them immediately. They were the three who had tracked him down like a dog and taken him to this place. The leader still wore his same trench coat. The other two argued as they pulled a limp body from the backseat and propped it upright. Jan saw faint movement as the prisoner tried to stand on his own. The two thugs holding him let him go, and he collapsed, falling forward and striking his head on the tarmac. The two thugs laughed.

"Enough!" the trench-coated man said. They picked their prisoner up under either arm and dragged him toward the elevator.

A bolt of hate and remembrance shot through Jan; angrily, he reached to pull open the partition between himself and his driver to tell the man to stop.

"No," Bridget said, close-by. It sounded as if she were curled like a kitten next to him. Jan felt the weight of her hand on his lap, working its way inside the coat to his belt. "Think about me, Jan. Think about what it will be like when we're together."

Jan's eyes were glued to the retreating image of the three men stumbling their prisoner toward the elevator doors.

"Think about me, only me," Bridget cooed in his ear.

Jan felt the beginnings of arousal. He glanced at his lap to see that she had placed his hand where hers had been.

"Think of me, Jan. All of me," she purred.

"Yes," Jan said, suddenly very aware of her presence, aware that she was everything to him.

"Yes . . ."

14. THE ASSISTANT

I'm going to kill her.

And after they had been getting along so well. The last two weeks, in particular, had been heaven. Bridget had warned him that there might be a little work coming up at the end of October, but in the meantime, he could enjoy the calm before the storm. A couple of trips upstate was all she had asked, stocking supplies, things like that, and the rest of the time he had had to himself. He had almost begun to believe that the "storm," the busy times she had talked about, wouldn't come at all.

And then—boom!—all at once. She had woke him out of a sound sleep, the first he had had in four nights, since Mr. Felligan liked to play blackjack until all hours of the morning. The old fool didn't get off work until midnight, and Gary had had to listen to stories till the sun came up about how Felligan would not be a night watchman forever. "Temporary! Temporary!" Felligan always reminded him, his bent finger in the air next to his head, his thin, balding head rigid, his foolish little dreamer's eyes lost in his dreams. "Ah, Gary, I can't tell you how wonderful it'll be, me a croupier in Atlantic City, ever since I seen that Burt Lancaster movie *Atlantic City,* Burt, that's me, me with that little redheaded piece of ass, what's her name, Sarandon—Susan Sarandon—the one in that baseball movie, yeah, that's me, Burt Lancaster, I'll be happy down there, did I tell you I was born by the saltwater, Gary, I can't tell you how much I 'ppreciate you helping me practice it and all, won't be long now, I can tell you, the money's in the bank, five hundred dollars and this time next year I'll be living off that boardwalk, one of them not too fancy boarding houses, just a few more hundred dollars if I could just stay away from the ponies, that goddamn exacta, guy that invented that should be shot for taking the money right out of my wallet, did I say five hundred in the bank? well, maybe like two hundred or a hundred, but it won't be long, Gary, no sir . . .'' It wouldn't be long before Felligan dreamed forever, the long dream. But then Bridget had woken him up out of that good sleep, his first in four nights, and told him there was work to do.

That hadn't gotten him so mad. She had done that before, always apologizing. She had this time, but there was an urgency to her that made him feel she was telling him, not asking him. That he didn't like. It was one thing for her to ask his help, another for her to tell him to drive upstate *right away* and get things ready.

And that was only the beginning. He drove around for her like a madman the next two days, which put Felligan completely on the back burner (''See you early next week, Burt''—*for the last time,* Gary didn't add, and Felligan had only snuffled and wheezed in the self-pitying, disgusting way he had, and said, ''If you *must,* Gary, if you *must* . . .).

But the thing that had *really* gotten to Gary, had made him decide that there might be a score to settle (unless she *really* made this up to him, which, so far, she had not), was her insistence that he suddenly turn *bellhop* and *chauffeur*. It had started out easily enough, with the arrival of the strange-looking girl from Ottawa who had driven down in an old Honda that smelled like spilled beer and piss. All he'd had to do was drive the foul-smelling thing around back and park it in the weeds.

But the next day he had been back up there, just waiting

like a bellhop until, about four-thirty in the afternoon, a limo half as long as the block had pulled into the drive, letting out a skinny young man in a topcoat and red scarf, speaking English with a foreign accent, with the craziest smile on his face Gary had ever seen.

Up till then he had put up with it. But the next day, after he had finally driven back down to the city, with an ache in the back of his neck, and parked out on the street, running up to his apartment to get a change of clothes before going out to meet Felligan, the phone had rung and she had told him to rent a van, *now*.

"My car's on the street. Let me just park it in the garage."

"*Immediately,* Gary."

That was the first time he had felt her order him to do something, instead of ask, the first time he had ever really felt her anger. That made him mad.

But what really made him mad was that it had scared him.

So he had gotten the van and picked up the third delivery at LaGuardia Airport. It was a cripple in a wheelchair, coked out of his mind, a twenty year old with the eyes of a hundred-year-old man (okay, so Gary understood why the van, he'd never have gotten the goddamn wheelchair in the Datsun), and then after driving all the way upstate and then back to the city again, he'd found that his Datsun had been towed.

He'd almost lost it, right there on the street. What he remembered himself doing was putting big dents in the side of the van with his fists and then whacking at it with a discarded umbrella, blood rushing to his eyes—then suddenly realizing what he was doing, that a crowd was forming. He had stumbled away and into his building just before real notice was taken of him (the crowd had mostly been interested, not alarmed, these were New Yorkers, you could have sold peanuts) and up to his apartment. Mrs. Fogelman had got on the elevator with him, appearing it seemed out of nowhere, her bland, self-absorbed face seeing but not registering his rage as she began her litany, "You know, Gary, your mother was a good woman. I wonder if they'll ever do something about the heat in this building. It's been a little cold the last few nights, don't you think? Your mother . . ." If Gary had had a weapon on him, he might have killed her, knifing her throat right out of her neck, *just to shut her up*. But he had managed to stumble out of the elevator to his apartment door, getting the key into the lock, opening the door, thinking all these bad thoughts about Bridget and the way she had been treating him—

The phone was ringing. Automatically, he picked it up, put it to his ear.

"Gary," she said, her voice subsumed in static. "You have to go out once more, tonight. There's a ship getting in from Bermuda at the Forty-sixth Street pier, the S.S. *Eiderhorn*. A boy on it named Ricky . . ."

Gary went blind with fury. *"They took my car."*

She laughed. "You'll have another car. All the cars you want."

Gary's anger was undiminished. "I want Felligan. Now."

Her voice hardened, the way it had when she had first frightened him. But he was too enraged to be frightened now. "When you've finished—"

"I said now!" Gary began to hyperventilate. A memory bolted through his head: himself at four years old, on the floor, face flushed red, pounding on the floor with his fists, his feet, getting up to punch the walls, his mother impassionately saying, "It will do you no good to throw a tantrum, young man," before turning back to talk intimately with the man who sat on the sofa with her, giggling laughter at something the man said into her ear as Gary screamed and railed and beat at his own body till he wept, curling in on himself, looking out at her on the couch as the man put his hands on her, and Gary wanted her *to look only at him* . . .

"You won't get me to do ANYTHING for you! Not ANYTHING!" he screamed into the phone.

He continued to scream.

There was silence on the other end of the phone when he stopped screaming. He didn't know how much time had passed. He looked out the window, through the slatted blinds. It was dark. He stretched the phone cord to the hall and looked at the round clock on the wall: eight o'clock.

He walked back into the living room, easing the phone

cord, and now registered the ripped carpet in the center of the living room, the scratches on the china hutch (his mother's china hutch) next to the phone. The wall around the phone was scored, chunks of plaster gone. On the floor under it was the tiny pocketknife he carried as a key chain. The blade was bent.

"Gary?"

Her tone had changed. She sounded the way she had when she had first called him. She sounded like a friend, someone who understood him.

"I treated you badly, Gary, and I'm sorry."

"It's all right," he said.

"Will you forgive me?"

How could he not forgive her? How could he hold anything back from her, who understood him, knew what was in him? "Yes."

She sighed, as if she had been afraid he would refuse her.

"Are you all right, Gary?"

"Yes, I'm all right."

"These past few days . . . I've been very thoughtless, selfish. I've just had so much to do. I don't want you to think that I ever don't appreciate the little things you do for me, Gary."

"Sometimes I do."

"That's why I'm sorry. You don't know how happy I was that day you broke into the house and I was able to talk to you. You don't know how long I had waited for someone like you. You have to admit you didn't recognize your greatness, your invincibility, until I told you of it. You're a great man, Gary."

He was silent for a moment. "Yes."

"Sometimes I forget that. Selfishness is a terrible thing."

"It is."

"You're invincible, Gary. Just like I told you. I may have been busy, but I haven't forgotten that."

"Yes."

"Are you very upset about your car?"

"No. It's all right."

"You could get it back tomorrow, you know."

"Yes, that would be all right."

"After tonight, Gary, I won't need you again. You'll be free to do whatever you want. I *want* you to do whatever makes you happy."

Gary was silent.

"Tonight is the last thing I'll ever ask of you."

"All right."

"Gary." The way she said his name, with pride, as if it meant something—formed a lump in his throat.

"I'll leave now," he said.

"Thank you, Gary. Thank you."

He heard her voice fade into the static, and he put the phone down. Felligan could wait one more night.

He put his change of clothes away, put his duffel bag back into his closet. He straightened the living room, sweeping the pulls from the carpet, putting the furniture back into place. By the time he got down to the van in the garage, he was whistling.

Invincible.

Maybe he wouldn't have to kill Bridget after all.

The Forty-sixth Street pier was jammed with traffic. He could see why: the huge, brightly lit S.S. *Eiderhorn* was just nosing in. But Gary was lucky. A minibus from an earlier arrival shot out of a parking space right next to the debarking area just ahead of him. He pulled immediately into it. He was whistling again as he got out of the van and slammed the door.

Huge ship, huge passenger list. There were families lined up like Noah's animals against the railing, smiling in the artificial light, searching for a sign of their newly tanned loved ones.

Gary waited next to the open door of the van. He wished the damn thing had a tape deck so he could listen to some good jazz. A momentary flash of anger bolted through him; all of his tapes were in his impounded car. He balled his fist, then relaxed it, slowing his breathing. He'd get the car tomorrow, no problem. He'd get the fucking car, and soon he would have any car he wanted, just like she said. He was invincible, and soon, *very soon,* he could have anything he wanted.

He saw someone that looked like his pickup.

At the top of the ramp, a young boy was leaning over the railing looking down at the pier. He looked confused. He moved in place, mingling with a group of tourists debarking the ship, disappearing in the midst of their bags and hats and loud laughing voices.

At the bottom of the ramp, just past the steward, he appeared again when the laughing group, gaily dressed, carnival in the sodium-vapor lamps, moved on, leaving him behind, staring into space.

Gary left the van and moved up close to him. This was the one. The kid stared up into his face as Gary took his arm, registering little. "Come on," Gary said, pulling him toward the van. He followed. He seemed weak, ready to stumble, light as a feather.

Whistling, Gary let go of the kid's arm at the side of the van and slid open the cargo door. "Get in," he said. The kid followed meekly, stumbling on the second step up into the cab. "Whoa," Gary said, laughing, and caught him under the arm, lifting him up onto the seat. The kid stared at him for a moment.

"Who are you?" he asked tepidly.

Gary shrugged, then laughed. "Maybe I'm your worst fucking nightmare."

The kid lay down on the bench seat of the van and stared glassily through the window as Gary slid the door shut with a bang.

Gary pulled out onto Forty-sixth Street and headed across town. He flipped on the digital radio, finding an all-talk show. He dialed up and down, looking for something listenable on the AM band, and finally gave up in disgust, leaving the radio on a country-western station.

They hit Broadway and Gary turned downtown as Bridget had directed. She'd told him to drive through the theater district. The lights got brighter. He felt a rustling from the backseat. When he checked the rearview mirror, the black kid was sitting up, staring out the window. They were crossing Forty-second Street now, and the sex show signs and movie marquees brightened and then gave way to theater marquees—The Shubert, the Nederlander.

Gary looked into the rearview mirror again and then turned around in his seat. The black kid had his face pressed against the glass of the side window. He was trying to clutch at the glass. Tears streamed down his face. He was making low moaning noises.

"What the fuck is wrong with you?" Gary snapped. He reached back, slapping at the kid's knees with the flat of his hand. He swerved back into the middle lane, just avoiding a taxi that had shot out of Thirty-fourth Street into his path. The moaning noises continued in the back.

"Shut up!" Gary screamed, turning quickly to hit at the kid again. But Ricky had already turned from the window and was quieting down, curling up onto the bench seat.

Gary shot crosstown to the FDR Drive, up the Third Avenue Bridge, and then the Deegan Expressway. When he got to the Saw Mill River Parkway, he played with the radio again. This time he found a station playing Dave Brubeck. He tapped out the rhythms of "Take Five" on the steering wheel. The station, a college one, Fordham or Columbia, then played an entire Art Farmer record.

By the time the college station faded into static, he was past Poughkeepsie. He snapped off the radio and checked the cargo in the back. The kid was asleep, tight in a fetal position.

Fifteen minutes later, Gary left the Taconic. He maneuvered twenty more minutes through town and out into the countryside. The moon was up; everything looked cold and clean. Gary passed a few houses with jack-o'lanterns on their porches and remembered that it was almost Halloween.

He caught a quick glimpse of the house from the rise that led down to its valley. The thin glint of silver from the stream shone in moonlight. Two windows were filled with illumination—one up at the cupola, the other on the ground floor: one of the living room lamps.

Five minutes later he pulled into the driveway, then off that to the half-circle offshoot that curled around to the front of the house. The porch light was off. He switched off the engine and got out of the van.

He slid back the door. The black kid stirred. The dome light was on. The kid shivered, tried to roll into a tighter ball.

"Ride's over, kid," Gary said. He punched the kid on the thigh.

Ricky shivered again.

"Get out."

Ricky began to cry. He wouldn't open his eyes.

Gary breathed deeply, trying to keep down his impatience. He pulled at the kid's pant leg. Ricky pulled his leg up tight, rolling into a more compact form.

Gary put his foot up on the step and reached into the van, yanking the kid up off the bench seat.

"Get the fuck out," he said.

"God no, God no," Ricky moaned, sobbing freely.

Gary tightened his fist and punched at Ricky ribs. He landed two solid blows. Ricky's answer was to pull himself up even tighter.

"Fuck!" Gary shouted. He breath turned ragged and hard. He stalked to the back of the van, yanked open the door. He put his hand into the back well, searching until his fingers closed around the cold shaft of the tire jack's crowbar. He hefted it out and took three hard steps back to the side of the van.

"Get out!" He pumped the tire iron over his head and reached in, pulling with all his strength. He jerked Ricky up onto the seat, then out of the van.

Ricky fell to the road and lay moaning.

"You little *fucker,*" Gary spat, raising the tire iron in one hand and then transferring it to two.

"Gary."

It was Bridget. He wheeled around, facing empty night.

"Leave him there," her voice said, somewhere close-by. "Go home."

"I'm fucking invincible!" Gary shouted.

"Yes, but you have to leave him alone."

"I don't have to do anything! You hear me? I DON'T HAVE TO DO ANYTHING!"

He shouted, raising the tire iron high and bringing it down with all his strength on the kid's head.

But Ricky wasn't there. The jack hit driveway. Gary grunted with the dull shock.

"Where the fuck—?"

"He's safe," she said. "I told you I need him."

"You fucking bitch—" Gary began. His words were cut in midsentence. The tire iron was pulled from his hands. It struck him on the left side under his arm. He heard ribs crack. He dropped to his knees.

His vision cleared as the iron bar hit him again. A hot pain tore through his right forearm. Almost immediately, his shoulder went bright with pain and then numbness.

"*Je-sus,*" he grunted, collapsing.

The tire iron hit him on his right ankle and again on his shoulder.

"Do you want more?" Bridget laughed.

"I'll . . . kill . . . you . . ."

The iron struck his left knee. A blossom of white pain opened in his leg.

"Listen carefully, Gary. Leave now. If you come back, I'll kill you." The iron bar struck across his back.

"I'm . . . invin . . . cible," Gary gasped.

She laughed. "You never were."

"I'm invin . . ." he insisted, but the fall of the tire iron on his right elbow ended his protestations.

"Last chance, Gary."

Groaning, he pushed himself to his knees. Holding the side of the van, he pulled himself to his feet. He stood gasping, then leaned his way around the van to the driver's side and crawled in. When he sat up straight over the wheel, his eyes went blind with pain. He sat breathing heavily over the wheel until he could see again.

"Good-bye, Gary," he heard her laugh, close-by his ear.

He twisted the ignition key. The engine roared out of sleep.

He slammed the shift into reverse, backing down into the driveway.

Clouds were moving in, and in the peek-a-boo moonlight, he saw Ricky. He was lying where Gary had left him, the tire iron next to him on the tarmac.

Gary gunned the van back down the long drive to the

street, barely missing a sturdy oak butting on the side of the drive.

Half doubled over, blinking sweat and grogginess from his eyes, he roared off toward the Taconic Parkway.

As it began to drizzle an hour later on the Major Deegan Expressway, he put the accelerator pedal to the floor and drove into the side of an overpass.

He awoke sometime later, alive. There was a fireman in a black slicker and hat standing over him. A cold rain was falling; red and white flashing lights reflected off the fireman's wet uniform.

"Buddy," the fireman said to him, "can you move?"

Slowly, Gary stood, only the retreating aches of the tire-iron beating making him wince.

In the cold rain, the fireman helped him up.

"You sure you're okay?"

"I'm fine," Gary said.

"Damnedest thing I ever saw," the fireman said. "You have any idea how far you were thrown?"

"No."

The fireman pointed at the still burning, smoking, black, ruined mass of metal that had been the van, twenty-five feet away.

The fireman patted him on the back. "You should be real dead, my friend. Whoever you pray to, I think you owe him thanks."

The fireman walked back to his truck, shaking his head.

Gary stood in the rain, watching the van burn blacker, and suddenly he laughed.

"I *AM* INVINCIBLE!" he shouted up at the rain.

And I'm going to kill her.

15. BRENNAN

He was at the circus with his father. They were sitting in wonderful seats, in the front row, and Ted had a huge box of popcorn in one hand and a magnificent pink wad of cotton candy on a stick in his other hand. It was his birthday, and he was nine years old.

He had looked forward to this day for two months. His father had promised him the circus, promised him he would free his schedule of surgery and spend the entire afternoon with him. They had gotten there early and watched the clowns practice their routines. One of the clowns had come over and stood before Ted and performed for him alone, juggling and lighting matches that disappeared into his mouth and then reappeared lit again and, finally, doing a trick with his hat that made it shoot off his orange wig with a popping explosion. It had been a wonderful afternoon, with three rings performing simultaneously, with trapeze artists and a lion tamer and a man who rode a motorcycle around the inside of a wire cage while torch flames licked at the tires.

And then, about halfway through the show, as Ted put the popcorn down between his knees to concentrate on the cotton candy, some of whose pink spiderweb strands were already stuck to his cheeks, he heard the one sound he had thought he would not hear today, the soft insistent sound of his father's beeper.

"Damn," his father said, taking his cigarette from his mouth and grinding it out with his shoe, reaching to push the button on the pager.

"You promised you wouldn't bring it!" Ted protested.

His father's face bore a mixture of remorse and worry. "I'm sorry, Ted, it's Mrs. Morris, who I told you about. I thought for sure that Dr. Parks would be able to handle it—"

"You promised! You promised!" Ted had risen from his seat, knocking the huge tub of popcorn over. His face was flushed red, his eyes filling with hot tears.

His father put his hand on Ted's shoulder. "I'm truly sorry, son. I'll call Mrs. Jacobsen, and she'll come stay with you the rest of the day."

"I don't want my nanny!"

His father squeezed Ted's shoulder, bending low, trying to quiet the boy. "Ted, please, I have to go."

"No!" Ted thrust the pink cloud of cotton candy up at his father, who warded off the blow with his hands, immersing them in the sticky mass.

Ted stood trembling, tears tracking his cheeks as his father quietly extricated himself from the cotton candy.

An usher appeared, and when Ted's father explained the situation, the usher offered to stay until Ted's nanny arrived.

His father began to move toward the aisle; as he reached it, he paused and glanced back at Ted, a pleading for understanding in his eyes.

"I want my mother!" Ted screamed. His father hurried up the aisle. "All of my friends have mothers. I want my mother . . ."

In the dream, the circus darkened, and now Ted was in a night place. He was very young. He heard a mixture of voices, away from where he was. He was on his back, and where he was was quiet and dark.

A crack of light appeared in the room, and he strained to see. When his eyes were open, he saw blurs; in the day, different colors, fuzzy blue and yellows. But the blurs were getting sharper. Today, for the first time, he had seen the edge of something hanging above him: a yellow thing smiling, with wings.

The crack of light widened; more light entered the room.

He heard voices, louder.

Someone crying.

He knew the crying voice; he became very excited when it came near. The other voices stayed back. He began to kick his legs, move his hands expectantly.

She was crying. She leaned down over him. She rose like the moon above him, her face, and she murmured something to him, a crying sweet thing, and then she came close and kissed him, a warm tear on his cheek, a blur, but as she pulled away the blur began to sharpen—

And then another voice came into the room, and came close, and put a blanket on him, and his mother's crying went away, and he become afraid, and for a moment as he was lifted, the blanket covered his just-focusing eyes, and he was blinded, and he panicked and began to scream—

Brennan awoke.

"God."

"You needn't call me that, sugar," a yawning voice said.

Brennan sat up in bed. Beauvaque rose from a chair in the corner of the room. He wore a long red robe. He stretched his arms up, then rubbed his back. "*Lord,* these chairs weren't meant to be *slept* in." His hooded eyes regarded Brennan. "You can *see* this morning, sugar?"

Full realization that he had regained his sight gripped Brennan. "Yes!"

"Ah."

Beauvaque brushed something from the chair he had been in. It was one of the cats, a black shorthair with one white ear. It jumped onto the bed, purring, and began to knead at Brennan's foot under the covers.

"I do believe he *likes* you," Beauvaque said, sitting on the end of the bed. He petted the cat. "I should tell you," he continued, fixing Brennan with a fiercely even look, "that he hardly likes *anybody*."

Brennan wondered briefly if Beauvaque was actually jealous of the cat's affection for him. He pulled his foot away beneath the covers, but the cat merely followed, pushing at it with his front paws, purring.

"My, my," Beauvaque said, pulling his hand away from the cat.

"Perhaps I should leave," Brennan said.

Beauvaque looked at him as if seeing him for the first time. "Oh, no, don't you worry about leaving just yet, sugar. I wouldn't *hear* of it. Not before you tell me just what happened to you yesterday. And I *must* insist on making you the finest breakfast you've ever had."

Brennan sensed that he, at least, was not the source of Beauvaque's anger, which suddenly flared again as Beauvaque rose from the bed and slammed his fist into his palm.

"Is something wrong?" Brennan asked.

Beauvaque turned away from him, bringing his knuckles up to his mouth. Brennan heard a muffled sob.

"Are you all right?" Brennan said.

Beauvaque waved a hand behind his back at him; his body heaved in short sobbing gasps.

"Don't . . . worry about . . . *me,* sugar."

Brennan felt trapped. Even the black cat seemed to have him, pouncing on his foot each time he slid it away, holding and biting at it beneath the sheets.

Beauvaque turned around. As abruptly as his outburst began it was gone. He wiped at his eyes with one hand, holding his robe tightly closed with the other. "Don't mind me."

"Are you sure—"

"I was just being foolish. And *old.*" He smiled, unconvincingly. "That's what I am, you know."

Brennan said nothing.

"Tell me," Beauvaque said, sitting back on the bed. His dried eyes were focused on Brennan with full attention. "What happened in that apartment yesterday?"

"I went blind," Brennan said.

Beauvaque motioned impatiently. "I *know* that already. Tell me what *happened.*"

Brennan considered, saw no harm in being honest (thumbnail of Beauvaque: old queen capable of spite and kindness but not dishonesty; likes gossip but doesn't like getting involved. Safe—thank God).

"I think," Brennan said, "I was attacked."

"Ah," Beauvaque said. He added, unblinking, "By *who*?"

Brennan sat up, putting his back against the backboard. The cat followed his movements, jumping twice at folds in the blanket before finding Brennan's foot. "I don't know."

"You think something didn't want you snooping in there, sugar?"

Brennan's mind, recalling the mixture of hope and fear he had felt the previous day, missed the urgency in Beauvaque's voice.

"Something . . . *bad*?" Beauvaque said, in a tone so sharp that Brennan's attention refocused on him.

"Yes."

"Ah."

Beauvaque rose, clutching his robe closed as he paced the room. He stopped before the blinds, toyed with the rod to open them, kept them closed. "Dr. Brennan," Beauvaque said, slowly, turning to face him. The look was the angriest he had seen yet from the landlord. "I . . ."

His face collapsed into anguish, and once again he bit his knuckles, so hard that Brennan was alarmed to see a thin trickle of blood run down the back of Beauvaque's hand.

"*God* . . . you just don't *know* how much it hurts, Dr. Brennan. *No one knows* . . ."

"Maybe if you told—"

"I'M *TRYING* TO TELL YOU!" Beauvaque shouted. His face, flushed red, was twisted in anguish. He thrust his bloody knuckles back into his mouth and then covered his face with his hands. A sobbing groan escaped him. "Oh, *God* . . ."

Brennan's fingers had strayed to rub the belly of the black cat, which had rolled onto its side in the hollow of the thigh, accepting his gift with typical feline nonchalance.

"I'm sorry," Beauvaque said. He lowered his bloody hand, dabbing at it with a handkerchief produced from the pocket of his robe. With relative success, he composed himself. He walked to the end of the bed, began to lower himself to sit on it, changed his mind. He stood straight; still uncomfortable, he walked stiffly back to the window. Once again, he fingered the rod that opened and closed the blinds, opening them a crack this time and staring out.

"I have a very strange story to tell you." He looked quickly at Brennan, catching his impassive look. "Will you listen?"

"Yes."

Beauvaque went to the club chair in the corner and sat down. His face fell in half-shadow. When he spoke again, his voice had assumed the dreamy cadence of painful recollection. He looked toward the window that held out the day, staring at it in a kind of trance.

"He was a beautiful boy." He cast a sharp look at Brennan. "Of course, that's how you would *expect* me to start something like this."

Brennan said nothing.

"But he *was* beautiful," Beauvaque continued, dreamily. "I don't think many people—even *gay* people—understand that a person can be truly loved for his beauty alone, without all the sexual business entering into it. Believe me, Dr. Brennan, it can happen."

Again Beauvaque looked to Brennan for reaction.

Brennan said, "I understand."

"This was almost four years ago. He lived in that apartment you were in. The one that girl was in. He was eleven then, he would not have been fifteen, yet."

Beauvaque paused. "You must remember how *hard* this is for me."

"Yes."

Beauvaque stared at the window. "He was so *beautiful*. When I first saw him, his mother was holding his hand. They were moving into a new apartment, and she kept him close to her.

"God, how I wanted to be that woman. I wanted to hold him the way she was holding him. He was the kind of boy who was lost. He needed to be protected. You could see that on his face, Dr. Brennan. Even his mother knew that."

Beauvaque took a deep, shuddering breath. "So they moved in. And I acted like a fool. The mother didn't see through me—at least not at the beginning. She was a fluttery type, so caught up in her own little problems that the rest of the world barely existed for her. But Jeffrey knew from the start. He *knew* why I was always making excuses to see the two of them, to check up on the apartment, make sure the heating was working, the plumbing was all right, to share a particularly nice flower I had found while walking. Oh, yes, I'm *sure* he knew about me. It was terrible of me, Dr. Brennan, but I just couldn't keep my eyes off him. I began to dream about him at night, about enfolding him in my arms like a baby. In my dreams I sang to him. Oh, *God* . . ."

He took another halting breath and, after a brief pause, continued. "Perhaps if I describe him to you. He was frail, but not short. Almost as tall as his mother. I never saw him play ball. I never saw his mother let him play with another child. For that reason alone I pitied him, because *I* would have let him play, would have encouraged him to make friends.

"It was his face that captivated me, Mr. Brennan. It had the beauty that only some Mediterranean faces can have. His skin was dark, his hair the deepest and straightest black I've ever seen. He was always pushing it up and to the side because it would hang down over his right eye. And his *eyes*. They were set deep in his face. They were the most liquid brown I have ever seen. They say it isn't the eyeball itself that makes the eye, that it's the expression of the facial skin around eyes that make them expressive, but in this case I would have to disagree. I would know those brown eyes, that color of brown, anywhere. I'm sure no one else on earth had those eyes.

"He liked to draw. I was able to study his hands. They were long-fingered. He bit his nails. I would have persuaded him to stop that terrible habit . . ."

He stopped; and Brennan took the opportunity to shift his back, which had begun to hurt. He moved his leg away from the lounging cat, which rolled farther onto its back than it wanted to. It gave Brennan a reproachful look before settling into a new position.

"Dr. Brennan, I must admit I had fantasies of stealing that boy." Beauvaque's voice was a near-whisper. "I went so far as to make a plan. I was going to take him to Vancouver with me, to a place where I had been once, a resort town that would be safe for us. I was going to raise him myself."

A smile touched and then abandoned Beauvaque's lips. "I never got so close as to actually try it, though. The planning was a way of relieving my agony. Then a real agony came, Dr. Brennan, which began as the sweetest time in my life."

Beauvaque rose, began to pace. "I began to see Jeffrey, on my own. His mother had come to trust me. When she started to work hours that would not get her home in time to meet Jeffrey's school bus, she allowed me to keep him company for an hour. She was *very* grateful, Dr. Brennan." Again the sad, fleeting smile.

"I don't think I'd ever been happier in my life. I don't think Jeffrey minded me. I think he sensed that I would be better at the job than his own mother. After a while I think he began to rely on me. We went places during our short time together each day. We went for walks or shopping at the market. He let me arrange his clothes. His mother even let me buy him clothing. His *wardrobe* certainly improved."

Beauvaque's voice softened to a chilling whisper. "And then he changed."

A line of cold crawled up Brennan's back. Beauvaque stood rigid in the half light, staring into nothingness. Brennan could almost physically feel the loss the other man was expressing.

"It happened quite suddenly, Dr. Brennan. At first, I became afraid that he had said something to his mother about my attentions, how I doted on him, or sang to him, or read him poems or brushed his hair. But that wasn't it.

"It was a Friday, I remember very clearly. His mother had asked me to keep him longer because she had to work late. I, of course, agreed. But I had to show an apartment, and so I arranged for Jeffrey to stay locked in his home between four and four-thirty. Then, I told him, I would take him for ice cream. That had seemed fine with him. I still remember his smile as he closed the door, promising not to open it for anyone else while I was gone.

"I was gone no longer than forty-five minutes. A young man and his bitchy wife went over every inch of the empty apartment, then began to haggle about the rent. After wasting all of my time, the woman—I can remember her bad blonde hair coloring: the roots showed mousey brown—took her husband by the arm and said, 'Let's go.' They left without a word of thanks.

"I was angry. By the time I arrived at Jeffrey's apartment, I was talking to myself, venting my spleen. I froze at the door because I heard voices within. Two voices. Jeffrey's and another. A woman's, but not his mother's.

"I knocked. I'm afraid I lost my composure. I was fearful he had opened the door to a stranger. I knocked very hard. I shouted, 'Jeffrey, open this door at once!'

"There was silence inside. I shouted louder. Then he opened the door and stared at me. He looked . . . guilty. As if I had caught him doing something bad.

" 'Jeffrey, who is *in* this apartment with you?' I said. I stormed past him to see who it was he had been talking to.

"Well, Dr. Brennan, the apartment was empty. I checked it top to bottom. When I confronted him, he shrugged evasively and said it was the television I had heard.

"I *knew* it wasn't the television. I *knew* it. I was sure he was lying to me.

"The rest of the afternoon was a disaster. I think my own mood eventually turned Jeffrey sour, also. We ended up not speaking to one another. Even his cow of a mother noticed that something was wrong between us when she got home.

"I don't know if he said something to her then. But for the next two weeks I barely saw him. His mother was on vacation and was there to spend time with him. But it seemed that something had happened to turn her against me. As the two weeks came to an end, I delicately asked if she would need me to watch him again, and she declined. She was gracious enough. I would have to say she looked genuinely perplexed. Which led me to believe the breakup was Jeffrey's doing.

"Of course I was in agony. I blamed myself for my outburst. I told myself I should have trusted him when he told me no one had been in the apartment. There is nothing worse than mistrust. I began to have terrible dreams of Jeffrey going away, leaving by himself, leaving me behind.

"Dr. Brennan, I took to doing terrible things. It was unbearable for me not to see him. I began to sneak around, trying to catch a glimpse of him. But during that two weeks he never left his apartment, and after that, he left only to go to school. He stayed in when he came home. His mother had not been able to find anyone to watch him for the hour after school, and so he locked himself in the apartment alone each day.

"I stood outside the apartment when I couldn't stand it any longer. I was like a lovesick adolescent. I suppose that's what I was. But then I began to hear that voice again and became mortally afraid. My vigils became motivated by fear for his safety.

"I never heard the words that were spoken between Jeffrey and that voice, Dr. Brennan. They were just below my threshold of hearing. I think they were back in that room where Miss Hutchins did those horrible things. I can't be sure. When I did see Jeffrey, as he left for school in the morning or returned in the afternoon, he looked terrible.

"He looked haunted, Dr. Brennan. As I said, he was not a healthy-looking boy to begin with, but now he looked as though what health he possessed was being drained out of him.

"I was frantic. One night, when I couldn't sleep, I snuck like a thief and stood outside their door. I think I wept. Then I heard that high, thin female voice, and Jeffrey's voice in answer, and I suddenly became very jealous and angry. I nearly pounded on the door.

"There was only one thing for me to do. The next evening, when Jeffrey's mother came home from work, carrying a bag of groceries, I was waiting by her apartment door.

"She would not look at me, Dr. Brennan. She tried to hurry past, as if I had some sort of disease. I think she was *afraid* of me.

"I tried to speak to her, but she turned red and tried to push me away from her with the bag of groceries.

"I tried again to speak to her. My voice was climbing to hysteria. She was trying desperately to fit her key in her door. She dropped her groceries and turned on me.

" 'Don't you ever touch my son again,' she spat at me. 'If you even go *near* him the police will visit you.'

"I tried to tell her there was something wrong with Jeffrey. But she pushed me away.

" 'You *disgust* me! You're little more than a *woman*!'

"Once again I tried to warn her about Jeffrey.

" 'Do you think you'd make a better mother than *me*?' she shrieked. 'I *hear* you at night, talking to him, singing to him, turning him against me. How do you do it? Are there wires in the walls? Do you use your *key* and sneak in? *I know you're stealing him from me!*'

" 'Please,' I said.

"She struck out at me with her fist. 'You can't have my boy! No one can take my boy from me!'

"With that, Dr. Brennan, she gathered up her fallen groceries and went into her apartment. She slammed the door in my face.

"I tried," Beauvaque went on after a few moments, looking down at his hands, "to talk to her again. I left a note in her mailbox. I tried to make her believe it wasn't me taking her boy from her."

He clenched his hands, hard. His voice remained almost a whisper. "Two days after his mother said all those terrible things to me, when he was coming home from school, he tried to run past me. I caught his arm. I couldn't help myself. I was scared for him.

"He had his head down as he rushed past. When I caught him, he looked up at me. I don't know if I'll be able to describe the look on his face—"

Beauvaque broke down. Brennan waited, stroking the cat, which had settled into a nap.

"I—the look on Jeffrey's face was like nothing I've ever seen on a human being before. He . . . *smiled* at me, Dr. Brennan. But it was such a *malevolent* smile.

"I let go of him. He continued to stare at me, smiling. Then he turned to go. But he stopped, turned, and said, 'She's better than you *or* my mom. *Much* better.'

"He ran away from me.

"I never saw him alive again.

"I wanted to go down to his apartment that night. I wanted to listen at the door. But . . . I didn't. I was afraid. Of everything. Of his mother, of that *voice,* of Jeffrey. I stayed in my room and cried like a fool.

"And, sometime during the night, Jeffrey's mother put a gun to his head and fired, and then she put the same gun to her breast. They were both gone. Jeffrey was gone . . ."

Beauvaque wept.

When Beauvaque composed himself, he stood at the foot of the bed. "So what do you think, Dr. Brennan? Do you believe in *bad* things?"

Backlit, with the shadows of its own flesh magnifying its inscrutability, Beauvaque's face became unreadable. Brennan felt as if he was being tested.

"Yes, I believe in bad things."

"Good," Beauvaque said. He went back into his dark corner and retrieved something from the floor next to the chair he had slept in.

He returned to the bed and held out a marbled notebook, the kind schoolchildren scribble their lessons in. "You shall have this, Dr. Brennan. I found it in Jeffrey's apartment, before the police could take it."

Brennan opened the notebook to the first page. He saw a well-executed pencil drawing of a young woman's face to the shoulder. She was pretty, with an odd, sad smile. Brennan found her strangely attractive. Beneath the picture, in neat script, was the name *Bridget.*

Before he could go further, Beauvaque touched his arm. "Later, Dr. Brennan. I want you to come with me." He smiled his weak smile. "I *do* make a wonderful breakfast. The cats"—at mention of the species the animal next to Brennan's leg leapt from the bed and began to rub Beauvaque's ankle vigorously—"have not been fed." He reached down to rub the cat's chin. "But first," he said, his voice serious, completely untheatrical, "I want you to make me a promise. My giving you my dear Jeffrey's notebook implies a great trust."

"What would that promise be, Mr. Beauvaque?"

"From what you've told me, you're looking for some sort of evidence that there's an afterlife." His voice was almost chillingly calm. "That's why I let that girl Laura Hutchins rent the apartment. Do you think there's an afterlife, Dr. Brennan?''

''I think there may be.''

''I want you to promise, Dr. Brennan, that if you ever discover an existence after this world, that you'll see if my dear Jeffrey is happy. I know that what happened to him was not his own fault. I only want to know that he's happy.''

Forty minutes later, Brennan sat in Beauvaque's ornate kitchen, finishing what *had* proved to be a wonderful breakfast, a mixture of Cajun and Canadian. Beauvaque had been born in Louisiana; had spent his early life in the South, his middle life in the East, and what he referred to as the *rest* of his middle life in the far North, where ''a man like me can be about as happy as is possible, Dr. Brennan. We're *all* haunted by *something,* sugar. Animal, vegetable, or mineral, there's something all of us want but can't have.''

When the phone rang in another room, Beauvaque politely excused himself to answer it, leaving Brennan alone with the marbled notebook that lay on the table next to his plate.

Brennan opened the notebook, studying the drawing of the girl named Bridget before looking at the following pages.

When he turned to the last page of the book, a shocked thrill went through him unlike any he had ever known. For a moment he couldn't breathe. Time stood still. It was as if a shadow he had chased for years, a shadow that had stayed just out of reach, insubstantial, had suddenly stopped dead, let him catch up, and whirled around to face him.

Then Ted Brennan began to breathe again, time went on, and the shadow was his immediate quest. Filled almost painfully with that amalgam of joy and dread he had felt the previous day, Ted Brennan stared once again at the page in the marbled notebook and said, barely believing his own words, ''My God, I've found it.''

TWO: THE COMPASS CROSS

16. WEST

For a few moments, Ray Garver felt his legs working.

He sat abruptly up in bed, feeling below his knees for what had been there in his head a moment before. He had been dreaming daylight, sun blasting slats of white light against the walls of his California home. He had jumped out of bed and shouted and thrown on his clothes and run out the front door to the lawn. The men were there doing the lawn, manicuring it to a green crew-cut, the way he insisted. He shouted to them to stop their work and come with him. They looked at him, puzzled, then dropped their tools and followed.

He ran to the garage, and there, behind the specially equipped Dodge Caravan with handicap plates that he never used, was an old tarp-covered wooden box. He pulled the tarp off the box and began to rummage through it, shouting like a boy on his first day of summer vacation.

There were old baseball bats in the box, some of them cracked from special hits. There were three or four footballs, some of them scuffed, all of them flat, various baseballs, and Spalding rubber balls, handballs, and Wiffle balls. He pulled them all out. There were three baseball gloves, stiff from disuse, craving oil, or, better yet, the Little Leaguer's cure: the glove closed over a hardball in the pocket and wrapped tight in rubber bands, then set in a bucket of water overnight. There was a yellow Wiffle ball bat with electrical tape wrapped around the handle right down to the scraped nub.

He found his basketball.

It was as flat as the football. He dug farther down into the box and came up, shouting, "Eureka!" brandishing a hand pump. It was a short-lived "Eureka!" since, naturally, there was no air needle screwed into the end.

After a moment of despair, he cried, "I know where it is!" and jumped up to feel around on the shelf above the wooden box. There was old fishing tackle up there, STP gas treatment, a small can of 3-In-One oil that had never been opened, a tube of Plastic Wood, a tube of Duco Cement still in its box.

He moved his fingers, careful as a surgeon, around the boxed tube of Duco. There, behind it, was the needle. "Yes!" He brought it down in his fingers and screwed it onto the end of the pump. He inserted the needle into the basketball and began to inflate it.

The gardeners watched all of this curiously from the edge of the garage door.

When the basketball was hard and tight, Ray pulled the pin from it and laid the pump back in the wooden box. "All right!" he shouted. He ran past the startled gardeners, cradling the ball, around the side of the garage to a flat, long, wide square of blacktop with a pole mounted on one side. An orange and white backboard was mounted on the pole, an orange rim mounted on the backboard, a white net hanging from that.

"Basketball!" Ray shouted, and the gardeners smiled and caught on, and took an early lunch.

He played; he was good. He was as good as he had been in high school, when he had played forward for two years before dropping the sport in senior year to concentrate on getting into college. He was better. The gardeners were good, and they formed two teams, and he played his heart and legs out, and then suddenly he realized, *realized,* that he really did have legs and bent down to touch them and sat up in bed.

A dreaming lie. His legs were gone and always would be. It wasn't even daytime; moonlight bled through the shuttered window at the end of his bed. He was not home in California, but in a small, bare bedroom in a nightmare house in New York. Suddenly, he wanted cocaine very badly.

He threw the covers off and lifted himself to the edge of the mattress. He found the wheelchair there and dropped himself into it, grasping the sides, wincing as always because he always hit the edge just a little off, banging his left side. He rolled the wheelchair purposefully to the dresser and pulled open the middle drawer. He reached in for the bag of powder.

It wasn't there.

He hitched his breath. He searched more carefully with his hand. He did not find it. He rolled to the light switch and flipped it up; the bulb behind a sallow lampshade behind him, on a bedside table, went on.

He went back to the drawer and searched.

The bag was not there. He had placed it in the drawer himself this afternoon, after his last hit. Now it was gone.

Oh, God, he thought, *what am I going to do?*

The dresser was a dark, enamel-painted monstrosity from the early 1900s, with big claw feet. He pulled all the drawers out, shaking his meager belongings from them. He put his head close to the openings, and looked for where the bag might have fallen.

It was not there.

"Jesus bloody God!" he shouted.

His body was demanding cocaine.

He sobbed, whacking at the place where his legs had been in the dream.

Cold sweat broke out on his forehead. He locked his eyes shut. He didn't want to look at anything in this room. He wanted to go back to that basketball game for a little while. The coke would do that for him. It would do anything he wanted, grow his legs back and let him play *real* basketball for a little while, let him think about destroying Bridget, if that's what he wanted.

He anchored his torso on the wheelchair, took the edge of the dresser in both hands and yanked it out from the wall.

His wheelchair rolled forward, into the dresser, and the dresser only moved a little out from the wall. He cursed and braced himself, then stopped to lock the wheels of the wheelchair and yanked again.

The dresser groaned, pulled out an inch or two.

He pulled again and again, until it was out six inches from the wall.

He unlocked the wheels and rolled to the wall, pressing his head against it to look along the back of the dresser.

There was nothing there.

"WHERE DID YOU HIDE IT?" he shouted, his head still pressed against the wall. "WHERE THE FUCK DID YOU HIDE IT?"

He heard the far-off echoing sound of laughter, the faint whisper of her voice calling his name.

"Ray . . ."

"WHERE?" he screamed, launching himself from the wall, pulling the dresser over with a crash on top of its drawers.

He rolled around the fallen dresser to the closet door. It had an old, oval hollow metal knob, greened with age. He twisted it, opening the door.

The closet was shallow in depth, dusty shelf paper curled on the empty top shelf, an old pair of man's wingtips butted against the back. There was nothing else. The floorboards were painted dull red.

He hoisted himself up off the arms of the wheelchair, grasping the doorjamb, and tried to reach at the top shelf. He just missed, and fell back. Filled with naked frustration, he bent over and took the wingtips and hefted one back and threw it at the shelf.

The shelf flew up off its wooden brackets and settled at an angle.

"SHIT!" he shouted. He threw the other shoe, knocking the shelf sideways, down onto the floor of the closet.

Ray examined the shelf, feeling along the edges for anything taped to it. He threw it down in disgust. He rolled the wheelchair to the bed. He pulled the coverlet away, then the blanket, the sheets, the underpad. He felt along every inch of the mattress top, then turned it over and checked the bottom.

He checked the box spring. He was pulling the gauzy covering that was stapled to it off to check around the inside of the foundation when his hand hit the bedside table holding the lamp, knocking the slim drawer in it partway open.

He pulled the drawer out.

There it was.

Now he remembered putting it there. He remembered taking out the plastic bag and laying a line on top of the bedside table, then putting the bag in the drawer. He remembered snorting the coke, then lying back on the bed for a little while, telling himself that this would be the last one, that he would get himself under control after this one.

He remembered thinking she would be sorry, after this one.

He had been thinking that for two days.

He pulled the bag open with barely controlled fingers, fumbled with the tiny straw, jabbing it down into the coke and then lifting the straw to his nostril and snorting it straight up.

He felt in back of him for the bed to relax on, found only the stripped foundation. *Ripped you off, man,* he thought, and began to laugh. He felt the coke untensing his muscles, his brain. He crawled over the box spring, pulling the mattress back on top of it. The covers were in a heap on the floor. *Hell with it.* He found the pillow and propped himself against the headboard, turning off the sallow bedside lamp. He studied the fading slats of moonlight against the wall, which abruptly disappeared into clouds.

"Handle you tomorrow, Bridget," he said out loud. *Soon as I get straight.* Then a better thought occurred to him. *I don't have to get straight.* He liked that better. He liked the sound and feel of it a hell of a lot better than the alternative. He would handle her just like this.

"As I *said,*" he spoke, to the slats of moonlight, "the alternative sucks."

Tentatively, he felt down below his knees. Dead, so far. Maybe he could reenter that dream and play basketball some more. He'd like that. *As I said, the alternative—*

There was a sound downstairs.

He heard the front door of the house open, close. Other times in the past two days he had heard sounds, comings and goings; at the height of a coke snort, he had rolled out onto the landing to see, through the slats of the railing, a girl enter the house. Silence after that; then later, after another line had gone up his nose, he had seen a tall person with a long coat and red scarf come in. Hurrying back to his room, he had heard a heavy tramp on the stairs and then a door opening and closing.

Another noise downstairs.

Sounded like someone bumping into things in the dark. A muffled shout, someone falling down. Weeping.

Bumped your knee? That's certainly not Bridget.

A rise of well-being flooded through him. This often happened to him on cocaine, especially on this wonderful Colombian stuff he'd had in the house for the past two years. For the next half hour or so nothing could go wrong. At home, at the height of his self-imposed "medical" treatment, he had tried rolling down the cellar steps in his wheelchair once, just to try it. Miraculously, he had bounced straight to the bottom, his hands working expertly on the wheels as brake and accelerator, without tipping over. After coming down off the drug, he had thought about it and couldn't stop shaking for an hour. He had even crawled back *up* the steps pulling the wheelchair behind him.

Let's try it again!

The weeping downstairs intensified. Whoever it was was banging on something and cursing.

Super Ray to the rescue! Giggling, he rolled to the door and pulled it open.

Darkness. A few bars of cloud-filtered moonlight colored the landing from the west windows. Rather than wait for his eyes to adjust to the deeper darkness, Ray willed himself to see. He rolled straight to the railing and looked into the vestibule below.

See. Nothing at first, the outline of a chair, the ponderous grandfather clock that loomed over the front entranceway.

He heard crying, saw the back of a person: feet and legs kicking feebly at the point where vestibule met living room.

SUPER RAY!

Grinning, Ray launched himself toward the top step. He

balanced nimbly. A quarter inch forward movement and he would be off the edge.

"Yaahhh-HOOOO!" His voice echoed through the open spaces below.

He pushed himself off into space.

He rode the stairs as expertly as he had the first time in his cellar. He was even disappointed; here, the steps were wide and flat and he hit no loose boards. After bouncing down five steps he stopped with a jerk. He leaned back in perfect balance.

Silence from below.

"Yaahhh-HOOOO!" He set off again, reaching the landing in four bouncing jerks before spinning a tight circle. He spun until dizzy. He couldn't decide whether to take the left or right stairways.

He jerked to a stop and rolled toward the right staircase. "No!" He stopped dead, spun around and rolled as fast as he could toward the left.

"YESSIREE!" He flew off the top step. For a brief moment ecstasy seized him. He was in midair. He had the oddest feeling that he might, if he wished, continue in a straight line and fly.

"SUPER RAY!"

He laughed. He felt the jolt of the wheelchair landing precisely in the center of the third step down the stairway. He yanked back on the wheels and stood perfectly still.

"YAAHHHHHH-HOOOOOOOOOOO!" He launched himself forward, bouncing down the remaining steps expertly.

He came to a breathless stop at the bottom. The wheels butted up against the tassels of the living room rug that began there.

"ALL RIGHT!"

The rush continued. He rolled up onto the rug, around to the front of the stairs. The cavernously dark parlor spread out before him, chairs and sofas and tables like obstacles.

"I'm coming, baby! Super Ray to the rescue!"

His voice died to echoes, and he listened.

Nothing.

He pushed ahead into the front room. He brushed a

Sheraton couch, nicking the end table next to it. The front entranceway became visible. It looked empty.

"Hey, where are you?"

He laughed, pushing the wheels harder, deliberately bumping, bouncing off of, a club chair. "Wheeeee!" he said, feigning a harder collision, spinning his wheels in opposite directions to make himself circle furiously. "I'm flying! Ha ha!" He stopped with a jolt and roared off, making car-revving sounds, toward the front entranceway.

The barred red stained-glass window in the top half of the front door was filled with a tentative gray glow. Dawn was approaching. There was a sprinkle of rain on the window. Ray turned to look into the parlor, saw that the shadows were lifting from the furniture, outlining them easily.

Down the vestibule, Ray heard a whimper.

"Ah-ha!"

He rolled furiously into the entranceway, stopping just before crashing into the front door. He heard rain spattering outside. He wheeled and surveyed the short hall.

"I *see* you!" he giggled. He jerked toward a shadowed spot between an empty thick wooden coatrack and the grandfather clock. The grandfather clock sounded, five deep bongs. Ray heard an intake of breath, saw a leg twitch out into the hall, then retreat.

Ray stopped at the spot and looked into it.

Abruptly, the edge left his coke high. He felt instant panic. Off in the recesses of the house he heard Bridget laugh. *The bag. Where is the bag?* His mind locked on the bag, saw it in the drawer on the bedside table.

He knew where the bag was.

Everything was fine.

He pulled in a long breath; the edge came partially back.

"Hey," he said, into the hiding place.

The shadow moved; formed into human shape, fell out into the entrance hallway.

Morning cranked up a notch: rose to dull scarlet. The figure stood up and pushed Ray away and ran off into the house.

Its face imprinted on Ray's memory starkly: young and black. The look was of a frightened animal, nostrils flared, lips pulled back over teeth. Ray already knew the look: it was his own.

The edge was gone, as if someone had reached down and switched it off. Her laughter came again.

Ray shivered. The light outside was cranking up. He thought of trying to open the front door, but knew that it was a waste of time. *Fools check in, but they don't check out.*

If only he had the coke with him now. If only it wasn't up in the room.

If only he had the coke, then he could face her.

Her laughter rolled around the walls, a faint echo, like the dawn, rising into his head.

"Ray . . ."

He rolled slowly back into the parlor, shivering. The furniture looked liked furniture now, a hint of chintz here and there, blue velvet visible on a wing chair. Everything looked ominous. He moved his wheelchair as if moving through a minefield. He rolled to the base of the stairs he had wildly descended.

Painfully, the cocaine leaving him by the minute, panic edging in around him, only the need for more of the drug spurring him on, he began to ascend the stairs, one crawling step at a time, dragging his wheelchair behind him.

Reaching the landing, he saw the fearful young black man regarding him from the depths of the still-shadowed hall leading to the kitchen.

"Don't worry," Ray said, soberly, knowing he was speaking to himself. "There's nothing super about me."

He continued his ascension.

A half hour later, as full light suffused the house, he reached the top landing, pulled himself back into his chair, and rolled, shaking, back to his room.

He slammed the door and moved hastily to the bedside table. He yanked open the drawer, pulled out the bag of white powder.

He laid a neat line across the table top, cut it with a credit card, and used the spoon he kept in his wallet to snort it up into his head.

There was an immediate, topping rush. He straightened

the bedclothes, hoisted himself into the bed and lay back, closing his eyes.

"Come on, come on," he said, the trembling in his body and mind melting, easing into half sleep. After this one, she'd be sorry.

"Please . . ."

And then he had it. He walked tall in the sunshine. There were men following him, and he felt his legs hard and sure beneath him. He threw the ball to one of the men, and then he made a move and one of them threw the ball back to him. He rose up, jumping on his solid legs into the air, and placed the orange ball—orange as the rising sun—into the round metal hoop, laying it as gently as a kiss . . .

17. THE ASSISTANT

As Gary Gaimes put his key into the lock of his Datsun, the hairs on the back of his neck stood up.

Somebody's been in here.

He glanced back at the cop in the caged-in booth who had just given him his receipt for the seventy-five-dollar impounding fee. The cop looked quickly away, but Gary was sure he had been staring at him. He turned to open the car door then spun quickly to catch the cop, who was still hunched over his desk.

Calm down. You're invincible.

But he couldn't calm down. The feeling of violation persisted when, wincing with pain at his taped ribs, he got into the car. *Somebody's been in here.* It just didn't feel right; it felt like everything had been gone over lightly and left just as before. He flipped open the glove compartment; all of his maps were in there, his flashlight, but it looked as if the flashlight had been moved from one end of the compartment to the other. A candy wrapper was on top of the maps. He was sure it had been on the bottom.

He began to shake with rage. He forced himself to be calm. *Easy.* He checked under his seat: the huge wrench he kept there was where it should be. The scatter of papers and empty McDonald's bags in the bag looked undisturbed. A quick glance out the window showed the cop attendant still ignoring him.

Take it easy.

He had already had to control his rage once today, when the rent-a-car bastards had refused to believe him outright when he'd told them something had been wrong with the steering on the van he had plowed into the Deegan highway overpass. *Have to be an investigation,* they'd said. *I'll give you an investigation,* Gary had wanted to say; *I'll tear your fucking eyes out and investigate the inside of your empty fucking skulls.* But he had kept cool then.

He'd keep cool now.

He pushed the key into the ignition. The dangling, empty string tied to the rearview mirror caught his eyes. He searched the seat next to him, sliding the flat of his hand down behind it, but found nothing. He put his hand back under the seat, moving it away from the wrench toward the middle, and he found what he was looking for: a pine-scented hanger, a blonde with her hands behind her head in a copy of the Marilyn Monroe red-satin *Playboy* magazine pose, naked to the waist, ample breasts (bigger than Monroe's) thrusting out like two big pine trees. He examined where the string had broken through; it looked as if it had been pulled, not worn.

Red rage engulfed him. He pushed open the car door, grasping the huge wrench before coming to his senses enough to leave it where it was. He got out of the car and stalked to the cage. The cop tried to ignore him.

"Is this how you *cops* take care of other people's property?" he sputtered.

The cop looked up slowly. He was young and looked just a little nervous. He smiled. "Is something wrong, sir?"

"Somebody went through my goddamned car while it was here."

"I'm sure—" the cop began.

A sudden realization came to Gary, and he threw the nudie air freshener down. "Forget it."

"Sir, if you'd like to file a complaint—"

A sudden, horrible realization came to Gary Gaimes. He

trotted back to the Datsun, got in, and yanked open the glove compartment door. He pulled everything out—flashlight, maps, candy wrapper.

It was gone.

The knife he had used on Marilyn Fagen was gone.

Shit.

He rammed the key into the ignition, turned on the engine, and pulled out. As he rolled past the cage he saw the young cop talking frantically into his phone, following Gary with his eyes.

Shit. Shit.

Gary pulled out into traffic. Immediately, a brown Dodge eased out behind him, two grim faces in the front seat.

Shit. Fuck.

Gary made a quick left, heading toward Chinatown. The Dodge followed. He prayed that Mott Street would be relatively empty; if he could get through that to Broadway he could lose the cops.

Mott was jammed solid, delivery trucks halfway out on either side. A UPS truck sat in the exact center of the street. The delivery man unloaded cartons from the open back. Gary came to a halt three cars behind him. The UPS man finished, took his time closing the truck up and getting his customer, a small excitable Chinese man who kept counting the boxes on the sidewalk and gesturing at the spot on the delivery man's clipboard where he was supposed to sign. The two cars in front of Gary began to honk their horns. The Chinese man and the UPS driver blithely ignored them, lost in their calculations.

Gary looked into his rearview mirror. The Dodge was four cars behind.

Fuck.

Gary turned off the engine, pocketed the keys, and pushed open the door to the Datsun just wide enough to slip out. Keeping down, he pretended to study the ground for something he had dropped. He made his way to the sidewalk, shielding himself behind the stack of cartons the UPS man had just delivered. He kept walking toward Broadway. Beyond the brown delivery truck, he stopped. He looked back over the crowd. The UPS man had finally gotten the Chinese to sign and was slamming the back door of his truck.

Down the street, the brown Dodge sat patiently, the two cops still in the front seat.

Invincible.

Smiling, Gary turned and walked to Broadway.

As he was about to descend into the subway, he changed his mind and hailed a cab. They would be watching the subway exits near his apartment.

He flagged a yellow checker, giving it an address, and watched out the back window for signs of pursuit. The brown Dodge was history. No other cars followed them. He lay his head back against the seat and smiled.

He left the car four blocks from his apartment. Two blocks away, in front of an entrance to Gramercy Park, he saw the first police cruiser. The two young cops inside looked more like they were on their lunch break then waiting for a big bust.

He backtracked, coming behind his apartment complex. There was an alley shared with the building behind that led to a locked door into the laundry room. It hadn't been opened since a mugger had beat up Mrs. Garfinkle and taken her husband's wallet ten years ago. At one time the residents had used the courtyard to dry their clothes. Now all the lines were gone, leaving only the skeletons of the metal hangers. There was nothing but garbage in the alleyway, in the courtyard, now.

Another blue and white police cruiser guarded the back street. Gary passed them on the opposite curb, crossed the street, and came back toward them. He slipped quietly into the alley of his building's twin. He moved crates aside, passed into the courtyard, negotiating it quickly and then passing into the other short alley. He stopped before the locked door and pulled out his key chain.

His mother had had this key since 1946, when she had first moved into the building. She had told the super it was lost when he collected them all. Gary knew that the lock hadn't been changed; the landlord was so cheap he had tried to charge Gary's mother for the lost key.

He fit the key into the lock. For a moment he felt panic

when it didn't move. Then he pressed it further in, finessing its age. Something clicked. The key turned and the door cracked open.

He pulled the door back. He was confronted with the white enameled back of a clothes drier, installed with its two brothers when the courtyard had been closed. He pulled himself up over the back of the drier onto its top. Before jumping down he pulled the door closed behind him.

As expected, the laundry room was empty. The old people in the building rarely used it before noon, coming down in packs.

It was well lit, as was the corridor outside. Gary went to the doorway of the laundry room and peered into the corridor. Empty. He made his way to the stairs and climbed to the lobby.

He heard voices before he eased the door open. Cops, talking football. One of them laughed and said, "Shit, yeah."

Gary left the door closed. Forgoing the elevator, he pushed open the stairwell behind him. The door made a grinding sound when it opened. Gary froze, listening. After a moment, he heard the same laughter coming from the lobby. Again he heard, "Shit, yeah."

He eased the door closed behind him and climbed. At each landing he paused, listening.

When he got to the third floor, his heart began to pound. He waited a long time, listening for the slightest sound. His door was only fifteen feet away from where he stood.

Nothing.

He was just about to push the stairwell door open when he heard a cough.

He pulled his hand from the door. Outside in the hallway, someone snorted, shuffled his feet.

Gary edged away from the door. Noiselessly, he ascended the stairs to the fourth floor. Once again he waited by the stairwell door, listening.

Nothing.

He waited a full count of sixty. Still nothing. Then he heard a door open, close. The rattle of a key chain. A hacking cough.

He edged open the door far enough to see into the hallway. Mr. Grumell shuffled to the elevator, stood before it, hacked again, muttered "Goddammit" under his breath.

Gary waited; the elevator came. Mr. Grumell got on; the elevator went down.

The hallway was silent.

Gary eased the door open and slipped into the hallway.

There was no one.

Gary moved down the hallway to apartment 4J. Empty, he knew. Mrs. Chapin would be working, a clerk at Alexander's on Thirty-fourth Street, until six o'clock.

Gary retrieved his key chain from his pocket and searched it. 4J. He and his mother had lived here before his father died. A two-bedroom apartment. After his father's death, his mother had moved them downstairs to the smaller apartment. "To get away from the memories," his mother had sighed. He'd known she was lying. She had been cheating on his father for years. It was to save money. The one bedroom was fifteen dollars cheaper in rent. "You may sleep on the couch, Gary," she had said to him.

He was filled with sudden rage at the memory. His hand began to shake when he tried to put the key in the door of 4J.

Bitch, he thought, finally getting the key in and opening the door.

The apartment smelled like it had. It smelled like his father. No. It smelled like cabbage and potatoes; his father had smelled like . . . aftershave. A spicy, outdoors scent. Being in here made him remember it. He had only smelled it once anywhere else, the first time he had gone to the house upstate. It was in the air there: a sharp, piney odor.

Bitch. He had only been five years old when his father died, before his mother laundered Gary's mind and eyes and nose and ears clean of him.

The apartment smelled like cabbage and potatoes. Beer. There was a half-empty case of Bud on a chair next to the front door. Mrs. Chapin wasn't the neatest of housekeepers. Dust balls in the corners. A sheen of dust along the ridge of the china cabinet in the dining room.

Gary made his way past the kitchen to the back rooms, pushed open the door to the second bedroom.

His room.

It was a mess; boxes and newspapers stacked, *Daily Newses* yellowing to brittleness. Hatboxes. Unreturned beer cases. A fading blue dress laid carefully over the arm of a frayed club chair.

Gary stared at the window. He vaguely remembered the view, remembered the cowboy wallpaper his father had put on the walls: the large rodeo lassos with a buckeroo's ten-gallon-hatted, smiling face in the center. There was faded red wallpaper on the walls now. It looked like old Christmas wrap. Gary looked at the edge curling near the doorjamb; he pushed the curl back with his finger. There, underneath, was the glue-encrusted, time-worn hint of a lasso rope.

Bitch.

He went to the other bedroom. An old unmade bed, the smell of unwashed panty hose. Dark. Too many curtains. Footpowder, Dr. Scholl's footpads, unopened, on the dresser.

Gary pulled back the curtains, tried to open the window. It was painted shut. Gary hit the window at the edge with the flat of his hand.

He pushed the window and it hesitated, then slid up.

The storm window was still in place. He pushed that up, too.

A chilling breeze struck him. Fresh air for the foot smell impregnating the room. He put his head cautiously out the window and looked.

Below, through the alley to the back street, the young cops stood near their car. They had gotten out, leaned against it.

They would have to consciously study the back of his building, where he stood, to see him.

No one below in the courtyard. No one on the other fire escapes on his building or the one behind. He studied the roofline of the building facing the back street and saw nothing.

One leg out the window, then the other. He was out on the fire escape.

He climbed nimbly down to the third floor. If there was a tricky part, this was it. Two apartments, two fire escapes, over. He climbed over the outside of the railing, measured the distance. He would not have to jump but would have to be sure with his footing to grab across and carry himself over.

He accomplished the first vault with no problem. His foot just snugged into the railing, his hands quickly following. He pulled himself over onto the landing and waited.

The cops on the back street were looking at each other; no one in his vision anywhere.

He crossed the landing, climbed the other side of the railing, prepared to repeat his vault, tipped his balance forward, and grabbed the railing bordering the landing outside his apartment with his hands.

When he brought his feet over, the bottom part of the railing gave way.

Gary held with all his strength as an entire section of the landing, rusted through, fell away to the courtyard below him. He closed his eyes, waited for the sound. None came. He opened his eyes and looked down. The rusted rails and metal bridgework had landed flush in the middle of an old mattress.

Invincible.

Gary gingerly pulled himself up and over the railing.

He stood away from the corroded section of the landing, near the window to his apartment. He put his head close to the window and listened.

Nothing.

He studied the rooflines, the other landings, checked the courtyard, the alleyway.

He put his hand on the window to raise it. A shout went up behind him. His heart froze. He turned, looking down the alleyway to the back street. The cops had stopped chatting. One of them shouted, "Hey!" The cop was pointing up the street, away from him. Gary heard young laughter fading, running footsteps. The cop pursued, up the back street, out of Gary's line of sight.

Gary put his hand back on the window and edged it up. Six inches, then he paused. He tipped his head to listen into the apartment.

Nothing. Only the electrical *tock-tock* of the digital school clock in the hallway.

He edged the window up another foot.

Tock-tock.

Using the middle and index fingers on both his hands, he slid the window up all the way.

Tock-tock. Tock-tock.

He entered the apartment.

He slid the window down behind him. The apartment became stuffy and close.

Tock-tock.

He went to the hallway, edged down it. The sound of the clock became louder until he passed it.

He edged his ears and then his eyes into the kitchen.

He heard voices.

A shuffle of tired feet, a clearing throat, a cough into a hand. The beginnings of a hummed tune, fading to boredom.

They were outside the apartment door, in the hallway.

Quietly, he entered the kitchen. Two things from here. A knife he had used and had kept, a bloody dishrag. He found and carried them into the living room.

He watched the knob of the front door. It didn't move. Silently, he went to the front door, picked up his duffle bag from the floor. He brought the duffle bag to the couch (watch the knob, watch the duffle bag), opened it, checked to make sure everything else was in there, put the two objects from the kitchen in and zipped it quietly closed.

He got up, walking over a photograph that had not been pushed under the couch (he looked at it, crinkled, black and white, 1964, the New York World's Fair, his mother in the front seat of a futuristic Ford heading to Tomorrowland, he in the backseat staring blankly at the camera, wearing a short-sleeve shirt that made him look like Wally Cleaver—which one of them had taken the picture?) and kept walking. He hesitated. The photo album was on the coffee table, open. The clippings inside, *Post* headlines, *Times* stories. A picture of Detective Falconi bending over a body. He picked it up, carried it under his arm, went to the bedroom.

Tock-tock.

He went to the window, looked out, saw nothing. The cops on the back street had regained their position next to their cruiser. They were looking at each other; he noticed that one of them was a woman. He put his fingers on the window, began to raise it slowly.

"Hello, Gary."

His heart stopped, began beating again. For the merest fraction of a second it had sounded like Bridget.

"Don't move, Gary," the voice said reasonably. That was why he had thought of her: the tone was the same reasonable calm. Controlled.

"Lower the bag," the voice said.

He lay the bag gently on the floor. The photo album was pulled from under his arm.

"Your hands on your head, Gary. Spread your legs."

Efficient hands moved up and down his legs, around his upper torso, over his arms.

"Place your hands behind your back."

He felt the cold circlets of handcuffs lock into place above his wristbones.

"Turn around, please."

He turned. He saw nothing for a moment. A shadow. Then a man in the shadow. The man was back away from the window light. The light refracted around him, giving only a shape in the shadow.

Gary knew him. He knew his face even as the man stepped out of the shadow into the light; the man's small, stocky frame, perfect, fussy clothes. The exact part in his thinning black hair. Piercing, serious eyes. As if he was his own father.

"Hello, Gary," Detective Falconi said. He stepped fully into light. Sunlight produced shadows on his face. Sharp, straight nose. Deep-set eyes. His voice was calm. He smiled, a self-satisfied gesture that managed to be free of sarcasm. "Let me read you your rights."

18. SOUTH

A dream.

Ricky came out of the shadows into day.

The parlor was filled with clearing sun from the departing rainstorm. But the light was filtering through tall stained-glass windows, making everything dreamlike.

It was in his dark metal closet in the belly of the S.S. *Eiderhorn,* during his two-day trip without food or water, that he had decided that he must be dreaming. Spook had said (he remembered what had happened to Spook—had that been a dream?) that dreams were a place where you went to do all the crazy things you couldn't do in real life. You could fly in your dreams; could be famous; you could fight battles with monsters. You owned your dreams, Spook had said.

So Ricky had decided that he was dreaming. It had all been a dream, the initial contact in Chambers House the day Mr. Harvey had been away, the shivering in his bed, the return with Spook to the house, Spook's death (yes, it *had* been a dream, hadn't it?), the ride on the ship to New York, the ride with the madman in his van down Broadway. What a nightmarish place Broadway had been in his dream! Not at all like it had been in the earlier dream with Ben Vereen—this Broadway was dirty, with pornographic movie houses and people who looked like they were crazy staggering about or sleeping over heating vents in the sidewalk as other people walked right by them. This Broadway was dirty, with too many cars and taxis, women who looked like prostitutes, people who looked drunk or on drugs. The lights were too bright, there were too many of them, and most of the lights had nothing to do with theater, selling Ninja costumes, hocked musical instruments, cigarettes, and lottery tickets. This horrible cartoon nightmare he had dreamed up was nothing like the real Broadway.

The ride up here away from the lights and over the endless highway had been a dream, with the moon rising over more trees than he had ever seen, the smell of the ocean vanished from his nostrils, the land flat and waterless. He had gone over a dream bridge, over something called the Croton Reservoir, had passed big shopping centers bigger than Trimingham's in Bermuda, but ugly, with bright lights flaring against their flat fronts, all the stores looking the same. In this horrible dream the van had stopped at a small booth, and the madman who drove the van, tapping his hand on the wheel to the jazz coming from the radio, had paid a toll and gone on. The night was so dark, the moon so sickle bright, the land so strange. They began to rise up out of the flat land, into mountains. The dream mountains had looked huge to Ricky. There were trees all around them, dropping leaves like orange and yellow snow in the stabbing lights of the van. The roads got narrow, there were trees all around, half-nude branches throwing leaves down at them. They passed houses, turned, passed more houses.

They turned onto a long, curving driveway, trees pressing close, and then the trees arched back, revealing a dream house: a looming rise of shadows—a deeper shadow against the dark night. It seemed to refuse moonlight, or reflect it back as darkness.

A dream house.

In the backseat of the van, he had begged for the dream to end, pinched himself, screamed at himself for the nightmare to end.

But it hadn't. The madman in the front seat had dragged him out and driven away. And then Ricky lay in the driveway with the dream house, *her* house, rising over him, and then the shadows had parted at the bottom of the house, and the door had opened. Moonlight had brightened to guide him in until the moonlight snapped off like a light and the door closed with finality and darkness came upon him again.

And now, in the day, somehow, his dream continued. Sunlight pushed into the house, dream-tinged through the long stained-glass windows, a red stained-glass circle above each like a halo.

Ricky walked into the parlor. The furniture that had looked frightening in the night, and ominous and sharp-edged in the early morning light, now looked old. Chairs with dusty coverings, rubbed frays on the arms. A pull of stuffing from one cushion on the damask sofa. A chipped corner on a side table. A maroon oriental rug worn through in trafficked spots.

Behind the railing that enwrapped the second floor upstairs, Ricky heard a sound.

Rabbitlike, he retreated to the hallway.

He waited for the cursing, rolling ferocity of the man in the wheelchair. But it was not his door that opened. It was one on the opposite end of the house. A man came out, closing the door behind him.

He was young, short, thin, with long brown hair in need of trimming. He wore a dark suit with a white shirt and red tie. As he descended the stairs his shoes made a loud, singular clopping sound.

Ricky backed further into the hallway.

The young brown-haired man hesitated at the bottom of the steps.

Suddenly he turned and stared at Ricky.

His eyes had a glassy, dreamlike flatness.

He began to speak in a foreign language.

Ricky searched desperately for a way out. At the end of the hallway was a door. He ran for it. It swung in when he pushed at it, swung closed behind him.

Ricky was in a kitchen, spotless white, trimmed in chrome. There was a long butcher-block table under a window at one end, Breuer chairs around it. A lengthy counter flanked the table; behind the counter, against the wall and under another window—clear glass with a thin strip of ruby stained-glass at the top—ran a chrome sink. More counter space next to that; under the counter, a dishwasher, more drawers.

Ricky heard the *clop-clop* of the foreigner's shoes negotiating the hallway. He ran behind the long counter next to the table, hid down behind it.

The stranger entered the room. Ricky heard the *swish* of the opening door, a returning *whoosh* as it closed.

He heard one *clop,* another.

A dream. A horrible, bloody dream.

There was silence. The heavy shoes were walking his way.

Clop. Clop.

Go away, dream.

The shoes stopped. Ricky opened his eyes. The shoes were planted in front of him, shiny black. He could see himself in them.

Go away!

Ricky looked up.

The foreigner's face smiled; his mouth said, "Hello?" in English.

Ricky fainted dead away.

He awoke on the dusty sofa, in the living room. He turned his head, into the fabric, and sneezed.

He sat up.

The brown-haired foreigner was sitting in a frayed chair on the other side of the coffee table. On the coffee table was a tray with a teapot on it. There were biscuits and a bowl of fruit.

The foreigner lowered his cup of tea to its saucer.

"I'm sorry I startled you," he said earnestly, in careful, excellent English. "I only wanted to say hello."

Ricky stared at the foreigner, at the food on the tray. He was suddenly ravenously hungry.

"Please eat," the foreigner said. He put his own teacup down and poured one for Ricky. "I hope you don't mind tea. I'm afraid I don't know how to brew coffee."

Ricky took the saucer, relishing the warmth of the cup. He sipped at the tea.

It was as good as Brook Bond tea, at home.

"My name is Jan," the foreigner said. He bowed his head awkwardly.

"I'm Ricky."

Such a strange dream.

The stranger reached out, took another biscuit.

Ricky ate a biscuit, then another. There were two apples in the fruit bowl. He took one. He broke a banana from its mates and devoured it. He finished his tea, poured more for himself.

"Where are you from?" Jan asked.

"Bermuda."

"Ah."

The conversation flagged. Ricky ate another banana, another biscuit.

"Are there others beside you?" Jan asked. "I arrived yesterday, late. I'm afraid I've slept until now."

Ricky didn't like the dreamy glaze in the foreigner's eyes. *He looks like he's dreaming, too.*

"There's a man. In a wheelchair," Ricky said. "I saw him last night—"

"There's one more besides me," a voice boomed above them.

Ricky saw the man in the wheelchair balanced at the top of the landing. He looked calmer. Slowly, one step at a time, he came down.

When he reached the bottom and rolled closer to them, Ricky saw that his eyes were still overbright.

A dream filled with dreamers.

"Is there coffee?" the man in the wheelchair said, loudly.

"Tea—" Jan began to explain.

"No matter," the man said. He plucked the remaining apple from the bowl, rolled his chair away from them.

"You were saying?" Jan said politely. "There's a fourth—"

"A girl," the man in the wheelchair said. "I saw her come in early yesterday. She's in the north bedroom." He smiled grimly. "I'm Ray Garver."

Ricky and Jan introduced themselves.

"You and I met last night," Ray said to Ricky. He grinned. "Sorry."

Ricky regarded him blankly. *Such a strange dream.*

"That's right," Ray said, fidgeting in his chair. "When the candy-man is home, nobody's alone." He smiled again. "Little poem of mine. Want to hear another?" He looked at Ricky with his bloodshot eyes. "Forget it. Have you tried the door this morning, sport?"

"No," Ricky answered.

"Go on."

Ricky rose, went into the front hallway. He took hold of the door. The knob wouldn't move. He looked for a sliding lock or deadbolt. There was nothing, no keyhole, no turning mechanism on the knob.

"Maybe it's *stuck,*" Ray said sarcastically. "Give it a *pull.*"

Ricky pulled at the door. It wouldn't move. He couldn't even get the knob to turn.

"Try the windows, too, if you want," Ray continued. "Down here, upstairs. It doesn't matter. They're all sealed. Actually, it's as if they aren't there. It's like they're part of the walls. I tried to put a piece of furniture through one yesterday. Nothing. Not even a crack. There's a back door, too. There isn't even a knob on that one. Nice big porch out back. White wrought-iron chairs. Nice table, too, with a hole in the middle for an umbrella. I bet there's a striped one somewhere, maybe in the cellar. Like to have your tea on the patio, sport?" He laughed, spinning his wheels in opposite directions to turn himself in a quick circle.

Such a dream!

"Don't call me sport," Ricky said. He was frightened and angry.

"Come on!" Ray said. "I'll take you on the haunted house tour."

Without waiting, he rolled off toward the kitchen.

Jan and Ricky followed.

"You've already found the food," Ray said rapidly, bursting through the swinging doors, pointing to the pantry. "Enough for an army. Don't know about you, but I haven't been all that hungry since I got here. There's a washer and dryer back there too, if you need it.'' He stopped abruptly, turned, rolled to a door opposite the sink, yanked it open, pointed to the darkness down a flight of stairs. ''Cellar down there. If you flip on the light, there's a big open toolbox filled with stuff near the bottom step.'' He slammed the door. ''Excuse me.'' He spun away, rolled to the kitchen table, pulled a plastic bag from his shirt pocket, and tapped a small mound of cocaine out. He produced a tiny straw, crudely lined the coke, and bent over it, snorting it into his nose. The bag and straw went back into his pocket.

''Where was I?'' he said, spinning around toward them.

Not waiting for an answer, he shot back through the swinging doors into the hallway.

''Guest room, sewing room, bathroom,'' he said, even more rapidly, knocking on doors as he flew by them. ''Plenty of space for the growing family. I heard noises or saw something you wouldn't like to see in every one of them during my little escape attempt yesterday.'' He looked back at Ricky and Jan. ''Just trying to save you boys the trouble.'' He smiled. ''Then again, maybe you had a reason for coming, like me. And maybe you haven't been able to think clearly since you stepped through the front door. You want any of this,'' he said, patting his shirt pocket, ''just let ole Ray know.''

He shot back into the parlor, heading for the right fork of the staircase. ''You've already seen the beautiful living and dining area,'' he said. ''Now for the best part.''

He stopped at the bottom step, turned the wheelchair's back to it, and began to climb the stairway, jerking the wheels back up each step, one at a time. The muscles stood out taut on his arms. When Jan tried to move around to help pull him up, Ray stopped, braking himself with one hand while holding the other up to ward the Pole off.

''No problem,'' he said. He grinned at Ricky. ''I think sport over there saw me do a pretty good job with the wheels last night. Eh, sport?''

Terrible, horrible dream.

''Don't call me—'' Ricky began, but Ray was already back at work, grunting with effort, sweating, humping up the second-flight staircase toward the top.

''I *love* this second floor!'' he said at the top, not even pausing for breath. Jan and Ricky could barely keep up with his race. ''Four lovely bedrooms, one facing north,'' he said, pointing at the door facing the stairway, turning to the right, tracing his hand over the top of the guardrail as he turned the corner sharply. ''One facing east,'' he said, rapping on Jan's door as he flew by, ''one south,'' he continued, taking the next corner even more sharply, grabbing the handrail for balance, then rapping on Ricky's door, ''and my own room, of course,'' he said, again cornering at high speed, ''facing west,'' tapping his fingers over his door as he sped past. ''Each with its own bathroom. There is also,'' he went on, braking abruptly at a thin closed door set in the corner between the west and north bedrooms, yanking the door open to reveal a narrow flight of curving stairs leading up, ''a lovely garret, topped by the lovely cupola you may have noticed on entering this spacious, thoroughly haunted residence.''

Ray slammed the door hard, turned his wheelchair to face Ricky and Jan. ''Tour lecture's almost done, gents.'' He fumbled the coke bag out of his breast pocket, stuck his straw straight into it, and took a quick, sharp snort. He put the straw and bag away. ''Now as to why—''

There was a sound, and the door to the north bedroom opened. A young woman came out of the doorway, ignored them, and descended the stairs.

The three stared silently at her. She was barefoot, dressed in a soiled T-shirt and jeans. Her hair hung in two long braids, like a little girl's.

When she reached the bottom of the stairs, she went to the hallway. She walked with a limp, favoring her right foot. They heard the door to the kitchen swing open, whack closed.

After a few moments, they heard the kitchen door open and close again. She reappeared, limped calmly to the stairs, and ascended. In her right hand was a long, wide, serrated bread knife.

She reached her doorway, went into the room, and closed the door behind her.

They heard the sound of a lock being applied.

After a moment of silence, the air was bisected by the keening, sustained sound of a scream.

Ray sat frozen, then suddenly gave a whoop of laughter. "This is a job for Super Ray!"

The screaming became almost inhuman. Sounds of begging were interspersed with wildly happy cries of, "Yes! M and P! Yes!" But then the screams began to dominate. They heard a harsh, grinding sound interspersed with cries of agony.

Bellowing wildly, Ray shot forward and rammed his wheelchair into the door.

The door buckled, held.

Inside, the screams climbed to an ear-piercing shriek. The rhythmic grinding noise continued.

Ricky and Jan threw their weight against the door. It held fast. Ray retreated to the edge of the stairway. Again he shouted for the other two to stand aside. Pumping his hands down against the wheels, Ray sped at the door. He tilted back slightly so that only the metal footrest hit.

The door rattled, burst open a half inch. It stopped against the inner chain that held it closed. The screaming increased in volume.

"Dammit, help me!" Ray grabbed at Jan's hands, put them on the handles at the back of the wheelchair. He screamed at Ricky. "Pull it back and ram it!"

They rolled the chair back a few feet and rammed it forward.

"YA-HOOOO!" Ray yelled.

The chain held.

"Again!"

They hit the door twice more.

The third time, the door burst inward.

"In! Super Ray to the rescue!"

The screaming was even louder as they entered.

Laura looked up at them from the bed. For a brief, horrible moment, her screams ceased completely. Her pale, pain-ridden face split into a beatific smile. "Hello." Then her eyes rolled up into her head, and her unearthly shrieks resumed.

She thrashed her head from side to side. Ricky gagged, turned away, and began to vomit. Ray stared, his smile gone. Jan, his face coldly white, turned his eyes away.

Laura sat propped against the headboard of her bed,

holding the bread knife in both her hands, working on the flesh and bone of her right leg above the ankle as if it were a recalcitrant tree limb.

A gasp escaped her as the foot fell away. It lay on the bed like a discarded doll. Blood pumped from the open wound, pooling on the bed. Hands trembling, she raised the knife away from her leg.

The room was strong with the coppery smell of blood.

"Jesus, oh, Jesus," Ricky moaned.

Laura's shrieks trailed down to a sudden groan. She struggled to focus her gaze. Her face was bone white and slack; her voice came out a ragged whisper.

She managed a tiny smile, the ends of her slackening mouth turning up. She turned the smile on Ricky, managing, through gargantuan effort, to brighten it. "I promise I won't run anymore, M and P. I promise—"

Her hands went limp. Her head fell back, her sightless eyes studying the ceiling. There was the hint of a smile on her face.

Off in the depths of the house, they heard a deep, satisfied moan. The house itself seemed to tremble, and a bright light flashed across the windows of Laura's room. A low, sustained hum began that did not cease.

Ricky stumbled from the room, vomiting the scant remains of his biscuit and fruit breakfast into the hall. He was followed by Jan, who made it to the stairway before steadying himself, leaning heavily against the banister, and sitting down. He put his head in his hands and closed his eyes.

Ray appeared in the doorway. He rolled out onto the landing, pulled the door closed behind him.

He pushed his wheelchair toward his own room, opened the door, then turned to face Jan and Ricky.

"Now, as to why we're here," he said, the rapid-fire coke cockiness of his voice gone, "she told me that. She said it didn't matter. She said she had us, all four of us, and that nothing we could do can free us. We can't leave and we can't make her go away."

Ricky looked at Jan, who stared ahead as if in a trance; with one of his hands, he was idly stroking his groin.

Terrible, horrible dream.

He tried to block out the humming noise but could not.

Ricky looked at Ray and pinched himself as hard as he could.

Please, Lord, let me wake up.

Tears came to his eyes, and he felt the pain of his self-inflicted bruise.

Ray turned and began to roll into his room and close the door. Ricky saw the bag of white powder and straw resting in his lap.

"The only thing we can do," Ray said, as Ricky did not wake up, "is die."

19. FALCONI

What Rich Falconi *didn't* need was the earnest young man standing on the other side of his desk.

"Look, Dr. Brennan," Falconi said, lifting a pencil and tapping the point gently against the pad of his thumb, "I've done all I can for you. If Minkowski hadn't given you a green light, you wouldn't have gotten this far. I let you see Gaimes, like you wanted. He told you some things you wanted to hear. You left him your phone number and address in case he wants to get in touch with you again and tell you more things you want to hear. That's wonderful. I'm happy for you. The rest of this, I don't have time for."

Brennan began to light a cigarette; at Falconi's scowl, he put the match out and slipped the cigarette into his pocket.

Falconi slammed the pencil down flat on his desk; his voice rose a notch toward annoyance. "You want to know what I had waiting for me when I got in this morning?" He counted off on his fingers. "One, a guy in an ill-fitting priest's costume, his wife dressed as a soiled nun. Two, a medium named Margie Firewater, who called on the spirit of someone named Atu to cleanse this city, all of it—we're talking about a *generous* spirit here—of, in her words, 'Filth, corruption, *and* littering.' Three, a special delivery letter from someone claiming to be Gary Gaimes's long lost father, written in *crayon,* for Christ's sake, from Reno, Nevada. Says he forgot all about Gary until yesterday, when he heard about him on the news. Wants to come here and have a reunion, *and,* as a favor, write down his life story—along with his own, of course, I imagine in crayon—then sell it to the highest bidder. Four—" he stopped counting with his hands, smacked at the copy of the *New York Post* that lay closed on his desk; the cover, with a blown-up photo of Gary Gaimes, head bowed slightly, smiling, being taken out of a police cruiser with his hands cuffed behind his back. The headline said "GAMES KILLER KAUGHT: HAD HELP FROM GAL GHOST!" "—I've got crap like this all over the place, from England, I got a call from *Stern,* the West German rag, from *Playboy* wanting my story, from the *Enquirer* wanting *anybody's* story, the janitor, the guy who brings coffee around on a cart, anybody. Never mind the *Post* and *Daily News* guys are practically camped out in front of the building."

He folded his hands, let his blood pressure subside, tried to look as reasonable as he could when his eyes met Brennan's again.

"So *please* don't tell me anything fucked-up, because I really don't think I can handle it."

Brennan, who had stood patiently through this tirade, made sure Falconi was finished, then sat down.

"Afraid I have bad news for you on that."

Falconi almost told the young man to leave. He would have, if Minkowski hadn't talked so highly of him after Brennan had called, begging to come in, begging to be let in to see Gary Gaimes. Minkowski was funny like that; there was almost no one else in his own field that he trusted, respected, or liked. Brennan was the first Falconi had ever seen who scored on all three counts. They had used some of Minkowski's approved colleagues before, and Mark had usually spoken, and briefly, about why he thought they should be brought in, but the mention of Ted Brennan drew from

Minkowski the absolutely only rave Falconi had ever heard from the man.

"He's top-notch. He's not afraid to fuck with his peers. I knew him in school and *know,* I *know* because I saw with my own eyes, that Ted Brennan mastered everything in his field before moving on. He didn't find a comfortable cubbyhole to stick his ass into. He went looking for something *beyond* what was going on at the time. In the popular press, he sounds like a kook. But if you read the few journal pieces there have been about him—and, more important, if you read the few, very few pieces he himself has authored in the journals—you find absolutely nothing shoddy or obtuse about his work. He plays by the rules, Rich, and he stays solid inside the borders—even when what he's looking at lies outside any borders." By now, Mark was pacing, talking to the four walls, waving his arms—a classic Minkowski lecture. "If you look at his early work, just out of school, you find nothing but brilliance. His studies of acute schizophrenia are masterful. They formed a groundwork for eight or nine much less talented drones to build solid careers on later. And he left it behind, because he had found out what he wanted to know. He could have stayed where he was and built his life out of any of that early work, but he didn't."

Minkowski stopped in front of Falconi's desk and put his hands on it. His face was slightly flushed. "Damnit, Rich, he's what I wish I had the balls to be. But I don't. So here I am. But whatever you do, take him seriously. No matter how wild it sounds. Because he knows what the fuck he's talking about."

Falconi, thinking of this conversation he had had with Minkowski that morning, and wishing it had never taken place, nodded sourly. "Go ahead, Dr. Brennan."

Brennan's agitation, which had been obvious from the beginning, but which he had managed to contain with patience, now erupted. He opened his briefcase, arranging papers from it across the length of the desk. He took out a black-and-white marbled notebook and turned it for Falconi's inspection, flipping it open to the first page.

"That's Bridget," Brennan said simply, pointing to a fairly accomplished pencil sketch of a girl's head and shoulders.

Falconi immediately began to have second thoughts about Brennan, and about Minkowski. Perhaps Mark wasn't so right after all; perhaps he, too, like this overearnest young man in front of him, was in need of the services of his own profession.

"It gets more fucked-up than this," Brennan said, noting Falconi's growing irritability.

"There isn't any Bridget," Falconi said. "We checked everything out about Gary Gaimes. He didn't have a girlfriend, he didn't hang around with or know any girl named Bridget. He says she told him what to do, made him 'invincible.' That's pure bullshit. There is no such person, except in his head. Even Mark Minkowski says he probably made her up."

"He didn't." Brennan tapped the open page of the notebook. "Neither did the eleven-year-old boy who wrote this journal.

"Lieutenant," Brennan said. His face looked almost too earnest, like he was busting his gut with a secret to get out. "I'm going to tell you something very wild. I'm warning you now. I could sit here for an hour getting you ready psychologically. I know all the techniques for that, I was very good at it. I wrote a paper on it once. I called it 'Shock Reduction.' If I shock you, there's a much better chance you won't believe me. You'll want to have me thrown out. But I don't have *time* to fuck with your head. So please just listen to me."

Falconi looked at Brennan levelly. He threw up his hands, leaning back in his chair. "Say whatever you want."

Brennan took his cue. He flipped past the pencil drawing of the young girl to the second page of the journal. On it, in thick crayon, was scribbled, "I love her."

"The boy who completed this," Brennan said, flipping through the journal randomly, "Jeffrey Ragani, is talking about the same Bridget that Gary Gaimes is. It's the same Bridget that a girl named Laura Hutchins became obsessed with while staying in the apartment that Jeffrey Ragani died in at the hands of his mother. Laura Hutchins was Jeffrey Ragani's cousin. She was only there five days before she seemingly went out of her mind, killed her boyfriend who had come up to see her, and stole his car. Her whereabouts are unknown."

Brennan told Falconi about Beauvaque, told him where to get in touch with the landlord. "He'll verify everything I've told you about Laura Hutchins and Jeffrey Ragani."

Falconi fingered the pages of the notebook, looked at the scrawls of professed love, the primitive love poems. He knew obsession when he saw it.

Brennan jerked the notebook away from Falconi, began flipping furiously through it to the back, stopping at a few spots on the way, pointing out the word "Mother" to Falconi. Brennan settled on a page near the end. On it were the words, "Will meet her at the house."

Falconi read them. "So?"

"Jeffrey Ragani was talking about Bridget."

"What house?" Falconi said.

Brennan leaned across the desk, hands on the notebook, and said, "That's what I have to get Gary Gaimes to tell me."

"Dr. Brennan," Falconi said, "will you please get to the point?"

Brennan turned to the last page of the notebook.

"I doubt you've ever heard of this," Brennan said. "On the paper, in almost architectural precision—Jeffrey Ragani had proved poor in penmanship but excellent in draftmanship—was an almost symmetrical cross. It resembled the German Iron Cross, only the spokes were much thinner. Above each spoke was sketched a point of the compass—N for north, S, E, and W. At the hub of the cross was a representation of a dragon with its mouth open, long tongue lashing. "It's called the Compass Cross. It's also known as the Cross of Charlemagne."

Falconi had settled back in his chair. "Go on."

"Charlemagne died in 814 A.D. Some said there was a cross fashioned for Charlemagne by an evil priest named Salomagni, and actually placed in his hand. The story is probably apocryphal. These things always gain embellishment every time they're written down or translated.

"The Compass Cross was a house that, viewed from above, was shaped like a cross, on land owned by Charlemagne's heirs.

"In 990 A.D. the house was destroyed. There is a prime

source, a French priest named Verges, who swears he got the story from the only survivor's mouth, on her deathbed, during her confession. The woman, whose name was Genevieve, gave him permission to publish the story. Verges believed her. Not only that, but he returned to the place where the house stood and studied the ruins himself."

Falconi, resigned to the fact that Brennan hadn't gotten to the point yet, waved him on.

"The reason Verges is so believable is that he wasn't a fool. He was a scientist and skeptic. He never fooled with heresy, but he insisted on seeing with his own eyes whatever could be seen. There's a quote in his work that, loosely translated, says, 'If it be, let me touch it, if it breathe, let me hear its breath, if it walk in shadows, let me throw light upon it. For all that God, Almighty Creator, has made He has made for Man to look upon, and all that is not of God Himself, to touch, and hear, and see.'

"What he described, in physical terms, was what we would now call a classic poltergeist encounter. Or rather the aftermath of one. As he walked among the ruins of the house he described feelings of dread, unaccountable loss, of rage. Standing on one spot, he says there was a definite drop in temperature; not believing this possible, or doubting his own senses, he had the townsperson who he had hired—at great expense, for the town had become deathly afraid of the place—to blindfold him and lead him randomly from room to room in the ruins of the house. When he reached the cold spot, he says he knew it instantly, and drew off his blindfold to find himself standing at the exact location he had been earlier.

"All of this makes a nice ghost story, until you consider what the dying penitent, in the sacredness of confession, told Verges had taken place in the house. Genevieve was originally from Trieste. She had been lured to France, so she said, by a handsome man named Paul, who promised to become her husband. Paul had made her the promise when she was fourteen, when she had visited a series of caves that the locals claimed were haunted. Her friends had run away, but she had stayed behind to behold the vision of this handsome man.

Paul said he would love her always, and that someday he would marry her.

"She ran from the cave, but periodically she was visited by Paul, who continued to profess his love. By her own admission, she was a homely girl, and on her deathbed, she confessed to the sin of lust.

"When Genevieve was nineteen, Paul appeared to her while she was working in the fields and said she must come to him now. She immediately set out for France.

"She found the house occupied by two men and a girl. One of the men was from Nantes, in western France, the other from Brussels. The woman was from a town north of Barcelona.

"What followed was madness. As much of it that Verges describes, I get the feeling that he left as much out. It was obvious some of it Verges found unspeakable, blasphemous, or just distasteful.

"All four of them, one from the north, one from the south, one from the east, and one from the west, had been lured there, either with promises of love—Verges hints at but never states that one of the men was homosexual—or mothering—the Spanish girl was only nine years old, an orphan; one of the men, a boy of seventeen, had lost his mother only six months before. All of them had had initial contact with Paul in a place considered inhabited by spirits.

"None were able to leave the house once they were inside. Genevieve described a kind of lassitude she and the others felt, as if they were caught in amber. Genevieve described not being able to think clearly, and what thoughts she had were focused and concentrated on the obsession that had brought her to the house. The others, she said, acted the same way, as if they had been caught in a web, stung with spider's venom, and were waiting for the inevitable end. She described visions, mass hysteria, hallucinations. There is a strong hint of sexual degradation. You get the feeling Genevieve told him everything in detail; you can read between the lines and pretty much reconstruct what happened. Verges knew how much he could get away with telling. Despite his own prejudices, he worded things in such a way that the truth could be deduced.

"Genevieve described to Verges, in detail, her participation in the dismemberment of the young girl, along with the faintest hint—again, Verges is circumspect—of cannibalism.

"Only Genevieve survived. She found herself holding out her hands to an apparition of Paul displaying himself on their marriage bed, beckoning her to come forward and consummate their union. A crack of summer lightning illuminated the hall at that moment, and Genevieve looked straight into her reflection in a window. She saw that, in reality, she was standing on a bench in the entry hall of the house, covered in the blood and entrails of the others, a length of hemp around her neck knotted to a beam above.

"With the disappearance of the lightning, the hallucination of Paul returned. Then a second bolt of lightning followed. This one, miraculously, hit the house, which caught fire. Genevieve, screaming, pulled the rope from her neck, threw herself through the flames, and escaped to the outside world."

Brennan looked hard at Falconi. "There were certain things, purely physical things, that Paul could not do. He could not bring food to the house, for instance. For this, Paul had recruited an assistant, a man from the nearby village, who was later hanged as a witch."

Brennan leaned forward. "That's what Gary Gaimes is, Lieutenant. An assistant. Somewhere in New York State, there's another Compass Cross. Gary Gaimes knows where it is. This time the spirit's name is Bridget, and Laura Hutchins is one of the four people she's summoned."

Falconi looked at Brennan. "Is *that* your fucking point?"

"Don't get angry," Brennan said. "I told you I didn't have time to prepare—"

"*That's* what this is all about? *Evil spirits?*"

Brennan fumbled his cigarette out of his pocket, lit it, took a deep pull. Falconi scowled.

"There's more."

Falconi continued to scowl.

Brennan butted the cigarette out. He leaned forward intensely, hands on Falconi's desk. "Genevieve confessed to Father Verges that in the midst of all the horrors taking place, Paul claimed that when the four of them had died in the house he would be able to come over from the other side in his true form. The human image he displayed to them was the possessed spirit of someone named Paul who had been driven to his death in the Compass Cross. This thing said it would destroy the world. And as Genevieve fled the house, it promised it would return in a thousand years—''

''I've had enough of this—'' Falconi said, beginning to rise from his chair.

Brennan leaned back, took out his cigarette pack, removed a fresh cigarette, and lit it. This time he ignored Falconi's black look. He let the smoke fill his lungs, blew it out. ''Bridget is real, Lieutenant. Whoever she is, she's the most unfortunate one of all in this, because she was in the wrong place at the wrong time. In a way, she hasn't even been allowed to die. This thing on the other side has been using her.

''Lieutenant, something has been guiding me toward the Compass Cross. Something beyond my own mind. It guided me to Father Verges's work four years ago, and it's been trying to make me find the Compass Cross ever since. I don't know how to explain it, it's not rational, but this force is there and it's been growing stronger in my mind.

''Ten years ago, when I was an intern, I had a schizophrenic patient die on me, then come back. A classic near-death experience. She described the standard womb-analogy, the tunnel, the bright light at the end. Then she described something *after* it. A place. She was dead when she was in this place. A day later, she couldn't even remember dying and was as mentally incapacitated as ever. But for that brief time, after she came back, she was more lucid than I had ever seen her.

''At the time I thought nothing of it. But now I believe that place is real. And something bad is trying to get here from it. I've been guided to the Compass Cross, and now, suddenly, I'm sitting right on top of it. Gary Gaimes won't tell me where the house is, but he told me there were four people in it now. Bridget—whatever is using her—set its traps, and now they're sprung. I don't know what that thing is—the boogeyman, Satan, the Three Stooges's little sister—but if those four people die in that house, you're going to have more problems on your hands than a serial killer named Gary Gaimes—''

Falconi noticed a florid-faced, uniformed cop with a blond mustache and thin receding hairline standing in the doorway of his glassed-in office.

"What is it, Guinty?"

Detective Guinty stood mute.

"Well?" Falconi bellowed.

"Gary Gaimes, sir."

"What about him?"

Guinty looked like he'd rather be anywhere else on earth. "He's gone, Lieutenant. He overpowered Martin while he was being fed. Cut him up with a sharpened spoon. Must have been working on it since his first meal—"

"*Jesus!*" Falconi roared. He stalked around his desk, pausing to glare murderously at Guinty before stomping into the hallway. He stopped, turned on his heel, and regarded Brennan. His voice came out with controlled fury.

"If I went by my gut now," he said, "you'd be a dead man. God knows what kind of shit you filled Gaimes's brain up with. I *personally* tracked this fucker for eight weeks, losing sleep every night, spending time away from my kid, my wife, just to suck him off the streets so he wouldn't slice anybody else up because his sick little mind told him to. I'd be willing to believe just about anything about him—that his old man put his head in a vise when he was five, his mother stuck lit cigarettes on his testicles, his neighbors came over every Friday and did things to him your average S and M nut wouldn't even know about. I'd believe anything, because his mind is twisted and that's why he did the things he did. I'd be willing to listen to anything about Gary Gaimes, because I'm interested in what turned him into the sick dog he is. If we find that out, maybe we can stop somebody else from becoming a sick dog and slicing people up because they think it's the correct thing to do." His face was scarlet with anger; he brought his index finger up to point at Brennan, then brought himself under control and lowered it. "I would love to believe you, Dr. Brennan. To know that there was some other place beyond death, that all of the pain and hate and murder, all the sick shit I see every day was just a prelude to something else, something better—well, that would almost make it all worthwhile. I would have to say it would make me happy. But I'm sorry. I have to draw the line somewhere. And believing this *creep* Gary Gaimes is girl Friday for some monster from beyond the grave is just not something I'm prepared to do.''

Brennan crushed out his cigarette and began to gather his material into his briefcase. ''If you don't help me, Lieutenant,'' he said, ''you'll be one sorry asshole.''

Falconi raised his index finger again, thought better of it, gave Brennan a baleful stare before stomping off down the hallway, shouting, ''Minkowski!''

20. THE SOVIETS

Viktor Borodin never tired of America. What he tired of was fools. And, it seemed that in America there were so many fools. It only made his job more difficult.

Today, though, he was forced to admit, *The fool is our own.*

In fact, he had rather enjoyed the report. Couched in hysterical terms, syntax that in the old days, perhaps even during Brezhnev's reign, would have stricken icy fear into the heart of any bureaucrat unlucky enough to have it land on his desk, the report was, in these new days, these days of perestroika, of glasnost, taken very seriously by Borodin. But he had also allowed himself to see the comical side of it. It was almost like French farce. Here was this third-rate *Pole,* sequestered in an underground detention camp near Treblinka that some idiot in Warsaw had decided to set up to study ardent Solidarity supporters, in order to come up with some way to break their spirit—and the union's—and it turns out this fellow was not the man the officials thought he was and should not have been taken to begin with! And not only that, here was this fellow, this *Polack,* after one month of near-isolation, mental torture, and physical abuse, not only escaping his detention, but murdering the camp commandant (another stupid *Polack*) and, not so funny, his visiting Soviet liaison. Then—and this was the most farcical of all—this crazy man takes the liaison's clothes, matches his mannerisms and voice, rides his limousine to the Krakow airport, where he boards an Aeroflot jet, flies to New York, and, rather than stopping in for a chat at the embassy in Riverdale, has the waiting limousine driver drop him at a private residence in upstate New York.

Beautiful, just beautiful. Funny as hell.

But, again, not all that funny.

Viktor could afford to laugh, and openly, because he knew that in a day or two he would have this Polish whelp by the collar, singing like a whippoorwill, stripped of his stolen clothes, and on his way to Moscow.

But there were other KGB agents who were not laughing, because the Soviet attaché had apparently been wearing an Italian suit, something he should not have been able to afford. There were all kinds of allegations, from bribery to spying, which also gave Borodin a hearty belly laugh, because all of Liukin's men at home—and Viktor, from this distance, thought of them as his dear, dear brothers in arms who had the bad luck to deal with bad Russian plumbing, rotten Russian food, terrible Russian television, atrocious movies, despicable weather, ugly women—were shaking in their boots.

Yes, he loved America.

Except for the fools.

Viktor tapped on the glass partition; his driver slid the small window back and cocked his ear. "Drive slowly for a little while, Mikhail. This is the nicest part of the Hudson Valley in the fall." As an afterthought, for fun, he added, "Don't you agree?" He watched as Mikhail, a proper public servant, nodded briskly to the order, but ignored, and properly so, the intimacy, the invitation to opinion. "Just drive," Viktor said heartily, and Mikhail, nodding briskly, at once shut the opaque window and slowed the car five miles an hour.

This was a lovely part of the country. One of the pleasures Viktor had allowed himself was reading Washington Irving, the short story writer and essayist, who had described this area of New York so perfectly. Viktor doubted that, at least at certain times of the year such as high autumn and June, there was a more beautiful spot in all of the United States. He had been stationed many places before coming to New York, and he had never seen the kind of foliage he was witnessing now: long vast valleys sloping off the Taconic Parkway to the near horizon, trees in blinding reds and yellows broken only by the occasional dairy barn or silo. He considered telling Mikhail to pull into one of the turnouts they were passing at regular intervals, so that he could get out of the car and feel, away from the confines of the automobile, the true sweep of the autumn vista. But that was not something he could do in laughter, because Mikhail, who watched him as surely as Viktor watched everyone else, would be safe to report that Viktor Borodin had not only taken it upon himself to slow his car down but wasted more time away from the business of the state by actually stopping the car to enjoy a frivolous view.

Viktor sighed; turning away from his view, he once again tapped on the smoked glass partition. When it opened, he said, in a curt voice, "We have wasted enough time, Mikhail. Find the house."

Which they did, soon enough. The directions had been excellent, for once; apparently the driver who had been fooled into bringing the Pole up here was so contrite—or, more to the point, so frightened—that he had provided each detail, down to the tilted mailbox on the corner where they last turned and the description of the way the trees suddenly parted to give a view of the house, which was well off the road, before swallowing it up again.

They slowed, the way the driver had told them to; and the trees parted as if drawn back by an invisible hand (the colors were breathtaking up here, the roads dusted with first fallings that only reflected and intensified the colors in the trees), and they found the narrow drive and were soon in front of the house.

A gloomy place, Viktor thought. He allowed Mikhail to open the door of the Cadillac for him (oh, these wonderful American limousines!) and to assist his bulk out. Leaning on his cane, he looked up at the front of the place.

Gloomy, unkempt. A big Victorian that may at one time have been very beautiful. Now it looked a little like the house in *Psycho,* that wonderful film of Hitchcock's American period. High attic cupola topped by a rusted weathercock. Chipped scrollwork under the eaves. Tall stained-glass windows needing a good cleaning. There was nothing as depressing as soiled stained glass. That was one thing the Church knew.

Viktor eyed the door: large, darkly recessed under a paint-peeled porch. It looked as though it hadn't opened in a long time.

It certainly had, at least once recently, to let in a daring, infamous, desperate Polack.

Viktor stepped toward the porch.

Mikhail, standing deferentially by the car, said, "Shall I come with you, sir?"

To himself, Viktor snorted. *Not to help, but to watch me, no doubt.*

"No. Stay with the car." He smiled, grimly. "He could escape, steal the car, and get away from us—and then what?"

The *then what,* meaning, *and then what would happen to our asses?* seemed to penetrate Mikhail's tiny mind, and he nodded sharply. Already he looked diligent, watching for wild Polacks leaping from windows or charging from the shrubbery.

Shaking his head in wonder, Viktor Borodin walked to the door and knocked on it.

There was no answer. But, then, he hadn't expected one. He knocked again, shouting, "Jan Pesak! We know you're in there! Please come quietly, I'm sure we can figure something out to make us all happy!"

Meaning, of course, that Pesak, if he had any more brains than Mikhail, would be long gone, would have contacted some Western agency by now, either the State Department or the press, and, at the very least, blabbed his story if not begged asylum. Then again, he might still be here.

He is a Polack, after all.

"Jan Pesak!" Viktor shouted again. When he put his hand on the door, it opened halfway, on its own.

Standing where he was, Borodin pushed the door open the rest of the way with his cane.

A dimly lit vestibule was revealed, with no one in it.

Viktor snorted, looked back at Mikhail, and stepped into the house.

Somewhere in the long distance behind him he heard the front door close. But when he turned in the sudden darkness to look at it, there was no doorway there.

There was sudden light.

He was walking on snow. He felt stone beneath; he was on a snow-covered stone walkway that widened out all around him. It was early morning. The sun was low in the east, rising filtered through gray clouds thickening overhead. They promised more snow later. Someone had his arm around him; when Viktor turned to see who it was, he was met by a bearish grin in a face that *seemed* like that of a bear, all covered with hair. The man's teeth were bad; it looked as though his gums bled. The eyes in the grinning face were as cold and flat as small black coins.

"*So*, comrade, it is so *good* to have you back with us." The man hugged Viktor with his arm, using his free arm to gesture around them at what, Viktor realized with a shock, was Red Square. "Doesn't it feel wonderful to be back?"

Dazedly—and because the man was gazing at him with such purpose—Viktor nodded.

The man hugged him close again. "Good," his huffing breath said; even in the cold, in the fresh air of morning, and at a discreet distance, Viktor could smell his bad breath.

They walked on. The Kremlin grew closer. There were guards, at rigid attention. They smacked their heels together and saluted as the man and Viktor passed. The man waved lazily at them and their saluting hands lowered to their sides.

They passed through a small courtyard, through an iron gate, into a building. Viktor, who had been to the Kremlin, didn't recognize it. Neither did he recognize the way they had come, the guard's entrance, the descending, darkly lit hallway they now passed through.

They walked for a long time. Viktor's companion had ceased speaking, and now he took his arm away from Viktor and began to walk in a more military fashion. Stealing a look at him, Viktor saw that his right ear was partly gone; it looked as though it had been bitten off, a ragged toothline of healed tissue ridged above the lobe.

Viktor was becoming short of breath; he desperately hoped they would reach their destination before he was beset by an emphysemic attack. His companion increased their pace, beginning to swing his arms at his side like a soldier, eyes straight ahead. Viktor did all that he could do to keep up. Suddenly he stopped, leaning on his cane, and said, "See here! You'll have to wait."

The other ignored him, marching on ahead, and soon was lost in the dim downward slope of the hall.

After a mental count of sixty, a common technique, Viktor Borodin had regained his breath to the point where he could rise off his cane and take in his surroundings.

The initial shock of finding himself here had worn off. He was left with more a sense of wonder than anything. Had he wandered into some secret experiment? Could the Polack Pesak be something much more than he had seemed, or that he, Viktor Borodin, had been told about? Viktor reached out to touch the walls, found them solid and real. Could this be an illusion? An induced dream? Temporal travel? Sensory deprivation? Something to do with Star Wars, SDI?

Amazing, Viktor thought, tapping the dull green concrete wall, the ceiling, with his cane. Absolutely amazing.

But in forty years, working for the people he worked for, he had seen things nearly as strange.

There was nothing to do but go on.

At his own pace, he followed the bearish soldier. He heard faint sounds up ahead, a door opening, closing. Another, familiar sound, between the opening and closing, which his mind did not solidify because of its brevity. He walked on.

The slope in the hallway gradually diminished, disappeared. The walls changed. They were no longer dull green; there was paneling covering them now, a rich, deep cherry shade. The bare floor changed to gray shag carpeting. There were more lights, the feeling of being in an entranceway rather than an endless hall.

He came to a door.

Two doors. He had seen their kind before, in America. The doors and the fleeting sound he had heard linked momentarily, dissolved into failed memory. The doors were tall and wide, with a curtained round window set in each.

He put his cane against the door on the right, pushed at it.

It swung inward, and at that moment he knew the sound and the kind of doors they were.

He pushed the door all the way open and walked forward cautiously into darkness. He heard a ratcheting sound off to his right. Suddenly, a beam of light stabbed the darkness past him and illuminated a movie screen set above a small stage. In the silvery radiance he saw rows of movie theater chairs, their seats sprung up. The theater was empty. The screen continued to show bare whiteness. Then, just as a countdown of numbers began on the screen, some in circles and some upside down, denoting the beginning of a picture, he saw, out of the corner of his eye, off in the back corner, a gray puff of smoke, heard a voice call him.

"Come here—sit next to me."

The voice held lazy command. On the screen, a black-and-white globe of the world appeared; around it flew an airplane with a propeller on its front. Viktor walked through the beam, was blinded by it.

"Hurry, you'll ruin the picture," the voice in the back said.

Viktor ducked under the low beam of the light. As he reached the darkened back corner, he felt a large hand take hold of him and press him into a seat.

He turned to see the face that possessed the hand, but between the natural darkness of the corner and the weak glare from the distant black-and-white film, Viktor could not make out the features.

"Watch the screen," the voice scolded. "The film is beginning."

The credits, which Viktor had paid no attention to, rolled off, and the movie began.

Viktor stared at the screen. He listened to the booming, hearty laughter of the figure in the seat next to him. He studied the screen and realized what he was watching. It was a Laurel and Hardy film. Stan and Ollie had fooled their wives into thinking they were going on a cruise for Ollie's health. In fact, they were attending a convention. An actor on the screen, whom Viktor recognized as another great comic, Charley Chase, bedecked in fez and smoking a cigar, held a crowd of conventioneers enthralled with his trick of dropping a wallet and then whacking anyone who bent to pick it up with a wooden paddle. Ollie, naturally, became a victim.

Viktor knew the sequence and the film well. Before long, he was laughing as loud as the man in the seat next to him. Later in the film, Stan and Ollie have been photographed by a newsreel camera while marching in a parade with their fellow conventioneers, known as Sons of the Desert. The film is then seen by their worried wives, who have found that the ship they were supposed to have been on for Ollie's health has gone down at sea.

The man next to Viktor, watching Stan's innocently, naively smiling face while their wives register shock and then vengeful anger, burst into coughing paroxysms of laughter, hitting his knee with loud slapping sounds in the dark, barely able to catch his breath.

"Are you all right?" Viktor whispered, doubtful whether the man's fit was still laughter or a fight for breath.

"Yes, yes," the figure laughed, smacking Viktor once on the knee before bursting into a fresh bout of uncontrollable mirth. "Oh, I tell you, these men are *geniuses*!"

Viktor, again caught in the mood of the classic picture, following the subtitles with keen interest, had to agree.

After much laughter, the film was over. Viktor watched "The End" flash. The screen then went dark. Viktor waited for lights to come up.

Nothing happened. The figure next to him had gone silent. Viktor felt alone in the dark. For a moment his eyes saw nothing. He thought he might once again be afloat in the space continuum, to be relocated who knew where. Perhaps he was heading back to the house in New York State. Perhaps on some further bizarre adventure.

But then his eyes adjusted. He saw the dark outline of the rows of seats in front of him, heard the man in the seat next to him shift and cough.

A small square of light went on behind him. Viktor turned to see a bulb shining within the projection room. A figure was moving in there, eclipsing the movie projector and then moving away from it again.

"What are we to have next?" the man beside Viktor called out, impatiently.

The figure in the booth, backlit, once again walked in front of the projector. "I have managed to obtain *Gone With the Wind*."

"Ah." The man beside Viktor lost his impatience. "*Excellent*. But let's finish with this piece of business first, shall we, Alexi?"

"Of course," the man in the projection booth answered.

Viktor heard a door open in the back. He saw a shaft of light cut off as someone entered the theater. A flashlight went on, bobbed toward them. The man holding it stopped at their row, counting to himself, and attempting to enter, bumped on the aisle seat. He gave a low curse.

The man next to Viktor chuckled. "Come along, Alexi."

"Yes."

The flashlight steadied on the floor. Viktor watched the figure approach. It stopped when the flashlight found his shoes in their beam. The man holding it cleared his throat.

The man sitting next to Viktor said, "Go ahead, Alexi."

The man holding the flashlight angled it up across Viktor's face to hold it under his own. It gave him a ghoulish appearance, lighting his face from below. But Viktor knew him. It was the hairy man who had met Viktor outside in Red Square and brought him here.

"Hello, again," Alexi said to Viktor, tilting the flashlight beam down directly into his face.

Viktor winced and turned toward the man sitting in the seat next to him. He saw the man's face, in faint illumination.

He gasped.

"Shall I take him now, Premier?"

Joseph Stalin, looking boredly ahead toward the movie screen, seemingly lost in thought and slitting his eyes slightly against the beam of the flashlight, nodded.

"Here, Premier?"

Stalin turned his hawk's eyes on Alexi. Viktor felt the man stiffen. Suddenly Stalin's attention waned; he turned disinterestedly toward the screen again. "Yes."

The man with the flashlight fumbled through his clothes.

The beam of the flashlight was raised into Viktor's face again. He felt something heavy and cold placed in his lap.

"Pick it up," Alexi said coldly.

Viktor put his hand on the object and pulled away from it. A pistol. He had not held a gun in twenty years.

"Put it in your hand and lift it," Alexi ordered.

Viktor sat frozen; suddenly he felt Stalin's large hand on his own, the same one that had slapped the premier's knee in humor during the movie. Stalin's hand patted his.

"Pick up the pistol like Alexi told you," the premier said quietly.

Nearly immobile with terror, Viktor turned to look into the face that had stared out at him from history books since he was a child. He was only twenty-four when Stalin died; when Stalin was still alive, his mother had scared him to bed with threats of the ogre getting him. The ogre had gotten enough of them. Viktor's uncle had been caught dead in one of the purges; another uncle had died in Siberia twenty years after being sent there for an infraction that no one, including the men who had dragged him away one night from his home, where he had been reading his paper, had ever been able to articulate. Viktor had had nightmares involving that face until he was in his thirties; in the KGB, there were stories that constantly floated, mostly by the old-timers ready to quit and anxious for any kind of attention at all as they sat behind their desks, about the atrocities Stalin himself had privately committed—the electricity in women's vaginas, the ritual unmanning of boys he had tired of. The stories were endless. Whatever truth they held was superseded by the need these old-timers had of expressing in some way the absolute terror that had reigned during those times. It was not bureaucracy, the stodgy powerful beast that could grind you up in its machinery but do it impersonally—that came later. It was much worse—a constant, gnawing paranoia, a perpetual state of war in which no one was safe from foe, friend, even family. It was not angst and desperation that had ruled Mother Russia during those years, it was pure chemical terror, wielded by this man sitting next to him, this vicious fox, murderer of Trotsky, murderer of the Revolution itself. They had taught many versions of this man in the history books over the years; it was even said that he was as much wildly loved as feared and hated. But no one, not those old men in their fanny-worn chairs, nor the prisoners, nor the men, like Khrushchev, who had placed themselves well by managing to avoid his eye, no, no one Viktor Borodin had ever spoken to, or witnessed testimony from—even those who had professed love—had ever spoken of Iosif Vissarionovich Dzhugashvili, the son of a peasant from Georgia who had grown up to become Joseph Stalin, in terms that didn't contain the word fear.

Victor Borodin felt that fear now. The man was godlike with it. He was plain enough looking, his flat face, piggish eyes, and full, florid mustache unremarkable separately; his plain dress, the drab olive coat buttoned to the neck—all of this unremarkable in part, but devastating in total. There had been similar stories, which Viktor had been more inclined to believe were folklore, of the power of Rasputin. Rasputin would have wilted like a cold rose had he ever met this man.

"Viktor Borodin," Stalin said, his hand still on Viktor's own, now pressing Viktor's fingers around the handle of the gun. "I want you to lift this gun and put it in your mouth." His slitted eyes looked somehow huge, piercing him with a light more powerful than the flashlight beam. "You have been judged, Viktor Borodin, and you have been sentenced. Believe me, there is no reprieve."

To Viktor's great surprise, he found himself lifting the pistol. His hand trembled. Stalin's hand steadied him.

"Put the gun in your mouth and pull the trigger."

The man was like a cobra. Viktor Borodin, even as the hand followed Stalin's instructions, brought the gun to his mouth, set it inside (it was cold, radiated cold even before it touched his tongue; he thought of tongue depressors, the cold breast of a spoon bringing cough medicine into his throat), thought about whether all of this was really happening. He wondered if he really could have traveled in time as well as space.

Even as he thought these things, staring into the blank, commanding face of Joseph Stalin, he pulled the trigger and found that what he experienced was real.

• • •

Outside the house, when Mikhail, Borodin's driver, heard the single shot, his first impulse was to find a phone and call for instructions. Then another thought penetrated his brain. If he called in to tell them he had let Comrade Borodin go into the house alone, a house where a dangerous enemy of the state was known to be, a desperate man, it would be, as Comrade Borodin might say, "his ass."

Mikhail opened the front passenger door to the limousine and flipped down the door on the glove compartment. He pulled on the plastic map shelf, and it popped out, revealing a lit well behind it.

Mikhail reached into the well and brought out a Kolnokov automatic pistol. He checked the clip, reached back into the well and produced a second clip, which he put into the pocket of his coat.

He slammed the car door and walked to the front door. He listened against it, heard nothing, stepped back to kick it in.

It opened on its own. Mikhail immediately slid to the side, cocked gun before him. He heard nothing. He waited a long time, then edged around, taking in larger and larger portions of the front inside hallway with his eyes. It was seemingly empty.

"Comrade Borodin?" he called into the hallway.

Someone moved out beyond the hallway; the house was damnably dark inside.

"Comrade?"

No answer.

In a quick, almost catlike movement, Mikhail was inside the house.

And falling.

Somewhere above him, he heard the front door close. He began to scream. Darkness below him turned into great height. He felt the air of the upper atmosphere rushing past him, throwing him downward toward the farm-checkered, colored landscape thousands of feet below. He heard the prop-roar of a plane; just droning away into the distance toward the horizon was the trainer he had been pushed out of. He remembered this scene; he was making his first jump, had been scared, and the instructor, a brash fellow his own age who would be killed a month later on a routine jump of his own, had called him a coward and shoved him through the opening, laughing down to him that he would either use his parachute or die not using it.

During that first jump, he had screamed, flailing around in the air. The ground had gotten closer; he had seen farm implements and had had a sudden horrible vision of himself hitting a tractor, smashed to atoms, flesh against metal. Desperately, he had reached for the rip cord, and it had been there. Now it wasn't. There was no cord, no straps, no parachute or backup. There was only the drab long coat he had been wearing a moment before.

Up high in the air, dropping, Mikhail screamed. The earth, pastel patches resolving into rows of wheat, a rising trail of dust becoming a ponderous yellow tractor, rose up toward him. Desperately, Mikhail began to beat himself with his fists, trying to wake up.

The ground rushed up like a sucking breath, and this time Mikhail hit the tractor.

21. EAST

Let him go, Jan.

Jan took his hands from the neck of the Russian driver, Mikhail. The body lay still as ice, the back of the head, where Jan had smashed it repeatedly against the floor, clotted with blood.

Pick up your gun, Jan. Put it away.

He did as she told him, removing the barrel of the pistol from Viktor Borodin's bloody, ruined mouth, idly wiping it on his pants and putting it in his pocket.

Jan, I have other work for you.

She told him what she wanted.

He tried to think through the humming sound, to put one rational thought next to another. It was difficult. She was so close to him now, the promise of her so all-abiding, that he could think of little else. He barely remembered coming to this house, owning another life before her. Had he had a mother once? Friends? He recalled names—Tadeusz, Jozef—but they were little more than words. He remembered an underground place, pain—but all of these vague images broke up and floated away from one another on the sea in his mind that was Bridget. His mind had her; when his body possessed her, he knew that he would cease to exist, and gladly so, because she was all that he knew.

They're bad, also. They want to hurt you, to separate us.

His face contorted in effort. He saw two faces, the boy, the man in the wheelchair, felt an odd kinship that defied his muddled examination. "No. They're not like these. I can't."

Jan.

He looked up for her, at the top of the stairs. He heard, through the hum, Ray laugh behind his closed door. Ricky, who had gone to his room after the death of the girl, hadn't even appeared when the Russians arrived.

Jan. Here. It's finally time.

He saw her briefly, beckoning to him from the open doorway in the corner between the north and west bedrooms.

Come, Jan.

He mounted the stairs to the second floor and stood before the narrow, curving staircase.

I'm waiting. I've waited so long.

He began to climb.

His head filled with thoughts of her. They came complete, as if he were already with her. He felt the heat of her flesh beneath him, her pulling intensity, her unfocused eyes staring into his face as her mouth, lost in need, made little urgent noises and said, roughly, "Yes, Jan, yes . . ."

He reeled, sat down on the steps. Their hardness brought him back to himself. He felt wood beneath his hand, not her flesh.

He blinked into the dim stairwell. The walls were very close.

Her voice said, "Come to me now, Jan."

He looked up. There she was. She was no vision, no mirage, this time. She was real.

"Bridget . . ." he said, his voice choked with wonder.

"Yes, Jan. It's me."

She was wearing a stark white satin robe, which contrasted sharply with the red of her hair. She let it drop from her shoulders. Her body was as he had remembered it, but real flesh. He saw the perfect mole on her right shoulder, and felt if he ran his finger down from her neck he would feel its bump beneath his touch.

"Come." She smiled. She turned and ascended the stairs ahead of him.

The curve of her buttocks, the heart-shaped roundness of their bottoms, the tuft of red hair visible below—he witnessed all of this, and his erection was instantaneous and overwhelming.

She was real.

At the top of the stairway Bridget opened a door.

He followed her into the same attic he had seen at the inn in Kolno. A round window of red glass suffused the room with rosy red light.

There was a mattress on the floor, made up in sheets with a quilt coverlet. Jan passed Bridget's robe coming into the room. He bent to pick it up.

"I don't need it, Jan."

She was there, real, in front of him. He felt her heat before he looked at her, felt the hairs all over his body rise. His erection was painfully hard.

She pressed herself to him, full flesh, and pulled at his belt.

"*Now,* Jan." She rubbed one leg up around him, pulled his face down to her mouth.

She worked his belt free and slid her hand into his trousers behind his underpants. "Yes," she laughed. She brought him kneeling to the bed. She pawed at the rest of his clothes, pulling his undershirt over his head. She pushed his trousers off, removed his shoes, his socks. Holding his face in her hands, kissing him, she moved him back on the bed against the pillows and straddled him.

She traced her tongue down his chest. Jan could feel himself building, the weeks of fantasy, the promises she had made, the desperate yearnings. He was like a new machine, rising to explosion. "Not yet, Jan." She rose above him, opened herself and took him inside her.

It was like Jan had dreamed; better. She was real. Her flesh was to him like his own. As he touched, explored her long, hard nipples with his hands, the hard flat flesh of her belly, her face, her hair, her mouth, it was as if he had always known her.

"No, Jan. Not yet."

She drew him deep into her. The pressure mounted. Jan held it back, crying out.

"Now, Jan."

He came. Her muffled, grunting cries mingled with his shouts of release. He arched higher; she went with him, holding him fast, pushing and draining him simultaneously. A river of hate and hurt and need flowed out of him. His orgasm went on. He was hers, completely. All that had been him roared out of him into her.

And then, suddenly, it was over.

He pulled her down to him, enfolded her in his arms. He felt her quick breath, her heated heart. Her flesh was real. She owned him. She was no vision.

"Are you happy, Jan?" she asked.

"Oh, yes," he sobbed, unable to cope with his feelings. "Oh, yes, yes."

"I love you, Jan."

"Yes."

"We're going to be together forever."

He squeezed her tighter, saw his happy new world through a shimmer of tears.

"Do you really love me, Jan?"

"Yes . . ."

"Do you need anyone else in the world, anything else in the world?"

"No . . ."

She looked up at him, love and adoration suffusing her face. "There is something you must do for me, Jan . . . ."

22. THE ASSISTANT

Invincible.

Gary Gaimes threw his hands over his mouth to stifle his laughter. All he felt like doing was laughing, because it had all turned out to be true.

He was invincible. Just as she had said, just as he had hoped, in the midst of all his doubts and fears. Whatever else she had done to him, whatever else she would have to pay for, she had been right about that.

Invincible. A blurt of laughter came up his throat. He was not quick enough to stifle it before it broke out of his hands. In-vin-ci-ble. He saw the stupid cop's face as he put the tray down and was met by an upthrust of sharp steel, his fishlike gasping as Gary pulled him to the floor of the cell, sitting astride his neck to keep the blood off the uniform, holding one hand over the cop's mouth while he finished him off. Twenty seconds. It had taken him twenty seconds to push the spoon handle back through the cop's eye into his brain while the breath pushed out of him under Gary's fingers in one long begging gasp.

The idiots outside the cell hadn't even looked at him.

Dinner time! Busy busy. Cap low over his eyes, a nod and a wave here and there, and then out the back, around the alley to the street.

Gone.

Invincible. IN. VIN. CI. BLE. Into the subway, another twenty seconds in a tunnel ("Excuse me, sir, may I see your identification please?" Who's going to question a fucking NYC cop?), and the man had a nice suit, too short in the legs, but a briefcase and even a nice driving cap with a snap brim. He kept the cop shoes, more comfortable. Then onto the D train, Rob Peters (or so the junk in the man's wallet said) paying for the token.

To . . . here.

Invincible!

Gary laughed again, stifled it this time. Was that a sound? No, it wasn't.

His laughter came, and he held both hands over his mouth to stop it.

What would he do after he finished here?

What would he do after he finished with Bridget?

He laughed again. What could an invincible man *not* do in New York City—in the world?

See the world?

Rule the world?

A laugh he couldn't stop burst out. He felt like a little boy again, hiding while that *man*, all those men, that long succession of men, did it with his mother in the living room, with that fucking record on, "The Games People Play," which she thought was *funny*, "My name being 'Gaimes' and all," (he thought of Meg fleetingly, 'Your name being Gary *Gaimes* and all.') clicking to the end on the fucking Victrola, then back again, clicking to the end—

He was grinding his hand into his other palm. He looked down, calmed. A little laughter escaped, he breathed back to easy—

A sound.

Yes, this time a sound. Finally. How many hours in the dark? Two? An invincible man (ha! The Invincible Man! Claude Rains!) could wait as long as it took. He wished he had that black kid from the S.S. *Eiderhorn* here, he could start on him right now, finish with the tire iron what she had made him stop. He'd start with the little fucker—

Key in the lock. Definitely. He wanted to laugh again, kept his dignity. Have to do this right. Be quiet. Falconi would approve . . .

A light on somewhere out front. Things thrown down. The *wish-wish* sound of a pulled-off coat. The coat down, too. A disgusted sigh.

Footsteps on linoleum, lost to the rug. A cabinet. Glass against glass, he's got the scotch or bourbon, glass in the same hand. Then down on a table. Pour. Close bottle. Drink the drink.

Ah.

Wish the little black fucker were here—

Another light on. The bathroom. Shit. He could be in there for a half hour. No. Flush, he's out, into the kitchen. Open door (refrigerator?), close door, open door (microwave?), close door. Good. Out of the kitchen.

Another light. Open the bedroom door, another light. Gary could see the hand on the light switch, four inches from his own hand.

Falconi would *like* this.

"Hello," Gary said, stabbing the screwdriver in his hand into the hand on the light switch, pinning it to the wall.

Brennan woke up groaning in the backseat of his car. It was night, and raining. He couldn't identify the pain at first; it enveloped him in a cloud, suffusing his consciousness; then, like a needle, it stabbed down into his right hand and stayed there, crying for attention. His hands were tied in front of him. He moved his left hand away from the wound as much as he could. The pain subsided slightly.

"Hurt?" Gary Gaimes grinned into the rearview mirror from the front seat.

"Yes," Brennan said, between clenched teeth.

Gaimes's grin widened. He turned back to the road, increasing the radio volume. Charlie Parker playing "Misty."

The pain in Brennan's hand lowered to an angry throb. He leaned back into the seat. They were on the highway, two lanes. Looked like the Hutchinson or Taconic. A few off-ramp signs would tell him.

Not thirty seconds later, they passed a green sign for upstate New York (Taconic Parkway) and Gaimes turned sharply onto the off ramp and got off.

The night blackened. No street lights. No comforting mall spots, industrial parking lots. Through the window, and his hurting hand, Brennan could see falling rain.

"Where are we going?" Brennan said.

Gaimes laughed shortly, turned down Charlie Parker. "Wanted to meet her, didn't you?"

Gaimes turned the radio back up.

Brennan was filled with a mixture of elation and dread.

The Compass Cross. He's taking me to Bridget.

"Maybe she'll eat you for breakfast," Gary Gaimes shouted, over the radio. He grinned in the rearview mirror. "Maybe *I* will."

Gaimes looked at Brennan a couple of times in the rearview mirror. Brennan stared back at him blankly.

Suddenly, Gaimes snapped off the radio.

"What's the matter, don't you believe I can do whatever I want?"

"No, I didn't say . . ." Brennan began in a soothing tone.

Gary gunned the engine. They were on a dark street somewhere, passing intermittent houses, a rolling road with a few turns. The car shot forward, hitting a bump that knocked the shocks badly. The car accelerated. A house went by, yellow dim lights back off the road. A pumpkin was on the porch, a cardboard skeleton's head in the window. They were doing forty-five, fifty, on a road that called for thirty, less when it rained.

Gaimes pushed the accelerator to the floor.

There were no cars ahead of them; they barely negotiated a gradual curve. Brennan could visualize the four nearly bald tires on the wheels of his Malibu, could see that jerk in the commercial holding his thumb and forefinger a quarter inch apart and saying that that was all that stood between you and the road, could see himself checking through his wallet two weeks ago, thinking about buying new tires and saying screw it, I'll get through the winter on what I have. Gaimes took another turn, a left one, the car gliding like an ice skater across the road.

Gaimes, hooting in glee, twisted the wheel, barely keeping the car on the street. The tires squealed, caught roadway.

Gaimes turned to laugh into Ted Brennan's face.

"Want to see if it's true?"

There was a straight stretch of darkness. Gaimes roared into it. Suddenly, he turned the wheel hard to the right. The car slid, caught on the tarmac, turned sharply. Wet, heavy tree branches thwacked the side of the car. The trees parted.

They roared into a driveway.

Through the left side window Brennan saw the dark outline of a tall house. It looked like all the lights were on in it. They sped past. There was a hard bump as they left the drive. The tires threatened to sink in wet grass, but forward momentum carried them on.

"Let's see!" Gary Gaimes screamed.

Something large loomed ahead of them. The tires spun, caught on dirt. They shot ahead. The looming presence resolved into a line of white birch trees. They grew closer. The headlights stabbed a single tree and pulled them toward it.

"Want to—" Gary Gaimes shouted, but then they hit the birch as Brennan threw himself to the floor in the backseat.

There was a crash, a grind of metal. A steaming sound.

A grunting shout from Gary Grimes.

Brennan rose up from the backseat. His tied hands made him move awkwardly. He felt rain on his face. To his right, the window had shattered. Driving rain pelted him. The front of the car had moved substantially toward the back.

Brennan wiped water from his eyes with his tied hands and tried to see into the front seat. The glove compartment had nearly met the passenger seat. The headlights had gone out; the engine had stalled with the loss of coolant. Red warning lights illumined the front driver's side.

He felt for Gary Gaimes, couldn't find him. He reached forward, found Gaimes's head slumped over the top of the steering wheel.

He put a hand to Gaimes's neck, searched for a pulse.

It was there, strong.

Gaimes's head snapped up.

Brennan yanked his hand away as Gaimes began to yell. Gaimes tried to grab Brennan, then threw his hands toward the dashboard and tried to push the steering wheel away from his chest.

"GODDAMN MOTHERFUCKER, GET THIS OFF OF ME! I'M FUCKING INVINCIBLE! I'M INVINCIBLE!"

Gaimes beat madly at the steering column, breaking the top part of the wheel off with his hands. Brennan tried the handle of the door on the driver's side. The handle moved, but the door wouldn't open. He slid back across the seat and kicked at it.

"YOU FUCKER I'LL KILL YOU! I'LL GET OUT OF HERE AND KILL YOU!" Gaimes held the broken steering wheel behind his head and tried to hit Brennan with it. Ted kicked at the door harder. It wouldn't move. The steering wheel caught him a glancing blow on the side of the head. He pushed it away, shifting in the seat to try the door on the other side.

It was crushed tight, wouldn't open.

"YOU FUCKER! YOU FUCKER! I'LL KILL YOU. I'LL KILL EVERYONE!"

Gaimes managed to turn half around in the front seat. He clawed at Brennan, struck at him in the cramped car interior with the curve of steering wheel. Brennan shouted as the wheel hit him behind the ear.

Clawing over the front seat, Gaimes pulled himself half free and grabbed at Brennan's shoulders. He moved his hands up to Brennan's face, gouging at his cheeks with his fingernails.

Brennan kicked at the glass shards in the window to his right, pushed them out into the rain. He stopped to pull Gaimes's fingers from his face. Gaimes flailed over him, pulling at his hair, grunting in effort to free his pinned legs.

"...KILL...YOU..."

Ted Brennan threw himself out of Gaimes's grasp and toward the open window, bound hands first. He closed his eyes, pushing his head through after his arms. There was a burning slice of pain up his left side. He kept struggling. Gaimes pounded at Brennan's legs with his fists, trying to keep him in the car.

"... FUCKER!"

Brennan's left arm throbbed with agony. He forced his hands against the side of the window frame and wedged himself out. He kicked at Gaimes.

Brennan fell out onto the grass. Rain pelted him. Fighting for breath, he pushed himself to his knees, then to his feet.

In the car, Gary Gaimes struggled and screamed. His voice became inhuman, a sound of rage like that of a wounded beast.

Ted Brennan lurched away from the car. Rain-darkened night assaulted him. A cold wind was blowing, a November gale filling the world with water. He stepped in puddles, began to shiver.

He stumbled to the driveway.

Behind him, the cries continued.

Brennan stood looking up at the house. It pulsed like a living thing, red lights through all the windows growing bright and then dimming. Brennan heard an unmistakable low hum that seemed to grow from the house into the ground itself. He felt as if he were standing on a generator; he could feel the vibration into his bones. Despite the rain, the tearing flame of the wound in his arm, the tight cold fear that Gary Gaimes would lurch toward him from the remains of the car and murder him where he stood, he was mesmerized.

The Compass Cross.

Terrified elation filled him.

Yes, the house said to him. *You've found me. Come see.*

Brennan heard a wrench of metal from the car in the back. Gary Gaimes shouted triumphantly.

Come see.

Brennan backed away.

Come . . .

"KILL YOU!" Gary Gaimes shrieked.

Brennan reached the wet street. Rain roared in torrents down the curbs.

Come . . .

Brennan splashed through the street river. The burning in his left side flared to unbearable heat. He collapsed, began to black out.

"No!" he shouted at himself. He rolled onto his back, in the middle of the street, rain soaking into his mouth. *No . . .*

His mind slipped. The rain soothed him, beat on his face like on a tin roof, lulling, singing to him . . .

No . . .

With his last tiny flare of consciousness, Brennan reached his bound hands over his body, straightened his fingers, and drove them straight into the open wound on his side. He screamed. He dug his fingers into the wound, raking pain up until his eyes opened and he rolled onto his knees, panting and crying.

"God, oh, God . . ."

Up the driveway, he saw the top of the house above the trees. The red glow brightened, dimmed.

Come . . .

Panting, Brennan rose and staggered on. His left side was numb. He concentrated on it, blocked everything else out, his shivering, the call of the house, Gary Gaimes's cries, his fear. When his eyes began to close, his knees weaken, he dug his fingers into the numb area, stoking pain into it like a waning fire.

He prayed for a refuge, a house, a school, a country store. There was nothing. Only night, whipping trees, the sky open like God's screaming wrathful mouth with rain, and wind, and cold. Pain.

There was a sound behind him. He turned, saw nothing.

There was a car.

It moved along the curb, slowly, lights off.

Brennan's heart moved into his mouth.

He crossed to the other side of the street. The car silently turned, rolled after him. It was closer to him now; he heard the humming purr of its engine.

"Sweet Jesus," Brennan sobbed. He dropped to his knees in the road.

The car moved closer.

Brennan forced himself to his feet. His left side had turned into hard, wet fire. He dropped to his knees, looked back. The car was nearly on him.

"Oh, God."

He saw through a haze of pain. The front of the car was

crushed, pushed back like paper to the driver's seat; through the windshield he saw Gary Gaimes's howling, triumphant face, one fist punching toward him in victory.

"Oh . . . God . . ."

Ted Brennan fell forward into the road, onto his right hand. The pain did not keep him from unconsciousness, which rose toward him like the wet road, enveloping him, taking him to hard sleep . . .

Soon after, consciousness pushed him fleetingly back into the world. He felt himself lifted. He opened his eyes. He saw the dull yellow dome light of a car interior. He cried out, then looked into a face that was not Gary Gaimes's—

He went back to unconsciousness. But as he dropped back to it he heard, like the volume on a radio turning down, Falconi's voice, not altogether filled with animosity, say, "Who's a sorry asshole?"

23. SOUTH

A dream within a dream.

On the bed in the dream house, Ricky slept. So tired. Could you sleep in your dream? Maybe when he woke up, all the dreams would be gone, and he would be back in his bed in his mother's house, and she would shake him gently and say, "Ricky boy, time to get up, lazy boy, no work today, a beautiful day outside, the sun is shining, the sky is blue, get up and smell the salt air, your friends are waiting . . ."

A dream within a dream.

He was with Spook, and Spook was not dead, and they were on the ferry dock with Reesa and Charlie. The sky was as blue as Paul Newman's eyes. His mother was right. He never had seen such a beautiful color of sky, or such a beautiful warmth on his skin, or a more beautiful touch of cool, mild salt sea air across his wet skin. He swam, and Spook and Reesa and Charlie swam beside him, and they were like a school of beautiful angelfish swimming in the cool and mild salt sea of his home. When he came up to the surface and shouted happily and pulled soft air into his lungs, he could almost smell the limestone of the houses on his beautiful island. He could almost smell the limestone of his own roof, on his own home, with his mother inside cooking dinner for him and singing because she was happy.

And then his mother was there in the water with him. She was swimming beside him, another beautiful angelfish in the mirror-clear sea, and she rose to the surface with him and shouted happily alongside him and pulled fresh cool-warm air into her lungs and smelled the limestone of the houses with him. She was happy with him. And all the world was happy in the blue sky with high small clouds, trouble so far away, trouble like tiny clouds so high in the sky that no plane could reach them. The blue of the sky overwhelmed the clouds and made them insignificant.

"And someday," his mother said to him, "my Ricky will be as famous as Ben Vereen, and sing on Broadway, and be on TV, and I'll watch you on the satellite dish, and I'll be so proud of my boy!"

"We'll all be so proud!" Reesa said, rising up to the surface next to him and pulling the fresh air into her lungs, and Charlie and Spook rose next to her and said, "Yeah!" and "Yeah!"

And then Reesa kissed him, and laughed, and dove down into the clear water, and Ricky watched her, and Charlie laughed and dove too, and said before he hit the water, "She's yours, Ricky boy! She loves you!" and Spook laughed too, and then his mother laughed and dove down, and he was about to follow when he looked up into the blue-bright sky, and a hand came over the sun, over the sky, high up in the tiny clouds, and grew big and dropped, blotting out the sun and beautiful sky, and a huge shadow of the hand fell across the water, and the shadow of the hand grew toward him as the hand fell toward him—

—and Ricky cried out and awoke, and the dream within a dream was gone as a hand hit him in the face, and a face stood over him, and he was back in the bad dream in the dream house and the hand rose up where the beautiful blue sky should be, and fell, and hit him again, and he cried out and tried to cover his face, and there was a terrible loud hum in his ears, and brightening red light all around, and he looked up to see a face he knew from that terrible dream hovering over him, a face that belonged to the man who had offered him tea and biscuits, and the man's hand turned into a fist and hit him again, and then again, and the terrible dream began to go away, and the hum receded, and off in the distance, he heard the sea, and saw, vaguely, the blue sky, and the hand pulling up away into the clouds, and he felt himself lifted as the dream within a dream returned—

—but now he was in Chambers House. He was alone, and it was night, and the house was locked tight and dark around him. Off in the distance he heard something break. There was laughter.

A door opened in front of him. The cellar. He saw light, saw a shape move across the light, occluding it.

"Come down, Ricky," he heard someone say.

He found himself moving toward the cellar door, descending the stairs.

"Come down, Ricky. Come down."

When he reached the bottom of the stairs, darkness descended on him again. Then he saw a light on at the back of the cellar. Again, someone walked in front of it, blocking it out.

"Come here, Ricky," a voice said.

He began to walk.

"Come . . ."

His legs kept moving, but he found it difficult to walk. He looked down. The floor was covered with blood, rising like a red tide over his shoes to his ankles.

"Come on, Ricky. Come on."

He tried to walk, but his feet could not move. Then suddenly he *was* moving, his feet pulled by the wash of blood like a sucking tide.

"Come . . ."

The tide of blood pulled him around into the cleared area of the cellar. Bright light blinded him. Then he could see.

Spook stood propped against the back wall of the cellar, holding his own head. The tide of blood washed away from Ricky over the floor and up Spook's body, pulled back into his open neck cavity.

Spook's head, the mouth smiling, said, "Time to go now, Ricky." One of his hands rose up, holding a hammer, which suddenly grew very large, the flat front expanding, filling Ricky's entire field of vision.

"Time to dance," Spook said—

—and Ricky opened his eyes as the hammer came down at his face. He cried out, trying to deflect the blow, but the flat of the hammer hit him square, and his cry turned to a dull gasp. His vision began to blur as the hammer rose away from him, and again he saw the face of the young Polish man above him. Such a terrible dream. The Polish man raised the hammer high, and then it came down quickly, and now the head of the hammer filled his whole vision again, and he barely felt the blow, and—

—suddenly he was dancing, on Broadway, at a real theater, not the horrible dream theater with people sleeping on the street outside, but a theater like in a Busby Berkeley movie, and there was wild applause, and there in the audience, in the front row, was his mother and Reesa and Charlie, and Spook cradling his head in his arms and applauding, they were all applauding, and somewhere above he felt another dull blow from the hammer again, but he danced, and when he looked to his right there was Ben Vereen, dancing with him, and to his left was Tommy Tune, and the audience was cheering as the three of them danced into abrupt hard blackness—

Jan raised the hammer, brought it down again, raised it up, brought it down. On the floor of the cellar, the hammer struck into the inert bony flesh of Ricky's head as if striking a wet sponge. And still Jan raised the hammer, brought it down—

"Mind if I have a try?"

The calm voice behind Jan startled him. Panting, dull-eyed, the thick, mindless hum of the house filling his mind, he turned to see a figure standing quietly behind him. A cold breeze moved over Jan's face. Behind the figure, a cellar window was broken open, the floor littered with shards of glass.

"Here," the smiling figure said, taking the hammer from Jan's limp hand, edging Jan gently back.

The figure turned to Ricky's body and shouted, "Yes, you fucker!" bringing the hammer up and down in quick short jerks, moving up and down the body. He began to laugh. The body moved dully with each strike of the hammer. The man moved to the head, the hammer came up high, rushed down.

"You see?" the man said to Jan, examining his work. He pulled the hammer from the body and turned, striking Jan square in the face with it.

Jan cried out and threw his hands up. The man hit him again, bringing the hammer around in a wide arc to strike at his ribs.

The hammer struck again, and Jan fell. Gary Gaimes howled. He kicked the body down flat, then jumped onto it, pulling the trembling hands away from Jan's face to hit a direct blow. Blood came up at him. Gaimes howled louder. He felt the hammer like a fist, a tire iron, an extension of his hand, his soul. He brought it down again and again until the thing under him was an unrecognizable mass.

"All right!" he screamed. "All right!"

Gary Gaimes stood. He raised his voice to a wolflike howl. His eyes behind his glasses were like two saucers in his face. Around him, deep red light began to pulse like a huge living heartbeat. The hum of the house became a throbbing roar.

Gaimes whirled and struck a final time at the lifeless body of Jan on the floor, then held the hammer up, muscles tight in triumph.

"ALL RIGHT, BRIDGET," he screamed, laughing. "LET'S PLAY!"

24. FALCONI

"I hardly know what to say, Lieutenant Falconi. A murderer, you said? To think that something like this could happen just down the street. . . . Well, I suppose it could happen *anywhere* these days, anywhere at all. Why, just in the *Times* the other day there was a story about a man who cannibalized his family. Killed them and ate them. Down in Georgia, I believe. Years ago, you would never have seen anything like *that* in the *Times* . . ."

The voice, gentle, slight, was a susurrus to Ted Brennan's ears. As he rose from unconsciousness, the voice sought to press him back down to it. For a moment he thought it was the voice of Beauvaque, and that he might rise to consciousness in the big bed in the big dark bedroom, with a cat on his lap and the landlord sitting in his dark corner. Then he thought it might be his mother, her face rising like the silver moon in the night over him as he strained to see her, before she was gone and blindness descended on him. . . .

He forced open his eyes, saw the wide, lighted furnishings of a country living room, homely clutter, a pink brocade chair, mahogany side table, thick velvet curtains over a wide front window, a wide shade drawn down over it. He edged up in his seat: a secretary to the right, open to a scatter of lavender writing paper, a stamp dispenser, an elegant pen laid aside. Dark oriental rug on the floor, an ottoman beneath his feet, his arms on a dark green chair, the left side of his jacket cut away, his side and hand taped with new bandage. There were rope marks where the bindings had been removed.

He groaned, sat up, turned his head to see Falconi, and a perfectly dressed petite woman with short gray hair who looked to be about seventy-five regarding him with her hands in her lap from a couch beside his chair. There was a tea service on the coffee table before her.

"Feel okay?" Falconi asked.

"I'm alive," Brennan answered.

The woman immediately rose, pouring and bringing him a cup of tea. He hated tea. He drank it down with wonderment at how good its heat tasted in his mouth. He had a difficult time raising his left arm without a burn of pain rushing through his side.

"Would you like something to eat?" the woman asked. She looked like someone you wanted to be your grandmother.

He started to shake his head, stopped, said, "Yes, please."

There were sandwich halves on the tea service. She arranged three of them, along with a cluster of Pepperidge Farm cookies, handing the plate to him. She poured him more tea.

Before he realized it, he had eaten and drunk everything.

The elderly woman stood, efficiently gathered the dishes and cups onto the tea service, and went into the kitchen.

"How did you get here?" Brennan asked Falconi.

"Minkowski thought Gaimes might fixate on you, because of your interest in Bridget. And you were dumb enough to tell him where you live. I drove up to your place just as he was hauling you off in the car. The son of a bitch almost lost me when he started driving like a madman."

"You have him?" Brennan said.

"He's in the house. There are ten cops, my own and locals, watching the place."

Brennan eyed Falconi levelly. "Why haven't you gone in?"

Falconi was about to answer when the woman returned. "Is there anything else you gentlemen need?"

"I don't think so, Mrs. Williams," Falconi said. He made as if to get up. "Thank you—"

"Mrs. Williams," Ted Brennan said, "do you know anything about the house down the street?"

"Oh, yes. I've lived here for almost fifty years." She sat petitely on the edge of the couch and folded her hands in her lap.

"Who lived there last?"

"Oh," she said, "no one's lived there for almost forty years. The last was the Simmons family. They were there for . . . six months. They said they heard noises and such. No one seemed to want to move in after them. The children around here call it the Haunted House, of course."

"Have you ever seen anything strange around the house?"

"I can't say I have. But the house is well off the road and there's a lot of space between houses around here. And I never was one for snooping. Others around here have claimed noises and lights, but it's hard to know how much of that is just spook stories."

"Who lived there before the Simmons family?"

"The Fitzgeralds. Very nice family. Two boys and a girl. Before them, the Rileys. They had eleven children. They were there when Carl and I moved here, in the early forties. No one heard noises then. He was a marine. I think two of the boys became marines . . ."

"Mrs. Williams, did anyone ever die in the house?"

She concentrated. "The Rileys, no . . . The Simmons's, no . . . The Fitzgeralds . . ." A flush of memory reddened her face. "Oh, yes."

"Can you tell me about it?"

Mrs. Williams closed her eyes. Brennan thought she was concentrating, but a tear had traced her cheek. She produced a handkerchief and dabbed at her eyes, demurely blew her nose.

She rose, walked to her writing desk and took something from the shelf above it. She returned to Brennan, handed it to him, and sat back down on the couch.

"The Fitzgerald's daughter gave me that music box the

year before she died,'' Mrs. Williams said. ''She was a wonderful girl. I'm embarrassed to say it's been too long since I've thought of her . . .''

Again she used the handkerchief. ''She was a beautiful young thing. She went with my boy Carl awhile in high school. That was when she gave me the music box. She loved the music it played.''

On the cover of the box was painted a night scene: a church in the foreground, tiny village houses on hills rolling down away from it. Dark blue night with pinpoint stars.

When Brennan opened the box, nothing happened. He turned it over, found a metal key on the bottom, and wound it. He turned the box over and opened it again.

The mechanism, visible beneath a thin pane of glass, began to play a plaintive lullaby. On the inside cover were lyrics, painted black on a white background:

Why do you weep?
The bells are not ringing,
The town is asleep.
The night at your window
Is nestled in deep.
The stars in the heavens
Are gently singing—
Why do you weep?

Brennan felt a strange stirring; felt himself on the edge of a precipice with revelation at the bottom. But he did not go over. When the lullaby ended, he closed the box, and saw that Mrs. Williams was snuffling again.

''Excuse me,'' she said. ''She was a lovely girl.''

''What happened to her?''

Mrs. Williams had folded her hands properly on her lap again. ''She and Carl broke up just before she went to college. It was a mutual thing. They had been more friends than anything, and they were heading to different schools. She was eighteen, I believe. That would have been . . . 1951.

''My Carl told me later that she had begun to act strangely just before she went away to school, as if something was bothering her. The only thing she ever said to him about it was that a voice was calling to her. Carl admitted that that was part of the reason they drifted apart.

"At Christmas that year, she came home from college for vacation. She didn't go back to school again. There were rumors, of course, that she was failing her grades, or had gotten in trouble with a boy. Carl even tried to see her, but the Fitzgeralds became very protective of her and wouldn't let anyone in. And then, in the following autumn, she apparently . . . killed herself. The Fitzgeralds moved away soon after, and then the stories began. I believe they even said in the beginning that that poor girl was haunting the house, keeping people away from it." Mrs. Williams's hands opened, sadly. "People can be so uncaring."

"You said she was a nice girl?"

"A lovely girl. Carl used to say she was *too* nice. A quiet, lovely girl."

"Was her name Bridget, Mrs. Williams?"

Mrs. Williams blinked in surprise. "Why, yes, it was."

"We have to go," Falconi said to Brennan. He stood, and so did Brennan, smarting at the pain in his side.

"Thank you for all the help, Mrs. Williams," Falconi said.

"That's quite all right, Lieutenant. I'm only sorry something like this had to happen. As I said, the *Times* the other day—"

Brennan held up the music box. "May I borrow this, Mrs. Williams?"

"I suppose so. It *is* a lovely melody. But may I ask why you want it?"

"As odd as this may sound," Brennan said, "I may be able to help Bridget with it."

In the car, Falconi started the engine and turned on the windshield wipers. Then he turned to Brennan. "I'll tell you why I haven't gone in to get Gaimes. I talked to the landlord Beauvaque in Ottawa. He doesn't much like cops, but he corroborated your story about Laura Hutchins. We found the car Laura Hutchins took from her boyfriend in the bushes behind the house. There's a limousine out front that brought two KGB agents here, looking for an escaped Polish prisoner. The Russians are missing. Also, we have two reliable eyewitness reports on Gary Gaimes; one that he picked up a young man at the Forty-sixth Street pier debarking a cruise ship from Bermuda, the other that he met a man in a wheelchair at LaGuardia Airport. From the terminal we were able to find the flight; there was only one passenger in a wheelchair, a man named Ray Garver from California."

Falconi reached under the seat and pulled out a dog-eared paperback world atlas. He opened to a two-page spread showing the world. On the map was a pencil line from Ottawa down to Bermuda. Another ran from the middle of Poland across the Atlantic, intersecting the first line in New York and continuing west to California.

"The two lines cross where we're sitting," Falconi said.

Brennan grinned. "You believe me?"

"I found out a long time ago that sometimes you have to turn things over to the experts. Minkowski convinced me that you're the expert. So I'm letting you go in with me. Also . . ." Falconi stopped, seemingly disconcerted.

Brennan waited.

Falconi tapped the spot where the lines crossed on the map. "There's just too much happening here that can't be coincidence. If you're right, if there is life after death, it would . . . make everything better. Give it meaning."

"Then trust me," Brennan said.

Falconi stared at Brennan for a few moments, his face still red with embarrassment. Then he turned, threw the car into gear and pulled away from the curb.

"Besides," he said, a slight smile creeping onto his face, "even if you're wrong, I still get Gary Gaimes."

25. WEST

Remember, Ray.

The house was coming alive. From the cellar there were screams; they melted up through the floors, were eaten and expelled by the walls and the ceiling into his ears. The walls themselves radiated light, were alive with red, pulsing blood-light, were veined and pumping with each earth-deep drum boom of the heart of the house.

The blood veins hummed, a deep, rushing, pulling flow.

The heart pushed the blood—a pounding death-clock pump.

The house was coming alive.

Remember.

Fighting to keep his thoughts, Ray rolled to the table next to the bed, pulled the drawer out, and removed the plastic bag. His hands shook. He held the bag up in front of his face, staring at the granules, seeing each individual grain, studying the power in it.

Remember, Ray.

With a pain-fed, growling sound, he clutched the cocaine bag closed and rolled the wheelchair to the bathroom.

He flipped up the toilet seat, which vibrated in his hand.

Take the cocaine, Ray. Make it easy. Remember.

With a wrenching, pained cry he threw the bag down into the toilet water and pulled the flush.

Should have taken it, Ray.

Immediately he wanted to thrust his hand in and retrieve it. He bit his knuckles, closed his eyes, rocking in his wheelchair until the flush was complete.

"Should have taken it, Ray."

He wheeled around to see Bridget standing in the doorway of the bathroom. She was outlined in red, pulsing light. She looked more substantial, flushed, her voice deeper, more resonant, as if coming from a fast-closing distance. Her smile was that of the surrogate mother she had used on him long ago. "I only want to help you, Ray."

He held his hands over his ears and screamed, trying to block out the sound of her voice, the lure of the cocaine. He could *see* her in his mind, even with his eyes closed, just as he had seen her that first day at the Haunted Hut, an eternity ago.

"Ray," she said. She crossed to him, stroked his head like a true mother. "My poor little Ray."

He saw her as if his eyelids had been sliced off, heard her as if his hands did not exist over his ears. He saw her as she was then, the kindness in her eyes, the understanding, the . . . love.

"It's time to remember, Ray," she said. She stepped behind his wheelchair, rolled it slowly into the bedroom.

"I have something that can help you." He saw, right through his hands, through his tears, the neat white bag of cocaine, identical to the one he had flushed down the toilet, on the bedside table. She stopped him before it.

"NO!!" He lashed out, sweeping the bag of white powder from the table top. It hit the wall and opened, a puff of powder rising from the bag to settle in the light of the room like red-tinted talcum to the floor.

"Are you sure you don't want it?"

"*Damn you!*" He rolled to the bag, picked it up, ripped it open, letting the powder fly out.

She pointed to the white dust settling to the floor. "Are you *sure*?"

Crying, he bent down and brushed at the powder, sending tiny clouds of it in all directions.

When he looked at her, his eyes were hard. "Without it, I can beat you."

She sighed. "You should have taken it." She put her hand on his head. "Remember, Ray."

Memory . . .

Tony's birthday. A day with a sky so blue that even Ray's unhappiness could not make it any less so. In the early morning, when the trucks started to come in with the tent and the bandstand, he had run away into the woods, despite Anne's having told him he had to stay nearby. "Your father will need you when he gets in from Washington, there will be a lot of people to meet," she'd said, and then added, when she saw his glare, "I know this might be a little hard on you, Ray, but *please* be good. I have a feeling Tony won't enjoy it, either; I'm sure he would much rather have the kind of small party you did. But you know the way your father is. It's an election year. Some things just get out of hand."

His glare hadn't left, and when she tried to put her hand on his head, he had slipped out beneath it and run through the back door, ignoring her cries after him.

But Bridget was waiting for him at the Haunted Hut, just the way she always did. Her smile widened to enclose him, her arms out, embracing him.

"How's my boy?" she said.

He sat next to her, his head down. "They're having a party for Tony today."

"Are they now?" The faint odor of rosewater reached Ray. "Does that bother you?"

He shrugged.

"Didn't we talk about that?" she asked mildly. "Didn't we talk about being jealous?"

"Yes, but . . ."

She narrowed her eyes in faint accusation. He could tell that she was ready to smile. "But what?"

"I can't help it," he said.

She put her arm around him, drew him close. "Oh, Ray,

there's so much you don't understand. Do you really hate Tony so much?"

"Sometimes I do . . ."

"And Anne?"

He shifted uncomfortably, but the scent of rose kept him close to her, drinking her in. "She's not that bad." He turned his head, looked seriously up into her face. "I wish *you* were my mother."

Her smile never faltered. "Oh, Ray! You know I love you. Isn't that enough?"

"No," he said.

"Well, then," she sighed, hugging him, "maybe we can do something about it."

When Ray got back to the house, the tent and bandstand were already up. The tent was huge: a circus-sized, yellow and white striped canopy with open sides. Beneath it, tables were being set up and decorated. The band was unpacking their instruments; one large black man already had his trumpet out, playing bluesy scales up and down. The drummer next to him said, "Better get that out of your system, now, Willy; you *know* Senator Garver ain't going to want any of that for his white friends tonight."

Willy laughed, lowered his trumpet. The drummer winked at Ray as he walked by.

The kitchen in the house was deserted. Ray poured himself a glass of lemonade from a pitcher on the table and went into the living room. Tony's playpen was empty. Then he heard the baby cry upstairs, Anne's giggling scold for him to be quiet and let her change him. In another few moments Anne descended the stairs, Tony following, holding her hand, a halting step at a time.

Tony smiled and said, "Ray-ray!"

Anne stared hard at Ray. "Didn't I tell you not to leave the house?"

"Yes," he said. Despite himself, he felt guilty.

The doorbell rang. The caterers arrived. Anne was swept up in a flow of metal trays and huge, round, plastic-covered hors d'oeuvre platters.

"We'll talk about it later," she said to Ray. "Right now I need you to keep an eye on Tony."

She stared at him until he nodded. She put Tony down in his playpen and ran off to investigate a crashing sound coming from the pantry leading to the kitchen.

Tony crawled to the side of the playpen, hoisted himself up, inched his way over to where Ray was standing. "Ray-ray!" he said, grinning, a trickle of drool escaping his mouth to land on the plastic playpen pad.

Ray ignored him. Sipping his lemonade, he went to the front window. A second catering truck had pulled up. Two girls were climbing out of the open back doors, balancing either end of an enormously long platter covered a half-foot thick in cold cuts. Behind them came a third girl bearing a huge birthday cake, seven decks, as tall as Tony himself, frosted in yellow and white.

Pulling up behind the catering truck, nearly hitting the girl with the cake, was a television news van. Behind that, his father's limousine. A moment later his father appeared. His father waited for the television cameras to set up, then let them follow his waving, smiling form up the steps to the front porch, into the house.

"Hey! Ray!" his father said, striding to where Ray stood. The senator tousled his hair. Before Ray could respond, his father's eyes had found Tony, and he was shouting "Tony boy! Birthday lad!" lifting the drooling, laughing baby up for the benefit of the cameras and lights.

Anne appeared, straightening her dress, and the three of them posed for the cameras as his father sang happy birthday and kissed Tony on the cheek loudly, laughing right into the lenses.

Ray went upstairs.

With the door closed, it was quiet in his room. The windows looked out on the front of the house. When he pulled the shades, he could almost make believe it was nighttime.

Maybe we can do something about it, she had said.

Ray lay down on his bed and soon was fast asleep.

• • •

He awoke in true darkness.

He heard what sounded like the hissing of snakes. For a moment he was afraid; he thought he had wandered into the woods, clouds had covered the night stars, Bridget had left him, and the snakes were slithering toward him and ready to strike. He'd killed a copperhead once; perhaps its family had come back for revenge—

He rubbed at his eyes, felt his clothes still on him, his bed beneath him.

The hissing continued. It was mingled with cheers. Someone said something in a loud, echoey voice. His father, speaking into a microphone.

More hissing; more cheers.

Ray rose from the bed, opened the door to his bedroom. He was flooded with hallway light. He squinted against it, rubbed his eyes some more.

Yawning, sullen, he descended the stairs.

Tony's playpen sat abandoned in the empty living room. A scatter of toys lay outside its perimeter. A discarded, changed diaper was rolled in its adhesive tabs next to a soiled pair of bib overalls.

Ray walked into the kitchen.

A fresh pitcher of lemonade stood on the counter. He drew a plastic tumbler, poured himself a glass, and walked out into the night.

He heard hissing, saw a streak of trailing fire cut the sky. Cheers greeted the high explosion of light that briefly illumined the yellow and white striped tent and the thick carpet of guests sitting on the sloping back lawn.

His father's voice boomed over his microphone again.

"My friends, I can't *tell* you how *good* it is to be with you tonight! This is a great occasion for me, and to share it with so many of my closest friends is something I will not soon forget!"

The senator paused. Ray moved down toward the tent and caught sight of him now: a large, tall, salt-and-pepper-haired man with a hand aloft, an open smile on his face, highlighted by a single strong spotlight mounted on a tripod at the back of the crowd. A television camera was filming. His father was transfixed by light. He looked, in the night, like a larger than life character on a movie screen.

Another rocket went off. The senator paused to turn and look at its sizzling flight, laughing with the crowd as it sputtered and popped, forgoing its explosion.

"My friends, my fellow citizens!" his father continued, turning back to his constituents, turning his face to sudden grimness. "I wanted you here tonight not only to share this great day with my family—" his body language indicated Anne, who stood with arms folded, hugging herself against the night's descending chill; and Tony, who sat at her feet, picking at grass, a bottle stuck firmly in his mouth "—but to share this great message that we hope to convey to *all* of our friends around this great state of ours. This is the birthday not only of my son but also of a new idea: that freedom, and goodness, and decency, have not left America!" His smile began to return. "That we will win again in November! I thank you!"

He put his hands into the air, like a runner crossing the finish line. The applause flowed over and around him, seemed to lift him from the podium. Ray saw his quick look and nod toward the man running the fireworks. His father kept his hands in the air, waiting.

The man threw a switch. Nothing happened. While Ray's father stood motionless, the man crouched down under his panel, studying a length of coiled wires. He climbed out and threw the switch again. Once more, nothing happened.

The senator lowered his hands and laughed into the microphone.

"So much for grand finales, folks—but I can *promise* you one hell of a grand finale to this campaign!"

Again he threw his hands into the air, receiving applause.

The senator stepped down from the podium, motioning curtly and angrily to the fireworks coordinator. The man immediately left his console, joining the senator for a heated exchange behind the podium.

Ray moved down closer to the console. He was fascinated. There was a panel with a row of switches, numbered one to twenty-five, illuminated by dim red bulbs. All of the switches were thrown. All the lights were on except number twenty-five.

Beneath the console, the tangle of wire separated and branched to the various firing platforms. Ray bent down and examined the wires trailing from switch number twenty-five. They led off to a huge, separate area, fenced off by garden string. *DANGER!* signs were taped to the string. Row upon row of huge thick rockets were mounted in firing cans.

Tony was crawling under the garden string, under the *DANGER!* signs, into and among the rockets.

Ray turned to see Anne watching the senator and the fireworks man. The senator was waving his arms excitedly, starting to attract attention. Anne bit her lip pensively.

She took a step toward the two men, then looked down, missing Tony.

Ray watched her search the area around her, then extend her search to nearby guests, all of whom shook their heads or shrugged. A few looked down at their feet as Anne moved on.

Ray turned back to Tony, who was now in among the rockets. He sat with his bottle still clamped in his mouth, patting his hand tentatively against one of the firing cans.

Ray turned back to the bottom of the console. There, standing out distinctly, was a loose black wire at one of the terminals on the back of switch number twenty-five.

Tony was now holding the firing can with both hands on its rim, steadying himself to stand.

"Tony!" Anne shouted, spotting him.

An immediate hush came over the crowd.

She ran toward him. She stepped over the garden string, into the middle of the rockets. She scooped Tony up in her arms, saying "Oh, Tony!"

"Ray, we can do something about it."

Bridget stood next to him; she reached under the panel and touched the black wire to its terminal.

The entire area where Anne stood was engulfed in fire, as the finale went off. Anne screamed. Ray watched her try to shield Tony from the incendiary flames. Fire and smoke blotted them out, but Ray could still hear Anne scream, could still hear Tony scream—

• • •

"Are you sure you don't want the cocaine, Ray?" Bridget said mildly. She pointed to the thin dusting of powder on the floor.

"Damn you! Oh, God, they're dead, they're all dead, my father and Tony and Anne, you killed them . . ."

Bridget put her red-outlined hand on his shoulder. "Poor boy."

"I hate you! I'm going to kill you!" He hit her hand from his shoulder. "YOU KILLED MY FAMILY!"

She sighed, her voice as tender as it had ever been. "My poor little Ray. You'll never know how much I did for you. It's true, I needed you, but you also needed me. Why didn't you tell the psychiatrists about me, Ray? Because they would have kept you there forever? Or because they would have found the truth?"

"I'LL DESTROY YOU!"

"Don't you think I realize that if you remembered the truth, you'd kill yourself?"

She placed her hand back on his shoulder, squeezed tenderly. "Are you sure you don't want the cocaine, Ray? Believe me, I'm trying to be kind."

"I'LL DESTROY YOU!"

"Remember the truth, Ray."

Memory . . .

He was back in the car with his father. The exit ramp appeared, curving into snowy darkness. He felt Bridget behind him, laughing. "Go ahead, Ray, you want to," she said. His father sat imperious, demanding, beside him, and suddenly he did want to. Deliberately, he put his foot to the accelerator. The car skidded sideways, the headlights pinning the bed truck parked on the ramp. He drove into the skid, recovered, hit the gas pedal, aiming straight into the dropped bulldozer shovel, ducking calmly as they hit—

Memory . . .

He was at his father's house, watching Tony try to stand in the midst of the fireworks, holding his hands up to Anne, smiling as she snatched him up. He saw the worried faces around him, his father's face frozen with real anxiety, the giant striped tent, the food, the remains of the huge birthday cake, the beautiful night that was not for him, the woman who was not his mother cradling the child that reaped all the love and concern from these people, the child that should have been him, the woman that should have been his mother. Hate welled up within him. He reached quickly under the console to touch the naked wire end to the switch—

"OH GOD OH GOD OH GOD OH GOD!!!" Ray pounded at his face, trying to drive the true memories from his head, to beat his brain until the memories were gone.

In the house of screams, of pounding blood, of the heat of death, Ray screamed.

"We needed each other," Bridget said, opening the door for him.

Ray's hand moved very fast on the wheels of the wheelchair. He was filled with a power greater than cocaine. The wheelchair flew from the room and hit the second-floor railing.

It broke through.

Ray screamed. And then he was laughing. He suddenly felt his legs. He was running, running down the slope of the living green lawn over the hills to the hot sandy beach. He felt the warm grit of the sand between his toes as he leapt into the water, feet first. He felt cold water on the pads of his feet and then up his legs, and he was no longer screaming but laughing in happiness, the water covering his head.

He kicked down and touched the white sandy bottom with the flat of his hand and then his face.

He couldn't push himself back up—

26. BRIDGET

"You ready, Brennan?"

Ted Brennan stood smoking a cigarette, staring through light, cold rain at the glow emanating from the windows of the house. Little sparks of red crawled around the front of the house, along the gutters, around the front doorway and windows. The low, insistent pounding thrum was beginning to bother his ears. "You say that glow's coming from every window?"

Falconi looked to Detective Guinty standing next to them for an answer. Guinty's red hair was plastered to his skull; his collar was up, his hands thrust into the pockets of his raincoat. He looked cold. "Every window, Lieutenant, even the ones without stained glass."

"Is it stronger anywhere?" Brennan asked.

Guinty glanced at the house. "It looks stronger upstairs."

"Thank you."

"Ready now?" Falconi asked impatiently.

"Soon as I get that equipment from my car."

As if by magic, another of Falconi's men appeared, holding a crowbar in one hand, Brennan's meter and a bulky handled box that looked like a slide projector case in the other. He grinned, looked at Falconi. "Keys weren't in the ignition. I did like you said."

"That's fine," Brennan said, taking the equipment.

The detective continued to look at Falconi. His grin turned tentative. "Sure you know what you're doing, Lieutenant? That local cop Carpenter's pretty steamed." He looked at the house. "And to tell you the truth . . ."

"Don't worry about it, Weaver."

Detective Weaver walked away, shaking his head, swinging the crowbar.

"Before you ask," Brennan said to Falconi, "the little box is just a meter. The big one I built myself, with the help of Radio Shack components." He checked a compartment in the bottom; fumbled with two large, heavy-looking cells. There was a spark. He fumbled again. "I hope to God the batteries are okay. They're strong, but they're kind of dangerous."

"Have you ever used that thing?" Falconi asked.

"No. But I think it works."

"You *think*?"

Brennan sighed. "Look, Lieutenant, let's get something straight. I never said I knew what the fuck I was doing. I know more than anybody about this—but so what. Father Verges didn't exactly give instructions." He stopped fumbling with the batteries, closed the case. "What this instrument does is deionize the air. There tend to be a lot of ions around so-called spirits. The meter measures ions. Hopefully, what it will do is stabilize the thing controlling the spirit of Bridget Fitzgerald, or even free her from it. If I can do that, it may give me a look at the other side."

Brennan threw his cigarette down. "But remember what I said, Lieutenant. The most important thing is to get any of the four left alive in there out of the house. Destroying the Compass Cross comes first, before you, before me, before *anything*." Hefting his equipment, Brennan turned and began to walk toward the house. "If we don't do that, we'll all find out about life after death the hard way."

The local police chief was waiting for them with Detective Weaver near the broken cellar window at the side of the house. He was Falconi's height, with a hound dog's face; he wore a plastic rain-shield over his hat. He looked at Falconi grimly. "I don't really like what you're doing here, Lieutenant."

"Chief Carpenter," Falconi said, putting his arm around the local cop's shoulder, "the last thing I want here is a territorial dispute. Do you realize all the media coverage this apprehension is going to get?"

The chief looked surprised. "Well, no, I didn't realize . . ."

"I think you should handle that end of it completely. The way the TV boys have been sticking to this case, and with all this ruckus, I wouldn't doubt they're on their way up here from New York now." He squeezed Carpenter's shoulder, motioning to Detective Weaver. "If you think it'll be too much, I'm sure Weaver can—"

The chief's uncertainty had evaporated. "No, Lieutenant, I can handle it. I'd better be out by the street to face them when they get here."

Straightening his tie, smoothing the lapels on his raincoat, he marched off down the driveway.

Weaver grinned. "Bastard is already watching himself on Channel Seven."

"No shit," Falconi said. He moved closer to where Brennan waited for him by the broken cellar window, smoking another cigarette.

"Remember what I said," he told Weaver. "Nobody goes in, no matter what. If daylight comes before we come out, do whatever you want. A-bomb it if you want to. But not until then."

Weaver looked doubtfully up at the house; a red streak cut up the side, disappeared under the eaves. "It's your show, Lieutenant."

"Let's go, Brennan," Falconi said.

Brennan threw his cigarette away. "One more thing," he said. "Once we get in there, we'll be on her turf and she'll try to make us hallucinate. She won't have the same power over us she has over her four victims, and if you're aware of it, you can fight it. But she'll do her damndest. I've got a thing with blindness, and she made me think I was blind in Ottawa. Is there anything she can get to you with?"

Falconi shook his head. "No."

"Are you sure?" Brennan persisted. "Mark Minkowski told me about a little problem you have with a picture you keep on your desk—"

Falconi's anger began to flare. "I said no."

"All right," Brennan said. "But stay together. If she gets us alone, she'll be stronger, because we won't have a reference point of reality."

Falconi crouched to enter the window.

Brennan stopped him. "Me first. I may not know much, but I know more than you do."

Falconi started to protest, then nodded. "Okay."

As Brennan entered the cellar, the dial on his meter flipped over to maximum and the faceplate shattered.

"Holy shit," he said. The cellar was rumbling like a steam turbine about to blow, veins of pulsing red fire crawling over the walls, ceiling, and floor.

Falconi jumped down beside him. "Jesus." He kneeled to study the two bodies on the floor, one barely recognizable, the other a torso in a suit, with a jelly-beaten head. In the pocket of the second corpse was a Russian handgun with a silencer. Falconi wrapped it in a handkerchief and put it in his pocket.

"Gaimes killed these two," Falconi said. He took out the .44 Magnum in his shoulder holster.

Putting the deionizer down, Brennan cried out suddenly, throwing his hands to his eyes.

"What is it?" Falconi said.

Brennan's breathing steadied. Slowly, he took his hands away from his eyes, blinking. "It's all right," he said. "I told you she could get to me like this. I'd still be blind if I didn't know it wasn't real. Just stay together, like I told you."

They went over the rest of the cellar, searching in vain for the weapon that had been used on the two corpses.

"Let's go upstairs," Brennan said.

Brennan bearing his equipment, they mounted the steps to the first floor. Falconi moved in front when they reached the top. "Now *I* go first," he said.

He eased the cellar door open. It hinged back, showing a kitchen with wildly pulsing walls. The hum was even louder.

His .44 out, held up in front of him, Falconi stepped out into the kitchen, turning his gaze from side to side.

He saw nothing.

Then he did. On the kitchen counter was a pile of severed human fingers that twitched, squirting blood from their cut ends, jerking away from each other, dancing over the countertop.

Falconi closed his eyes; opened then. The fingers were gone.

"Shit," he muttered, checking to see that there really was only a clean countertop where the fingers had been.

"Another hallucination," Brennan said, entering the kitchen behind Falconi.

They heard rattling chains, the drag of metal across the floor, thumps, echoing moans.

"Welcome to a real haunted house," Brennan said.

The sounds abruptly ceased.

"Let's check the pantry," Brennan said.

Falconi heard a sound at the cellar door behind him.

He wheeled, looked into the cellar opening.

He was no longer in the house.

He was on a roof on East Thirty-third Street, in New York City. A wind was blowing. It was 1973, the last week in March. He was a rookie and there was a tight knot of fear in his belly.

The woman in the picture on his desk was standing not five feet from him.

They had told him how to handle these things at the academy, but he had never done it for real. She looked less scared than he was. In fact, she looked calm. She was overweight, and she wore a housecoat, and her hair was in tangles, blown by the blustery wind.

A windy March day. The sky was deep cold blue, warming toward spring. The day before, the temperature had risen to fifty-five degrees, but now it was back down in the forties. There were fat round clouds blowing through the blue sky.

"Don't come any closer," the woman said, matter-of-factly. Standing on the ledge of the brick wall, three feet above the roof, she looked like she could touch the clouds if she wanted to.

He inched his foot closer, trying to keep a reasonable look

on his face, and said, "Why don't you sit down on the wall and we'll talk about it?"

She calmly turned away from him.

He was supposed to keep talking, to wait while his partner got the jump team in place with its nets, but he was sure she was about to go.

He lunged, catching the fabric of her housecoat at the shoulder as she stepped off. He dug his fingers into the housecoat. The top of the ledge hit painfully into his underarm, but he held on.

She pried at his fingers, trying to make him let go.

His arm was turning numb. He edged his face up and over the wall. She looked up at him.

"Help me," he said, breathing hard. "Hold on to my arm and help me. *Please*."

The calm look never left her face. "I told you not to come any closer." She let go of his hand, shrugged herself out of the housecoat, her arm pulling past the shoulder he held tightly, and fell soundlessly to the pavement below.

He stood up, gasping for breath, trying not to cry, shaking, holding the housecoat. He looked over the wall, saw her bent body in the street, the jump team looking up at him, their nets half out of their van, a crowd already forming around the body . . .

He looked over the wall; the March air was so cold. He climbed up on the wall, looked down. He let go of the housecoat, watched it flutter down in the wind.

You were wrong, a voice told him. *You killed her* . . .

"Yes . . ."

Jump . . .

He stepped—

"Lieutenant!"

Falconi looked down the cellar steps, felt himself losing his balance. A hand was on him, steadying him.

He turned around. Brennan pulled him back away from the cellar opening.

"What the hell happened?" Brennan asked.

Falconi looked into the cellar. "The woman in the picture. I killed her . . ."

Brennan shook him. "Falconi!"

Falconi's eyes, his mind, were elsewhere. "I *killed* her, it was my fault, *I should have waited . . .*"

Brennan shook him again. "Falconi!"

Tears were streaming from Falconi's eyes; he stared into the black opening of the cellar. *"My God, I didn't listen, I was wrong, I killed her . . ."*

Falconi blinked; he turned toward Brennan and his eyes seemed to refocus on his surroundings. "Jesus," he said.

"Listen to me," Brennan said. "If she can get to you with this, she'll use it again."

Falconi had come back to himself. He shook Brennan off, took a shuddering breath. "I'm all right," he said.

Brennan looked at him levelly. "Are you sure?"

Falconi seemed himself again. His gaze was as level as Brennan's, "Yes." He edged past Brennan, away from the cellar door.

Brennan took him by the arm. "Stay with me."

Falconi nodded.

They checked the kitchen, the small pantry, laundry room behind it. In the windowed dryer door Falconi saw a severed head, bobbing languidly from side to side.

He closed his eyes; when he opened them, the head was gone.

They moved cautiously through the swinging doors of the kitchen, checking the rooms down the hallway. All were empty. The noise was almost deafening. The walls brightened; veins of red lights bulged out with each crimson beat. The hum deepened to a rumbling roar.

When they edged out into the living room, Falconi discovered two more corpses just inside the parlor, near the foyer leading to the front door.

Falconi examined papers on the bodies. "The missing Russians," he said, raising his voice to be heard. He studied the bullet wound in Viktor Borodin's body, an entrance in the throat out the back of the head. "Gaimes didn't do this. He never used a gun. He never would, according to Minkowski. Too impersonal." He took out the gun he'd found on the body in the cellar, studied the barrel. "The fellow with the suit on downstairs must be the Pole."

Brennan said, "The other one in the cellar must have been the kid from Bermuda. That leaves Ray Garver and Laura

Hutchins. West and north. Your man Guinty said the glow was stronger from the west bedroom.''

"We'll check them both.''

One step at a time, they mounted the stairs to the second floor. Falconi held his .44 ready in front of him.

The north bedroom faced them. Brennan stood before the door, examining the cracks in it.

"Get back,'' Falconi said. He stood with both hands on the .44 and pushed the door open.

Ready to fire, Falconi moved quickly into the room. "Jesus.''

Brennan followed him in, and gagged at the sight of what was on the bed. He turned to lean on the doorjamb.

As Falconi joined him he said, "Ray Garver's the only one left.''

From the west bedroom came a scream, followed immediately by another.

Falconi and Brennan ran toward the west door. The screams built to a frenzy. Falconi, holding his gun up, motioned Brennan to stand on the opposite side.

Falconi was turning to kick the door in when it flew open. There was a burst of screeching within. A man in a wheelchair hurtled by them. The chair hit the second floor railing and burst through. The man rose out of the chair in midflight, hands before him like a diver, and plunged to the floor below, hitting hard.

Falconi was moving to the stairway when Brennan grabbed his arm. Falconi turned to look into the doorway of the north bedroom.

The figure of a young girl with red hair stood there. She was almost solid, floating just above the floor, her feet nearly touching it.

Red lines of force from the walls and ceiling were concentrating, flowing and rising up through the floor into her.

"Soon . . .'' she said, her voice a deep, echoing well, at one with the rumbling generator's roar of the house.

"Go downstairs,'' Brennan said to Falconi, "and get that man out of the house.'' He set the deionizer down, quickly opened the case and turned it on.

Falconi's eyes were riveted to Bridget, who floated serenely in the flowing web of red energy.

"Move!" Brennan said, pushing Falconi until he turned and stumbled down the stairs.

Brennan turned up the deionizer, and suddenly the flow of energy to Bridget diminished. The serene look on her face vanished and she focused her eyes on Brennan.

"You can't stop me . . ." the bottomless voice said.

"Where is Bridget?" Ted Brennan said.

"In here. In the tunnel between worlds. She's been here all this time. Soon the fourth will be dead, and then I will enter this world." The thing, using Bridget's lips, smiled. "This *life*."

"Let me speak with her."

"No." The thing stared malevolently at Brennan. "Soon you'll die. You'll *all* die."

The thing began to moan, a low, rattling, grinding sound. Once again, the red flow of energy began to increase.

Brennan glanced down at Falconi, who was bent over the prone body of the man in the wheelchair. "Well?"

Falconi looked up. "He's still alive. I think his neck's broken. If I move him, he might die on me."

"If you don't get him out of the house, we're *all* dead!"

Falconi lifted the man gently under the arms and tried to straighten his broken body.

Brennan adjusted the deionizer; once again, the flow of red fire to Bridget diminished.

This time, when Bridget's eyes focused on Brennan, the malevolence was gone.

"Bridget!" Brennan shouted.

Bridget opened her mouth. "Yes . . ." a tiny, weak voice spoke from a great distance.

"Bridget," Ted Brennan said, "you have to fight it!"

"It has me trapped, in the tunnel . . ."

Brennan fumbled the music box from pocket. "Listen to this, Bridget."

The mouth opened, but no whisper of sound came out.

Brennan wound the music box and opened it.

"Do you know this song, Bridget? Do you remember it?"

"Yes . . ." Suddenly the voice was stronger. Tears tracked her cheeks. As the melody began, she looked at Brennan and sang in a sweet, sad voice:

"Why do you weep?
The bells are not ringing,
The town is asleep.
The night at your window
Is nestled in deep.
The stars in the heavens
Are gently singing—
Why do you weep?"

"Do *you* remember it?" Bridget said, beginning to cry.

A gate opened in Brennan's mind. "My God." He knew the song, now. He saw the soft, indistinct face looming over him, heard the resigned sadness, the infinite sorrow in the voice.

He saw the face of his mother.

It was Bridget.

"My God. My God." Brennan fell to his knees. He looked up at her, and she was smiling through her tears. "Mother . . ."

"Yes," she said. "When this began, when this horrible thing took me so long ago, I began to call you. It took so long for you to come. So long . . ."

"My father . . ."

"His family had money. They took you away from me. My family agreed. It was so easy to listen to the sounds in my head. Before I killed myself, I wrote your father a note asking him to never tell you who I was. I was so ashamed. Your father loved me as much as he loved you, and he followed my wishes. I was so wrong. But I got through to you. I got through . . ."

Her voice became urgent. "You must get the fourth out, now . . ."

Brennan turned to see Falconi struggling with the body of Ray Garver. He had carefully dragged it halfway to the front hallway.

"Falconi!" Brennan shouted, "You've got to get him out!"

The red color in the walls deepened, and suddenly the veins of power began to flow again.

Brennan turned back to see the thing once more in control

of Bridget. It stared at him coldly. The bottomless voice spoke. "I won't let her go."

It reached down, took the deionizer by its handle and hurtled it the length of the house. The instrument smashed against the railing in front of the east door, raining debris down on Falconi.

A spark shot from one of the smashed batteries, touching the dry, dusty fabric of a damask chair, which began to burn.

"Mother," Brennan begged, "you have to force it out!"

He rewound the music box.

The thing in his mother's spirit glared at him with pure hatred. "I'll tear the bones from your body." Her eyes filled with a blood red color. Her voice was like the rasp of a file. "I'll burn you alive," she said. "I—"

Suddenly, her face changed to that of an innocent, lost young girl.

"Mother," Brennan shouted, "make it leave!"

"Yes . . ."

"Force it out!"

"Yes . . ."

She made a gagging noise in her throat. The lines of red force vanished. Her eyes rolled up into her head. Her body ceased floating, touched the floor. She flopped down backward, bucking in an epilepticlike fit.

"Ahhhhhh, ahhhhh," she said, trying to push herself up.

Bridget's body went limp. Something huge, deep, and black rose slowly out of it, hovering like a cloud.

"Jesus, I think this guy's dying!" Falconi shouted from below.

Brennan looked. Falconi had dragged the broken man to the front hallway. He stopped, as Garver went into a series of convulsions, vomiting up blood.

The damask chair was smoking, tiny flames licking its arm up to its back.

Brennan screamed down to Falconi, "Get him out, now!"

"Ahhhhhh, ahhhhh . . ."

A shrieking, whistling sound came from within the roiling mass, which moved up above his mother's figure to the ceiling. It formed and reformed into a huge, dark dragon's head with a long, red whiplike tongue and blank, empty white eyes. Veins of crimson fire ran and pulsed around its outline.

"Ahhhhhhhh, ahhhhhhh . . ."

"Move!" Brennan screamed down to Falconi.

Below the dark cloud, Bridget's body began to disappear. As she became insubstantial, she opened her eyes, looked at Brennan, and smiled peacefully.

"Son, I'm going, I'm finally going . . ."

Holding her hand out to him, Bridget vanished.

"No!"

Gary Gaimes ran out of the door to the attic, straight at Brennan. *"She was mine!"* He raised the claw hammer, striking Brennan a solid blow on the side of the head.

Brennan dropped, lifeless, to the floor. Gaimes turned to the stairs and staggered down them, waving the hammer above his head. "I'm invincible!" he shouted. "INVINCIBLE!"

Falconi stood and fired the .44 into Gaimes, who reached the bottom of the stairs and kept coming.

"INVINCIBLE!"

Falconi fired again, hitting Gaimes square in the chest. Gaimes grunted, went down on one knee next to the burning chair, rose again, still holding the hammer. A flame jumped to his shirt, began to burn up the arm. He grinned at Falconi and staggered forward, raising the hammer above his head.

"I'm invin—"

Falconi fired four quick shots, and Gaimes collapsed before him, the hammer falling from his twitching hand.

Flames spread from Gaimes's shirt to the floor, from the burning chair to the nearby tables and rug.

Near the ceiling at the top of the stairs, the black cloud grew. The rumbling, deep sounds within it intensified.

Ahhhhhhhhhh, ahhhhhhhh.

"Shit," Falconi said. He felt for the pulse in Ray Garver's neck. It was barely evident. He began to drag Garver carefully toward the front door. "Fuck it," he said, lifting him roughly under the arms and hauling him down the hallway.

When he looked up at the second floor, the cloud was gone.

"Damn!"

He dragged his burden another yard, felt back, and found the front doorknob with his hand. He began to turn it.

"Falconi. Wait."

Falconi looked back into the house. Ted Brennan's form was calmly descending the stairs through growing flames, leaving its dead flesh behind. The side of Brennan's head where the hammer wound had been was whole.

Falconi said, "Shit," again. He fumbled for the knob, felt it turn in his hand.

"*Wait,*" Ted Brennan repeated. He approached, held his hand out.

Falconi heard the click of the opening lock—

"Stop."

Brennan stood beside him, put his cold hand over Falconi's on the doorknob.

Falconi turned, looked into Brennan's dead face. Something that was not Brennan stormed in his eyes.

"I believe you have something of mine," he said, his mouth releasing putrefaction.

He bent down and touched the crippled man at Falconi's feet. Ray Garver screamed, his eyes opening, blood pushing from his mouth and nostrils.

Falconi tried to pull the man from Brennan's grasp.

Brennan stood. His face was inches from Falconi's own. His grotesque smile quivered. Falconi saw something in Brennan's eyes, a black, roiling thing with the tongue of a snake. And then he was on the roof on East Thirty-third Street in New York City again, looking down at that poor, desperate, quiet woman, and she was pulling herself from her housecoat, pulling herself from his grasp, letting go, letting go . . .

Let go, the thing told him. *Let go, or the world will be destroyed, and you'll be wrong again.*

Falconi let go of Ray Garver.

"Falconi!"

He looked into Brennan's open eyes. The roiling thing was gone, pulling back into the recesses of the pupils. It was the real Ted Brennan facing him.

"Take him!" Brennan shouted, removing his hands from Ray Garver's dying body.

Falconi pulled the door open, lifted Ray Garver under the arms, and fell backward, out of the house.

As they hit the outside air, Ray took a long, moaning whisper of breath and let it out in expiration. "I'm sorry . . ."

Falconi felt for his pulse. There was none.

"Jesus," Falconi muttered, "that was close."

Ahhhhh . . .

Brennan stood in the doorway. In the back of his throat, trapped behind his eyes, something roared in rage.

ahhhh . . .

The roar faded to silence.

Brennan faded gently, seemed to float on air.

"Listen . . ." Brennan whispered. He looked at a place above Falconi's head. "Destroy the house, and this thing cannot come back. I'll release it at the other end of the tunnel . . ."

He was barely an outline in the air. "A light at the end . . . I'm through! A place . . ." His face suddenly lit with a beatific smile. "The woman in your picture . . . You're forgiven . . . Everyone is forgiven . . ."

Brennan was almost gone. He steadied his gaze on Falconi. "Tell Beauvaque . . ." His smile was angelic. "Tell him Jeffrey is happy . . ."

Brennan filtered to nothingness.

There was a hissing roar. The house burst into flame. The red, glowing windows blew outward. Fire licked up the walls, engulfed the roof, roared over the attic.

Guinty was at Falconi's side, aiding him. "We're calling the fire department, Lieutenant."

"Let it burn." Falconi looked up at the house. There was a strange smile on his face. Idly, he reached into his pocket, took out a book of matches, handed it to Guinty. "If the rain puts the fire out, start it up again."

"But, sir, the Russians, someone from their embassy is here, the television cameras are here—"

Falconi shook off Guinty, began to walk away. "Fuck television. Fuck the Russians. Fuck everybody. I have a message to deliver."

The house turned to flames behind him, reached fiery hands to heaven.

Falconi walked on, blithely ignoring the shouting voices, the rain, the cameras, and looked for a telephone.

ABOUT THE AUTHOR

AL SARRANTONIO's fifty short stories have appeared in such magazines as *Heavy Metal, Twilight Zone, Isaac Asimov's Science Fiction Magazine, Analog, Amazing,* and *Whispers,* as well as in such anthologies as *The Best of Shadows, The Year's Best Horror Stories, Great Ghost Stories, Razored Saddles, Under the Fang, Obsessions* and *Visions of Fantasy: Tales from the Masters.* He is the author of the horror novels *October, The Boy With Penny Eyes, Totentanz, Campbell Wood* and *The Worms,* the science fiction novel *Moonbane,* the mystery novel *Cold Night,* and a western, *West Texas.* He has edited three volumes of humor, *The Fireside Treasury of Great Humor, The Fireside Treasury of New Humor* and *The National Lampoon Treasury of Humor,* and is the author of columns for the Horror Writers of America newsletter and *Mystery Scene* magazine. He lives in New York's Hudson Valley with his wife and two sons, and is currently at work on his next horror novel, *Skeletons.*